IMPERVIOUS

IMPERVIOUS

CITY OF ELDRICH — BOOK ONE

LAURA KIRWAN

BURNT BARN PRESS

ISBN: 0-9913023-2
ISBN-13: 978-0-9913023-2-1

CHAPTER 1

S TEAM ROSE GENTLY from the iron cauldron. Huddled over it, in the dim light cast by the flame beneath, two cloaked figures muttered and swayed. One raised a hand, gasped a few unintelligible words, and dropped something into the cauldron.

The flame under the cauldron flared and steam billowed into the air.

The figure threw back the dark hood and shook out her auburn ringlets. "Okey doke. It needs to simmer a bit, then all done."

The second figure pulled off her dark robe and dropped it on the floor. She wrinkled her nose. "That robe stinks. How long since they've been washed?"

The first woman fluffed her curls with her fingers. "It's been a while. Sorry. I thought we needed some ceremony. Hang on a sec." She picked up a cell phone from the gritty linoleum floor and held it out in front of her. "Sierra, you still there?"

The phone squawked. "Damn thing," she muttered as she stabbed a button and put it to her ear. "You there? . . . Yeah, sorry. I had you on speaker. It's this building, you know how it gets. Magnifies the magic but makes my cell phone all wonky. Did you get it? . . . Awesome. You're the best. Tell the coven I said hi." She pulled off her robe and slipped the phone into the back pocket of her jeans.

The second woman, younger, with shoulder-length fine straight hair somewhere between dark blond and light brown, scowled at her companion. "You said all the ritual was crap for the tourists."

The first one sniffed her robe. "Ooh, that's bad." She balled up the dark robe under her arm. "Well, yeah, to a certain extent. If you're good you don't really need any of this. I guess we could have put a cup of hot water on my desk and stuck in a pair of scissors. But it's Matthew's daughter. Didn't want to chance it by being loosey-goosey. This far away and if she's like her dad? That's why I included Sierra and some of the Sedona girls in the spell. Like an antenna. To give it a little boost from closer to home, you know?"

The younger woman shook her head. "I'm not comfortable with this, Natalie. Are we doing the right thing?"

"Matthew can't do the job anymore and somebody's got to step up before it gets all crazy again."

"But she's not stepping up. She's being dragged."

Natalie sighed. "Kady, what do you want me to say?" She glanced at her watch. "Another minute or so." She looked back at Kady. "I mean, yeah, I know, but it's for a good cause."

Kady's scowl deepened. "I know all that. But it's her life. We're messing with her life. Is it ever right to meddle like this?"

"From what I hear, it's not much of a life. And I've been scrying her aura so I can see how much she hates her job. We aren't dragging her. We're merely nudging things along."

Kady snorted. "Scrying her aura? What the hell does that mean?"

"Viewing her aura from a distance through a crystal ball. Or a mirror."

Kady rolled her eyes. "Mirror, mirror on the wall, who's the most burnt out lawyer of them all? Give me a break. She's like twenty five hundred miles away. You can't read her from that far. If she's really like Matthew, you couldn't read her if she was in the next room. Not with magic at least."

"Fine, you got me." Natalie pointed at Kady's discarded robe. "Hand me that. I'll take them home and put them in the wash."

Kady leaned over, picked up the robe, and handed it to Natalie, holding it between thumb and index finger as if it might be contagious.

Natalie continued. "You're right. I can't read her aura from here. But come on. That place she works is a circus."

Kady raised an eyebrow. "And this isn't?"

Natalie laughed. "Not even in the same dimension. Maybe I can't use a scrying mirror to read her, but I can read the Arizona news online. She's just like Matthew and you know how he gets. It's only a matter of time before she tells that grandstanding jackass she works for what she really thinks of him. And then buh-bye employment. And besides it's not like we're hexing her, not technically."

"Only because we can't," Kady said. "I'm not sure I see the difference."

"The difference is we're hexing her boss. And a few other people. Not her. It doesn't matter whether we can't because we aren't. And it's too late to stop it, so you'll just have to live with it." Natalie checked her watch again. "All done."

Natalie bent and shut off the flame under the small cauldron. "This is so much easier with the camp stove. Now we leave it until it cools then dump it down the mop sink." She straightened up and looked at Kady. "If you think about it, we're doing her a favor. She needs a change of scenery. Bad. Don't let me forget to take the knife out before we dump the cauldron."

"Got it. Don't forget to take the knife out before we dump the cauldron."

Natalie sighed. "I walked right into that didn't I. I gotta get back to the phones. Go downstairs and get a can of pop. Take a few minutes. This was heavier magic than you're used to. Sugar and caffeine will help you recharge."

"I still don't feel good about this."

"It'll be fine," Natalie said. "Trust me. She'll love it here."

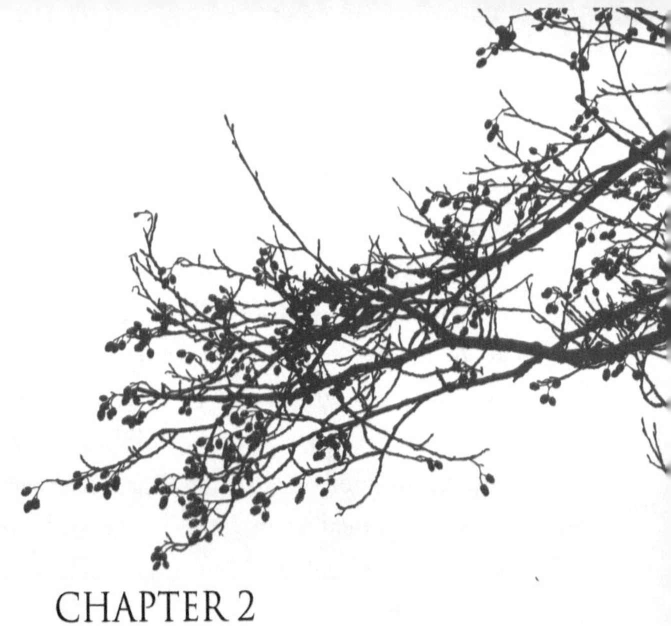

CHAPTER 2

EIGHT HOURS INTO her fourth day on the road, Meaghan Keele was tired. She'd started in Arizona and now—finally—neared her destination, her new home. Pennsylvania was too green for her desert-adapted eye. Too many trees closing in around her, overhung by a solid slab of dreary gray clouds. Already she missed Phoenix, missed the blue skies, the heat, the treeless vistas.

Meaghan began missing Phoenix the moment she started the car to begin her cross-country drive. She sighed and turned up the radio. Thank God for satellite. The country up here near the New York state line was a black hole. No radio stations or large cities. Only small towns separated by miles of mountains and claustrophobic forests.

She was headed for the town of Eldrich to become its new city attorney, or solicitor as they termed it in Pennsylvania. The job was a godsend, really, but she wished she were happier about it. She wished it felt more like a choice and less like a summons.

The timing had been fortuitous, almost eerie. Meaghan lost control at work and shouted at an elderly constituent who had denoted her the corrupt face of Evil Big Government. This encounter led to a second shouting match, this time with her boss, which didn't end well. Her outburst could be blamed in part on her frustration with the latest round of political scandals to break in the office, but the real reason was the call she had just received from her younger brother, Russ.

"Dad has Alzheimer's, Meg. I need help," Russ said in a flat emotionless voice, without a greeting or any attempt at small talk. Given the combustible nature of Meaghan's relationship with their father, she and Russ both knew there was no point in sugarcoating this request.

"Where are you?" she asked, feeling sick.

"In Eldrich, in his house. I've been here for a while and it's too much for me to do alone." Still the flat tone, the lack of emotion.

"Well, what do you expect me to do from out here?" Meaghan hadn't seen her father in more than ten years. She saw her brother more often, but he hadn't made his usual winter trip out to Arizona the last couple of years and now she knew why. Russ emailed her with news from time to time. She knew that Russ's third marriage had fallen apart within months of the wedding, but he'd never given her even a hint about their father's illness.

"Damn it, Meg, don't get all lawyer on me," he said. "I can't do this on my own anymore. It's too much. I need you to move back home."

Eldrich isn't my home, she thought, but knew enough not to say it aloud. "Are there any nursing homes or facilities you can put him in?"

"I tried that. It was a disaster. He begged me to take him home."

She could hear the naked plea in Russ's voice. He was near tears. "Meg, he asks for you all the time."

Trying to put a tough veneer over her growing fear, Meaghan said, "Yeah, Russ, I just bet he does."

"I am so goddamn sick of this shit between you and Dad," Russ said. "He's dying and we both need your help." He took a few ragged breaths. "Your part in this family didn't end when Mom died."

Meaghan clung to the phone, staring at her feet, her face hot with anger and, she had to admit, shame. "You have my attention, Russ. But you're asking a lot. I can't simply pick up and leave. I've got a job. And a house."

And, she could barely admit to herself, nothing more. A government law practice that was slowly killing her and a house she hid in to recharge from her dreadful job. She had friends, of course. She'd lived in Phoenix for more than thirty years. But her closest friends all found husbands and had babies before their biological clocks ran out while she hadn't, and the gulf between them grew wider and wider. There was, she had to admit, almost nothing to keep her in Arizona.

But move in with her father? In Pennsylvania? It was the last thing she would choose to do, all things being equal. But they weren't equal. Her father was dying and her brother wanted her to step up and do her share.

"Meg, I know it's a lot to ask. But if it helps, the city's lawyer quit a few weeks ago and they need a new one. They still talk about how much they miss Dad. With your experience, if you want the job it's yours."

Matthew Keele served as Eldrich's solicitor for nearly two decades and retired, with great reluctance, when his health began to fail. The city had gone through a couple of lawyers since, both of whom washed out quickly, and Matthew continued to hold the job in spirit and legend if not in actuality.

"Russ, I . . ." She was, for once, at a loss for words.

Russ relented. In a softer voice, he said, "I know this is a lot to spring on you all of a sudden and if it wasn't so bad, I wouldn't ask. Think about it. Okay?"

"Can you get any help in town? A nurse or something?"

"Some of the neighbors are helping. Dad has a lot of friends here, but . . ."

For a long moment neither of them spoke. Russ broke the silence. "Could you at least come out for a visit? It might calm him down a bit. He's pretty agitated about wanting to see you."

Meaghan sighed, not sure if she dreaded more the thought of seeing her father or staying away and never seeing him again. "Sure, I can fly out for a few days, but I'll need to reschedule some stuff. Let me figure it all out and I'll call you with the dates. Give me the best number to reach you."

Russ gave her his up-to-date contact info and the call ended as abruptly as it began.

A few minutes later, Meaghan got into her shouting match with the elderly conspiracy theorist. Her boss, the elected head of her office, had been looking for an excuse to knock her down a few pegs. He summoned her into his office and more shouting ensued. What miniscule respect Meaghan once had for the man had devolved over time into pure contempt. When he called her unprofessional, she called him twenty pounds of shit in a ten-pound bag.

And just like that, Meaghan severed one of the two tethers holding her in Arizona. As she cleaned out her office under the watchful eye of a security guard, her cell phone rang. Seeing an Eldrich area code, she answered. It was the mayor of Eldrich offering her the city solicitor's job.

The pay was adequate for the middle of nowhere, particularly if she lived in her father's house. She would supervise a deputy solicitor and two support staff. The county handled all criminal matters. The deputy solicitor handled any civil litigation, mostly defending claims against the city for sidewalk slip-and-falls, civil rights complaints against the tiny city police force, cars being nicked by snow plows, that sort of thing. A small law firm in Williamsport, Hallam and Associates, provided backup when needed.

Meaghan would advise the mayor, the council, and city staff members on all legal matters. She would prepare contracts and ordinances and manage litigation, which she took to mean supervising her deputy and reviewing the bills whenever the town hired Hallam and Associates as outside counsel. She didn't even have to take the bar exam to get admitted to practice in Pennsylvania. The mayor must have spoken to Russ before calling her, because he made sure to point out that the job would give her the "flexibility to take care of things at home."

She couldn't say no to a gift-wrapped job offer ten minutes after getting fired. They even threw in a moving allowance.

So, less than twenty-four hours after her brother's call for help, Meaghan found herself unemployed in Arizona, soon to be employed in Pennsylvania, and talking with a realtor about selling her house. Twenty-four hours after that, before the house was even listed, a cash investor made a generous offer sight unseen.

She said goodbye to friends and acquaintances. They expressed sadness at her leaving despite having spent very little time with her during the last few years. A mere two weeks after Russ's cry for help, Meaghan hit the road, with thirty plus years of life reduced to the contents of a small moving container to be delivered to her father's house in Eldrich.

Things happened so fast, it wasn't until she was actually driving that she had the chance to think about what she'd done and regret it. She wanted to turn back before she hit Albuquerque, but pressed on. By the time she got to Denver, she had convinced herself that it was a temporary move. If her father was declining at the rate Russ claimed, he wouldn't live much longer. She'd stick around to settle his estate, work at the city job at least a year to keep her resume from looking too flaky, and ponder her next move.

Crossing the Great Plains, despite her best efforts, she couldn't talk herself out of the realization that the ease with which she shed her entire life proved how empty and pointless that life had been. She'd been restive and unhappy for a while now, but when she thought of changing careers, she couldn't figure out what else to do. Meaghan was her father's daughter and a lawyer to the bone. Without a husband or kids, the job was all Meaghan had. If she wasn't a lawyer, what was she?

She hit the Rust Belt too tired to think and simply drove. Now she was in Pennsylvania at the exit from I-80 that would take her north to Eldrich. Russ had told her to stay on that road for about nine miles until she got to an abandoned gas station and then call him and he'd guide her in. When she told him she'd use her GPS, he laughed and said, "Good luck with that." The deep twisting valleys and ravines were not amenable to GPS. Trust the satellites, he told her, and she'd find yourself at the bottom of a quarry or on a rutted lumber road mired in the ever-present mud. He wouldn't even give her written directions, claiming it was easier to simply talk her through it.

Meaghan drove north. More green, more trees crowding to the very edge of the road. It was like driving through a leaf-covered tunnel. Lumber was big business around here, but to her it looked like they hadn't made a dent.

She shivered. The dim forests hemmed her in on either side. She felt a visceral stab of longing for the open desert stretching to meet the bright clear Arizona sky.

"What the hell have I done?" she muttered aloud for about the hundredth time. As if in answer, her cell phone rang. She jumped in her seat with a yelp, jerked the wheel, and almost swerved off the road.

The caller ID showed Russ's number. With a vicious stab, she hit the dashboard button that connected her to her cell phone.

"What?" she growled.

"Enjoying our drive, are we?" Now that he had Meaghan trapped and knew help was on the way, he was far more jovial.

"Bite me."

Russ laughed. "Where are you?"

"The heavily forested ass end of nowhere."

"You off the interstate yet?" He could barely conceal his glee, the bastard.

"Um . . ." She squinted at the odometer. "About

eight miles up Witch Hollow Road. Who comes up with these names?"

Ignoring her crack about the road name, Russ said, "Great. Stay on the phone and I'll guide you in. If the call drops, pull the car over and I'll find you."

He was making her nuts with this. "Russ, give me some damn directions already. I just drove across America. I don't need an escort."

"Do it my way for once, please?" Tension crept into his voice. "If you get lost out there, we'll never find you."

"I'll toss bread crumbs out the car window, Hansel."

"Ha. Ha." Russ's voice dripped sarcasm, but with a hint of worry. "I'm serious. People disappear out in those woods. You make a wrong turn, run out of gas, and all we find is the empty car. Humor me, all right?"

Meaghan sighed in disgust. "Fine. Okay, I'm passing the closed gas station. Now what?"

He talked her in by phone, like an air traffic controller. She would never admit it, but she was glad he had insisted on it. The thick woods obscured all landmarks and her sense of direction abandoned her. She now believed that people could be swallowed up by all those trees and simply vanish. Driving after dark must be a nightmare out here, she thought.

Just as she felt something close to claustrophobia coming on, she came around a blind curve, and the forest ended. The road wound into a lovely green valley. Eldrich lay below, tiny and perfect. A green square, surrounded by ornate buildings, anchored the town. Grand Victorian mansions lined the streets north of the square. To the south and west sat tidy bungalows and cottages. On the east side of town, a river flowed like a ribbon. Rolling farmland surrounded it all.

The sun finally made an appearance. A single beam shone through the thick clouds. The river sparkled for a moment, and then the clouds closed again. But it raised Meaghan's spirits a bit. In spite of her homesickness, she was dazzled. A charming little town, Eldrich shone like a bright jewel after the miles of dark forest.

Despite Russ's concern, the call didn't drop and he still spoke to her from the dashboard. "So?" he asked. "What do you think?"

"Damn. It's stupid pretty. You didn't lie."

"Wait until you see Dad's house, Gretel. You'll want to eat it up." Now that she was out of the woods, he gave her directions to the house on Holly Lane and hung up.

Meaghan drove through the quiet streets. In the warm Sunday twilight, a restful calm presided over the town. She'd expected things to be a bit shabbier up close, but no. It was even more charming when she saw the details. Her mood lifted. This might be okay after all.

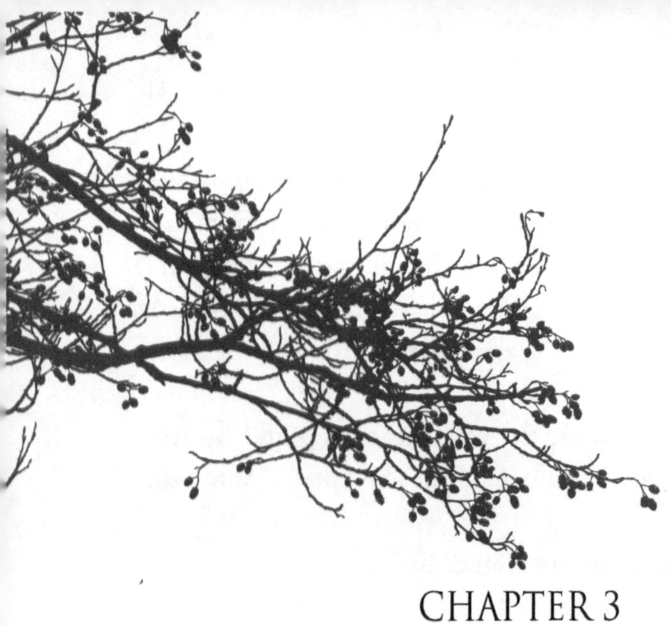

CHAPTER 3

RUSS HADN'T LIED about the house, a Victorian gingerbread fantasy meticulously restored and maintained, surrounded by the shiny holly bushes that gave the small dead-end street its name.

And he hadn't lied about their father's condition.

Meaghan remembered Matthew Keele as a tall man, imposing, with a head of thick, unruly white hair and dark brown eyes set deep in a hawkish brow. He could generate a blistering glare, a skill she had inherited, along with a natural dexterity with words and the tendency to let tenacity degenerate into pig-headedness.

All her life she'd been told that her problems with her father were because she and Matthew were so much alike. Her father had always intimidated her. Her natural inclination to hopscotch over fear right into anger made that intimidation play out as sullen defiance.

Over the last four days, she'd steeled herself to face the

man she remembered. She'd expected him to be a bit frailer, a bit vaguer, but still her father.

She barely recognized the man in the chair by the living room window. The white hair no longer sprang from his head like he'd just come out of a bracing wind. It now hung in lank strands. Underneath, she could see the pink of his scalp. The dark eyes that used to glow with fiery intelligence were milky now, and bloodshot. He was a husk of a man, so fragile he could be blown away with a gentle breath.

"Dad?" Russ said in a loud voice. "Look who it is. It's Meg. Meg's come home."

"Meg?" the old man quavered. "Meaghan? Meaghan's my daughter."

Russ grabbed her arm and dragged her close. "This is Meaghan, Dad." He held her hand out to Matthew. "Meaghan's right here."

Matthew squinted at her and recognition flared. He beamed at her, a joy on his face she'd never seen before.

She felt the hot prickle of tears and willed them away. "Hi, Dad. Here I am."

Matthew squeezed her hand and began to cry.

She wasn't sure later what unnerved her more. His physical decline or his joyful tears at seeing her. Sniffling, her own tears now flowing, she hugged him. "I'm home, Daddy. I'm home."

For the moment, all was forgiven. Her fatigue and his dementia opened a door through the imposing emotional wall between them. She knew it probably wouldn't last, but for right now, the past was forgotten.

Even Russ cried, Meaghan noticed. But then emotion had always been easy for him. He was like their mother that way. Kind, open, forgiving. Everything that Matthew and Meaghan so often were not. Russ smiled at her, then headed for the kitchen to check on supper. Another way Russ was like Mom. He was a great cook.

Meaghan held her father's hand, sniffing back her tears. After ten minutes, he dozed off.

She untangled herself and went out to her car, parked in the driveway beneath a large oak tree, to get her overnight bag. The rest of it could wait until tomorrow. The early summer twilight lingered, soft and golden. In Arizona, sunsets, although spectacular, were harsher and faster. The sky turned pink, then orange, then red, and the sun dropped like a rock behind the horizon. Night fell like a curtain at the end of a play.

But in early June, this far north, twilight lasted awhile. She took a few minutes, sitting on the front steps, to be alone and calm down a bit. All her expectations had been turned upside down. Her father was thrilled to see her. After the forbidding forests, the town was lovely and welcoming.

For the first time since Russ's call for help, Meaghan felt good. She hadn't even realized the dread she carried until it lessened. It wasn't all gone, but it was better.

Out of the corner of her eye, she saw a flash of soft light. She glanced towards it and saw another. And another.

Fireflies. Lightning bugs, she and Russ called them when they were kids.

She watched them, transfixed. Like gentle sparks, the fireflies floated in the air. Fireflies didn't exist in Arizona or anywhere in the west and she'd forgotten how magical they were. She and Russ had spent many warm evenings as children running through the soft twilight catching the flashing insects. They carried empty jam jars filled with grass and leaves, air holes punched in the lid, to hold the captured fire-flies. Meaghan liked to fall asleep with the flashing jar next to her pillow. Once she'd drifted off, her mother would slip into her room, take the jar outside, and shake the fireflies back into the soft night air, to be caught another time.

Then Matthew had his breakdown and there were no more fireflies. His drinking escalated out of control, and she, Russ, and Mom fled to Arizona. She was thirteen and Russ was eleven. Soon after, Matthew got fired from his law firm in Manhattan and ended up in Eldrich.

Mom sued for sole custody with no visitation and Matthew didn't contest it. By the time Matthew cleaned himself up, quit drinking, and reached out to his kids, it was too late. For Meaghan, at least. She was a junior in high school by then and wanted nothing to do with her father.

She relented a bit over time, elevating their relationship from non-existent to severely strained. At some point —she didn't know the details—Russ made his peace with Matthew. Probably after Mom died from an aneurysm, a death that occurred quickly, painlessly, and way too soon.

Russ responded by reaching out to his father. Meaghan, who was starting law school, stuffed her grief deep inside and buried herself in work. The door Matthew had managed to pry open a crack slammed shut again.

After Russ's first marriage failed, he moved back East at Matthew's invitation. Russ had lived in Eldrich on and off for twenty years. Dealing with their father came easier for Russ because he was so much like Mom, and Mom and Mat-thew had complemented each other well. Yin and yang.

Meaghan and Matthew were more like fire and gasoline. Or the rock and the hard place. So many years later, Meaghan had to accept that she was as much a failure at relationships as her father. Actually more of a failure, because her father had managed to be married for fifteen years, some of them happy.

There had been men in her life over the years. She'd almost married once. But things always went wrong. By the time she reached her fortieth birthday, after another relationship blew up in her face, she decided she was done with love, with all of it.

Single was lonelier sometimes, but so much easier. Giving up on romance freed up a lot of emotional space in her head. She still looked for a man, sort of, but nobody flared even a tiny interested spark within her.

Ten years passed, and now she lived in a tiny little town in the middle of nowhere. If she couldn't find love in the sixth-largest metropolitan area in America, she didn't like her odds in itty-bitty Eldrich.

Russ interrupted her thoughts. "Want a glass of wine?"

Meaghan craned her head around to look at him. "There's wine? What about Dad?"

"He's not interested anymore. But if he starts drinking again, so what?" Russ plopped down on the step next to her. "We send him to rehab?"

She smiled. "Yeah. I mean no, I guess not." She sighed. "Wine would be great."

"Chicken for dinner. Got a few nice bottles of white in the fridge." He took her hand. "You okay?"

She felt the tears well up and pushed them back down. Russ was a good guy. Always had been.

"Yeah," she said. "That's as good as it's going to get, isn't it."

"Well . . . for the two of you, yeah, maybe." He watched the fireflies for a moment. "That's actually the best I've ever seen you get along. And he still has the occasional lucid moment, so don't give up hope."

"Why didn't you tell me about this sooner? When did he get sick?"

Russ sighed. "He didn't want me to tell you."

Meaghan snorted. "Of course not. I know you think the shit between us is all my fault, but he hasn't exactly been father of the year. Ever. Not to me at least."

Russ shook his head. "It's not like you've ever given him the chance. I think he didn't want you to feel obligated or think that he thought you owed him something. He always knew how bad he'd screwed up with you, but he didn't know how to fix it."

Meaghan let go of Russ's hand and stared into the distance. I will not cry, she told herself. I will not start crying again.

Russ gave her a moment then continued. "It wasn't only you. He didn't tell anybody he was sick for a long time. He did a really good job of hiding it. Masking is what they call it. Natalie—his secretary—she noticed it first. He was having a hard time remembering stuff and keeping track of time. Everyone covered for him, hoping, I think, that it was only a temporary slump."

"How long has this been going on?"

Russ squinted, thinking. "Natalie first started seeing odd stuff a little over four years ago. It was another six months before she called me. I was down in Philly. I still had the restaurant and didn't want to move back up here. And he kind of plateaued for a while. For almost a year. He couldn't work anymore, but there were enough folks keeping an eye on him that I didn't need to be here. Then he got worse and I tried to put him in a care facility. I told you what a disaster that was."

Meaghan nodded.

"But at the time, I didn't know what else to do. I didn't think moving him down to Philly was a good idea."

"And you got married," Meaghan said.

"Yeah." Russ rolled his eyes. "There's some great timing. Darla. What a girl." Darla was Russ's third ex-wife. "They say the third time's the charm. But for me I think it's three strikes, you're out."

Meaghan laughed. Russ wasn't much better than she was at picking partners, but Meaghan was smart enough not to marry them.

"And then she took off," Russ continued. "And the restaurant tanked and here I am. Almost two years now. I thought about opening a cafe or something, but realized in a hurry that I had a full-time job here at home."

"Huh. Yeah. Well, I'm finally here. Not sure what help I'll be."

"You'll be company for both of us. I need someone lucid to talk to. And someone to keep an eye on him so I can have the occasional afternoon off. I know you don't believe it, but he really wants you to be here."

"Okay." Meaghan stood up and grabbed her overnight bag. "I gotta pee, then let's get that wine. Where's the bathroom?"

They stepped inside. In the warm glow of the hallway light, Meaghan took a long look at her brother. His hazel eyes were bloodshot and beneath them dark circles stood out like bruises. His warm brown hair was shot through with white. Lines she hadn't seen before etched his cheeks and forehead.

"I'm a crappy sister," Meaghan announced. "Through all this, I've never asked how you are."

Russ laughed. "That's because I started shouting at you over the phone, remember? I didn't give you a chance to ask before I started whining."

"Seriously. Are you okay? I am sorry about you and Darla. And the restaurant."

He shrugged. "I'm okay. You're here now. As far as Darla goes . . ." He paused, weighing his response. "Her taking off so fast saved us all that tedious hating-each-other time."

Without thinking, Meaghan threw her arms around him. She wasn't much of a hugger, so even she was surprised.

Russ hugged her back, laughing. "Whoa. Down, big sis. You're freaking me out. First you and Dad crying all over each other and now this." He pulled away. "Bathroom's on the left past the stairs and the kitchen's at the end of the hall. I'll run your bag up, check on Dad, and be back in a flash."

She nodded. "Where's the wine?"

"In the fridge, glasses on the counter."

"Corkscrew?"

"Screw cap. Don't be a snob," he added, seeing the look on her face.

CHAPTER 4

THEY GOT THROUGH dinner. Matthew, while not overcome with joy like he had been when he first saw Meaghan, remained calm and seemed to know who she was. He could still feed himself, Russ had told her, but never had much of an appetite.

Meaghan ate two huge plates of food, drank three glasses of wine, and, glassy-eyed, made her way up to her bedroom around nine.

It was a large room, containing simple furniture and no personal touches, a small bathroom, and a huge bay window with a window seat. I'm hiding in my room like a teenager, she thought. She laughed and then segued smoothly into weeping. Big, gasping sobs shook her.

The stress of the last few weeks broke over her like surf. She sat on the bed, face buried in a pillow, crying her eyes out. When the tears tapered off, she hiccupped a few times like a small child. She staggered into the bathroom, grabbed a wad of toilet paper, and blew her nose. She looked at herself in the mirror. Red and splotchy. Swollen eyes. And she had to pee again.

"Stupid wine," she muttered. "Three glasses and I have a meltdown."

Finished in the bathroom, Meaghan wandered out into the bedroom, a roll of toilet paper stuffed under her arm. Her eyes were still leaking and her nose running and, from experience, she knew it would last a while. She made a mental note to buy a box of tissues. She unpacked her small bag and went back into the bathroom to brush her teeth. Then she pulled on her pajamas and crawled into bed.

She hadn't slept well since Russ's call for help—she expected to toss and turn in the dark awhile. She didn't. Next thing she knew, sunlight was streaming through the white lace curtains in the bay window. She glanced at her cell phone on the night stand. It was 8:33. She'd been asleep almost eleven hours.

Her new job didn't start for another week, but she wanted to stop in today and at least look around and introduce herself. And she had to unpack her car. And figure out where her storage pod was and when she'd get it. And get a Pennsylvania driver's license. And register the car and find a bank and check on her law license application and . . .

After a night's respite, her churning thoughts resumed. She had so much to do, she didn't know where to start.

Then she smelled bacon. And coffee. Her stomach growled. Distracted from her frenzied thoughts, she pulled on jeans and a T-shirt, peed out the rest of the wine, and patted down her short silvery hair with wet fingers. The messy short do was the best thing that ever happened to her. She didn't even need gel to make her hair stand up. Another legacy from her father.

Good enough, she thought. She clattered down the stairs and back to the kitchen. Russ was already cooking her breakfast. She grinned at him. "What a good brother you are."

"I heard you stomping around up there and decided to get a head start. Here." He set a plate down in front of her.

Russ had heaped her plate with bacon. Meaghan loved bacon. Thick sliced and cooked exactly how she liked. Crisp but still with some chew. Knowing Russ, it was probably from a hand-fed organic hog raised locally and smoked according to some ancient family recipe.

"So, let me guess," she said, inspecting her plate. "Organic uncured bacon and free-range eggs, from local farmers, scrambled with a locally sourced, hand-crafted cheddar. Did I get all the buzzwords right?"

"Yup," Russ said.

Meaghan was used to bagged salads, grocery store rotisserie chickens, and street tacos from the cart outside of her old office. "Trying to fatten me up, Hansel?"

"No, just trying to feed you actual food for a change."

"I eat actual food."

"Not like this you don't." He set a steaming mug of coffee next to her plate. "Cream's in the pitcher if you want it. And I got some early strawberries from Natalie's garden."

"Cream?" Meaghan said through a mouthful of bacon. "Real cream?"

"Yes. Real cream. That fake crap is an abomination." He set down a small bowl of strawberries. "It's good on the berries too."

"Uhn," Meaghan answered. She chewed a bit and swallowed some of the food in her mouth. "Is there toast?"

"Toast? *Toast?* You want more food?" he said in mock outrage. A moment later, he brought her a plate of heavy brown bread she knew he'd baked himself, toasted and smeared with butter.

"There's no place like home," Meaghan said with a grin before diving back into her breakfast.

A few minutes later, she leaned back in her chair with a groan. "You don't do breakfast like that every day, do you?"

Russ poured her more coffee and finally sat down. "Nah. There's a little fatted calf killing going on here. I'm glad you're back, prodigal sister."

"Where's Matthew?"

"*Dad*," Russ answered, "is out on the front porch."

She knew it drove Russ nuts when she called their father by his first name.

Russ continued. "He usually wakes up pretty early, six-thirty, seven." He sighed and stared at her hard for a long moment. "The thing you gotta understand is it might be a good day, or it might be a bad day. Or it might be both. He may not recognize you today. He may think you're someone else."

He stood up, grabbed Meaghan's plate before she could protest, and set it in the sink. "You can't take any of it to heart. It's got nothing to do with you. It's the disease clogging up his brain."

Again, Meaghan saw the fatigue etched into her brother's face. And for the first time, she also saw the grief. "Russ, I know I've been hard on him over the years. And I know I overreacted a lot." She traced her finger through a drop of coffee spilled on the table top. "I . . . it's not . . . I'm not the person I used to be. And he's not who he used to be, I get that. Last night was . . ." She waved her hand in the air, lost for the words. "Last night. I won't stomp off in a huff, okay?"

Russ nodded, but still looked worried. "Okay. But you might hear some weird shit coming out of his mouth. I'm just warning you." He picked her plate out of the sink, rinsed it, and put it in the dishwasher.

"That was an awesome breakfast, by the way," Meaghan said, trying to lighten the mood. "But please don't feed me like that every day or I'll get huge."

Russ smiled. "Okay, Gretel. No more gingerbread cottage for you." He held out his hand. "Let's go remind him again who you are."

It was a good thing Russ was there. Despite her promise not to get upset by anything her father said, if Russ hadn't been there to calm her down, she would have run for the car and not stopped driving until she hit the Pacific.

Matthew had come back into the house and now sat in the living room.

"Dad," Russ said. "Meaghan's here to see you."

"Meaghan?" The quaver was gone and some of the sharpness had returned to his milky eyes. "What the hell does she want? Here to tell me again what a bastard I am?" He turned his glare from Russ to Meaghan. "Who the hell are you? I don't need a nurse," he said, his voice tight with anger.

Russ gave her a reassuring smile. "Dad, this is Meg. She's here to see you. She came all the way from Arizona."

Skeptical, Matthew squinted at her. "Too old. Meaghan's a young girl and besides she hates me. Quit lying to me!" he shouted, furious, spittle flecking his chin. He raised a shaking hand and pointed at her. "Your magic won't work here, witch. Get out of my house. Go!"

And Meaghan went. Out the front door. No car keys. Barefoot. She sprinted to her car, blinded with tears, feeling like a teenager again.

She tripped over the low stone border along the front walkway and sat down hard, pain shutting off her tears like a switch. Cradling her right foot, she saw the blood already pooling under the big toenail. "Shit, shit, shit," she said, rocking back and forth. "Shit."

Russ trotted up. "Let me see. Is it broken?" He knelt down next to her. "Can you move it?"

She wiggled her toes with care and circled her foot. "I'm gonna lose the nail, but I don't think it's too bad." She looked into her brother's concerned eyes. "He hates me."

"No, Meg, no. That's what I was trying to warn you about. I'm sorry you got such a vivid example of it." He tried to help her up.

"Wait, give me a sec." She took a couple of ragged breaths. "He sure sounded like he hates me. Or at least he used to."

"Yeah, once, maybe. For like five minutes." Russ squeezed her hand. "These fits are like snapshots, random moments that flare in his head and then burn out."

Meaghan nodded. "I guess."

"It's like he's . . ." Russ pondered a moment. "It's like he's unstuck in time. He still knows where he is, but he doesn't know when. Let's get some ice on that. Ready?"

She nodded and he helped her up. She put some weight on her injured foot. "Nothing broken, I don't think. What the hell was that witch and magic stuff?"

"Don't know," Russ answered and for a moment she had the overwhelming sense he was lying. "A book, a movie? There's no way to tell."

With Russ's assistance, Meaghan limped back to the house. So much for all the running around she planned to do today. She wouldn't even be able to get a shoe on for a couple of days.

The front door opened and Matthew stepped out of the house. Meaghan stiffened.

"Wait," Russ whispered.

"Hey, there, young lady. You took quite a tumble," Matthew said, smiling. "Russ, you bring her into the living room. Let's get her some ice. And an aspirin." He held out his hand. "I'm Matthew Keele, dear. And you'd be?"

Meaghan stared, mouth open. How did Russ keep up with this shit? "Um, I'm Meaghan?" She held out her trembling hand.

Matthew took her proffered hand in both of his and shook it. "How about that? That's my daughter's name." His smile broadened. "She's a lawyer, like me."

"I . . . I know?" How was she supposed to respond to this?

Russ rescued her. "Dad, this is Meaghan. She lives with us now."

Matthew looked at Russ, surprised. "She does? Well, that's great!" He seemed thrilled with the news. He turned his attention back to Meaghan. "You'll like her. She has the same first name as you." He beamed at Meaghan, with no sign of recognition.

"You get it now?" Russ muttered out the side of his mouth. "Why I'm so fried?"

Meaghan, eyes wide, looked back and forth between her father and brother and nodded.

CHAPTER 5

ANGRY MATTHEW DID not make a return appearance that day. He was cheerful and friendly and utterly
without comprehension that the woman on the sofa with the
swollen foot was his daughter. He went on and on about how
proud he was of Meaghan, how she was a lawyer, how she'd be
along any minute, and they could all laugh about her having
the same name as the injured passerby.

It was, in many ways, Meaghan realized, worse than being
snarled at and mistaken for a witch.

Meaghan had spent her whole life certain that she never
quite measured up in her father's eyes. But clearly that wasn't
the case, at least not for this version of Matthew. Either she
had been wrong all this time or he had changed his mind.

Not that it mattered. The past was gone and so was the
man she had loved and hated all those many years. She could
make peace with the addled old man who dwelt in his place,
but he was a mere shadow of her father. Matthew, the man

she remembered, was vanishing before her eyes, so much of him now gone that true reconciliation seemed impossible.

After an hour of amiable chatter about his "little girl," Matthew began yawning and rubbing his eyes like a child and Russ led him upstairs for a nap.

"You see?" Russ walked into the living room and flopped into the easy chair by the sofa. "He doesn't hate you. I told you. For years I've been telling you." He rubbed his hand over his face and grimaced. "I need to shave and take a shower. Dad's never hated you. Except for a few minutes here and there when you were being a total bitch."

Meaghan opened her mouth to protest, then closed it. He had a point. She knew she'd been awful to her father over the years. Worse than he'd been to her.

Russ smiled at her, obviously pleased to see her accepting what he had to say instead of fighting it. "Want a cup of tea? You look kind of beat up."

"I *am* kind of beat up."

"Yes. You are."

"And it's all self-inflicted, isn't it?"

"Yes." Russ reached over and squeezed her shoulder. "It is."

"You don't have to be so damn happy about it," Meaghan said. She could feel her face redden.

"Sure I do. It's a long time coming—you finally pulling your head out of your ass."

She laughed in spite of herself and threw a pillow at him. "Jerk face."

He caught the pillow, laughing too. "How's your foot?"

"The ice is all melted. And I have a lot of stuff I should be doing today."

Russ nodded. "Which you won't be doing."

"But, I—"

He cut her off. "God, you're as stubborn as Dad. Just sit. One day. The world won't end if you chill out for one day." He stood up and plucked the ice bag from her foot. "I'll get you more ice."

"And the tea? Anything to go with that?"

He nodded. "Got some muffins."

"Would you get me some ibuprofen?"

"Sure." Russ walked out of the room.

"And my cell phone and laptop?" she called after him. She could almost hear his eyes rolling in response.

The day grew warmer and right after her tea and muffin, which Russ turned into an early lunch by adding a bowl of chicken soup, she hobbled out to the wide front porch. Matthew still napped upstairs while Russ showered. The house had no Internet connection, so her laptop was useless. She tried to access the net on her phone and it was so slow she finally gave up. No 4G service, or 3G service for that matter, on Holly Lane.

For years, Matthew had paid a hefty fee to have the *New York Times* delivered. But now he didn't care about the news and Russ had let the subscription lapse. Eldrich had a small weekly newspaper, but Russ didn't subscribe to that either.

Like all small towns, Eldrich ran on gossip. The important information was disseminated orally, either on the phone or in person. Russ learned all he needed to know gossiping with his organic farmers and artisan cheese makers and anyone else he encountered throughout the day. The newspaper contained sports scores and classified ads, and the community relied on it mostly for lining hamster cages and catching paint drips.

Meaghan tried to read a couple of the mystery novels Russ brought out to her. But she almost always figured out who did it after reading the first few chapters and then ruined any hope of reading further by jumping to the final chapter to see if she was right, which she almost always was. Years spent working with politicians and the public had given her an ultra-sensitive, finely-calibrated bullshit detector. She could spot liars and schmucks, even fictional ones, from a million miles away.

With nothing else to do, she fell asleep. And dreamed.

Meaghan almost never remembered her dreams. What little she could recall was fuzzy and disconnected—random images with a feeble narrative imposed upon them. Her usual dreams were synaptic housecleaning, nothing more.

But this dream—this was different. Vivid. And she knew she was dreaming, something she'd never experienced before. In her dream, she was in the same place she'd been when she fell asleep. On the porch curled up in the wicker settee with her foot propped on an ottoman. She sat up and looked around. At a glance, things looked normal. But with a longer look, things were not quite right.

The forbidding forest she had driven through the day before now surrounded her father's house. The front yard had become a tidy island surrounded by looming trees. She could see movement within the tree line, but couldn't make out what was moving. The sunlight shimmered, like heat rising from a hot asphalt road. Within the shimmer she could barely make out a distant figure walking towards her.

But the perspective was all wrong. The trees crowded

around the house, but the walker appeared to be miles away, on an open plane.

And then the shimmer evaporated and in the front yard stood her mother, real and solid.

Meaghan felt a rush of joy and then a stab of grief, so powerful she gasped. She hadn't felt grief like this since the day her mother died. For, even in her dream, with her mother standing before her, Meaghan knew, in her bones and in her gut, that her mother was dead.

The mom figure smiled and waved her hand. "Hi, sweetheart." She remained standing on the lawn.

"You're dead," Meaghan replied.

"Well, yes. Have been for a while." She gave a small nervous laugh.

"What do you want? How are you here?" In the dream, Meaghan could feel her heart pound.

"You're dreaming, Meggy. That's how I'm here." The dream Mom sighed. "Why I'm here . . . this is kind of complicated. Mind if I sit down?"

With a trembling hand, Meaghan pointed at the chair beside her.

Her dead mother ascended the porch steps and sat down, on the edge of the seat, back straight, smoothing her skirt with her hands. Meaghan recognized the skirt. Blue and green cotton madras plaid, faded, sensible. It had been one of her mother's favorites. Far more ladylike than her daughter, Elizabeth Keele always wore skirts, even to work in the yard and mow the lawn.

"This is a dream," Meaghan said.

"Well, yes, sweetheart it is. How's your foot?"

This was too much, even for this dream. "You aren't real.

You're a . . . I don't know. A sign that my brain's starting to melt like Matthew's."

Elizabeth frowned. "I wish you wouldn't call him by his first name. It hurts him so when you do that."

"You. Aren't. Real." Meaghan's voice shook now, along with her hands.

"Well, I may not be real, but I'm still your mother." Elizabeth reached over to pluck a strand of hair from Meaghan's forehead. "This haircut is adorable, by the way."

Meaghan pulled away. She wasn't sure how to accept a compliment from her own subconscious, which was what this had to be.

"Fine, I'm your subconscious," Elizabeth said, reading her mind. "Your brain isn't melting. You've merely had a very busy few weeks." The smile vanished and she leaned forward. "Real or not, I don't have a lot of time and there are things I need to tell you. Stop analyzing and listen, okay?"

"You aren't real. I'm dreaming."

Elizabeth rolled her eyes, like Russ always did. "Exactly like your father. I'm not real, we've established that. I'm simply a manifestation of your subconscious mind. Please. Hush and listen to what you're trying to tell yourself, okay?"

Elizabeth commenced her skirt smoothing, a nervous habit of hers, Meaghan recalled.

"The thing is, sweetie," Elizabeth said, "your dad needs you now in more ways than you know." She grabbed Meaghan's hand in both of hers before Meaghan could pull away.

Her mother's hands felt warm and lightly calloused—from gardening without gloves, Meaghan remembered. In that moment, it didn't matter if the figure before her was real or not.

"Mom," Meaghan whispered, her eyes filling with tears. Elizabeth leaned forward and put her arms around Meaghan and hugged her tight. Meaghan could smell Dove soap and lavender and that sunny warm smell Mom always had after a day in the garden.

Elizabeth squeezed in next to her on the settee. "Meggy," she said, stroking Meaghan's hair. "I'm so sorry I had to leave you and Russ like that. Without saying goodbye. And I'm so sorry for taking you from your father."

"He abandoned us," Meaghan said, sniffling.

"No. He didn't. That's one of the things I came here to tell you." Elizabeth pulled back so she could look Meaghan in the eye. "I abandoned him. When he needed me most. Because I couldn't accept what was happening. I refused to believe what my own eyes showed me and I fled. With you and Russ."

"But, he had a breakdown," Meaghan said. "I remember —"

Elizabeth cut her off. "You remember the version I told you and everyone else. He had a breakdown because we left. Because I left. Not the other way around."

Meaghan shook her head, refusing to believe this version of events. "But he let you take us. He didn't fight for custody or come visit or anything."

"Because it wasn't safe around him anymore. The war had started and your father was neck deep in it. He couldn't risk you and Russ getting hurt."

War? What the hell was she talking about? She pulled

away from her mother. "You were so mad at him all those years. Now I know you aren't real. You can't be."

Elizabeth released her hold on Meaghan, and turned away, her face in her hands. Shaking her head, she said, "I didn't know. I couldn't see—*wouldn't* see—what was happening to him. Because I didn't want to believe it." She raised her head and looked over her shoulder and spoke to someone who wasn't there. "I need a minute more. Please . . . I know . . ." She nodded. "I'll be quick."

She turned back to Meaghan. "Meggy, it's almost time for you to wake up. Listen now." She scooped up one of Meaghan's hands and gripped it so hard it hurt. "Trust your eyes and your ears. Soon you'll be dealing with some strange things. Your father was supposed to ease you in, but he got sick so fast there was no time."

Elizabeth stared at Meaghan with an intensity Meaghan never remembered her mother displaying in life. "Believe what's in front of you," Elizabeth said. "Even if you don't know why and it seems crazy. Trust your gut. And don't be afraid. You have power you don't know about yet. And allies."

She pulled Meaghan back into a tight embrace, kissed her daughter's cheek, and whispered, "Remember." The world dissolved and Meaghan woke up.

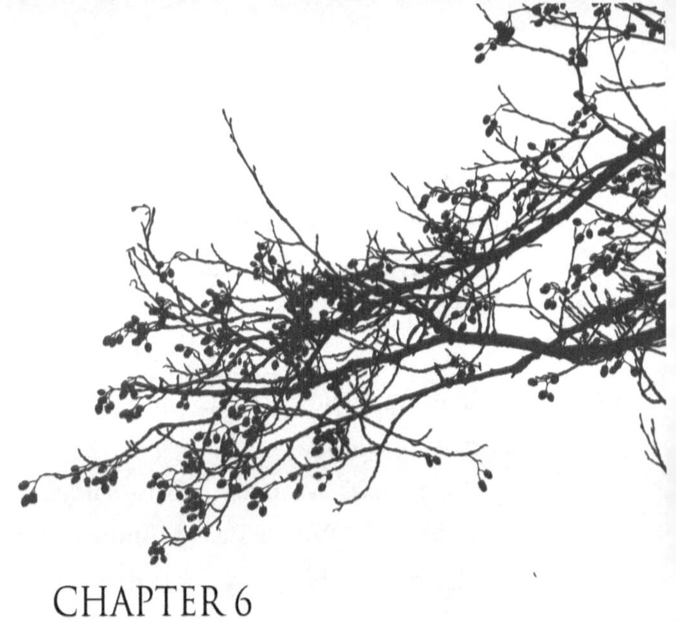

CHAPTER 6

MEAGHAN WAS LYING on her side on the settee, injured foot at an awkward angle on the ottoman. She pushed herself up. Groggy and disoriented, she looked around the yard. The dark forest of her dream was gone.

She fumbled for her cell phone on the floor boards under the settee. It was almost four. She'd been asleep for over an hour. That dream, what the hell was that? She recognized the hollow grief she hadn't felt in years. For her mother. Waking felt like losing her all over again.

Meaghan shivered. The porch, now heavily shaded, was chilly without the early June sunshine. She stood up and tried putting some weight on her foot. Experimenting, she discovered she could walk on her heel, avoiding the rest of the foot, without too much pain.

She limped into the house. She stopped in the hallway bathroom, patted her nap-disheveled hair back into some semblance of its normal shape, and went to find her family.

Matthew and Russ sat at the kitchen table. Matthew worked on some kind of puzzle while Russ read a cookbook.

"Hi, Daddy," Meaghan said, squeezing his shoulder. An unfamiliar wave of tenderness broke over her as she looked at him.

"I did my homework," he said with pride. "All done, Becky, take a look."

"Dad, that's Meaghan," Russ said, not looking up from his cookbook. "We see Becky tomorrow. At the hospital."

Matthew sighed and looked up at her. "I don't know what's happening anymore."

Meaghan leaned her cheek on top of his head. "I don't know what's happening most of the time anymore either."

Matthew smiled up at her. "Becky's never met Meaghan."

Russ shook his head and put down the book. "No, Dad. She hasn't. Maybe Meaghan can go to the hospital with us tomorrow."

Matthew nodded, then sat up straighter. "Car in the driveway." He jumped up with a spryness belying his age and headed for the front door.

Russ sighed. "Half the time he can't hear you even if you shout in his ear, but he always knows when someone drives up. It's like Duke and the fridge door."

Duke had been their childhood dog. A scruffy German Shepherd mix, by age twelve Duke was stone deaf, except for the refrigerator door. He could be sound asleep upstairs under a bed, but if someone opened the fridge even a crack to peek in, Duke came running.

Russ got up to follow Matthew to the front door. "It's probably Jamie. He said he'd stop by with some stuff for you to read when I told him you'd jammed your toe and wouldn't be by for a few days."

"Jamie?" Meaghan asked, in shock. "Jamie Smith, my *deputy?* Oh crap, Russ. Look at me."

"Relax. You look fine. It's Eldrich, not Manhattan. Nobody expects you to be all dolled up."

Meaghan scowled. "I'd settle for bathed."

Russ dismissed her with a wave of his hand. The doorbell rang. Russ trotted out to help Matthew with the front door.

Meaghan hobbled after him. So much for a professional first impression.

She knew Matthew had known Jamie since he was a boy. It was Matthew who encouraged him to go to law school and Matthew who gave him his first legal job clerking part-time in the solicitor's office.

After several hours of relatively normal behavior, even if he still didn't recognize his daughter, Matthew got weird again. She had a moment to register Jamie—tall, young, athletic build, wearing khakis and a black golf shirt, shy smile—standing in the hallway. Nervous to meet his new boss, she thought.

Then Matthew swept into a deep bow in front of him and said something in a language Meaghan had never heard before. He straightened up and smiled. "Welcome."

Jamie blushed. "Matthew, it's me. It's Jamie."

"I know who you are, Jamie. Your father is well?" Matthew accented Jamie's name oddly, making it sound something like "szhumay."

Meaghan gave Jamie a sympathetic smile while Russ came to the rescue. "Dad, it's Jamie. Your old law clerk. He works for Meaghan now."

"Russ, don't interrupt," Matthew said. "I've known the prince since he was a boy." Matthew bowed again. "I am, as always, at your service."

Jamie's nervous grin smoothed into a deeper smile. He bowed his head. "For which I am always grateful, my friend." He spoke in a slow, rich voice. He glanced up at Meaghan and winked. His eyes were dark indigo blue. If he were twenty years older, I'd be in trouble, Meaghan thought. Too young for her tastes, thank God, but a honey, no doubt about it.

Satisfied by this response, Matthew patted Jamie's arm with a smile. "I'll leave you kids to talk shop." He ambled back to the kitchen.

Jamie took a couple steps toward Meaghan and held out his hand. "You must be Meaghan. I'm Jamie Smith. Welcome to Eldrich."

Meaghan shook his hand. "I never thought of playing along. All day long he's thought I'm somebody else. This morning he thought I was a witch. At least you get to be royalty."

Russ coughed. Jamie stiffened for a moment, then shrugged. "It seems to make him happy."

Again, she had the quick intuition of a lie—some shared information her brother and this young man didn't want her to know. Too much stress, she thought. It's making me nutty.

Russ served them lemonade and a plate of cookies, and left them alone in the living room. Jamie had brought her a copy of the city ordinance book along with some other documents—budgets, memos, a city organization chart. He had the Pennsylvania Code on a flash drive until she could access the online version at city hall.

Meaghan needed to get better acquainted with the specifics of Pennsylvania law, but it was familiar stuff after all the years she'd spent working in local government. With just over five thousand residents, Eldrich was small enough to keep the politicians from getting into expensive trouble. Shallow pockets meant less of a fiscal safety cushion, but also limited the range of bad ideas available to elected officials. A $100,000 boondoggle was much easier to clean up than a multimillion dollar one.

As if reading her thoughts, Jamie said, "Eldrich is kind of sleepy. Must seem like Mayberry after Phoenix. It's not a badly run town, but things have slipped a bit since Matthew left."

Meaghan shook her head with a smile. "I never actually worked for Phoenix itself. I worked for a couple of smaller cities and the county."

"But it's basically all one big city, right?"

"Yeah, sort of, I guess. Not as self-contained as Eldrich."

Jamie chuckled. "Not as dinky, you mean."

"Ouch. Am I that transparent?"

Jamie smile widened, his eyes crinkling. It was a freer happier expression than the nervous grin in the hallway or the smile he'd given Matthew. In that moment, she could see the boy he had once been. It was extraordinarily disarming.

He must be magic with a jury, Meaghan thought. What's he doing in Eldrich handling municipal slip and falls?

"No," he said. "You aren't transparent at all, but I remember how I felt coming back here after law school in Philadelphia."

"Which school?"

"Temple. Not in a great part of town so it was even a bigger shock to come back to Eldrich."

Meaghan smiled. "Well, I'd be lying if said I wasn't suffering Internet withdrawal and all the trees didn't freak me out a little."

Jamie leaned forward, now serious. "It's hard to see your dad like this."

It wasn't a question for her, she realized, but a statement about Jamie.

"You've known Matthew since you were a kid?"

He nodded. "It was a bad time. We had to leave . . ." A moment's hesitation. "We had to leave the place we lived really fast and got here with nothing. Matthew helped us get on our feet."

"How old were you?"

"I was twelve."

"And you've lived in Eldrich since?"

He sat back. "Not the whole time. I went to Mansfield University for undergrad. It's real close so I got back to Eldrich on weekends a lot. And then the three years in Philly."

"But you came back."

"I did. I feel at home here. It's safe. My wife had some culture shock at first. But she's good with it now.

If he'd known Matthew for what must be almost twenty years, Meaghan calculated, then he must know something of their turbulent history. Best to deal with it right away.

"I guess you know Matthew and I haven't been very close over the years."

Jamie's face flushed. "Uh, yeah . . ." He stopped, embarrassed.

Now it was Meaghan's turn to blush. "I'm sorry. I put you on the spot there. It's just . . ."

Just what? It would help to clear the air if she had to

work with this kid every day. But beneath the pragmatism, she realized, lay jealousy, coiled like a snake. Jamie had found Matthew in his life at about the same age Meaghan had lost him.

She continued. "I know you've been closer to him than I have. I figure it's better to deal with that upfront than tiptoe around it."

Jamie nodded. "I get that." He looked away from her. "I don't . . . my father and I . . ." He met her gaze again. "I understand how things go wrong. And it's none of my business anyway." He smiled again, but it was restrained, sad even. "But you're here now."

He looked so woeful for a moment that Meaghan felt a pang of . . . maternal instinct? Like I'd know what that felt like, she thought. "I'm here now."

The conversation was more casual after that. Less about work, more personal details, but easy. Two people getting to know each other.

His wife was named Patrice. He had two small children. His daughter, called Liddy, short for Elizabeth, was four and his son, Ben, was not quite two. With pride, he pulled out his cell phone and showed her some photos. Patrice was petite and lovely, with a determined set to her jaw. Liddy had wild curly red hair and Ben had his father's blue eyes.

They lived in a pre-war Tudor cottage—another story-book house, Meaghan thought—in the newer part of town, within walking distance of city hall. Patrice worked as a nurse at the local clinic. By Eldrich standards, they were doing well. They didn't need Patrice's paycheck to get by, but Jamie said she loved her job and it kept her from going small-town bonkers.

In spite of herself, Meaghan's cynical heart warmed. Jamie was a good man, with a good head on his shoulders, who loved his wife and his kids. He liked to fly fish and play softball. He was a normal, well-adjusted, all-American guy. With a wonderful little family. In a wonderful little town that was his refuge from whatever domestic nightmare he'd grown up in. His hasty arrival in Eldrich and his stammering references to his father suggested a troubled start in life.

And it hit her. The war. What her mother—what her *subconscious*, Meaghan corrected herself—had been trying to tell her. Did she hear somewhere through the years that her father was working with refugees? Given his age, maybe Jamie was a refugee? From somewhere like Bosnia or Kosovo? One of the countries in the post-Yugoslavian mess? The time-line fit.

That had to be it. She had found a highly dramatic way to put some disconnected bits of memory about Matthew and Jamie together. That meant her dream was not an omen of incipient dementia. She breathed an internal sigh of relief. Her mother delivering it and telling her to give her father a break was nothing more than familial guilt for not having been a better daughter.

Jamie's English was flawless American and his name sure didn't sound eastern European. But dropping the accent and picking up a quintessentially western name—honestly, James Smith? He might as well be named John Doe. Both acts fit a traumatized kid fleeing an ugly civil war and a messed-up family life.

He didn't mention any other family and Meaghan knew well enough not to ask. She'd ask Russ for the details over dinner.

Jamie looked at his watch. "It's after five. Gotta pick up the kids from day care." He handed Meaghan a business card with his cell number and told her to call him if she needed anything, asked her to give his best to Russ and Matthew, and hurried out the door. She hobbled over to the window to watch him go. He got into a minivan—of course, Meaghan thought, I bet it's full of stale Cheerios, broken toys, and softball equipment—backed with care out of the driveway and drove down Holly Lane.

Well, good for him, she thought. To get out of whatever post-Soviet hellhole he'd been born into and build himself a nice little life here in Eldrich. The perfect little American dream. Somebody ought to have one. She was glad it was him.

CHAPTER 7

MEAGHAN TRIED AT dinner to push Russ for details about Jamie's past, but he and Matthew were reticent, to say the least. She could barely drag speech out of them at all until she'd finally dropped it and changed the subject.

What were they not telling her? Was Jamie here illegally maybe? His father was wanted for war crimes? What was the big secret?

Meaghan resigned herself to waiting for now. In another week she'd be neck deep in office gossip and would hear all the ugly details soon enough.

By the next morning, the swelling in her toe had subsided enough so that Meaghan could wear flip-flops. Right after breakfast, Russ and Matthew trekked off to the hospital in Williamsport, for Matthew's weekly session with Becky, the occupational therapist. Meaghan was left alone for the first time in her new home.

With no Internet connection for her laptop and the cell

signal still spotty, she used the landline phone in the kitchen. She scheduled her storage pod to be dropped off on Thursday despite resistance from the Williamsport trucking company that now had it. At first, they flat out refused to drive to Eldrich, despite its inclusion on the service area map on their website. Meaghan changed their minds by informing them what she did for a living, reading them the part of the contract about delivery, and threatening to call the corporate office.

Then she called the city's human resources department about filling out her employment paperwork. A motherly woman named Gretchen told her not to worry about it yet. She advised Meaghan to get settled in at home and they could take care of it all next week.

That was all she could do with a sore foot and no Internet. The day yawned ahead of her, empty. The pace of small town life would take some getting used to. Meaghan sighed and poured herself another cup of Russ's excellent coffee and topped it off with a dollop of fresh cream. At least the food was really good.

She sat back down at the table and took a sip, wondering what to do with herself. A firm rap on the back door made her jump. She spilled the almost-full cup of coffee onto the table.

Meaghan grabbed up her laptop, clutching it to her chest, before the spill spread under it.

Another rap on the door, more tentative than the first.

Meaghan hobbled around the table, holding her laptop to her chest like a sleeping baby, and peered through the window in the kitchen door.

A man stooped on the back porch, pulling amber jars

from a cardboard box and setting them with care in a line next to the door.

One of Russ's foodie guys.

Meaghan pulled open the door. The man stood up fast and took a step backward.

"I . . . I bring the honey for Russ," he said in a thick accent. Tall, with a strong build, he had indigo eyes, like Jamie's, but rheumy and bloodshot. He had once been quite handsome, she could see, but the effects of too much drinking lay over his face like a veil, muddying his features. He looked about her age, with shaggy dark-blond hair shot through with gray.

He looked familiar. And it hit her. He looked like Jamie with twenty extra years and a drinking problem. This man had to be Jamie's father.

"Hi, um, Russ and my dad are at the hospital right now. Do I need to pay you or . . ."

He shook his head. "Nuh. Russ leave the money for me." He pointed at an empty flower pot next to the door. "In there."

"I'm Meaghan," she said. Juggling her laptop to her other arm, she held out her right hand.

He didn't take it. He gave her a small shy smile, like it was something he seldom did, and shook his head. "My hand is dirty. From the bees." His exhausted eyes met hers for a moment, then darted away.

Her gut fluttered and she felt her face grow hot. She flashed on her observation from the day before when she met Jamie for the first time. *If he were twenty years older, I'd be in trouble.* It hadn't been an observation, she realized. It had been a prediction.

She was in trouble.

Still know how to pick them, she thought. Some things never change.

Now, she wanted him gone. Fast. An attraction to Jamie's alcoholic father was drama she didn't need. She saw a battered, rusty white pick-up truck parked in the narrow access alley.

"Okay," she said, realizing she still didn't know his name. "I'll tell Russ you were here."

"It's good for your father you're here." His accent was unlike anything she'd ever heard before. Like Scandinavia mixed with Russia by way of Central America. With a stop in Jamaica.

Bosnian, she thought. Or Croatian. Or something. Close enough.

He met her eyes and she felt the heat again. No, she thought. Bad Meaghan. Don't go there.

"Thank you," she answered. Leave, she thought. Please leave.

As if hearing her thoughts, he said, his voice now gruff, "Tell Russ to call me if he wants more." He turned away from her and marched back to his truck.

She fled back into the house, her heart pounding. A door slammed. She heard the truck cough into life and head down the alley.

Meaghan waited a few moments, then peeped out the window to make sure he was gone.

She gathered up the jars of honey and brought them into the kitchen, lining them up on the counter. She unscrewed a jar lid, dipped the tip of her finger into the thick amber liquid, and tasted it. She'd always thought of honey as sweet but otherwise flavorless. But this stuff—it tasted like roses and cut grass. And sunshine.

Meaghan sighed. Of course it was the most amazing honey she'd ever tasted. Because the world always conspired against her that way if inappropriate romance was involved.

She didn't fall in love often, but when she did, she fell hard. And it always—*always*—started with that flutter in her gut, that moment of heat. She liked to believe that love was a conscious choice, something she could control.

Except when she couldn't.

Jamie's father—she didn't even know his name—Jamie's father was a fixer-upper, exactly what she'd sworn off of for years. A sad, broken man in desperate need of rescue. Signs of a drinking problem normally short circuited any spark of attraction she might feel for a man. Yet here she was with honey on her fingers and butterflies in her belly.

"I'm not freaking St. Meaghan," she muttered as she screwed the lid back on the honey jar. She remembered the spilled coffee on the table, sighed, and grabbed a wad of paper towels to clean it up. There's no such thing as love at first sight, she scolded herself as she mopped up the coffee. Just sexual instinct and people recognizing each other's dysfunctions. He was a drunk. Her father was a drunk. She'd been ambushed by lingering codependent daddy issues masquerading as attraction. Nothing more.

Besides, Meaghan had good reasons for being cautious. All she had to do was look in the mirror at the faint scar above her right eyebrow to be reminded. Her one, and only, experience with domestic violence. A boyfriend from long ago with a drinking problem and, as it turned out, a heavy fist. She'd moved in with him too fast and it didn't take long for him to throw that first punch.

Meaghan returned from the hospital with a black eye and five stitches where he'd caught her with his college class ring. Greg wept and begged for forgiveness, swearing it would never happen again. He made a brief show of AA. She took him back. It was only a matter of weeks before the heavy fist made a return appearance after a session of hard partying with his college buddies. Before his swing had a chance to make contact, Meaghan ducked under his arm, elbowed him in the throat, and drove a knee into his groin.

He wept and begged again, clutching an ice pack to his crotch, while Meaghan packed her bags. He made a few half-hearted attempts to win her back, and then tried threats. He called one evening to say he was on his way over to hurt her like she'd hurt him.

Meaghan borrowed a pump shotgun from a neighbor. She loaded it with birdshot, turned off the porch light, and waited in the dark. Greg, drunk, stormed onto the porch. Meaghan, a calm voice from the shadows, explained her rights under Arizona law to use deadly force to protect herself, told him to leave, and then racked the shotgun. At the sound, her would-be attacker whimpered, wet himself, and ran like hell.

Meaghan never saw him again. But she never forgot the lesson she'd learned. At the first sign of an inclination for violence or a drinking problem in a man, she was out the door. No explanations, no pleas for forgiveness, no acts of atonement were sufficient to overcome her determination to protect herself.

She mopped up the last of the coffee with a sigh and

poured herself another cup. She took one sip and realized she didn't want it anymore. Meaghan hadn't expected something like this to ever happen to her again. She'd thought that particular part of herself was dead, that the nerve endings required to fall for a man had been fried beyond repair. There had been men on and off over the years, but she always found a reason to stop things before they got too serious. And there hadn't been anybody since Michael, ten years earlier. A few dates here and there, but nothing more. No sex. No love. No attraction. Not even a hint of it.

Michael had been different, or so she thought at the time. Meaghan believed then that she was in love with Michael, but she'd finally had to admit to herself that what she'd loved was not him, but what he could give her.

She had wanted a child. Desperately. With Michael, she'd thought she'd managed to pull it off, to have it all. She thought she'd found a husband and had time to squeeze out a baby, maybe even two, before her biological clock ran out.

They hadn't even managed to get married before Michael started cheating on her. By the time the whole sad mess had fallen apart and Michael was gone, the heavy uterine bleeding had begun. Her gynecologist informed her that her uterus was so rotten with fibroid tumors the only treatment option was a hysterectomy. Her ovaries were salvageable so she wouldn't be thrown immediately into the hormonal symptoms of menopause, but her fertility was gone, probably had been for a while.

Putting on a brave face, Meaghan asked her friends to throw her a fibroid shower. Instead of baby stuff, she received stretchy pajama pants she could pull over her distended abdomen and DVDs to keep her entertained while she healed.

She told everyone how relieved she was to have the whole "will I or won't I" motherhood question behind her.

And without a word, without even admitting it to herself, Meaghan grieved. She liked her friends' kids well enough, but many days, too many days, the photos and parenting stories felt like a knife to the heart. Had she been able to acknowledge her pain, it might have made things easier. Instead she insisted she was fine and all was well.

She began deflecting invitations and stopped reaching out to people. She worked her miserable job and went home to her silent house. She joked about how she had no business being a mother and how it all worked out for the best. But, no matter how she rationalized it, she felt like a failure as a woman and mourned the child she couldn't conceive.

Her friends drifted away as a regular presence in her life. She felt less and less connected to the world around her. By the time the pieces fell into place for her move to Eldrich, there was nothing to keep her from leaving. She had isolated herself so effectively that leaving everything she knew could be accomplished with barely a pang.

And now, the first man she'd felt any attraction to in years was a careworn beekeeper with a drinking problem and an estranged son she had to work with every day.

Oh, yeah. Some things never changed.

CHAPTER 8

WHEN RUSS AND Matthew got home, around lunchtime, Meaghan was waiting.

"The honey guy came by," Meaghan said, arms folded across her chest.

"Um," Russ replied. After a moment he added, "You met him?"

"I did. He said to call him if you need any more."

Russ started making a sandwich for Matthew's lunch. Matthew walked in with a beaming smile, waved a drawing at Meaghan, and wandered past into the living room. "Dad," Russ called. "Lunchtime."

Matthew shuffled back into the kitchen. He smiled at Meaghan, introduced himself and shook her hand, with no recognition, and sat down at the table.

Meaghan stared at the back of Russ's skull, willing him to turn around.

Russ sliced the sandwich in half and put it on a plate with

a pickle spear. He set the plate in front of Matthew with a glass of apple juice. Matthew eyed it with suspicion.

"Turkey. You like this a lot."

Matthew nodded and picked up a sandwich half. He took a bite and, smiling as he chewed, gave Russ a thumbs-up.

Russ puttered for a minute, ignoring Meaghan, and then turned to face her. "All right, fine. Quit the lawyer stare. What do you want to know?"

"The honey guy. He's Jamie's dad, isn't he?"

Russ sighed. "Yes, John is Jamie's father."

Meaghan snorted. "John Smith and James Smith? You couldn't help them pick out better names?"

Russ raised an eyebrow. "Pick out names? What are you talking about?"

"Russ, damn it, will you stop it with the cryptic crap?" Meaghan pulled out a chair and sat down. "The guy has an accent that thick and his name is John Smith?"

Matthew, who appeared oblivious to the conversation, stood up and put his empty plate in the sink. He walked toward the living room.

"Dad," Russ called after him. "Where are you going?"

"To the sofa," Matthew called back. "I'm sleepy."

"So?" Meaghan asked.

Russ sighed. Meaghan never let stuff like this go and they both knew it. "Fine, his name hasn't always been John Smith."

"Where are they from?"

Russ coughed like he was choking on something. "Where do you think they're from?"

"Bosnia. Croatia. Kosovo. Somewhere like that."

"Yeah, somewhere like that." Russ turned to the fridge. "You want lunch?"

"Yes. And don't change the subject. I have to work with Jamie. And you and Matthew know him like family. It would be nice to be let in on his history, even a little."

Russ started assembling two sandwiches. "Put the kettle on, would you? I need a cup of tea."

Meaghan got up, and with far more stomping, banging, and clanking than necessary, filled the kettle, slammed it down on the stove, and turned on the burner. At least now maybe she was going to get some answers.

She sat back down at the table. "So, what's the story on those two? They're refugees, right?"

"Did Jamie tell you that?"

"No, I figured it out on my own. I'm right though, aren't I?"

"Yeah, you are." Russ brought the sandwiches over. "Eat. I'll take care of the kettle."

Meaghan examined the sandwich. Turkey, it looked like, with red leaf lettuce and mayonnaise. "Did you make this mayo from scratch or scoop it out of a plastic jar like a normal person?"

"It's criminal that people eat that processed crap when it's so easy to make." The kettle whistled and Russ filled two mugs with hot water and tea bags. He carried the mugs over and sat down. "Let it steep a minute," Russ said. "Want some honey?"

When Russ said "honey" she felt her face grow hot. "Yes. Then stop fussing and talk to me."

Russ fetched a jar of honey and two teaspoons. "Fine," he said, sitting back down. "John and Jamie are refugees from . . . Bosnia." He seemed to be tasting the word, trying it out to see how it sounded. "Somewhere like that." He took a bite of his sandwich and chewed for moment. "Look, Meg, the thing you got to know is they left a damn horror movie behind them. Jamie was only a kid and he watched his mother killed right in front of him. John was a prisoner and they tortured him for days. Jamie had to watch that too. It was so bad. You can't imagine how bad."

Meaghan felt her impatience and indignation evaporate. She'd been so obsessed with getting the details that she'd never considered how awful they might be.

"God," she said. "Poor Jamie." This was so much worse than she'd imagined. "He seems so normal. Happy. I never would have thought . . ." She trailed off. Twelve years old and watching that happen to his parents. Her respect for him grew. That kind of resilience required phenomenal inner strength.

"Yeah, amazing, isn't it," Russ said. "He was like a wild animal when they first got here. It took Matthew six months to get him to even speak. But when he finally did, it was almost flawless English. He told me later he learned it watching TV. The guy is smart as hell. And tough."

"How did Matthew get involved?"

Russ's face flushed. "I don't really know. I wasn't here for all of it. I got here right after they did."

"Did he sponsor them or something?"

"Um." Russ set his sandwich down. "Not exactly. They kind of came here outside official channels."

Meaghan raised an eyebrow. "John's not a war criminal, is he?"

Russ shook his head. "No, no. Well, I guess it depends which side you were on. There was a fight for control and

John lost. I don't know all the details. From what I do know, the other guy was the war criminal. Complete bastard."

"And he took his revenge," Meaghan said.

"Yeah. He did." Russ shoved his plate away, his sandwich half eaten. He opened the honey jar and stirred a spoonful into his tea cup. "This stuff is so damn good. You taste it?"

"I did," Meaghan said, trying to keep her voice flat. "It's good. So they're here illegally?"

"Yeah. Matthew got them set up with new identities."

Meaghan nodded. "John never really recovered from what happened to him, did he." It was a statement, not a question.

Russ sighed. "No. I guess he didn't. He drinks. A lot. How did you figure out he was Jamie's father?"

"The eyes," she said. "They have the same eyes."

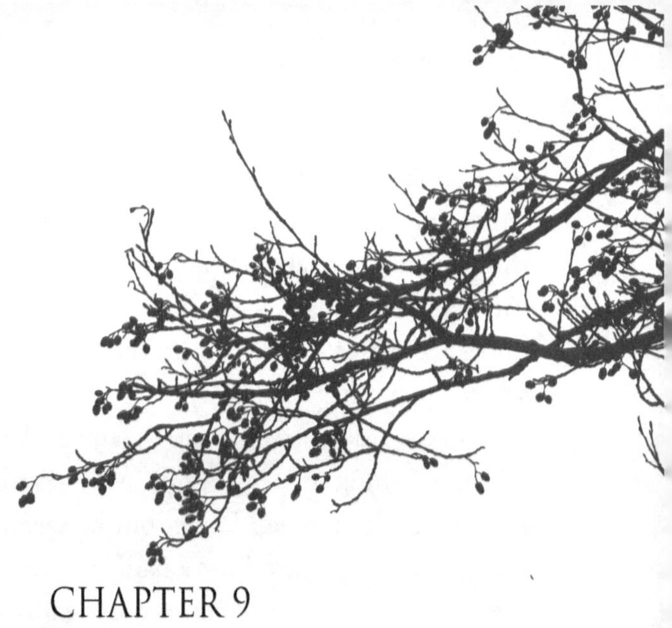

CHAPTER 9

HER STORAGE POD arrived Wednesday afternoon. Meaghan could tell the delivery driver didn't want to be there. He got the pod off the back of the flatbed truck and into the driveway as fast as he could, thrust a clipboard at her with shaking hands, and told her to sign it. His impatience and anger couldn't mask the body language betraying his fear.

She remembered her mother, in that stupid dream, warning her to trust her gut. Fine, she thought. The moving company probably let the pod fall off the side of the truck somewhere along I-80, all her stuff was broken, and they knew she was a lawyer. That would explain his fear.

Meaghan took her time reading the form, signed it, and handed the clipboard back, grateful she'd had the foresight to pay extra for damage insurance. He ran to the truck, scrambled in, and roared off with screeching tires. Yeah, they'd smashed up her stuff. That had to be it.

She spent the next few days unpacking and, despite her

prediction, everything was intact. After three days she was almost moved in, except for a few boxes. They weren't anything critical, merely artwork, photos, that sort of stuff. But she couldn't bring herself to unpack them. If she still had unpacked boxes in the corner, then she could convince herself the move was temporary.

On Saturday, Jamie came by and picked up Matthew to take him fishing for a few hours. Matthew didn't fish any longer, he merely watched Jamie, but he seemed to enjoy it and their fishing trips gave Russ a badly needed respite. Russ used the time to escort Meaghan around Eldrich, which to Russ consisted of the weekly farmers' market in the town square and the food co-op. A shiny new supermarket sat on the edge of town, but Russ avoided it unless absolutely necessary.

"But the co-op's gotta cost more, right?" Meaghan asked. "What's the difference?"

Even as the question came out of her mouth, Meaghan regretted it. For the fifteen minutes it took them to drive downtown, he lectured her about the "food-industrial" complex and the evils it wrought upon the world and how nobody should eat stuff produced farther than ten miles from home.

"Fine, I get it," she finally said. "Local good, distant bad. I will never question your hunter-gatherer creds again. Can we stop for coffee? Or is coffee evil too? I know they don't grow that within ten miles of our house."

"Um," Russ said. "Well, you have to make some allowances for certain things . . ."

"Like coffee," Meaghan said.

"Yes, but I buy only fair-trade organic—"

She cut him off. "I don't care. I want caffeine. They can grow it in crude oil in a lab for all I care."

Russ wrinkled his nose in disgust. "Pathetic. You have so much to learn about food. There's a great little place next to the co-op if you can wait a couple of minutes."

Car parked, a cup of coffee in hand from Eldrich Brew, the funky little coffee shop next to the co-op, Meaghan followed Russ across the street to the farmer's market in the town square. Russ planned to hit the co-op on their way back to the car.

Unlike some of the farmers' markets she'd been to in Phoenix, which were mostly craft fairs with the token produce table for the look of things, the Eldrich farmers' market was the real deal. Pickup trucks surrounded the square, fronted by stands laden with produce, fresh bread, cheese, eggs, and all sorts of jams, jellies, and preserves. She saw several signs for organic meat.

"Does John Smith sell his honey here?" Meaghan asked Russ.

"Why do you ask?" He wore a knowing smile.

She wanted to smack that cheesy grin off his face as she felt her cheeks grow hot. "No reason. Merely curious."

"He should be here. Unless . . ."

"Unless what?"

"Um. Unless he drank too much last night."

Now it was Russ's turn to blush, Meaghan noticed, feeling satisfied and disappointed at the same time. John was trouble, and Russ just confirmed it. But as victories went, it felt pretty hollow.

"He's not a bad guy," Russ said. "He could be a really great guy if he sobered up. But it's not hard to understand his compulsion to drink considering all he suffered."

"Oh, bullshit," Meaghan said. "Drinking is a choice. Plenty of people suffer and still manage not to pickle themselves."

"Wow. Way to feel the compassion," Russ responded.

"Fine. I get that it's a disease, but it's the only disease I know of where the cure is simply telling yourself no."

"Simply?" He shook his head.

"Jamie lost his mom. He suffered and he's not a drunk, is he?"

Russ shook his head. "No, but—"

"Don't ever expect me to have sympathy for this shit. Not after Dad and Greg. Been there, done that." She tapped the white mark above her eyebrow. "Got the scar to prove it."

Feeling bolstered by her tough talk, Meaghan turned away from Russ only to see John sitting about twenty feet away on the lowered tailgate of his truck, counting money. A table stacked with honey jars sat in front of him. As Meaghan watched, a couple of older women walked up and made a purchase. He gave them his shy smile, but barely looked up. The two women whispered something to each other and giggled as they walked away.

"Oh, look, Meg," Russ said, noticing John. "Let's go kick him in the balls and then tell him how his drinking is a choice."

"You know I'm right," Meaghan said, her face flaming again. "I'm not trying to be mean. I know he went through something awful, but he drinks because he chooses to. No other reason."

"Yeah, but I think he's salvageable."

"So, what's that got to do with me?" She felt her face get even hotter.

"Well, I thought, maybe, if he had someone to motivate him—"

"Oh, Russ, please. Tell me you aren't thinking of trying

to fix us up. Not. Gonna. Happen. Just because you make bad choices doesn't mean I have to." It was out of her mouth before she could stop herself.

Russ gave her a frozen look and walked towards John.

"Russ," she called after him. "I'm sorry."

He ignored her.

"Oh, nice one, Meg," she muttered as she followed him.

"Hey, John," she heard Russ call. "How's business?"

John looked up from his money counting, saw Russ, shoved the bills into the pocket of his worn jeans, and smiled. He saw Meaghan a moment later. His face turned red and he stared back down at the table.

Russ walked up, hand out. John shook it, still looking down.

"The last batch you dropped by was awesome," Russ said. "How are the bees doing?"

John shrugged. "They seem happy. I added more hives. In the lower clearing."

"You met Meaghan, I hear," Russ said, throwing her another frosty look.

"I did," John said.

Standing near him, seeing him up close, Meaghan felt a rush of shame for her glib remarks. She could see faint scars around his wrists and on his forearms. A big man, he did all he could to appear small. He carried himself cautiously, with a slight crouch, arms held close to his sides, ready to flee or curl into a protective ball at the slightest sign of trouble. He reminded her of the abused dogs a friend in Phoenix used to foster, the fight beaten out of them, expecting every human touch to hurt.

"Well," Russ said, breaking the uncomfortable silence. "I

guess we'll be moving along." He grabbed Meaghan's arm and tugged her away from the table. "Good to see you, John."

"Did you meet my son?" John asked. Meaghan turned. John was staring at her, a hungry look on his face.

"I did. A few days ago," Meaghan said, forcing herself to look in his eyes. Trying to be tough and smug with John about being a drunk would be like kicking a frightened puppy, Meaghan thought. Goddammit. It would be a lot easier to smother her attraction if she could feel scorn for him. But up close, it was impossible.

"Is he well? Is he happy?"

"Yes," she said. "He seems to be."

"And you met his family, the babies?"

Again she saw the hunger in his eyes. You do not need a man to save, she told herself. Don't go there. "Only saw pictures."

"I see them around town sometimes, but they don't know me." He returned his gaze to the table. "It's better this way, I think. For them."

Meaghan felt the tears begin to build. They were always close by since she'd arrived in Eldrich. She clenched her hand and dug her fingernails into her palm, forcing them back down. She had no idea how to reply to him.

Russ jumped in. "Jamie took Dad fishing. We'll see him later. I'll tell him we saw you."

John shook his head. "Don't. It only upsets him." He tried to change the subject. "Your father, he is well?"

Russ shrugged. "As well as can be expected. I'm sure Dad would be thrilled to see you if you want to drop by. Think about it, okay?"

John nodded. A knot of people stopped in front of the table and began asking him questions about the honey.

Russ pulled Meaghan away. "Yeah, he should simply tell himself no and then he'd be all better."

"Russ, I . . . I'm sorry. I let my mouth get out in front of my brain back there."

"I forgive you, Meg, but I don't understand you," he said. "When did you get so hard?"

She had no answer for that. "He really doesn't know his grandkids?"

Russ shook his head. "And Jamie would go ballistic if John tried to make contact. When they got here, John was . . . well, he was in no shape to raise Jamie, so he let Dad step in. Jamie doesn't want anything to do with him now. Sound familiar?"

Meaghan stopped walking and let the crowd flow around her. She could no longer keep her tears at bay. "My coffee's cold and I barely drank any," she said in a small voice. "Can we go home now?"

He handed her the car keys. "I've got a couple more stops here and then the co-op. If you aren't in the car, I'll look for you in the coffee shop." He relented a bit. "I'm sorry. That was a cheap shot. Guess I've gotten a little hard too." He pulled a bandana out of his pocket and handed it to her. "It's clean. Blow your nose and I'll see you in few minutes." He took a few steps away, but turned before melting into the growing crowd. "Sally—the one with all the tattoos—will be happy to warm that coffee up if you ask nice."

Meaghan nodded, and then he was gone.

CHAPTER 10

MONDAY, MEAGHAN'S FIRST day on the new job, dawned cool and rainy. Jamie had assured her that the dress code in City Hall was casual, but she put on the black power suit anyway. After a moment's hesitation, she opted for the trousers instead of the skirt. She'd never make it all day in heels with her still tender big toe, so trousers it was.

Meaghan checked herself in the mirror. She looked good for fifty. She had taken care of her skin, protecting it from the Arizona sun, and her silver hair made her face look younger in comparison rather than aging her. She was a swimmer since childhood, an avid hiker, and remained strong and fit.

Too many angles to her face and the hawk-like brow she'd inherited from her father prevented Meaghan from being pretty in the conventional sense. But she was striking, she knew that. A Victorian novelist would have termed her a "handsome woman."

Her face had been rounder when she was young. Aging

had carved out cheekbones that fit better with her heavy brow. She really did look better now than when she was younger. Too bad, she thought, that modern culture only values twenty-five-year-olds.

"All right, Miss America," she said to her reflection. "Good enough."

Russ had a simple breakfast waiting and had packed her a lunch. "I'm sure they'll take you out, but in case they don't, here you go." He handed her a tiny soft-sided cooler.

She peeked inside. Sandwich, apple, green salad, and some cookies. Good old Russ. "Thanks, Mommy," she said.

Russ made a face and pointed at the door. "Go and lawyer, smart ass."

She'd seen city hall, which sat on the block north of the town square, on her trip to the farmers' market but hadn't taken a close look.

City hall rose three stories with a clock tower rising an additional two stories above the roofline. A stone layer cake of a building, city hall looked like a Gothic castle. Gargoyles sprang from the roof and ornate carvings covered the stone walls. Around it lay another lush green square, with huge old trees, a fountain, and iron benches.

Meaghan found her assigned parking space in the small circular drive that led up to the building. Most city employees parked in a lot across the street, but as city solicitor Meaghan got to park up close, along with the mayor, the council members, and a handful of high-ranking staff.

For a city as tiny as Eldrich, Meaghan thought, walking in the main door, it was a bit much. The architectural excess continued inside. A reception desk sat in the corner of a large vaulted lobby. An elderly security guard greeted her with a beaming smile.

"I know who you are," he quavered. "You have your dad's eyes. How is Mr. Keele doing these days?"

Meaghan wasn't surprised he recognized her. She doubted more than a handful of unfamiliar people walked by his checkpoint each day. "Well, he has good days and bad days. You know how it is." She held out her hand across the desk. "I'm Meaghan."

"Oh, where are my manners?" He shuffled from behind the desk towards her. "Rainy days are hard on the knees." He took her outstretched hand and shook it warmly. "Moyer. Meb Moyer, Miss Keele. Call me Meb."

"Only if you call me Meaghan." He was, she realized, more akin to a Walmart greeter than a security guard. "Good to meet you, Meb. Can you point me towards the solicitor's office?"

He showed her the elevator and told her to go the third floor. She told him she'd rather take the stairs. With a nervous grin, he told her the tiled stairs were slick and wet shoes made it worse and with the ceilings so high it was really more like climbing five stories than three. He gestured again toward the elevator.

It was like Russ and the drive through the woods. "Do people walk up the stairs and disappear never to be heard from again?" she asked, before she could stop herself.

Now poor Meb looked panicky. And miserable, like he wanted to tell her something he knew he couldn't.

She let him off the hook. "I'm kidding." She smiled at him. "I'm sorry. You reminded me of how nervous my brother was the first time I drove up from the interstate."

Meb relaxed. "Why climb the stairs when you don't have to?"

"Why indeed," Meaghan answered. "You have a good day, Meb." She walked to the open elevator and stepped in. She felt an odd prickle on the back of her neck. She knew she was being silly, but it felt like people were trying to keep a big secret. She thought of her dream and her mother's cryptic warning to trust her gut. She shivered.

Enough, she thought, disgusted with herself. She'd worked before in organizations poisoned by the dysfunctional antics of a few difficult personalities and she knew what was going on. Matthew had, no doubt, crossed swords with some half-baked martinet or queen bee. Everyone was waiting for the fireworks to being anew now that Meaghan had arrived. What they were hiding from her was the common knowledge that her new job was going to be a monumental pain in the ass.

CHAPTER 11

W ITH A JERK, the elevator car stopped and the door slid open on the third floor.

Like many old buildings, city hall was rumored to be haunted, with the third floor at the center of most of the stories. Meaghan didn't care. She'd known people over the years who had experienced unexplainable things. She hadn't. Whether that had more to do with them or with her, she wasn't sure. Meaghan would worry about ghosts if and when she saw one. And if she was right about the fireworks to come, at least a few of the living people in the building were scarier than the dead ones.

Haunted or not, city hall was a beautiful old building, rich in detail and character, unlike the ugly sealed brick-and-glass boxes she'd worked in before. The windows even opened. Encounters with the supernatural seemed a small price to pay for fresh air.

A few steps from the elevator, a glass-and-wood door

marked "City Solicitor" in ornate gold script stood open. Meaghan walked into an open reception area containing two desks. A young woman sat behind one of them. The nameplate identified her as Kady Cressley. The nameplate on the other desk read "Natalie Segretti."

Kady gave Meaghan a glowing smile and jumped to her feet. "Ms. Keele?"

Meaghan smiled back. "That's me. And it's Meaghan, okay?"

"Got it." Kady walked around the desk. "I'm Kady." She wore jeans and a plaid hoodie. "We are so happy you're here. Especially Jamie. I don't think he wants to be the big boss anymore."

"Yeah, I got that feeling. He was way too eager to bring me stuff when I hurt my foot."

Kady tried to muffle a laugh. "Oh, he's so ready not to be in charge. Let me take you to your office. Natalie's around here somewhere. She's the office manager."

A four-person office needed a manager? Meaghan wondered if Natalie could be the queen bee she suspected lurked somewhere in the building. But that wasn't the feeling she got from the way Russ and Jamie spoke about Natalie. They seemed to like her quite a bit.

Kady led Meaghan down a short hallway and gestured at the open doorway. "Here's your office. Not as big as the downstairs offices but a lot more fun." She giggled. "At least I think so."

Meaghan walked through the doorway and her mouth dropped open. The small office was round. Meaghan realized she was in one of the turrets. Light streamed in from three directions through six windows, tall and narrow to compensate for the curve of the walls. Even with the gray rain clouds hanging in the sky, the office was filled with natural light. Meaghan couldn't wait to see how it looked on a sunny day.

"Do those windows open?" Meaghan asked.

"They sure do," Kady said with obvious pride.

"Wow. I've never had office windows that open before." Meaghan laughed, delighted with the space. "I've never had a round office either."

"Not big."

"Who cares," Meaghan said. "It's round."

Meaghan had never fallen in love with a room before. The space felt right. It felt good.

It felt like home.

She shook her head, chalking up the rush of feeling to the general weirdness that seemed to be swirling all around her. It was stress-induced, she was sure, manufactured by the too-rapid transition from the life she'd long known, a bad case of nerves caused by being abruptly dumped into a whole new life.

Kady giggled some more. "I know, right? That's what I thought the first time I saw it. A bitch to furnish, though." She stopped and looked at Meaghan, waiting for a reaction. "Sorry."

Meaghan raised an eyebrow. "You know, I've heard that word before. Even used it a few times. Sometimes I use much worse words."

Kady relaxed and her smile returned. "That makes things easier. Natalie and I both swear like dock workers. Drives poor Jamie nuts."

Meaghan dropped her purse and umbrella behind the desk and Kady took her on a tour of the rest of the small office suite. They crossed the hall to the small copy room and smaller file room. According to Kady, the door at the back of the file room led into a larger storage area carved out of the unfinished attic. It was always kept locked, more for the safety of people who might enter than to protect anything inside. The storage area was only partially finished and surrounded by unreinforced floors and exposed stone walls. One wrong step and you'd find yourself dropping in, literally, on the mayor, whose second floor office sat below.

Natalie, Kady told her, kept the attic key. They found her in Jamie's office, which sat next to Meaghan's.

Natalie sat in Jamie's desk chair, staring at his computer with a scowl. She muttered under her breath, reached down, and whacked the computer tower with her hand. "Work already, you evil piece of shit."

Kady cleared her throat. Natalie turned to look at Kady and Meaghan standing in the doorway and smiled. She was in her early thirties, with wild auburn hair, curled in ringlets, and the greenest eyes Meaghan had ever seen.

Natalie hopped to her feet and came around the desk with her hand out. She was tall and curvy, like an ancient fertility goddess. Renaissance artists would have killed for the chance to paint her. "Hey, boss. Welcome aboard. Just knocking some sense into Jamie's computer."

Meaghan shook her offered hand. Natalie's grip was firm and her hand so warm it felt like a heating pad. Jamie hadn't been kidding about it being casual dress around here, Meaghan thought. Like Kady, Natalie wore jeans. She also wore a lavender T-shirt with "Humboldt Hydroponics" written in dark green Gothic script punctuated with a pot leaf, a spangly knit scarf around her neck, and black engineer boots.

Meaghan liked her right away. She never cared what her administrative staff wore, only that the work got done. Despite her wild hair and stoner T-shirt, Natalie exuded competence. According to Jamie, Natalie always got the job done, on time and with minimal drama.

"Kady give you the tour?" Natalie asked.

"Sure did." Meaghan hesitated. What the hell was she doing here? At that moment, the realization of the enormity of the changes she'd undergone in the last few weeks, of how far she was from what she thought of as home, hit her like a fist. The room began to spin, gently at first, and then picked up speed, and now Kady and Natalie were easing her into a chair.

Meaghan, her eyes screwed shut, let the room come to a stop.

She felt Natalie's warm hand on her shoulder. "You okay?"

Meaghan opened her eyes. "Yeah, better." She took a few deep breaths to steady herself and then tried to make a joke. "And I'm not even in the round office. I may need hand rails in there."

Natalie laughed, but it sounded forced and she looked concerned. She and Kady exchanged a meaningful glance. Again, Meaghan sensed an unspoken conversation.

"Seriously," Meaghan said. "I'm fine. Just got a little woozy for a sec."

Natalie frowned. "Does that happen often?"

"No," Meaghan said. "Not since high school choir. Don't worry. I won't be swooning all over the office. I'm fine."

Natalie's frown relaxed into a smile. "Has anyone ever told you you're exactly like your father?"

Meaghan grinned back. "No. Not ever once in my whole life."

"Yeah, right," Natalie shot back. She turned to Kady. "Would you get Meaghan a cup of . . ." She turned back to Meaghan. "Coffee? Tea?"

"Coffee," Meaghan told her.

"On it," Kady said, and headed down the hall.

"Okay, lady," Natalie said. "Let's get you into your office and see if the computer guy did his job."

Meaghan rose with care, but the dizziness was gone. A small fountain of fear bubbled in the back of her mind. She *was* exactly like Matthew. What if she was getting his disease now too? Did Alzheimer's have a genetic component?

The fear must have shown on her face. Natalie said, "I don't know if you believe in any of the ghost stories, but you're not the first person who's gotten woozy in that office. Bob, the guy before you, always got the wobbles in there. If he had to talk to Jamie, he'd stand in the doorway but wouldn't go in. Otherwise he'd end up on the floor."

"You're saying it's ghosts?"

Natalie laughed. "Oh, hell. I don't know. But Bob had a bunch of tests done, an EEG and some other stuff, and they never found anything wrong. And he didn't have the problem anywhere else."

"So I shouldn't worry," Meaghan said.

Natalie nodded. "Right. You shouldn't worry."

And for whatever reason, maybe Natalie's kind, open face, Meaghan felt the cloud lift.

She felt better as soon as she entered her little round office. "I'm fine in here," she told Natalie. "No ghosts?"

"Oh, God. I never should have said that. Now you think I'm some crazy crystal grabber."

Meaghan laughed and plopped into one of the side chairs in front of her desk, gesturing to Natalie to take the desk chair. "I'm from Arizona, remember? There are as many people down there packing crystals as there are packing guns. Ever been to Sedona? Maybe it's an energy vortex."

Kady appeared in the doorway with a white mug. "Energy vortex? There's an energy vortex?" She looked worried.

"Nope," Natalie replied. "Meaghan was telling me about Sedona."

Kady and Natalie exchanged glances. There it was again. The unspoken conversation.

Kady handed her the mug. Meaghan had been expecting the typical crappy office coffeemaker sludge, but this smelled wonderful. Kady plopped a metal spoon, a couple of little white tubs of half and half, and a few sugar packets on the desk.

Natalie moved behind the desk, sat down, and leaned over to turn on the computer. Meaghan thanked Kady for the coffee. Kady then left to answer the phone, although Meaghan didn't hear anything.

"Ears like an owl, that one," Natalie said. "How's the coffee?"

"Freaking fabulous. Got a Starbucks downstairs?"

Natalie let fly a booming laugh. "Oh, I'm better than Starbucks. It was your dad who started us on the high-end coffee habit. I replaced the espresso machine a few months ago, but he got us the original one."

"Espresso machine? You juicing the whole building?"

"Nope. Just us. Sally and Nate over at Eldrich Brew

would go out of business without city hall, but our coffee maker was here first, and we're too lazy to walk across the street. Sorry about the plastic tubs. I had to pinch those from the mayor's office. Leftovers from a reception or luncheon or something. We usually have a pitcher of cream, but I didn't make it to the food co-op last night."

"Cream? Actual cream? You're as bad as my brother."

At the mention of Russ, Natalie looked up at Meaghan and then looked down fast, her face red.

I'll have to keep an eye on that, Meaghan thought. Her brother sleeping with her office manager could be awkward, to say the least. But Russ couldn't unzip his pants without proposing marriage, so maybe Natalie merely had a crush on him.

Natalie scowled at the computer. "I told Eddie last week to get this damn thing set up." She muttered under her breath, and smacked it, like she had Jamie's computer. "There we are. Good to go." She stood up and gestured towards the chair. "All yours, boss."

"Where's Jamie?" Meaghan asked as she sat down behind the desk.

"He had a hearing over in Williamsport. He'll be back at lunchtime." Natalie walked out of the office, then turned in the doorway. "Check your calendar. You've got a meeting in the mayor's office at ten, and then you and Jamie have a two o'clock with the council director." Natalie grimaced. "Emily."

Ah. There was the queen bee. "That's Emily Proctor, right?"

Natalie nodded.

"Down there or up here?"

"Oh, up here. I made a point of it," Natalie said, venom in her voice.

"Good. Based on the look on your face when you say her name, I'm betting she's a great big pain in the ass?"

Natalie snorted with laughter. "That's what Matthew used to call her. He always made her come up here. Totally pissed her off."

"But it makes a point. Anything else I need to know about? What about lunch?"

"The mayor will probably offer to take you out. We'd do it ourselves, but we wanted to wait until you got settled a little and Jamie's around all day."

"What's the mayor like?"

Natalie sighed. "You want tactful or honest?"

Meaghan raised an eyebrow. "Let me hear honest."

"Everyone calls him Mayor McCheese."

Meaghan laughed so hard she almost spit out the sip of coffee in her mouth. "Oh, hell. That's funny. Sad but funny. So, let me guess. Oily but kind of hapless?"

"Yup. He's not a bad guy, just a schmoozy booster type. You know. Lots of rah-rah with the chamber of commerce but not enough spine to stand up to the council."

"To Emily, you mean. Natalie, if you've got nowhere to be right now, shut the door, sit down, and give me the dirt."

Natalie smiled and shut the door.

CHAPTER 12

EMILY HAD WORKED for the city for more than twenty years. She'd started out as a part-time secretary for a council member and ended up running the show. Why a city the size of Eldrich even needed professional staff for its council members was never mentioned.

Emily built her empire with deliberation and care, and now, under the guise of separation of powers, was accountable to no one, except the council members whose egos she stroked and whose secrets she kept. She controlled the flow of information in and out of the council offices with an iron hand and tolerated no dissent. All contact between council members and the rest of the city had to go through her. Council members who balked found themselves, through some electoral alchemy they didn't understand, serving only one term.

"She even used city funds to buy a high-end coffee maker to keep the council members from going over to Eldrich Brew before meetings so she can keep an eye on them," Natalie said. "She's that much of a control freak."

When Matthew was city solicitor, he kept Emily in check. Her reign of terror extended only to the council members, her tiny administrative staff, and the occasional new, low-ranking city employee who made the mistake of thinking Emily was bound by the same rules as everybody else.

Emily hated Matthew. He was impervious—that was the word Natalie used—to Emily's machinations. And so a fragile detente emerged. Matthew talked with the council members any time he damn well pleased and Emily stayed out of his way. In return, Matthew didn't actively lobby the council to fire her.

Then Matthew retired and without his monolithic presence on the third floor to thwart her, Emily made her power grab. The two successive city solicitors hired following Matthew's retirement had been terrified of her, particularly Bob, Meaghan's immediate predecessor.

Bob was a former partner in a large Manhattan law firm. He'd left his wife of twenty years for a gorgeous trophy wife. The trophy wife decided she wanted to make artisan goat cheese in the country and that's how they got Bob.

He was a good lawyer but a weak manager, with no government experience, and no match for Emily. Despite Natalie's and Jamie's attempts to bolster him, Emily pinned Bob squarely under her thumb.

Jamie took the brunt of it. Despite being a young attorney, with only a few years of experience, Jamie got dumped with every project Bob feared might somehow anger Emily. Instead of protecting Jamie, Bob threw him to the council, like raw meat, then shrugged and smiled and hemmed and hawed, while Jamie was savaged for trying to do his job.

The more local the politics were, Meaghan had learned over the years, the more brutal and dirtier the fighting got.

From what Natalie said, it sounded like Emily had it out for Jamie, in a personal nasty sort of way. When Meaghan asked about it, Natalie looked blank a moment, then said, "Yeah, she doesn't like him." She didn't elaborate.

Mayor McCheese,—Anthony "Tony" Diebler—was elected right before Matthew retired. It was Tony who'd hand-picked and appointed Bob, and like Bob, Tony was terrified of Emily. The council now had their hands in daily adminis-trative decisions that far exceeded their legislative authority. Emily bullied and harassed staff, eviscerated funding requests as punishment for perceived transgressions, and engaged in destructive email campaigns against people who crossed her. Her control over the council was now absolute. Emily had become, in the vacuum created by Matthew's retirement, the single most powerful person in city hall.

"Well, that explains it," Meaghan said.

"Explains what?" Natalie asked.

"All the weirdness. I've had the strongest sense that peo-ple weren't telling me something. Now I know what it is. This job won't be the cakewalk I was led to believe it would be. I'm going to have to earn my paycheck."

"You okay with that?" Natalie asked.

"Sure. I love a good fight. Emily's not going to know what hit her."

Natalie looked thoughtful. "Oh, I think she already knows exactly what she's dealing with. I think she's down-stairs right now stewing about it. Meaghan, I know it's a small town and you've dealt with much bigger stuff, but watch out for her. She's more dangerous than she appears."

Meaghan laughed. "Yeah, yeah. I know. And so are the woods and the stairs and blah blah blah. You know, I'm not completely helpless. I've seen her type before. I can handle Emily."

Natalie glanced at her watch, her face bright red.

Mystery solved. Exactly what Meaghan had thought. A big messy personality conflict on the first day. That's what everybody wasn't telling her.

"You need to get downstairs to the mayor's office," Natalie said. "It's almost ten. Take the elevator down to two."

"I'll take the stairs," Meaghan said, watching Natalie for a reaction. "I need the exercise."

"I'll walk down with you. I need to drop something off with Annie. The mayor's secretary. I can introduce you before his Cheesiness makes an entrance."

Okay. Meaghan had merely given herself a bad case of the heebie-jeebies, induced by stress. Nothing more. She'd dealt with plenty of people like Emily before. And in a town this tiny, she thought, how bad can city hall politics really be?

Annie, a smiling blond woman a few years older than Natalie, greeted them from her desk in the reception area. The mayor was running a few minutes late. She told Meaghan to have a seat and chatted with Natalie a moment. It sounded like they were neighbors.

Small town, Meaghan thought. They all know each other. Another change she'd have to get used to. Phoenix was a sprawling community full of people from somewhere else, some of whom only lived there during the winter. Meaghan had lived in her last house for ten years and had never met the people who lived across the street.

Natalie left Meaghan in Annie's care and headed back up the stairs.

Annie busied herself with something on her desk and Meaghan waited. The office was silent except for the tick of a large antique clock above Annie's desk and the occasional muffled voice from somewhere further back in the office suite.

"He's back in the building," Annie announced after a couple of minutes. "He should be here any time now."

Meaghan wondered a moment how Annie knew that. The phone hadn't rung. She wasn't near a window or working at her computer. Meaghan didn't see a cell phone or tablet anywhere. Then Mayor Diebler bustled into the room and schmoozed Meaghan into his office before she could think about it further.

Tony Diebler was pleasant enough, but his nickname fit. Meaghan had gotten a hint of it when he'd called her in Phoenix to offer her the job in Eldrich. Middle-aged and divorced, Tony liked to flirt with women far too young for him. He wore too much cologne. He had good hair, which Meaghan could tell he was proud of, and described himself as an "innovative problem solver."

Meaghan thought he'd be easy enough to manage. They were about the same age, which made her at least twenty years too old for him. No worries there. Tony merely needed to be reassured from time to time that he was the boss, the alpha male. He needed the illusion of authority, not the substance, and as long as Meaghan allowed him that illusion and stroked his ego a bit, he'd stay out of her way.

They chatted for about twenty minutes about the city and Tony's general goals as mayor. Lots of grandiose ideas but no obvious boondoggles on the horizon. Natalie had been wrong about the lunch invitation. Tony already had lunch plans he claimed he couldn't break, and Meaghan returned upstairs, relieved, and grateful for her sack lunch. She didn't think she could tolerate Tony's cologne much longer. Besides, she needed the time to prepare for her meeting with the notorious Emily Proctor.

CHAPTER 13

MEAGHAN PORED OVER the city code, reviewed Bob's files, and quizzed Natalie and Kady about what they knew, heard, or suspected about various projects. It was all standard municipal stuff, except that since Matthew's departure, the city seemed incapable of completing anything.

In each project, Emily's thwarting presence was obvious. Nothing got done because at the last minute the council got cold feet. Somewhere in the file, there'd be a nasty email from Emily, sent out to far more people than needed to be involved, blathering about "frustrating legislative intent" or "usurping legislative authority."

And, damn, she hated Jamie, absolutely despised him. It had gotten to the point where the council, urged on by Emily, were trying to insert themselves into how Jamie handled his court cases and threatening to fire him if he didn't comply with their every whim.

That stopped as of today. If Emily didn't like it, too

bad. Meaghan would try to be tactful, but considering that Emily had a history with Matthew and likely already hated Meaghan because of that history, she wasn't going to waste time building bridges. There was no excuse for the way Emily bullied Jamie. He was a good kid and he didn't deserve it.

Meaghan sighed. She'd just thought of a handsome thirty-year-old man as a kid. "God, I'm getting old," she muttered.

By one thirty, Meaghan was ready. She didn't have all the details, but enough to make her point. She'd try to keep things civil as long as she could, but she planned to make it crystal clear to Emily that the legislative meddling stopped today. Meaghan would not be bullied or pushed.

Jamie rushed past Meaghan's open office door about one forty-five carrying a huge file box. She heard him drop it on his desk and then he appeared in her doorway. He looked worried.

"I'm sorry," he said in a rush. "Court went long and I had to grab lunch. I need to talk to you about the meeting with Emily, and there's a lot to go over—"

Meaghan cut him off with a raised hand. "Breathe. Okay? Take a deep breath. Let it out." She pointed at the chair in front of her desk. "Sit down. It's all good. Natalie told me everything." Jamie's eyes widened in shock. What, did he think she couldn't figure this stuff out? "I know Bob didn't protect you. I will. Count on it."

Jamie's face broke into that wide disarming grin. "Oh, that. Bob. Yeah. Thank you."

Oh, that? What else was there? "Let me do the talking," Meaghan continued. "If I can keep things cordial, I will, but that's not my top priority. Things are changing. As of today. And she'll know that by the time she goes back downstairs."

"She won't like it."

"I don't care. I cannot emphasize enough how much I don't care."

Jamie sagged into the chair, relief wafting off him like steam. "Will Natalie be there?"

Meaghan smiled. "Safety in numbers?"

"Something like that."

"She'll be there. I need her institutional memory. And judging by the files, Natalie and Emily have gotten into it before. And Natalie's won."

"She holds her ground, yeah," Jamie said, nodding.

Two minutes before two o'clock, Meaghan, Jamie, and Natalie walked to the conference room across the hall from the solicitor's office. Meaghan's stomach fluttered with nervous anticipation. She noticed Jamie's hands shaking and Natalie looked apprehensive. Their anxiety was palpable.

She took each of them by the arm before they entered the conference room. "Let me do the talking," she said in a low voice. "Don't be scared. I've dealt with her type before. Her bullshit ends today."

Emily was waiting for them. Based on her fearsome reputation, Meaghan had been expecting a cross between Grendel's mother and Lady Macbeth. Instead, Emily was petite, with chin-length dark hair, not a strand out of place. She wore all pastels. A pink cotton sweater set. A pale green, pink, and powder blue plaid skirt. Pearls. Sensible tan flats. She looked like she'd stepped out of an LL Bean or Talbot's catalog.

Emily smiled, a forced cheery grin that didn't reach her eyes. "Hello, Meaghan," she said in a little girl singsong. She held out her well-manicured right hand. On her left hand, she wore a gold wedding band with a large diamond. "I've heard so much about you."

And in the same way Meaghan liked Natalie right away, Meaghan disliked Emily. She was the type who smiled and chirped and was oh so *nice,* while she stabbed you in the back over and over with a rusty knife.

Emily had a limp fish handshake. Meaghan took her hand for a moment, then dropped it. Looking her square in the eye, Meaghan answered, "And I've heard so much about you, Emily."

Emily's eyes narrowed, she frowned for a quick moment, and then the artificial smile reappeared.

Once they were all seated, Emily gave a speech about how great it was when everyone worked together, but how city government only worked if both branches, executive and legislative, were kept separate and boundaries respected.

Meaghan broke in. "Excellent point, Emily." Meaghan leaned back in her chair and smiled. Here we go, she thought. "It's been my experience in local government that the judicial branch doesn't have the same 'check and balance' power it does at the state or federal level. This leaves a power vacuum unless you have a city attorney—solicitor, I mean, still getting used to the terminology—unless you have a city solicitor who functions as that third player."

Emily's fake smile was gone.

"A strong city solicitor," Meaghan said, "is important to keeping the council and the mayor in check. Without that third pole of power it becomes tug-of-war. Or a shoving match, if one side is too powerful."

Jamie stared at her, in open admiration.

Emily scowled. "And I suppose you think that's you."

Meaghan nodded. "Yes. I do. You remember my father. We're a lot alike."

Emily stood up in a huff. "I don't like what you're insinuating."

"Emily, please, have a seat." Meaghan gestured at the table. "I'm not insinuating anything. But with regard to boundaries, you're right. There's been a power vacuum in this office for a while now and it's thrown the relationship between branches out of balance." Meaghan took a deep breath to steady her nerves. "It's nobody's fault. The work needs to get done, I understand that. But now that I'm here, we need to discuss the council's practice of inserting itself into executive functions, particularly with regard to my office."

Emily still stood, her face red and her voice thick with rage. "You have no authority over the council."

The hairs on the back of Meaghan's neck stood up. She hadn't discovered anything in her research suggesting Emily was mentally unbalanced, but her anger seemed far out of proportion to the conversation. She could see now why everyone feared Emily Proctor.

"I have the same authority with the council that I have with the mayor," Meaghan said, trying to keep her voice calm. "Under state statute and city ordinance, my duty is to advise both branches, legislative and executive." What the hell, Meaghan thought. She's already pissed off. Might as well go for it. "Which means I plan to speak directly with council members—without going through you first."

"You can try to sidestep me, but my council members won't talk to you," Emily hissed. "They respect my opinion on everything, including hiring and firing." The affable civil servant was gone. Emily looked wild with fury. "Don't forget.

You serve at the pleasure of the council. If I want you gone, you'll go."

Feigning calm, Meaghan replied, "No. That's not how it works. Read the ordinance. I serve at the pleasure of the mayor. Alone. The council had to consent to my being hired, and even you couldn't stop them on that one. But they don't have any say over when I leave." Meaghan gripped the arms of her chair so Emily couldn't see her hands shake. How did things get so ugly so fast? "And I suspect," Meaghan continued, fighting to keep her voice steady, "the council members would be troubled to hear you brag about how well you control them. You have no authority *whatsoever*," she accentuated each syllable, "over the terms of my employment. Much like you have no authority over my deputy and no right to tell him how to do his job."

Meaghan glanced at Jamie and Natalie. He stared at the table, his face red. Natalie gripped his trembling hand and glared at Emily.

Emily sneered. "Your *deputy*," she said. "You don't even know what he is." She paused. Her eyes narrowed, then she threw her head back and laughed. "I don't believe it. You really don't know. The great Matthew Keele's precious daughter has no idea what she's walked into."

She lifted a hand towards Jamie and began to utter unintelligible syllables. Natalie rose now, hands out in front of Jamie and chanted something in response.

What happened next played out in Meaghan's mind later in slow motion, like the moments leading up to a car crash. Time slowed and she could see everything unfold, but, as if paralyzed, she couldn't move in time to intercede.

Emily raised her other hand in a sweeping motion and

Natalie fell back—was pushed back—from the table and fell to the floor. Emily now swept both arms upward and Jamie looked like he was yanked out of his chair. She slashed her arms downward and Jamie's chest slammed to the table top and then his body rolled as if shoved. He sprawled on his back.

Natalie jumped to her feet and shouted, "No!" She threw herself on top of Jamie but was thrown to the floor again.

Pinned under invisible hands, Jamie struggled but couldn't sit up. His head rocked as if struck and a red line opened on his right cheek.

Emily, triumphant, leaned over him and hissed something. He groaned and struggled but couldn't move. She tore open his shirt and pulled out a dark stone on a leather thong. She yanked hard and the thong snapped.

A bright flash blinded Meaghan for a moment. Then she saw Jamie was gone, the table empty except for his shirt and tie, which lay there like rags. Emily held up her arm, the stone dangling from her fist. She smiled at Meaghan, her face alight with malice.

"Your turn," Emily said. She raised her hands again, chanting the strange syllables and swept her arm at Meaghan the way she had at Natalie and Jamie.

Nothing happened. Emily's eyes widened in fear. She turned and fled, still clutching Jamie's necklace.

CHAPTER 14

NATALIE STRUGGLED TO her feet and ran to the conference room door, which she slammed shut. Meaghan stared at the empty table where she'd last seen Jamie. She couldn't move or speak or think.

"Meaghan, I—"

The sound of Natalie's voice acted like a bucket of cold water. Meaghan's paralysis snapped.

"What just happened?" In her mind, Meaghan saw for an instant her mother's face and heard her voice. *Trust your eyes and ears. Believe what's in front of you.*

She had seen Natalie and Jamie tossed around the room, seemingly upon Emily's gesture. She'd seen Jamie slammed to the conference table, unable to get up or defend himself. She'd seen his head rocked like he'd been struck hard and a wound open on his cheek without a hand touching him. She'd seen Emily pull a necklace from his throat. And then there was a flash of light and he was gone, except for the white dress shirt and paisley tie left on the table.

Meaghan turned her eyes to Natalie. And she saw him.

Her mind wanted to shut down. It was not possible. It could not be. She stood and looked over the table. The rest of Jamie's clothes lay in a pile on the floor.

Something fluttered by Natalie's head.

No. Meaghan's brain fought against her eyes. No.

Trust your eyes and ears.

"Meaghan," Natalie said again.

Believe what's in front of you.

"Am I seeing what I think I'm seeing?"

"Meaghan, I—"

"Goddammit, Natalie. Am I seeing what I'm seeing? Is that Jamie next to you?"

Natalie looked around the room, eyes darting frantically.

"Natalie!" Meaghan barked at her. "Tell me right now what the hell just happened!"

Like a raw private responding to an angry drill sergeant, Natalie said in a rush, "Me and Emily are witches and Jamie's not exactly human."

Meaghan took a deep breath. *Believe what's in front of you.*

"Okay. And that's him?" With a shaking hand, Meaghan pointed at the thing fluttering around Natalie's head.

It flew closer and hovered in front of Meaghan's face.

It was Jamie. About eight inches tall. With wings.

And he was naked.

Unable to stop herself, she glanced down a few inches. Whatever he was, he was anatomically correct. Very much so, in fact.

Amidst the clamor of panicked voices in her head, the

lawyer chimed in. She had just sneaked a peek at her male employee's genitalia. It wasn't the biggest problem she had at the moment, but years of sexual harassment prevention training kicked in even as the rational underpinnings of western civilization collapsed beneath her feet.

Meaghan plucked a tissue from the box on the table. She looked at Jamie again, keeping her eyes glued on his tiny face. He leered at her in a way she couldn't have imagined him capable, at least not when she thought he was human.

She held out the tissue. "Cover yourself up. Now."

A tiny hand yanked the tissue from her. He wrapped it around himself like a bed sheet and zipped away.

"Meaghan," Natalie said. "I know this must be hard to take and . . ." She trailed off.

Trust your eyes and ears.

"It's the necklace," Meaghan said, staring at Jamie's empty clothes. "Right? It makes him our size and Emily knows that."

Natalie nodded.

"How do we get it back?" Meaghan asked.

"I don't know. I've never seen her this strong. She's a lot stronger than I am right now." Natalie's face crumbled into tears. "I'm sorry. I couldn't stop her. I couldn't fight her. I promised Matthew I'd keep him safe."

Meaghan handed the box of tissues across the table to Natalie. There was a banging at the window. Jamie was hurling himself against it. He looked more feral and less human by the moment.

"He wants to get outside," Natalie said. "He's . . . it's been a really long time since the last time he changed and he didn't have any time to prepare. He's all primal urge right now. It'll pass, but we've got to get him someplace safe."

Meaghan nodded.

Kady pushed open the conference room door. "I heard . . ." She looked around the room, saw the pile of clothes on the floor, and registered the looks on Meaghan's and Natalie's faces.

"Oh. Crap," she said. She slammed the door shut behind her. Jamie zipped over. Her face crinkled into a smile. "Ooh, he's so cute!"

The tiny winged Jamie hovered right in front of her face.

"He's waving his itty bitty middle finger at me." He pulled open the tissue he was wearing. Kady's smile evaporated. "The little fucker is flashing me!" She peered closer. "Damn. He's hung like a tiny little horse. No wonder Patrice is so happy."

"Kady. Not helping." Natalie snuck up behind Jamie, muttered something, and waved her hand. His wings sputtered and he fell through the air. Kady caught him before he hit the ground. Natalie scooped up his shirt and threw it around him like a net. "We need to get him back across the hall. He'll only be out for a minute or two."

Kady gathered up the rest of his clothing and they hurried across the hall into the office suite. Meaghan locked the door behind her and leaned on it. Kady dumped out a cardboard file box and they placed the stunned Jamie inside it.

"Take him back to the file room. Weight the lid with something. It won't hold him for long so get out of there fast and lock the door," Natalie said.

Kady nodded, grabbed the box, and ran.

"He's still all muddled from the change," Natalie said,

"but he's going to get crazy strong real soon. She had to do it up here, the bitch. It makes it so much worse. Let's hope his head clears first. There are no windows in there and both doors are steel, so he should be okay for now."

Meaghan was still leaning against the door. "Why couldn't Emily get me? She tried right before she bolted."

Natalie sat down in her desk chair and rubbed her temples. "This isn't how we wanted you to find out about your . . . about what Matthew really did around here." She looked up and met Meaghan's eyes. Natalie's eyes were red and puffy, but she'd stopped crying. "You truly are your father's daughter."

"Why couldn't she get me?"

"Because magic doesn't work on you. You're impervious," Natalie answered.

Believe what's in front of you.

Meaghan nodded. "That means I'm the one who has to go get Jamie's necklace back."

"Amulet," Natalie corrected.

"Amulet. Will she go back to her office?"

Natalie nodded. "Yeah. I think so. She's got it rigged with some big magic to keep her safe. From me." Natalie looked down. Her voice thickened like she was choking back tears. "Like she needs to worry about me right now."

Meaghan needed her to stay on track. "Magic that won't work on me?"

"Yeah. I think. It didn't work on Matthew." She raised her gaze again. "But please be careful. Even if she can't hex you, she can hex everything around you."

Meaghan raised an eyebrow. "What, like drop a piano on my head?"

Natalie flashed a weak smile. "I don't think she has that much imagination. She was crazy strong back there, but she'll need time to recharge."

Meaghan gave her a grim smile in return. "I'll be careful. She was scared back there. Of me. That gives me something to work with."

"You're taking this surprisingly well," Natalie said.

"No, I'm not, but I don't have time to fall apart right now. I need my deputy back. Lock the door behind me. If there's anything you can do from here to back me up—spells, voodoo dolls, whatever—get on it."

Meaghan strode out the door. Time to tour the council offices.

CHAPTER 15

MEAGHAN TOOK THE stairs. As she neared the second floor landing, she felt the hair on her arms stand on end and a slight stab of nausea for a moment and then it passed.

She felt her anger rise, her typical response to fear. But still she felt detached, like she was watching someone else stomp down the stairs, someone else who had just had the rug of reality yanked from under her feet.

Under the detachment, her mind sifted and sorted the events of the last week. The unspoken conversation was now loud and clear. She'd been right. Everyone *had* been hiding something from her, although it was several orders of magnitude weirder than she could have imagined.

Meaghan expected at some point before the end of the day she'd find herself weeping and assuring herself that it was only stress and she couldn't possibly have seen what she saw. But for now, she had to get Jamie back. Make him human instead of . . . what? A fairy?

Her mind rebelled at the thought. Only fifteen minutes ago, she knew there was no such thing as fairies. But now, who knew? The whole world had turned upside down. But that couldn't be it. Weren't fairies supposed to be all sparkly and pretty and childlike?

Jamie had merely been a smaller version of himself, with wings. Based on the full frontal naked view Meaghan had gotten, there was nothing in the least childlike about him. On the contrary, that leer he'd given her—if he'd been his normal size, she'd have kneed him in the balls and run like hell.

And he'd flashed Kady, pulling his tissue toga apart like a greasy raincoat. After he'd flipped her off.

Definitely not Tinkerbell.

The council office was on the second floor, at the opposite end of the hallway from the mayor's office. Meaghan pushed open the door and strode in. A young woman—chubby, plain, wearing glasses, her brown hair in a ponytail—sat at a reception desk.

"Where's Emily?" Meaghan barked.

Her voice quavering, the girl said, "Emily's not available right now. If you'd like to make an appointment . . ."

Meaghan felt a stab of pity for the girl. Hurricane Meaghan had to be nearly as terrifying as Emily in full wicked-witch mode.

Trying to sound a bit less enraged, Meaghan said, "She's going to see me now if I have to kick the goddamn door down. Please call her and tell her that." With a quick smile to reassure the girl, Meaghan swept past her and into the office suite.

Another young woman waited, this one blond, and so

tall and thin that she'd adopted the sad slouch shy girls got trying to hide in the crowd.

With a shaking hand, she pointed at the closed wooden door behind her. "In there," she whispered. "Be careful."

Meaghan smiled at her and nodded. Poor kid. Emily had handpicked assistants she could easily terrorize.

Bitch, Meaghan thought. A witch and a bitch. That thought was followed by the fervent prayer that Natalie was right about the impervious-to-magic thing. Meaghan pushed down her fear. After an entrance like she'd just made, there was no going back.

"Emily," Meaghan shouted at the closed door. It flew open with a bang, but the doorway was empty.

Meaghan snorted. "Show off," she muttered. She stepped through the doorway and looked around. Please, she thought, give me a break. The office walls were covered with cheerful motivational posters. There was a cutesy, crafty dried flower wreath on the wall above her desk with a placard dangling from it reading "Welcome!" She could smell potpourri.

My first encounter with an actual witch, Meaghan thought, and she's freaking Martha Stewart.

Emily stood behind her immaculate desk. Jamie's amulet lay in the middle of the gleaming glass desktop. Emily sneered at Meaghan, but Meaghan could see the fear behind the bravado. Emily began waving her arms and chanting. She raised her arm and made a throwing motion.

Meaghan felt a tiny shock, like walking across the carpet in socks and then touching a doorknob, nothing more.

Emily's eyes widened. Her chanting grew louder and more guttural. She lifted both arms and made the same downward slashing motion Meaghan had seen upstairs.

Not even a shock this time.

More chanting and more arm waving. And still Meaghan stood there, unscathed.

"You done?" Meaghan asked, hands on her hips and eyebrow raised.

"You . . . you," Emily sputtered, inarticulate with rage. "You have no idea what you're dealing with."

Face impassive, Meaghan said, "Let's see. You and Natalie are witches and Jamie . . . hell, I don't what he is. I just know he can't stay that way."

Emily's jaw dropped.

"And I'm sure there's a bunch of other supernatural crap going on too." Meaghan waited a beat. "Oh, and I'm impervious to magic. Like my father. There's a whole lot of detail I still need to pick up, but I think I have the general outline."

Emily, her face brick red, stared back without reply.

Meaghan took a step closer to the desk. Emily took a step backward.

Gotcha, Meaghan thought. "I know you can't hex me, but you can still magic all the stuff around me. But you need to understand. You drop a desk on me, you'd better make it count because if I get back up again I'll kick your ass all over this building."

She dropped her hands onto the glass desktop and leaned forward. Emily cringed backward. Meaghan glared at her. "Don't ever come at me through my staff or anyone I care about again. You've got a problem with me, you take it up with me."

Emily refused to meet Meaghan's eye. With a stiff nod, she pointed at the amulet.

Meaghan scooped the amulet off the desktop. A subtle surge of energy seemed to flow through it. Heavy for its size, it felt warm in her hand, alive.

"Thank you," said Meaghan. She held the amulet tight in her fist, feeling it throb like a tiny heart. "You and I have gotten off to a bad start. I'm not sure what you hoped to accomplish here, but since you've decided to now be reasonable, this one time I'm going to overlook you assaulting my staff members."

As Meaghan turned to leave, Emily said, her voice tight with anger, "You may be safe from magic but that doesn't mean I can't make your life miserable. Politics can get pretty ugly around here and . . ."

Meaghan stormed back to the desk, silencing Emily in mid-rant. Emily backed up so fast she almost sat on the credenza that covered the wall behind her desk.

Again, Meaghan placed both hands on the glass desktop and leaned until she was at eye level with Emily. With icy calm, Meaghan said, "You may be a big bad-ass witch, Endora, but I've spent my entire government law career in Maricopa County, Arizona, which is, in many ways, still the Wild, Wild West." She leaned back and stared down at the cowering Emily. "I know uglier politics than you've ever seen. Bring it, sweetie, and I'll take you to school."

Meaghan turned on her heel and strode out. The two timid girls in the outer office looked at her with something approaching adulation. Meaghan smiled back. She stopped a moment and said, "She gives you any shit, come see me."

Eyes wide, they nodded, as Meaghan swept out the door and down the hall.

CHAPTER 16

MEAGHAN TOOK THE elevator because she wasn't sure her legs would support her. She slumped against the back wall of the car, eyes shut, her whole body shaking. The amulet thrummed in her hand.Kady had been posted as lookout. When she saw Meaghan, she unlocked the office door. "Did you get it?"

Meaghan opened her hand and displayed the amulet.

"Oh, thank God," Kady said. "Natalie has to keep hexing him so he doesn't knock the file room door down." A metallic boom echoed through the office suite. "There he goes again."

Meaghan ran back to the file room. Natalie was leaning against the door.

Boom!

Natalie looked grim. "The hexes aren't working anymore. He's too strong. And still crazy. City hall's about the worst place for him to change."

Meaghan held up the amulet. "How do we get this around his neck?"

Boom!

Natalie turned her head and shouted at the closed door. "Damn it, you little shit, we're trying to help you!"

"What if you magic the door open from behind me and I'll be waiting with the amulet to throw it over him and you can try to net him with my trench coat if I miss."

Boom!

Natalie shook her head. "Won't work. If you miss, he'll blast through that coat like a bullet and we'll never catch him."

Boom!

"Or." They heard Kady behind them. "We can use this." She held a Taser gun. "I was hoping it wouldn't go this far."

Natalie glared at Kady. "I told you to leave that at home."

"And aren't you glad I ignored you?"

"You know how to use that thing?" Meaghan asked.

Boom!

Kady nodded.

"Can you hit him with it?" Meaghan asked.

"Oh, yeah. I've taken classes," answered Kady. "And I practice at the range. I'm a real good shot."

Boom!

Meaghan leaned against the door with Natalie. "He's so small," Meaghan said. "Won't that much electricity fry him?"

Natalie said, "No, the mass he's lost has been converted to magical energy. It would take a lot of juice to really hurt him."

"Should affect him like it would at his human size," Kady

said. "I'll need to get close or the probe spread will be too wide to catch him."

Boom!

"How close?" Meaghan asked.

"Give me a second," Kady said. Eyes narrowed, she paced several steps from the door, and stopped about seven feet away, then nodded. "He'll come straight out at me and then I need to pop him when he's a little closer. I'll go for his wings, so I need to hold it sideways."

Boom!

"Okay," Meaghan said. "Natalie, get the door and Kady, zap him. I'll get the amulet around his neck. If the first blast doesn't drop him or Kady misses, we all dive on and try to wrestle him to the ground."

Natalie unlocked the door and pulled it open. Jamie zipped out, once again naked. Kady squinted, aimed, and pulled the trigger. The wires shot out, caught both wings and—zzzt. He convulsed and dropped to the ground like a rock.

Meaghan dove on top, threw the amulet around his tiny neck, and rolled away. A flash of bright green light filled the hallway.

And there was Jamie, full size and lying naked on the hallway carpet.

The Taser probes lay on the floor on either side of him. Kady retracted them back into the gun while Natalie grabbed Jamie's tan raincoat out of his office and threw it over him.

After a few tense moments, his eyes fluttered open and he groaned. "Oh, that sucked." Awareness flooded back and his face grew bright red. "Oh, shit, I'm so sorry. Is everybody okay? Did I hurt anybody?"

Kady crouched down and rubbed his shoulder. "No, dumb ass. You shook your junk at us and flipped me off but no harm done."

"Oh, shit, shit, shit." He curled into a ball and pulled the raincoat over his head. "Where are my clothes?" he asked, voice muffled.

"In your office, hon," Natalie said. "We'll all go out front and give you some privacy. Take your time getting up. Kady just Tasered you."

"Thanks," Jamie's muffled voice responded. He pulled the raincoat off his head and looked at Kady. "You Tasered me?"

"You flashed me," Kady said, with a broad grin. "And may I say, wowza. Nature has been generous."

Jamie turned a deeper shade of red and groaned. He dove back under the raincoat.

"Kady," Natalie said. "Still not helping." She grabbed Kady by the arm and pulled her down the hallway. Meaghan turned to follow.

Jamie pulled back the raincoat and called after her. "Meaghan, I'm . . . I don't . . . I'm sorry I wasn't honest with you."

Meaghan stopped and looked back at him, lying curled up on the floor. There was dried blood on his cheek from the gash Emily had inflicted. "Get dressed and we can talk about it. And don't worry. I think that was something I needed to see to believe." She continued down the hallway after Natalie and Kady, and followed them to the front office.

"Okay," she said, and the room began whirling around her again. Natalie led her to a chair and sat her down.

"Head between your knees, deep breaths." Natalie hovered over Meaghan, rubbing her back.

In a few moments, the spinning in Meaghan's head stopped and she sat up. She closed her eyes and rubbed her temples. She had a pounding headache. Opening her eyes, she saw Natalie and Kady staring at her, as if waiting for her to detonate.

"Okay," Meaghan said. "Let's try this again. I guess we have a lot to talk about."

They all fell silent for several long moments. Meaghan didn't have a clue where to start. Natalie and Kady avoided her eyes. Kady stared at her shoes and spun her chair in tight half circles. Natalie stared at the ceiling. Now with the immediate panic over, nobody knew what to say.

Meaghan finally broke the silence. "What time is it?"

"Three thirty," Kady answered in a small, subdued voice.

"I think we're closing up shop early today," Meaghan answered. "Is there any alcohol stashed away up here? I could use a drink."

Natalie reached into the file cabinet behind her desk and, with a guilty grin, pulled out an unopened bottle of Irish whiskey.

Meaghan raised an eyebrow. Irish whiskey had been Matthew's beverage of choice during his drinking days.

"I found it tucked into a box of really old files in long-term storage," Natalie said. "It was really dusty and the label is faded. It's never been opened. I think he stashed it when he first got here, just in case, and forgot about it."

Meaghan nodded. It made sense. If his first day on the job had been anything like hers, then drinking again might have seemed like a good idea.

"Let's crack it open," Meaghan said. "I think we need it."

Natalie nodded. Kady pulled some plastic cups out of

another file drawer and Natalie poured a stiff shot into three of them.

The women lifted their drinks and stared at each other. Meaghan raised her cup. "Here's to the absolutely weirdest first day on the job I've ever had." She drained it in a single gulp and began coughing. Meaghan's usual drink was white wine or the occasional fancy mixed cocktail. She loved the smell of whiskey, but it tasted like liquid fire going down.

When Meaghan's coughing subsided a bit, Kady said, "You're taking this all really well." She took a careful sip of her drink. "Why aren't you freaking out? I've lived with it all my life and it still freaks me out sometimes."

"You know, I don't know," Meaghan answered. She paused, mulling what to say. "I knew there was something going on, this whole silent conversation everyone seemed to be having around me." She shook her head. "I kept getting the creeps, but thought I was overreacting from stress. Russ was so weird about leading me through the woods when I first drove in. And my dad calling me a witch and bowing to Jamie, and Meb downstairs not wanting me to take the stairs. And that dream, my mom . . ."

Meaghan stared into the empty air. "Oh, shit. Did my mother really come see me? Are there ghosts too?"

Kady nodded. "Oh, yeah. Especially in city hall."

Meaghan nodded. Of course there were. "And Jamie," she said. "I thought he was a refugee from somewhere in Eastern Europe."

"I was a refugee," Jamie said as he walked into the office. "But not from there." He had his clothes back on, except for the tie, and his shirt was untucked, but he looked normal again. Except for the haunted look in his eyes and the cut on his cheek. He'd wiped off the blood. The cut appeared shallow, but his eye had started to bruise and swell. He walked with a stiff gait, like he was in pain.

Natalie said. "I don't know how much you remember, but you're gonna be one big bruise the way you were banging on that steel door."

"I think I already am. Got any ibuprofen?" He sat on the edge of her desk. He wouldn't meet Meaghan's eye. Natalie gave him the requested pills and he swallowed them dry with a grimace. She tried to examine his cut cheek and swollen eye, but he waved her away. Again silence fell. The three women stared at Jamie. He stared at the floor.

After a long silent moment he said, "I'm fine. I'm sore and beat up and embarrassed as hell, but I'll be fine." He looked up at everyone. "Quit staring me at like that. Please. It's bad enough without you all acting weird. Is that whiskey? Can I have some?"

Natalie poured him a cupful. He took a healthy gulp, made a face, and said, "I guess a margarita was too much to hope for."

Natalie and Kady sagged with relief at Jamie's attempt to make a joke. "Yeah, ha ha," Kady said. "Blender's on the fritz."

More awkward silence descended. Again, Jamie spoke first. "I'm so sorry. I know what a shit I can be when I'm . . . that way. I'm just relieved I didn't hurt anybody."

"It's not your fault," Meaghan said. "Quit apologizing. It's Emily's fault. She's the one who's going to be sorry if she pulls something like that again."

The silence returned.

Meaghan took charge. She was the boss, after all. "Natalie, send the phones to voice mail. Kady, put a sign on the door that says we're closed for a staff retreat."

"Already made it," Kady said. "While you were downstairs."

With the phones forwarded and the closed sign on the door, Meaghan grabbed the whiskey bottle, told everyone to bring their cup, and led them back to her office.

CHAPTER 17

THE SMALL OFFICE, with its round walls and big windows, felt safe and welcoming. It smelled good too, Meaghan realized. Lavender and some other scents she couldn't identify. When Meaghan commented, Natalie pulled a small bag out from behind a book shelf. "Hex bag," she said. "Keeps the bad juju out. They're all over your house too."

Another round of drinks poured, her staff arranged in front of her desk, Meaghan leaned back in her chair and took a deep breath. "Okay. Spill."

The universe, they explained, was a far weirder place than even quantum physics suggested. Eldrich was—for lack of a better description—a hole in the fence of reality. Worlds, most of them magical in some way, collided here. Energy leaked in from other dimensions, feeding the paranormal. Ghosts and witches predominated, but there were many other things roaming the woods where the gateways were located.

Supernatural creatures that existed in the human world were drawn to Eldrich like moths to a porch light.

"So," Meaghan interrupted, "what's the deal with city hall?"

"It's not a gateway, exactly," Natalie said. "More like a big radio tower for supernatural energy."

"Is it why I got woozy in Jamie's office?"

Natalie nodded. "It happens a lot in there. I goosed Jamie's amulet so the energy doesn't affect him. Basically, a bunch of mystical whatsits converge here and the building was designed to amplify them."

"Whatsit? Is that the technical term?" Meaghan asked, with a grin. "Is this like Sedona?"

"Um. Sort of but not really," Natalie answered. "Like Sedona. Not the technical term thing. Sorry. Just know that if you get wobbly it's probably that and not something you need to worry about."

Meaghan nodded. "So, why'd they build it like this?"

Natalie shrugged. "The founder of the town was nuts? He wanted to talk to his dead wife and got sick of being conned by fake mediums, so he decided to cut out the middle man and build a big phone and talk to her directly."

"Did he?" Meaghan asked. "Talk to her?"

"Not that way. He died before the building was finished," Natalie said.

"But does it work?"

Kady snorted. "Oh, it works, only not as planned. You really need to get more of the basics before city hall makes any sense."

Meaghan nodded. "Okay, you were talking about witches before I interrupted."

Natalie continued. She was training Kady, who had been raised by her widowed father and was a bit of a late bloomer, but generally the craft went from mother to daughter. Natalie came to work for Matthew when her mother, Vivian, died. Vivian had worked for Matthew since he first came to Eldrich. It was Vivian who made Jamie's first amulet, when he was still a boy.

"So is it only women who do magic?" Meaghan asked.

"Well, it doesn't have to be, but for some reason in Eldrich it is."

"Why is that?"

Natalie thought about it a moment. "I don't think there was ever any intent to exclude men. It just sort of happened over time because they weren't as interested and now everyone assumes only women do magic. Since no boys in the past learned how to do it, there are no men to pass it on. So for now, you have to learn it from women, and boys with raw talent take one look at their mom's pack of crazy friends and decide to try out for Little League instead."

Those residents so inclined saw the ghosts, felt the magic, and came to accept the supernatural as merely another local quirk, like the rain and the problems using GPS. Those not so inclined did their best to ignore the weirdness swirling all around them, or left town. The end result was a town full of people who either accepted the paranormal or were so skillful at denial they could overlook it.

"And those who flee tell stories about their strange experiences," Meaghan said. "That's why the trucking company didn't want to deliver my storage pod and the driver was in such a hurry to get away. I thought it was because they broke all my stuff."

Natalie and Kady nodded. Jamie gazed out the window behind her, a blank look on his face.

And then there was Matthew. And now Meaghan. Being impervious to magic in a magical place gave Matthew a unique power. He was the perfect mediator for disputes within and between magical worlds. He couldn't be hexed. He couldn't be charmed or manipulated. He couldn't be glamoured or confused. With a powerful witch at his side to spot attempts to hex the things around him, he stood alone and above the fray.

He was also the perfect gatekeeper to protect the human world from those who saw humans as easy prey. Humans were clever—frighteningly clever—which is how they thrived as a species even while surrounded by more powerful magical entities. But humans, despite their cleverness, were vulnerable—their general lack of magical ability, coupled with their susceptibility to magical influence made them easy to manipulate and confuse. In Matthew, magical bad actors had to contend with human ingenuity without the accompanying human frailty, and it terrified them.

Being impervious to magic was rare and only occurred among humans. When Matthew lost his capacity to continue, order began breaking down. Species who'd stayed clear of the human world now saw opportunity.

"Think about what happened to Europe when Rome fell," Natalie said. "The Dark Ages. That's why we . . ." She paused and looked away from Meaghan. Her face flushed pink.

"You tell her or I will," Kady said. "She deserves to know."

"Tell me what?"

Natalie lifted her head and met Meaghan's steady gaze.

"That's why we did a spell to nudge some people and events in ways to make it very easy for you to decide to come here."

Meaghan let this sink in a moment. Magic didn't work on her, so they had to go after the people around her. Her former boss? Russ? The Canadian real estate investor who bought her house in Phoenix for cash sight unseen?

"You hexed my boss," Meaghan said. She wasn't angry, which surprised her a little. She'd been bombarded with such weirdness for the last couple of hours that she thought she no longer had the capacity to react to anything.

"Yes. We did." To her credit, Natalie continued to maintain eye contact. "And the grumpy old guy who picked that fight with you. And the guy who bought your house."

"Russ?"

"No. Not him. It was kind of Russ's idea to do it."

Meaghan's blank gaze shifted into the fearsome glare. Now she was angry. "He knows about all this? And he had you cast spells to get me back here?"

Natalie withered under Meaghan's stony glare and looked down at her feet. Her face was bright red.

Jamie broke his silence. "Of course he knows. It took you a couple of days to figure out something was weird about this place. He's been here on and off for nearly thirty years." He scowled at her. "He needed you to step up and he knew there wasn't any other way. Russ has been there for Matthew for a long time."

And you haven't. Meaghan could almost hear the unspoken words. Now it was her turn to blush and look away.

No one spoke and Meaghan felt the numbness return. Her own brother had blown up her entire life. With magic. So she could protect the world from scary things from other dimensions. Anger seemed pathetically inadequate to convey what she was feeling at the moment. She poured another shot of whiskey into her empty plastic cup and drained it in one gulp. She didn't even cough this time.

"The mediator thing," Meaghan said, looking at Jamie for his reaction. "That's how Matthew got hooked up with you and your father?"

Jamie nodded. He refused to make eye contact with anyone, Meaghan noticed. He looked ready to bolt at the slightest provocation.

"How did you know we were refugees?" he asked, staring at his knees.

"I figured it out the first time I met you," she said gently. "Russ told me the rough outlines of the story when I asked, but I knew you'd fled from somewhere and the generic name . . ." Meaghan took a deep breath. No point in shying away from it now. "And something my mother told me in a dream I had right before I met you. About the war starting."

Jamie glanced up at her. He was more than merely wary, she realized. He was ashamed. Of what she might think of him.

"The war?" Natalie asked in a high choked voice. "We . . . don't . . . that was something else entirely. The war . . ." She fell silent under Meaghan's withering glare.

Meaghan saw Jamie and Kady exchange confused glances. They didn't know what Natalie was talking about either. No time to worry about it now, Meaghan thought. She wanted to know about Jamie.

Meaghan continued. "I figured I'd found a highly dramatic way of telling myself something I already knew. I hit on Bosnia, that general conflict, based on your age and appearance and when you got here."

Jamie nodded, allowing her to hold his gaze.

"And your father's accent seemed to confirm it," Meaghan said.

Jamie's brow furrowed in a scowl. "You met my father?"

Meaghan nodded. "He dropped off some honey at our house for Russ and then we saw him at the farmers' market."

Jamie's eyes narrowed and his jaw tightened. "Was he drunk?"

A rush of maternal feeling for Jamie swept through Meaghan. They'd taken both his parents from him. His father had, for all practical purposes, died at the same time his mother had. But John kept walking around as a broken reminder of what Jamie had lost.

"No," she answered. "He appeared to be sober. Both times."

"Something new," Jamie said, his voice bitter.

After a long moment, Meaghan said, "I'm sorry. There's no tactful way to ask this. But I have to know. What are you?"

Jamie's mouth twitched into a humorless grin. "Not human. But I guess you already figured that out."

"Well, yes," Meaghan said, unsure how to respond. "The . . . uh . . . wings kind of gave it away. And your . . . height."

Kady snorted, choking back a laugh, and the tension broke. Unable to contain herself, Kady burst out laughing and Natalie joined her. Jamie grinned for the first time since before their meeting with Emily, and started laughing too.

The weirdness of the day broke over Meaghan and she lost it. Huge belly laughs shook her. She could feel the tears not far behind, but she resisted them. She could weep when she got home. Right now laughing was what everybody needed.

Guffawing, as tears streamed down her face, Kady slapped Jamie's arm. "The wings," she gasped. "Your height." She choked unable to say more.

Natalie and Jamie laughed so hard they couldn't speak. After a bit, Meaghan started coughing and everyone settled down as she caught her breath.

"I needed that," Jamie said, dabbing his eyes with his shirtsleeve.

Meaghan grabbed a tissue out of the box on her desk, then handed the box to Jamie. Everyone wiped their eyes and blew their noses and regained a bit of composure.

She sat back in her chair and surveyed her staff. Jamie, in particular, looked much calmer. "So," she said. "Now that we all feel better—"

Jamie finished her sentence for her. "You still need to know what I am."

Meaghan nodded.

Jamie nodded in response. "Okay." He took a deep breath. "Here goes. I'm one of several different species that are the source of human stories about . . . fairies, pixies, gnomes . . . et al."

Meaghan smiled. "Et al? You may not be human, but you're definitely an attorney."

Jamie grinned back. "There's a lawyer joke in there somewhere."

"So," Meaghan said, not letting him get off track. "You're a . . ." For a moment she saw him in her mind, as clear as a photograph, hovering naked in front of her, leering. She felt her face get hot. "You're not Tinkerbell, I know that."

"No. Not by a long shot," he said. "We call ourselves a name I can't really say with human vocal cords. When I'm . . . like that I have an extra set and can make sounds humans can't make."

"Is there something approximate in human?" She'd never referred to "human" as a language before.

"Your dad called us Fahraya."

"Is that the source for the word fairy?"

Jamie shook his head. "No. Fairy legends existed long before we showed up. Our contribution to the folklore are the wings. Our name sounds different when we say it, but with human vocal cords and preconceived notions . . ." He shrugged.

Meaghan nodded. The Southwest was full of bastardized Spanish and Indian names for things that sounded very little like the original word. If English speakers could screw up Spanish that badly, imagine what they could do with a language that required an extra set of vocal cords to pronounce.

"The name I get," she said. "But you . . ." Again she had to push the image of naked, flying Jamie out of her head. "I wouldn't describe what you looked like as a . . . well, you know. The whole Peter Pan 'I do believe in fairies' thing. Not at all like that."

Kady jumped in. "More badass, less pixie dust."

Jamie looked out the window behind Meaghan's head, the look of shame back on his face. "More brutal. And more blood. So much blood. Think the Stone Age with wings." He shook his head. "Yeah, it's a mystery. The first time I ran across the human conception of fairies, I decided you were all crazy."

He looked back at Meaghan, meeting her gaze. "When I got here, I was filthy, wearing untanned skins, matted greasy hair down my back. Your father and your brother had to teach me how to be human. How to sleep in a bed, bathe, use a toilet, eat at a table." He looked down at his feet, his face flushed. The shame was back.

Meaghan gave him a few moments, then continued her questioning. "I assume you weren't always called Jamie. How did you pick that?" She wanted to ask about John too, but he was obviously a sore topic, so she let it go.

"My Fahrayan name was . . . I can't really pronounce it without the vocal cords. With a human voice it sounds something like 'Zhu-may.' It's what Matthew called me that first day we met. So, Matthew and Russ started calling me Jamie. When I was ready to go to school and Matthew had to get paperwork forged, I wanted a normal human name." He poured the last of the whiskey into his cup and drained it in one gulp. "Matthew had already gone with John Smith for my father—something to do with a friend of a friend dying and them being able to use his identity, so Matthew chose James Smith for me. I wanted Keele, but . . ." Jamie paused, staring past Meaghan's shoulder and out the window. "I guess he figured my father had lost enough and he didn't want him to lose me too." He snorted in disgust. "Like he gives a shit."

She knew how that felt, so she didn't contradict him. *But I'm pretty sure you're wrong*, she thought. "So," she said, trying to lighten the mood, "how does the amulet work?"

Natalie jumped in before Jamie could answer. "It's magic," she said.

They all broke up laughing again.

CHAPTER 18

BY FIVE O'CLOCK, everyone was exhausted and Meaghan decided to call it a day. She planned on grilling Russ hard when she got home. She still couldn't process how she felt about his involvement in bringing her to Eldrich.

Jamie had walked to work that morning, his standard practice on the mornings he didn't take the kids to day care, and had used a city car to drive to court. He drank more of the whiskey than the others and was in obvious pain from the battering he'd given himself trying to escape the file room, so Meaghan drove him home.

"Do you want to come in and meet Patrice and the kids?" he asked as they turned onto his street.

"Okay, but only a quick visit. I have to get home and pummel my brother. I assume she knows about . . . you know?"

Jamie smiled and nodded. "She knows. She wants to meet you. Just for a minute."

Meaghan parked the car in front of Jamie's house. It had

a picket fence. A white picket fence. The All-American guy. Except he wasn't.

Meaghan grabbed his trench coat and briefcase from the backseat while he climbed out of the car. Patrice waited on the front porch, still wearing her blue scrubs from work. Small, no more than five foot two or so, with dark hair pulled back in a ponytail, she was even lovelier in person than in her photo.

She had her arms folded across her chest, her lips pressed tightly together. As Meaghan got closer, she saw tears in Patrice's eyes as she watched Jamie limp up the front walk.

"Hi, honey, I'm home," he said with a weak smile. He had finally allowed Natalie to dab a vile-smelling salve on the cut on his cheek, and it looked better. But the salve hadn't done anything to reduce the beginnings of an impressive shiner.

"Natalie called and told me what happened," Patrice said. "Let me see your eye."

He tried to wave her off the way he'd waved off Natalie.

"James," she said. "Hold still."

It was a command and Jamie obeyed. She probed the injured tissue with gentle fingers, scowling.

"Why didn't you ice this?" she demanded.

"There was a lot going on," Jamie said with a sheepish look.

Patrice snorted. "If I ever get my hands on that bitch Emily—"

"She's dangerous," Jamie said, his voice sharp. "Stay away from her." He pointed over his shoulder. "This is Meaghan, by the way."

Patrice gave her a warm smile. "Thank you. Natalie told me what you did. It's . . . I know it's a lot to take in."

"Yes," Meaghan said. "It is. I'm glad to meet you, but

right now you need to take care of your husband. We can visit another time."

"Where are the kids?" Jamie asked.

"Over at Annie's," Patrice said. Meaghan wondered if it was the same Annie who worked in city hall, the woman who just seemed to know when the mayor entered the building. Maybe she used a crystal ball, Meaghan thought. My deputy can fly and my office manager keeps hex bags around to protect us from the spell-casting city council director and the resident ghosts, so why not? She shivered and turned her attention back to Jamie and Patrice.

"I figured you might need a little quiet," Patrice continued. "Come on, big guy. Let's get you into a hot bath." She pulled his arm over her shoulders and turned back to Meaghan. "We'll have you over for dinner when the dust settles a little, okay?"

"Sounds great. I'll see you then." Meaghan started down the front walk to the car. She turned back to the house and said, "Jamie, if you need tomorrow off, take it, okay?"

He nodded and waved. Patrice led him into the house as Meaghan drove away.

She barely noticed the road, driving on autopilot while her mind churned. She intended to interrogate Russ when she got home. He, at the very least, owed her some answers. But the person Meaghan most wanted to talk with was her father. It was bad enough finding out that the fairy tales were true, in a dark horrible way, and the world really was full of monsters and magic. But Meaghan had also learned that she had a destiny. A big one. Protecting the world. And the one person who truly understood what lay before her no longer recognized her and slipped further out of reach every day.

When she got home, Russ was waiting on the back porch with a glass of white wine and a nervous look on his face. Natalie must have called Russ after she talked to Patrice.

"Hey, sis." He held the wine glass out to her. "I thought you might need this. Weird day at the office?"

Meaghan glared at him, ignoring the offered wine as she walked past him into the house.

"Meg, I—"

She cut him off. "Back off. I need to change my clothes and I need a few minutes alone."

"But, I—"

"I can't deal with you right now," she said, feeling her anger at Russ come roaring back. "You blew up my entire life. You didn't trust me enough to even try to tell me the truth. You never gave me a chance to choose this life. You just dumped it on me. A glass of wine isn't going to fix it."

Meaghan stomped up the stairs to her bedroom. She pushed the door shut behind her, kicked off her shoes, and leaned against the door frame, her eyes shut. The flare of anger faded away and she felt numb again.

She pushed herself away from the door and dropped her bag on the bed. The black suit went back into the closet and she pulled on jeans and a T-shirt. She used the bathroom and washed her hands, unable to look at herself in the mirror.

Walking out of the bathroom, she noticed the cardboard boxes lined up along the base of the window seat. Five of them, old, battered, and dusty. These weren't boxes she'd brought with her from Arizona.

She heard a quiet knock on the door. She squeezed her eyes shut and took a deep breath. Don't rip his head off, she told herself.

"Come in, Russ."

The door creaked open a few inches. Russ stuck his head in. "I'm sorry to bug you. You have every right to be angry with me. And we can talk about it whenever you're ready. But in the meantime, do you want to come down for dinner? I can make you a tray if you'd rather be alone."

Meaghan realized she didn't want to be alone. If she had a Destiny with a capital D, she wanted to spread the burden around as much as she could. She turned to face him. "I'll come down. I'm still really mad at you, but not as much as I thought I'd be." She pointed behind her at the boxes. "What's this?"

"Some of Dad's stuff. Journals and photos and stuff. I brought them over from his office."

"Office?" Meaghan asked. "In city hall?"

"No. The room over the garage. It's been locked up since he got sick. He kept notes on everything and I thought since you can't talk to him about it, this was the next best thing."

Matthew could help her after all. She felt relief flood over her followed by the crushing wave of emotion she'd been pushing back all afternoon.

Here's the freak-out, she thought, and then conscious thought left her and the tears turned into shaking sobs. Russ helped her to the edge of the bed and sat her down. He sat next to her, an arm around her shoulders. He didn't try to tell her it would be okay or that she shouldn't cry. He merely let her wail. It occurred to her, when the storm began to pass, that he'd been here himself, once upon a time, trying to come to terms with a rational world blown to pieces.

When the crying slowed to sniffles, Russ got up, grabbed the box of tissues from the bathroom, and handed it to her.

"I've cried more in the week I've been here than I have in years." Meaghan blew her nose hard, several times. "Let's go eat. I'll look at Dad's stuff later." She looked up at her brother, at the worried look on his tired, lined face. She took Russ's hand and squeezed it. "I haven't forgiven you yet, you big doofus, but I will. And it's not like I would have believed you if you'd tried to tell me. I'm scared and weirded out and I have a zillion questions, but right now I need some normal. For a little while at least."

He smiled and nodded. "Okay. Not that things are ever very normal around here. C'mon. I made meatloaf. With bacon on top."

"Bacon is good," she said in a small voice. "It's not magical bacon, is it?"

"No more magical than usual," he replied.

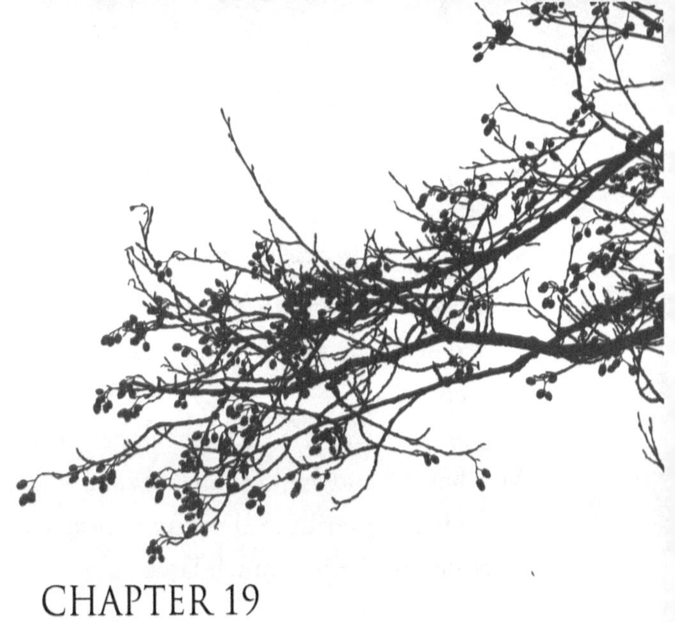

CHAPTER 19

MEAGHAN GOT THROUGH dinner in a haze. Russ didn't try to engage her in conversation, and Matthew still didn't recognize her, so what little talk there was concerned Matthew's weekly visit to his occupational therapist the next morning.

The food helped, though. Russ had made quintessential comfort food—meatloaf and mashed potatoes. The prosaic hominess of the heavy meal grounded her in a way the whiskey at her office hadn't.

She offered to do the dishes, dreading the moment when she was alone with her thoughts again. The warm water and the clatter of the plates and cutlery as she rinsed them and loaded them into the dishwasher soothed her raw nerves.

Dishes done, she said goodnight to Matthew, who would be asleep before too long, and left her father and brother in the living room watching TV. She'd planned to grill Russ, but now she intended to go to the source—Matthew's journals and files.

Meaghan flipped on the bedside lamps and the lamp next to the window seat and took a closer look at the boxes. They were dated. She picked the oldest box, dated from 1976, and opened it.

On top was a sealed envelope with her name on it in Matthew's handwriting. She opened it with care. The paper was much newer than the stuff beneath it and it appeared to be added to the box much later.

> *January 1, 2011*
>
> *Dearest Meaghan,*
>
> *If you're reading this, Meg, it means I'm either dead or so far gone I may as well be. I'm sorry I can't convey this story in person, that I can't be there to help you. But considering our history, maybe that's for the best.*
>
> *I'm sorry, so sorry, that I couldn't be a better father to you. The distance between us breaks my heart, but I made it, I know that, and now I fear it's too late to fix it. But please know how much I love your mother and you and Russ. I made so many mistakes, but the greatest sin of my life was pride. I believed myself alone with this burden, that I somehow stood above everyone, and had to bear it on my own. Meg, you aren't alone. You are surrounded by people who will love you and help you if you let them. Don't make the same blunder I did and try to lone wolf it.*

I suppose the best thing I can do now is shut up and let you wade through these boxes. There's more stuff in my office—ask Russ—but these journals and files are enough to get you started. I kept a regular journal and hung onto every photo, article, book, whatever. It's all out in the garage. You'll need to do the same thing for whomever succeeds you. People like us are out there. Do yourself a favor and start looking now for your replacement. Don't make this job a life sentence like I did.

Don't ever doubt your abilities, Meg. Always trust your gut. And don't let the crazy magical bastards grind you down, because they will certainly try. Russ knows all about this stuff. Let him handle the hospitality duties. You concentrate on kicking tail and taking names. They won't know what hit 'em.

All my love,

Dad

Meaghan felt her eyes fill again with tears. She sniffed them back. Enough with the crying for one day. She had work to do. She set the letter aside, not sure whether to go through the boxes chronologically or dig in and look for stuff about Jamie and John.

Curiosity overcame organization and she tipped the box on its side and pulled the folders and notebooks onto the carpet.

Good old Matthew. Every folder was labeled, every notebook dated. She fanned the folders across the floor looking for references to Fahraya.

Nothing.

"Duh, dumbass," she mumbled to herself. She did some mental math. John and Jamie hadn't gotten here until at least 1995.

She shoved the files and journals from the seventies aside. Jamie first. Then she'd go back and figure out how Matthew got involved in the first place. She suspected there would be some painful memories in that box and she decided she wasn't ready.

Mid nineties . . . the box right in the middle. She pulled it open. Bingo. There were several accordion files with "FAH-RAYA" scrawled across the front in black marker.

Meaghan soon discovered that while Matthew had been good at dating his journals and getting stuff from the same general time grouped together, inside the individual manila folders, chaos reigned. Matthew's meticulous record keeping had slipped over time. Some files were labeled, some weren't. None had dates.

She grabbed an accordion file and pulled the folders out. She fanned them across the carpet. She spotted one labeled "Photos" and opened it.

Twelve-year-old Jamie scowled at her, standing on the back porch of the house in which she sat. He was wrapped in a blanket, but his hands were visible. The nails and fingertips were black with grime. Ugly red welts marked his wrists. His face was bruised and his upper lip swollen.

She could see the amulet around his neck, and wondered where his clothes were. This must have been taken right after he arrived. He said they got here with nothing. The size difference, she realized—his clothes wouldn't have survived the change and any objects would be Barbie-doll sized.

There were several more photos of Jamie. His hair hung

in matted dingy blond dreadlocks halfway down his back. More bruises covered his back, legs, and arms. He hadn't come through his parents' ordeal unscathed. He'd been restrained and beaten.

The only clean spots on his body were two strips of skin, each about an inch wide, running down his back next to his spine and along his shoulder blades. The wings, she thought. That's where the wings would be attached if he still had them.

She pulled out another envelope of photos. These were Jamie, still young. The top one showed him clean, hair short, wearing jeans and a T-shirt, smiling shyly at the camera. Matthew, a broad grin on his face, stood next to Jamie, an arm draped across his shoulder.

Meaghan felt a stab of . . . grief? Jealousy? When she'd been that age, Matthew had been spiraling out of control, alternately terrifying his family and avoiding them.

Every photo in the folder included Jamie. Russ and teenaged Jamie showing off the fish they'd caught. Jamie playing with a dog she didn't recognize. Jamie graduating from high school. Jamie living his life with Russ and Matthew, growing happier in each photo.

This wasn't an historical record. It was a family photo album. Her father had no photos like this of her. She hated herself for being jealous of Jamie, and tried to remember the traumatized child in the earliest photos and how lucky he had been to find a loving family.

John wasn't anywhere. He didn't appear in any of these photos. He was as absent from Jamie's life as Matthew had been from Meaghan's.

At the bottom of the file, she found an envelope labeled "Fahraya—J'han." With trembling hands she opened it.

The first photo showed a bleak, stony, utterly foreign landscape. And underneath that one, there was a photo of John. Pre-exile.

Matthew had called Jamie a prince. So, John must have been the king. Despite the grime, the skins he wore, and the matted dreadlocks, John looked like a king. He smiled regally, his wings extended to their full span. He stared into the camera looking strong and confident.

She felt a tingle in her gut and her face grew hot.

In the second photo, John, wings pulled in, stood with a protective arm draped over a young Jamie, who stood in front of him and wore a shy smile. Another young boy, a few years older, crouched next to them, looking up at John with a broad grin. She turned the photo over. On the back, she recognized Matthew's uneven scrawl. "J'han with son (center) and nephew."

In both photos, John looked a lot more like grown-up Jamie than he looked like the man she had met. Whatever they'd done to him must have been horrific to degrade this magnificent man into a sad, defeated wreck.

The next few photos confirmed it. John was still in Fahrayan form, but must have been in the human world. He was tiny, lying on a towel over someone's knees. There was no part of him not cut or bruised or lashed. His wings were gone and in their place ran two ragged mounds of bloody flesh, following the same general line of the clean skin she'd seen in that first photo of Jamie.

They'd cut—hacked—his wings off.

The last photos showed him cleaned up, his hair cropped, wearing an amulet similar to Jamie's. Matthew must have taken them soon after John's arrival. The photos documenting his injuries showed barely faded bruises and stark red scars running along his spine where his wings had been. Unlike the photos taken in Fahraya, where he'd looked confidently into the camera, now he stared at the ground. The power he exuded in the earlier photos was gone.

No happy family pictures of John. He had slunk away into a bottle and let Matthew and Russ raise his traumatized son.

It was the wings, she thought. When they took away his ability to fly, they took away from him what made him a Fahrayan man. It wasn't only his throne and his queen they'd stolen from him.

Meaghan's brief jealousy over Jamie was long gone. Sad and exhausted, she left the files strewn across the floor and crawled into bed. She still had a day job and it was getting late.

CHAPTER 20

THE REMAINDER OF the work week passed in a blur. Under the guise of reaching out and introducing herself, Meaghan got the scoop on the city's stalled projects and did what she could to push them along. As the city solicitor, she wasn't supposed to involve herself in policy decisions or administration of city business. Her job was to advise her clients how to do things within the parameters of the law and to defend the city when they failed to do so. But the story of her confrontation with Emily had swept like a tornado through city hall, and everybody was happy to let Meaghan intervene, even those staffers who weren't aware of the magical details.

Nobody liked Emily, it seemed.

Emily took the rest of the week off. There was no council meeting scheduled and she may have been planning to take the time anyway. But her absence allowed everyone in the solicitor's office to breathe a little easier.

Jamie took Tuesday off but was back Wednesday. Other

than a black eye, he appeared unscathed. Meaghan asked how he was, he said he was fine, and then he briefed her on his cases and a couple of small things being handled by Hallam and Associates, the city's outside counsel. No mention was made of the events of Monday beyond a quick mention that Buzz Hallam, the firm's founder, had grown up in Eldrich, was an old friend of Matthew's, and understood how things worked.

Natalie and Kady didn't push either. On Tuesday they told her who was "clued in," Eldrich code for being aware of the supernatural and otherworldly. Most of the support staff were clued in, but many of the higher level officials were not. Mayor Diebler didn't "have a clue about anything," Kady added when Natalie mentioned him. Likewise, none of the council members were aware of Eldrich's paranormal elements. In Meaghan's experience, the ability to function in a constant state of denial was something many politicians excelled at, so it didn't surprise her.

Jamie, Natalie, and Kady all told her they'd be happy to answer any questions she had and then left her alone. Focusing on her legal job, Meaghan let the week slip by without a single question or comment about her strange new world. After that first day of weirdness, work was . . . work. It was normal municipal law. Jamie went to court. Natalie and Kady kept things humming along. Meaghan reviewed contracts and attended meetings.

Bob's hasty departure had created a backlog that kept her busy enough during each work day that she could almost forget the other part of the job. On Tuesday morning, she thought she would spend the day anxious to get home and dive into Matthew's files. But by the end of the work day, she couldn't face them. Instead she watched TV with Russ. She told herself she'd return to Matthew's files on Saturday. One job at a time.

After one of her usual disjointed dreams—Matthew's file boxes had grown feet and were chasing her up and down the stairs in city hall—she woke Saturday morning to the sound of voices and laughter in the kitchen. It sounded like several people, not only Russ and Matthew. More of Russ's food people? *John?*

Hating herself for the swoop of giddy excitement she felt at the thought, she climbed out of bed. Go and see, she told herself. If it's him, then deal with it. Instead of throwing a bathrobe over her pajamas, she pulled on her usual jeans and T-shirt, but not wrinkled ones from the foot of the bed or the top of the hamper. These were clean, from the dresser.

"Oh, girl, you got it bad," she mumbled. She spritzed some water on her sleep-twisted hair, combed it back into place and resisted the urge to put on makeup—what was she, sixteen? She forced herself to take a measured pace down the stairs. If it was John, he'd likely flee as soon as she got there. Besides, it wasn't like she wanted to impress him, she tried to convince herself, so no need to make a fuss.

It wasn't John.

Russ and Matthew sat at the kitchen table with three . . . she hadn't a clue. They were blue, like Smurfs. Only taller, the size of ten-year-olds maybe. With piggy looking faces and small tusks. And wearing a weird mix of trendy children's clothes. Gender was indeterminate.

Everyone stopped eating and talking and turned to stare at her.

She stared back. And stared some more.

"I'm going back to bed," she announced, then turned and walked down the hall and back up the stairs.

About ten minutes later, Russ came up with a mug of coffee and a plate of toast.

On the unmade bed, Meaghan lay curled in a ball, her pillow wrapped around her head. "Friends of yours?" she asked, her voice muffled.

"Yeah, they are friends. Once you get used to the blue skin and the tusks and their unique fashion sense, they're a lot of fun. I'd have introduced you if you hadn't run away."

Meaghan threw the pillow onto the bed and sat up. "Sorry. I . . . it's . . . sorry," she stammered. "They're blue," she added.

"Yeah," Russ answered. "We've already established that." He handed her the coffee and set the plate on the table. "Come eat your toast."

With a sigh, she took the mug and moved to the table. She had to shove aside a pile of files to sit down.

Russ picked his way through the papers and folders covering the floor, stepped over a box, and sat down on the window seat. He surveyed the mess in silence, letting Meaghan drink her coffee and eat a slice of toast.

This was their mother's old trick, Meaghan realized. Sit quietly, look sad, and wait for somebody to crack.

Not me, she thought, and held firm in her resolve for a good ten seconds before she folded.

"Fine," she snapped. "It's a big mess, I know."

"That's not the problem," Russ said, still gazing at the floor. He looked up at her. "The problem is your utter refusal to deal with this. I've been talking to Natalie. And Jamie."

Meaghan felt her face grow hot. "Checking up on me? Enlisting the employees to spy?"

Russ refused to take the bait. "Nope. They called me. They're concerned. The world blows up on Monday. And then nothing."

"What were they expecting?" she shot back. "A big show?"

He still refused to react. "No. Questions. We all expected a lot more questions. Any questions at all, in fact, would be an improvement."

"I've been waiting until today. I do have another job you know." Her face grew hotter. "The one I thought the city hired me to do, remember?"

"Which," Russ countered, "you can do with your hands tied behind your back and hopping on one foot. Leaving plenty of time to deal with this." He waved his hand at the scattered files.

"You don't understand," she whined. "It's —"

Russ cut her off. "I don't understand? I've been dealing with this shit for nearly thirty years."

"But you don't have . . . the *Destiny*," she said. "It's not all riding on your shoulders."

"It's not all riding on yours, either. I may not have the special family mojo, but I'm the one who stuck around, who gave Dad a chance," Russ said, his voice growing louder with each word. "I'm the one who moved back to Eldrich to help with Jamie. I'm the one who's down there cooking breakfast. Where the hell have you been? Not here. As usual. Dad knew you'd get like this. That you'd pull the all-by-myself martyr routine."

"Oh, nice," she shot back. "Nice to know what you both really think of me."

"Here we go. Poor little Meaghan, all by herself 'cause Daddy doesn't love her." He rose to his feet. "I'll go tell everybody her Highness can't deal so the whole universe will have to piss off."

He tried to storm out of the room while picking his way with care through the strewn files. His feet, not sensing the contradiction, tried to do both at the same time. Russ tripped, did a graceful spin, and then sat down hard on the floor.

The tension broke. Meaghan hopped out of her chair and knelt beside him. "Are you okay?"

"Yeah, I'm fine. So much for my grand exit." He didn't try to get up. "Seriously, Meg. I shouldn't have dumped on you like that, but you gotta get your shit together. Ignoring it won't make it go away."

"I know," she said as she stood up. "And I know that you've been doing way more than your share when it comes to Dad." She held out a hand to him but couldn't meet his eyes as she helped pull him to his feet. "Are the blue guys still downstairs?"

"Yeah, I'm sure they are," Russ said. "They're rotten little gossips, so I can't imagine they'd want to miss a good fight."

Meaghan rolled her eyes. "Oh. Wonderful. So everybody's going to be buzzing about this?"

Russ smiled. "Oh, yeah. Which is why you need to get down there and give them a better story."

"Is this the hospitality stuff Matthew mentioned in his letter?"

Russ nodded. "The Troon are important. You want them to like you."

"So the gossip is positive?"

"Yeah. They also serve as translators. Between the worlds. You need them."

Meaghan pondered this a moment. "Translators? Isn't there some magical thingy that takes care of it?"

Russ snorted. "Like the Tardis? The babel fish? Space aliens and magical creatures who conveniently speak English?"

Meaghan smiled. "Well, yeah."

"So, how would that work out for you, Miss Impervious -to-Magic?"

"I didn't think of that," she answered. "So, what's the deal with the . . . what are they called again?"

"Troon."

"There's a fancy-pants golf resort in Scottsdale called Troon North," Meaghan said. "They don't golf, do they?"

Russ stared at her a moment. Meaghan knew that look. It was the save-me-from-idiots look. "No," he answered. "They don't golf." He thought a moment. "At least as far as I know."

"So, how did they get the translator job? Some magical ability?"

Russ shook his head. "No. You know how Fahrayans have an extra set of vocal cords?"

Meaghan nodded.

"Well the Troon have like three extra sets. Their language is crazy complex. Everything else is easy for them to learn." Russ smiled. "And they're nosy little shits. Like to know everything that's going on."

"Nosy?" Meaghan asked. "There are nosy aliens?"

Russ made a face. "Don't call any of these folks aliens. Major faux pas."

"So, what do I call them?"

"Call them Troon. That's what they are. And sure, other

species can be nosy. People are people, you know? Even when they're not."

Meaghan laughed. "Russ you should have been a litigator. Or a politician. 'People are people even when they're not,'" she intoned, trying to imitate his voice.

They laughed for a moment, then Russ got serious.

"Meg, what I said to you, I —"

She cut him off. "Don't. It's fine. We're good."

"I'm sorry."

"Don't be. As usual you were right."

Neither spoke for a long moment. Then Meaghan said, in a voice so low it was almost a whisper. "What if I can't do this? What if I'm not good enough?"

Russ put his arms around her and gave her a tight hug, kissed her on the forehead, and stepped away. "You're good enough. You may even be better than Dad was. But you won't know unless you try. If you don't at least try, then failure's a sure thing."

Meaghan nodded, her eyes full of tears. She sniffled. "Well, I'm certainly better than Matthew at crying all the time."

Russ shook his head, smiling. "So, you have to stop kicking ass once in a while to blow your nose. Big deal. I'll go down to the kitchen first and tell them you're on your way. Fix yourself up and then make a grand entrance. Throw around some charm and the Troon will love you."

CHAPTER 21

RUSS WAS RIGHT. With a big smile and some self-deprecating comments about not being a morning person, Meaghan rehabilitated her image. After a cup of coffee and some more breakfast, the Troon—Wally, Sid, and Melanie—were her new best friends. Based on their names, the Troon had distinct genders, but Meaghan was damned if she could see the difference between them.

Russ was also right about them being a lot of fun. The three Troon specialized in human languages, particularly English, and Wally and Sid, at least, were enamored with American pop culture. The third, Melanie, was very quiet through breakfast, following the conversation but not participating in it.

Wally and Sid had flawless American accents. And they were wickedly funny, with a biting, catty sense of humor. In spite of herself, Meaghan was in stitches. If she'd been led into the room blindfolded, she would have sworn she was sitting at a table with a pair of bitchy drag queens channeling Joan Rivers.

Matthew had wandered off for a nap. He seemed to be sleeping a lot more lately, but, according to Russ, he was calmer and happier than he'd been in quite a while. As much as Meaghan wanted to talk to him, she wanted to talk to a version of him that hadn't existed in several years.

The Troons' pop culture talk lasted about half an hour until Wally, the older one, got down to business.

"So, Meg, darling," Wally oozed, "we hear Witchiepoo Procter's been a very bad girl. Taking amulets that don't belong to her. Using borrowed magic."

Meaghan frowned. "Borrowed magic? Natalie did say Emily was a lot stronger than usual."

Sid—who liked his coffee black with a lot of sugar— jumped in. "She was juiced big time. But we don't know where she got it from. Yet." He threw back the rest of his coffee. He had a wild over-caffeinated gleam in his small orange eyes. "Jamie's such a sweetie. Why would she want to do that to him? But on the plus side, we hear you got an eyeful." He let out a wicked cackle. "And there was a lot to see."

Wally sat back and surveyed the laughing Troon. "Sid, what did I tell you about the coffee? Shut up and let me tell the story."

Sid snorted with laughter and gestured dramatically towards Wally. "Fine, your Naginess. Sorry to steal your thunder. Proceed." Sid leaned back in his chair and winked at Meaghan.

"Yes, borrowed magic," Wally continued. "She had some help. Natalie says—"

Sid jumped in again. "Ooh, I love Natalie. She's a firecracker."

Wally glared at him. "As I was saying, Natalie told me she could feel something big. Bad. Evil." Wally rolled the word "evil" across his tongue like a fine Bordeaux. "New player. Nat swears on it."

"New player?" Meaghan asked.

Wally nodded. "Partly at least. She also smelled . . ." He paused for dramatic effect. "The Order."

Now it was Russ's turn to frown. "The Order? Who the hell are they?"

Sid answered him before Wally could speak. "Russell, honey, you don't know about the Order? You've been around almost as long as they have."

Russ shrugged. "I'm only the caterer, remember? If I don't feed them, I don't know them."

"Well," Sid said. "Then you are never gonna know those freaks. They don't eat."

Wally sighed. "They do so eat."

Sid snorted. "Bugs. Sticks. Mud. Nothing good. Not like Russy makes."

Wally sighed again, louder this time. "Would you shut up already and let me tell Meaghan the story? Without interruption?"

Sid threw his hands up, sat back in his chair, and folded his arms across his chest. "Fine, Mr. Thinks He's in Charge but Isn't Really."

Wally ignored him and continued. "The Order are wizards for hire. They have this crazy code they live by. Big time ascetic types. No possessions, barely any food, constant magical training. Gung. Ho." Wally leaned forward and lowered his voice as if sharing a shameful secret. "And, they don't believe women should do magic."

Russ winced like he'd been slapped. "*What?* Women have always done magic. Where do these whack jobs come from?"

"From here, if you can believe it." Wally shook his head in disbelief. "They're human."

"So," Meaghan said. "What's their deal? If they don't believe women should do magic, why did they help Emily?"

"Good question. Must have been for a job. The mystery evildoer Natalie sensed."

"How long have they been around?"

"Not more than twenty or thirty years," Wally said. "That's like being a newborn by magical standards."

"Has Matthew dealt with them?" Meaghan asked.

Wally shrugged. "No idea."

"Wait," Russ said. "They aren't those half-starved guys in the gray robes, are they?"

Wally nodded. "That's them."

Russ groaned. "Oh, not them. They're complete assholes. Dad had to deal with them once about ten years ago." He paused, looking thoughtful. "They have actual power? Dad thought they were just wannabes."

The third Troon, Melanie, who had been silent throughout the meal, joined the conversation. "Emily Proctor isn't the only one operating on borrowed magic. The Order have found a patron, it seems." Unlike the So-Cal teenage inflections adopted by Sid and Wally, Melanie spoke with an upper crust British accent. She didn't appear any more female, or male for that matter, than the other two.

"The big bad thing Natalie sensed?" Meaghan asked.

"Yes. It appears so." Melanie shook her small blue head.

"The Order are zealots. Without much power, they were merely tiresome. But with real magical ability . . ." She stared into space for a long moment, then shivered.

Meaghan broke into her silence. "Zealots about what? Besides not eating. And let me guess. They aren't fond of women."

Melanie sighed. "Purity. They're zealots about magical purity. Or so they claim. And while they aren't fond of anyone, they have a special lack of regard for women. Misogyny, I believe, is the technical term."

Russ broke in. "But how can they do magic and hate women? Magic requires a strong flow of feminine energy to work right. To do it safely, you have to draw yin power from the earth. At least that's what Natalie always says."

"What power?" Meaghan asked.

"Yin and yang, you know, the Chinese concept?"

Meaghan gave him a blank look.

Russ rolled his eyes. "You know, the black-and-white circle thingy? The duality of the universe? Hot and cold? Light and dark? Earth and sky?"

"Yeah, Russ, I'm not an idiot," Meaghan said. "I'm familiar with the concept in a general way, but I don't understand how it applies here. A week ago, I didn't even know magic existed. Give me the dummies version."

Russ sighed. "A lot of people think yin and yang are opposites. But they aren't. They're complementary halves required to make a whole. Yin is considered feminine, dark, cool, rising from the earth to the sky. Yang is the masculine, bright, hot, flowing from the sky down to the earth."

"So, wait," Meaghan said. "The Chinese invented magic?"

Russ shook his head. "No, no. Well, some of the ways to

use it, yeah. But nobody invented magic, it's just there. The yin and yang concept just works really well to explain it."

Melanie joined in. "Think sprouting seeds and sunshine. The earth is warmed by the sun, which causes the seeds to sprout. The shoots push up through the earth and convert sunshine into energy for more growth. Seeds without sun lie dormant. Sun without seeds results in barren desert."

"So then how does magic get by only with yin?" Meaghan asked, confused.

"It doesn't," Russ said. "It uses both. But without the yin grounding, the magic gets too heavy on the yang side. Too hot. A lot of power but no control. Think lightning. Awe inducing but deadly, unless it's properly grounded."

"So magic is like electricity?"

Russ thought about it a moment. "Yeah, it kind of is. And electricity can give you light and cook your food or it can kill you."

Meaghan nodded. "So, you need the yin, but without the yang, magic has to be kind of weak, right?"

"Not weak," Melanie said. "Think lightning bolt versus household current. Both are flows of electricity. Both powerful, but in very different ways. Yin magic is more subtle and slow to work, but much easier to control. And remember yin and yang qualities exist in everything in varying degrees. Complementary, rather than contradictory. Yang magic tends to come more naturally to men. They can do yin magic, but generally require training. Conversely, most women must be taught yang magic, but they're naturals at the yin."

Russ jumped in. "And, unfortunately for men, the yin is the side you need to master first so you don't blow yourself up."

"Huh. Natalie said it was because boys with talent are scared off by their mother's crazy friends and decide to go out for sports instead," Meaghan said. "How does that work?"

"Mom puts a grounding spell on him until he's past the worst of puberty and the raw power fades and she only trains her daughter," Russ replied. "Or somebody else's daughter. Which means more women than men end up being practitioners because the yin side doesn't need yang as much as the yang side needs yin." He shook his head. "Saying that made me kind of dizzy. Did it make any sense?"

Melanie smiled at him for a long moment, then reached out and squeezed his hand. "Yes, it did. And that's what frightens men drawn to groups like the Order."

"Great," Meaghan said. "So the Order's like the Taliban of magic?"

Sid, unable to stay silent a moment longer, piped in with "The Taliwho?"

Wally gave Sid another look, shook his head, and hopped down off his chair to refill his coffee cup.

"Taliban. Human politics," Melanie said, in a soothing voice. "On the other side of this world."

Sid nodded, without comment. He deferred to Melanie, Meaghan noticed, in a way he didn't defer to Wally. Was it a gender thing? Women were the boss among the Troon?

Melanie returned to her conversation with Meaghan. "The Order shares the Taliban's zealotry and intolerance. Different ideology but the same fear."

Meaghan nodded. "It's hardly a new phenomenon, men fearing women to the point of hate."

Wally worked his way around the table refilling everyone's coffee cup, except for Sid's. "They don't like Troon, either," he added.

"Only female Troon or all of you?" Meaghan asked.

Everyone but Meaghan burst out laughing. "Did I say something wrong?"

Melanie smiled at her. "We're simply Troon. We're neither male nor female. Or more accurately, we're both."

Sid cackled again. "Imagine what the Order thinks of *us* . . ."

"I'd better read Matthew's journals," Meaghan said.

CHAPTER 22

AFTER BREAKFAST, SID and Wally were picked up by Gretchen, the city's human resources coordinator.

"They're making the rounds," Russ told her. "Getting the gossip."

"And spreading it?" Meaghan asked.

Russ merely smiled.

"So Gretchen's a witch too? Are there any women in city hall besides me who aren't?"

Russ shrugged. "A few. Annie down in the mayor's office isn't. It's why Emily's such a bitch on the political stuff. It's the only place where she's got any power. Magically, she's totally outgunned. Unless she's juicing and catches you one on one."

"Like Natalie."

Russ nodded. "Natalie's pretty bad ass. Emily won't get another shot at her. Not like that. Let's hope you scared her enough so she behaves herself."

Melanie offered to stay behind with Meaghan and organize Matthew's journals and files. Meaghan accepted with an inward sigh of relief. She hadn't realized how daunting she found the prospect of digging through the mess alone until Melanie offered to help.

There was something calming and grounding about Melanie. Sid and Wally were fun but exhausting after a while. It may not have been gender, but there was clearly something different about her.

Meaghan decided that she would continue to think of Melanie as "her" even if she was technically an "it."

A world without gender—Meaghan couldn't wrap her brain around it. And apparently the Troon couldn't either. The gay vibe Sid and Wally gave out was definitely a *male* gay vibe. But Melanie—she reminded Meaghan powerfully of her mother.

Upstairs, Meaghan hurried to make the bed and jam the pile of clothes on the floor into the hamper. Melanie stood in the doorway as Meaghan tidied. When the room was somewhat presentable, Melanie walked to the table and sat on the chair not covered in paper.

"Where would you like to begin?" Melanie asked.

Meaghan surveyed the piles. "Um . . ."

"You're handling this all rather well, you know," Melanie said.

"No. I'm not. It's been almost a week and look at this. I ripped a few boxes apart digging out stuff on Fahraya Monday night and then just left it." Meaghan gestured at the paper-strewn carpet. "And I'm sorry I was so rude this morning. I . . . Russ set me straight. Like he always does."

Melanie smiled up at her. "This is why you need to start at the beginning. You and Russ were still quite young when

Matthew first learned of his ability. And then you left." Melanie looked sad for a moment and then brightened. "I was there. Trust me. You're doing remarkably well with the news." She pointed at the other chair. "Please. Sit with me."

Meaghan moved a pile of folders from the chair and sat.

"What do you remember from that time?" Melanie asked.

"Not much. Matthew was working all the time. We never saw him. When he was around, he was drunk or getting there. I don't remember him and Mom fighting, but there was a lot of tension."

"They would leave the house so you and Russ wouldn't hear," Melanie said. "You mother feared for his sanity."

Meaghan remembered what her mother had told her in the dream. How she couldn't accept what was going on. She nodded. "And then we left."

"And then you left," Melanie said. "Your mother did what she thought was best for you and Russ. Your father's behavior was increasingly erratic and he was telling your mother things she was unable to accept."

"So Matthew knew before we left about all . . . this?" Meaghan pointed toward the piles on the floor.

Melanie nodded. "And his response was to drive his family away and drink himself into mental collapse. At any time during this past week have you feared for your sanity?"

Meaghan, taken aback, took a moment to answer. "No. It never even occurred to me that I might be nuts. When the thing with Jamie was happening I didn't have time. Then everyone kept wondering when I'd flip out. I wondered too."

"Why then do you think you've avoided learning more since that day?"

Meaghan thought for a long moment. "I looked at a

couple of things that first night. Some pictures of Jamie and his father I found. And after that, well, yeah, fear I suppose. But not for my sanity. I mean, I saw what I saw. And so did everyone around me. And I knew they were hiding something from me." She smiled. "It was just a lot weirder than I could have imagined. So, the world isn't what I thought it was. There's no point in going crazy over that."

Melanie reached across the table and took Meaghan's hand. "Do you understand how rare that is?" Melanie's small hand was warm, dry, and a bit scaly. "To accept what you see? To step out of your lifelong conception of reality into a new world as easily as you have?"

Meaghan squeezed Melanie's hand. "God, you remind me of my mom."

Melanie laughed. "I'm a blue-skinned, tusked hermaphrodite from another world."

"Mom was a vegetarian. But we never held that against her."

They both laughed.

"I think," Meaghan said, when their laughter subsided, "what I'm afraid of is not being able to do the job. And . . ." She took a deep breath. This wasn't easy to admit. "I'm so jealous of Jamie. I keep trying to remember that beat-up, traumatized kid in the photos I found, but I can't forget all the happy family shots with Matthew. With my father." She looked at her feet, ashamed. "Jamie got my dad at the same age that I lost him. That's what I fear. All the bad memories that might be waiting in those boxes."

"Or maybe," Melanie said, "you'll discover the world wasn't what you thought it was."

"Maybe," Meaghan said. "Maybe." She stood up, grabbed

the first box in the line by the window seat, and set it on the table. "How do you want to do this?"

"Pull out the journals. Start at the beginning. You read while I start organizing the rest by topic."

Meaghan nodded. She pulled out the notebooks. "Take the table. I'll use the window seat."

Meaghan moved to the window seat. She organized the journals by date, opened the earliest one, and started reading.

CHAPTER 23

MEAGHAN READ ALL day. Russ brought up sand-wiches around noon, and tea and snacks throughout the day. Melanie worked quietly at the table, organizing files and writing up an index.

After having to get up for the second time to fetch a tissue to blow her nose, Meaghan brought the box back from the bathroom with her. Every couple of pages, she read something that made her tear up.

Like the entry from October 20, 1980:

Back from Arizona. Meg wouldn't see me or even talk to me on the phone. Liz won't talk to me either. We had to do it all through her lawyer. But at this point I'll take what I can get. I wish I could tell Meg and Russ about my life, about the reality of the world we live in. But after how Liz reacted, I know I can't. Not yet.

Russ was the only one happy I was there. He accepted all my bullshit without question, even if I could tell he didn't believe it. But Liz only gave me an hour with him, and I could only see him with a court-appointed babysitter there to make sure I didn't say or do anything crazy. So bullshit it had to be.

Russ knows I'm hiding something. I don't know what Meg suspects. She's a smart girl, too smart for her own good in some ways, and sensitive. I do know she hates me. For good reason and I don't know how to fix it, and if she hates me now, what's it going to be like if she gets stuck with this whole mess? If the trait is genetic—I only hope I can find somebody else to take the job or I can somehow mend the distance between us enough so I have time to prepare her. Nobody should have to walk into something like this cold. If only I'd met Vivian sooner, if Lou had found me sooner, maybe I wouldn't have scared my family away.

Melanie had been right. The world of her childhood wasn't what she thought it was. The names and details of the species Matthew had worked with were a jumble—she'd have to go back and do some indexing of her own, and she still hadn't found anything about the war her mother and Natalie had mentioned. But what did come through, with aching clarity, was her father's loneliness. With the exception of Vivian, Natalie's mother, Matthew had, as he called it in his letter to Meaghan, "lone wolfed" it. While he grieved for his lost family.

No wonder he was so eager to step in and raise Jamie.

But that was still years away. The Matthew who wrote these early journals was barely sober, lonely, and full of self-loathing and regret. How had she never seen that in him? Because she refused to look, she realized. She buried her pain—her standard coping mechanism—and cut herself off from her childhood. She moved on. She'd have left Russ behind too, after Mom died, if he hadn't fought to keep her from slipping away.

He'd done the same thing with Matthew. After Meaghan had given up on their father, Russ kept in touch by letter. Somehow, after Matthew's visit, fourteen-year-old Russ had gotten himself a post office box and been clever enough to hide the letters from their mother. Russ hadn't waited to restore contact until after Elizabeth died. There was nothing to restore because he'd never really lost contact in the first place.

Around four o'clock, she finished reading the journals from the seventies and early eighties, and decided she'd had enough for the day. Her head hurt and her eyes burned from all the crying.

But the fear was gone. Melanie was right. Meaghan was handling the shock of Monday remarkably well. For all her fear that she'd never measure up to her father, she realized now that she owned deep inside herself a clear-eyed strength that even he lacked. He had questioned things he'd experienced in a way Meaghan hadn't. He struggled for years to let go of long-held beliefs despite being surrounded by evidence to the contrary.

Meaghan had yelled at her brother, cried a lot, and dog paddled in denial for a few days. The most self-destructive things she had done in the past week were drinking a few extra glasses of wine with dinner and watching too much bad TV.

She had always been pragmatic and unsentimental, but even she was surprised at the ease with which she'd fallen down the rabbit hole. Or maybe going through the looking glass was the better analogy. Everything—with a few striking size, color, and anatomical variances—looked about the same as it had before.

Some fantasy world.

"Melanie," Meaghan said. "I'm tapped. No more reading for me today. Let's go get a glass of wine. Or whatever you like to drink. You staying for dinner?"

Melanie set down her pen and surveyed the now tidy piles of paper surrounding her. "Wine is good. Bourbon is better. And dinner would be wonderful. Your brother is one of the best cooks in all the worlds."

"You know you can't live in Arizona as long as I did without developing a taste for good margaritas. What's the Troon stance on tequila?"

"Olé," Melanie said with a wink.

"Let's see if Chef Russ has the ingredients." Meaghan stood, stretching and yawning. "My brain hurts."

She paused a moment, staring at Melanie. Meaghan was about to mix up a blender full of 'ritas for a blue-skinned hermaphrodite from another dimension. Or was it a different planet? She wasn't sure which. And it seemed like the most natural thing in the world. "I really am taking this well."

Melanie nodded. "Yes. You are. Let's see if Russ can make us some nachos to go with those drinks. And we need salt. I can't abide a margarita without salt."

Russ—assuming that Melanie would be joining them for dinner, along with Sid, Wally, and Natalie, who was their last gossip stop of the day—had already begun his dinner preparations.

"I also invited Jamie and Patrice and the kids if that's okay. I thought we could do burgers on the grill. It's really nice out there." He gave Meaghan a cautious look. "You okay with so much company?"

"Absolutely," she said. "Sounds fun. I could use some fun." She threw her arms around him and kissed him on the cheek. "How did you get a post office box at fourteen?"

Russ laughed. "Crap. There goes another family secret."

She stepped back. "Where's Dad?"

Russ's eyes widened in surprise. Meaghan always called their father by his first name. "On the front porch, I think."

"I'll go check on him, then I promised Melanie a genuine Arizona margarita if you've got the stuff."

Russ nodded. "Might have to improvise a little, but it's doable."

"She wants nachos too," Meaghan called over her shoulder as she walked down the hall.

On the porch, she found Matthew dozing in one of the wicker chairs. She sat on the settee and looked at him, really looked for once. A wave of tenderness broke over her and she felt her eyes fill again. He was so frail. But, she hoped, no longer alone. She couldn't bear the thought that he still carried that loneliness within him.

Meaghan knew about lonely. She'd lived the last ten years there. It occurred to her, watching her father sleep, that the man who had written the journals she had just read had been several years younger than she was now.

Please, let him recognize me, she thought. After a few moments, his eyes fluttered open.

"Meg?" he said, still groggy. "Is that you? What are you doing here?"

She smiled. At last. "I live here. With you and Russ. I'm doing your old job."

He looked cautious. "Which job is that?"

"City solicitor. And," she added, hoping she wasn't going to trigger any odd behavior, "the other job."

Matthew's eyes widened. "Russ?" he shouted. "Would you come out here?"

"I'll get him," she said, but Russ must have been waiting right inside the screen door because he was there before she could stand up.

"Russ, does Meg know about . . . you know?" He whispered the last two words.

"She knows, Dad. She saw Jamie change. She's been reading your journals. I gave her the boxes of files you put together for her."

"And she's still here?" Matthew asked out of the side of his mouth.

"Yes, Daddy. I'm still here. No more secrets."

Matthew sighed. "Well, that's a goddamn relief. How long you been here?"

"Almost two weeks."

"Where you been hiding?" he asked. "Or have I been . . . fuzzy?"

Russ reached down and squeezed his shoulder. "Fuzzy, Dad." He gave Meaghan a meaningful glance, and then turned and went back into the house. This must be one of those almost lucid spells Russ had mentioned.

Matthew looked up at Meaghan and smiled. "So you live here? That's great. Both my kids home at last."

Meaghan leaned forward and took his hand. "Yes, Dad. Home at last."

"Did Russ say you'd seen Jamie change? Did you see him fly? Helluva thing. You should see them when you're their size." He shook his head. "Fairies," he spat. "People are so damn stupid. How they got fairies out of those brutal unwashed bastards is beyond me."

"Jamie said the same thing."

"He back to normal? Why'd he take the stone off?"

"Emily Proctor ripped it off his neck during our first meeting and ran down to her office with it. But I got it back and we got it on him. He's fine now. He's coming over for dinner."

"The little shit's a prince, you know," Matthew said with a proud smile.

"I know, Dad," Meaghan said.

Matthew yawned. "That was a good nap." He stared at her, a furrow in his heavy brow. "I wish we had more time, but I'll probably get fuzzy again. Don't let that bitch Emily push you around. She scared of you?"

"Yeah, I think so."

"Good girl. Keep her that way." He yawned again. "Don't think I'm done sleeping." His eyes fluttered shut and then he opened them with effort. "Wake me up for dinner. Keep Vivian close. She'll take good care of you like she took care of me."

And he was asleep again. Meaghan wondered who he'd be when he woke up.

CHAPTER 24

THE MARGARITAS WERE a hit even if they weren't quite what Meaghan was used to. They had to replace her favorite prickly pear syrup with some of John's honey, which, she had to admit, made them even better. She, Russ, and Melanie had a nice mellow glow by the time the rest of the dinner guests arrived.

When Jamie walked in laden with a diaper bag and a giant tossed salad, Meaghan couldn't resist giving him a hug.

"What's that for?" he asked, grinning.

"I've been looking at some old pictures. Looks like we're family."

Jamie grimaced. "You didn't see the really old ones, did you? With the hair?"

Meaghan chuckled. "The hair and the dirt. You weren't kidding about that. Don't regrow the dreadlocks, okay?"

"No worries there. I get cranky if it's touching my collar."

A small girl ran into the kitchen. She was wearing a purple-and-orange striped polo shirt, a blue-and-yellow flowered skirt, and red cowboy boots. Her curly red hair spilled off her head in a tangled cascade to her shoulders. She stopped short when she saw Meaghan.

"I don't know you," she said to Meaghan. "Are you a stranger?"

"I don't think so. I'm Meaghan. I live here. I'm Russ's big sister."

The child perked up. "I'm a big sister too."

"Are you Liddy?" Meaghan asked. "Are you Ben's big sister?"

Liddy looked cautious again. "How do you know me?"

"I work with your daddy."

She thought about it a moment. "Like Natalie?"

"Like Natalie."

"Well, that's okay then," Liddy said. She did a twirl. "Do you like my outfit? I picked it out all by myself."

Meaghan smiled at her. "I'm sure you did. Very nice."

Liddy nodded. "Daddy, is Melanie here?" she asked Jamie.

"What do you say to Meaghan for complimenting you?"

Liddy sighed dramatically. "Thank you, Meaghan."

"You're welcome, Liddy."

Jamie rolled his eyes. "So gracious."

"Melanie's in the living room," Meaghan said.

Liddy ran down the hall.

"She loves Melanie," Jamie said. He set the salad bowl on the counter. "So I hear you've met the Troon."

Meaghan nodded. "It's been an interesting day. You and Natalie will be relieved to know that I'm finally coping."

"Good," he said, eyeing her like she might explode. "And how's that going?"

"Better than I expected. I want to meet your other kid. Do you and Patrice want a margarita?"

Jamie nodded. "God, yes."

More margaritas emerged from the blender. The burgers were great. Matthew appeared lucid, although he continued to act with happy surprise every time he saw Meaghan, and kept calling Natalie "Vivian." The kids crawled all over him and Meaghan heard him call the baby "Russ" on several occasions. Still, he seemed to be content and enjoying himself.

And, boy, did he love Jamie. Matthew beamed with pride at the sight of him. Meaghan felt the last dregs of her resentment melt away. It was clear to her that Matthew hadn't been lonely for a long time, and much of that was due to Jamie. Despite her sadness for all the lost time, the jealousy was gone, replaced with gratitude that her father hadn't spent that time alone.

Over dinner, Meaghan tried to get to know Jamie and Patrice better. The dynamic was becoming familiar to her. It was a slightly different take on the oddness she'd felt when asking Melanie to stay for dinner. Then she'd been struck about how normal the conversation sounded despite Melanie's obvious physical differences.

Sitting in the backyard with Jamie and Patrice asking about their children *looked* like a normal conversation, but the things being discussed shoved the whole thing off the deep end. Like trying to find a tactful way to ask the young parents if their children were completely human.

Patrice divined right away what Meaghan was trying to ask. "When I got pregnant with Liddy, we checked it out. We did a lot of ultrasounds with a local doc who's clued in.

To make sure, we had an amnio done. Completely normal human DNA."

Jamie jumped in. "Natalie assured us the amulet makes me human. It doesn't only change my appearance. But . . . well. Better to make sure."

Meaghan nodded. She spared them having to explain what they would have done if Liddy had wings or extra vocal cords. Or if she were only a few inches tall.

"So," she asked Patrice, "what does your family think of all this?"

Patrice shrugged. "Don't have any other family as far as I know. I was raised in the foster care system. Down in Harrisburg."

Meaghan blushed, embarrassed. "God, I'm sorry. I didn't know."

Patrice shook her head. "Don't be. I did okay. I don't have any foster care horror stories. I had good placements. I got bumped around enough that I didn't really settle in with any one family, but I liked most of them. I still send Christmas cards to a few. And it's certainly made all this easier. I'm not sure how we'd explain Jamie to the in-laws if he had any."

"Just a normal all-American guy," Jamie said, with a big cheesy grin.

Patrice smacked him gently on the cheek. "Smart ass. It's what made us so close so fast. We both understood what it was to feel different. To not have a so-called normal childhood."

Fascinated, Meaghan pressed tactfully for details.

Jamie had told Patrice only days after they met about his "condition," as he called it. "I knew the moment I met her she was the one," Jamie said. "I almost dropped to one knee and proposed right there."

"You did look kind of dazed," Patrice said. "Like Cupid hit you with a shovel instead of an arrow."

"So how do you have that conversation?" Meaghan asked. "'Hey baby, wanna see my wings?'"

Patrice snorted with laughter. "He wasn't that smooth."

"He didn't just rip the amulet off, did he?"

Patrice shook her head. "No. Natalie was there to help him."

"Natalie?" Meaghan asked.

"Yeah," Jamie said. "She followed me to college and law school. The amulet needs the occasional tune-up. The closer she is, the easier it is to sense if something's going wrong. "

"We met in Philly. I was finishing up my nursing degree. He was in law school. I thought Natalie was an ex who didn't want to let go. It was kind of a relief to discover she was actually his magical babysitter."

"That's relief?" Meaghan asked and laughed.

"Well, it took me a little while to get there."

"Before things went any further," Jamie broke in, "I thought she should meet little Jamie—"

Patrice raised an eyebrow.

"Not that little Jamie," he muttered, blushing.

Meaghan thought of him naked and blushed too. Little was really the wrong word. "Moving on," she said.

Patrice laughed, a deep throaty chuckle that bordered on salacious.

"But," Meaghan said, eager to change the subject. "How did that work? You were totally nuts when it happened last week."

"Part of that was the city hall effect," Jamie said. "Magnifying the magic. And I didn't have time to prepare. My control is much better if I have time to center myself first. And Natalie built a magical . . . cage, I guess, before I changed so I couldn't take off and so she could get the amulet back on."

"Without a Taser?" Meaghan asked.

"Without a Taser. Thank God. I felt wrong for a couple of days after that."

Meaghan had much less success chatting up Natalie. She wanted to talk to Natalie about the Order and the other force she'd sensed, but Natalie didn't give her the chance. She dodged Meaghan whenever she got within speaking distance.

Natalie didn't seem to welcome the news that Meaghan had started working through Matthew's journals and files. Every time Matthew called her Vivian, she started and looked guilty for a moment. And Meaghan caught Natalie and Russ exchanging a couple of meaningful glances.

Which meant they were hiding something. It was either more occult crap or they were sleeping together. Since the big secret had already been revealed, Meaghan was betting on sex. *Just so long as he doesn't propose,* Meaghan thought. *I don't need my office manager and head witch to be another ex-sister-in-law.*

After Matthew almost fell asleep at the table, around eight thirty, Russ and Jamie helped him up to bed.

Meaghan chased lightning bugs with Liddy for a little while, then the Smiths headed home, Liddy sound asleep in Jamie's arms as he carried her to the car. Ben was likewise asleep. Jamie and Patrice made the rounds, saying good night to Russ and Meaghan, the Troon, and Natalie who bolted out the door right behind them.

"Are the Troon staying here tonight?" Meaghan asked Russ.

Russ shook his head. "Nah. They're going home. I need to drive them out to their gateway."

"Gateway?"

"Some standing stones out in the woods."

"Is that the hole in the reality fence?"

"One of them," Russ said. "I'd bring you along, but somebody has to stay with Dad in case he wakes up. And you can't drive them out there alone because you don't know the woods well enough to get back on your own."

Meaghan simply nodded. After her drive through the forest the day she arrived, she was no longer inclined to argue.

Melanie and the "boys"—Meaghan couldn't help thinking of Sid and Wally that way despite their pan-gender status—cleaned up the kitchen while Meaghan and Russ put the folding tables and chairs back in the garage.

The Troon said their goodbyes, Melanie promised to return the following weekend to do more indexing, and they and Russ were out the door.

CHAPTER 25

MEAGHAN TOOK A couple of ibuprofen, refilled her water glass, and headed out to the front porch. She wasn't drunk, not really, but she'd had a lot of tequila throughout the evening and knew from experience how crappy she'd feel the next day if she didn't drink a few glasses of water before going to bed.

This was the first time she'd sat outside at night since arriving in Eldrich. She shut off the hall and porch lights to see the fireflies better. The only light came from the kitchen at the back of the house. The moon hadn't risen yet. No one else on Holly Lane had their porch lights on, and there were no streetlights in this part of town. Meaghan was surprised by how dark it became once night descended.

She stepped off the porch and gazed up at the stars. They were softer here, twinkled more. In Arizona, the dry air made the stars look like holes of light punched into black painted steel. Hard stars. No nonsense.

Meaghan felt a sudden, overwhelming pang of homesickness for the desert. In June, Phoenix was only beginning to experience the full heat of summer and it would stay that way until early October. For now, Eldrich was a fine place to be. But she dreaded the cold and dark of a northern Pennsylvania winter.

Maybe she could sneak away for a January visit, but she wouldn't be living in Arizona again anytime soon, she suspected. Meaghan couldn't imagine Phoenix had much magical activity going on. Phoenix seemed as impervious to magic as Meaghan herself. Too much new stuff.

With a heavy sigh, she sat on the porch steps. You never really want to be somewhere until you aren't there anymore, she thought.

As Meaghan's eyes adjusted to the darkness, she began to see more than the flashing fireflies. After a few minutes, she realized that what she had assumed was a shrub, sitting next to the driveway four houses down across the street, was actually a figure. Crouching motionless, watching her. A figure in a dark cowled robe.

Her heart lurched. The tequila fuzz evaporated as adrenaline surged through her.

The Order. The women-hating bastards were staking out her house. Her eyes darted around trying to spot more of them as the panic rose within her.

And like a loyal fierce dog, the anger rose with it. The bastards were watching her house. With her father asleep upstairs. They were stalking her. They were coming after her in *her own home.*

"I see you," she whispered. "I know who you are and I see you watching me." She wasn't sure why she knew, but she knew he could hear her. The dark figure, startled, scuttled away and dissolved into the night. If there were any others around, she hoped they had also heard her and fled.

Feigning calm, Meaghan picked up her water glass and strolled into the house.

Once inside, she shut the door, twisted the deadbolt, and closed and locked every open window she saw on her way back to the kitchen, flipping on lights as she went. Heart pounding, she rushed to the kitchen door, slammed it shut, and locked it. She pulled a giant chef's knife from the block next to the stove, and, shaking, sat at the table to wait for Russ.

Cell phone, idiot, call his cell, she thought after a few frozen moments. Warn him. Hands shaking, she dialed his number on the kitchen wall phone. After five rings it went to voice mail.

"Russ, the Order, I think it's them, are watching us. Get home now. I'm locked in the house. I think I scared away the one I saw, but I don't know if there's more. Hurry. Please. Call me on the landline."

Meaghan hung up and returned to her seat at the kitchen table, clutching the knife in her trembling fist. After two very long minutes, she called Russ again. She got a recording this time saying the phone was out of the service area. The panic bubbled back up until she remembered that Russ was driving through a forest where cell phone coverage was notoriously spotty.

"Get a grip," she told herself in a stern voice. "Think it through." She forced herself to take several slow deep breaths. Panic wouldn't help.

She'd seen one guy, only one, and he fled the moment

he knew she'd seen him. That suggested reconnaissance, not attack. Besides, why come after her and Matthew? In his addled state, Matthew was no threat. Neither was Meaghan, for that matter, this early on the job. Besides, both of them were impervious and the house was filled with Natalie's protective hex bags. If they couldn't attack Meaghan, why watch her? And why tonight?

Jamie, she thought. Emily had attacked Jamie. What if her actions had been about more than scaring Meaghan away? If Emily had simply wanted to pull the rational world out from under Meaghan's feet, she could have turned someone into a toad or whatever the hell it was bitchy witches did to show off. But, she'd gone after Jamie. With borrowed magic. Emily knew that Matthew and Meaghan were both impervious. Yet, she'd been visibly shocked when she couldn't hex Meaghan.

It made no sense. Unless somebody told her the borrowed magic would overcome Meaghan's imperviousness. The Order were mercenaries. But who had hired them? Between Emily and the unnamed baddy that Natalie had sensed, Meaghan's bet was on Big Bad.

Natalie said that Matthew's absence had made some bad actors bolder. Was Fahraya blowing up again? Although Meaghan didn't know the details, there'd been a power struggle and John, the king, had lost. He could never go back without his wings, but Jamie was still intact and the rightful heir to John's throne. Which made him a threat to somebody.

Heart in her throat, she ran upstairs for her cell phone. She didn't know Jamie's home number, but had his cell number programmed into her phone. Before heading back downstairs, she looked in on Matthew. He snored, his breathing soft and steady, sound asleep.

Meaghan crept back downstairs to call Jamie. She got one ring, then right to voice mail. She hoped he was on the other line and hadn't shut the phone off for the night.

"Jamie," she said, walking into the kitchen. "It's Meaghan. Russ is taking the Troon home and I've got a little trouble. We're okay, but call me as soon as you get this." She didn't mention the Order because she wasn't sure he knew about them.

But Natalie knew about them. And Meaghan really needed to hear a familiar voice right now, to calm her down if nothing else.

More voice mail. Considering how weird Natalie had been acting earlier, she might be screening.

"Hey, Natalie, it's Meaghan," she said to voice mail. "I've got a problem. One of those Order guys is skulking around—"

The back door exploded open, the glass inset shattering with the force. Meaghan screamed and dropped the phone.

A figure in a dark gray robe stood in the broken doorway. The deep cowl hid his face. She could tell it was a he by his large hands, which he held out in front of him. He laughed, the sound cruel and full of malice.

A mistake, she reflected later, always made by bad guys when dealing with those they perceived as weak. Her rage rose up like a monolith, smooth and huge.

"Get the fuck out of my house."

Instead, he stepped further into the kitchen, muttering and waving his hands. Time seemed to slow in the same way it did when Emily attacked Jamie and Natalie in the conference room.

With detached calm, Meaghan observed every detail of his appearance. He was about the same height as Meaghan, but thin, his forearms bony where they protruded from the sleeves of his robe.

She even had time to remember the old trope about vampires requiring an invitation to enter a home. Something to do with the protection provided by a threshold.

So much for that idea. The man in the gray robe strolled in like he owned the place.

Which angered Meaghan even more. Her vision began to get red around the edges, but not the red she sometimes saw behind her eyelids if she stood up too fast or looked at the sun too long. An angry red, a murderous red, framed the wizard.

So that's where the cliché comes from, she thought, watching the man come closer. The rage left no room for fear. Meaghan surveyed the kitchen for a weapon. The cowled figure stood between her and the knife she'd left on the kitchen table. Judging by his scrawny arms, the man took his asceticism to heart. He was a skeleton with skin. And because he relied on magic, she bet he didn't make much effort to take care of his body, while Meaghan ate well and kept fit. In a physical confrontation, she knew she could take this guy.

He continued chanting and waving, seemingly unaware that magic didn't work on Meaghan.

Time to clue him in. She grabbed a small saucepan out of the dish drainer. Russ only used high-grade commercial cookware, solid stuff made out of stainless steel. With riveted handles and heavy, reinforced bottoms. This particular saucepan had a copper disk in the bottom, sandwiched between two thick steel layers. It was a lot heavier than it looked, but small enough for Meaghan to wield with ease.

The hooded figure, now standing directly in front of her, finished his chant with a guttural cry and one last flourish of his hands.

Nothing happened.

He gasped and stepped back fast.

Meaghan stepped forward. "Nice try, Mr. Wizard," she snarled. With a firm backhand, she slammed the bottom of the saucepan into the center of the cowl. She felt a satisfying crunch and heard a bubbling gasp of pain. He bent over, face buried in his hands.

Broken nose, she thought. Not good enough. With a savage, wordless cry, she swung the pan with both hands, hitting him square on the temple.

He crumpled to the ground. Meaghan kicked him a few times until her rage began to wane. She pulled back the cowl and looked at a half-starved boy of about seventeen, his face covered in blood from his mangled nose.

Meaghan's anger evaporated. He was only a scrawny kid. What the hell?

With shaking fingers, she checked his pulse. It was strong and steady. At least she hadn't killed him. She rolled back his eyelids. Both pupils were the same size.

Now what? First thing, she had to restrain him. The strong pulse and equal pupils assured her she didn't need to rush him to a hospital. She wanted some questions answered first, while she still had leverage.

Meaghan's cold pragmatism startled her. What if he was seriously injured? She realized she didn't care. He attacked her in her own home and she defended herself. She decided she could be appalled by her callous indifference later. Right now she had more urgent things to worry about.

She yanked open the junk drawer. Duct tape. Perfect. She pulled out the roll and stared at the body on the floor, considering the best way to proceed when another bang, accompanied by a flash of light, shook the kitchen.

This time it was Natalie. And Kady. And several women Meaghan didn't know. All suddenly materialized around the table.

"Wow," Meaghan said. "That was fast. Help me duct tape this guy to a chair, okay?"

Kady, her eyes wide, said, "What did you do?"

"Hit him with a saucepan," Meaghan said.

One of the other women, older with a tidy silver bouffant, stared at Meaghan, somewhere between impressed and disbelieving. "You did that with a saucepan?"

Meaghan shrugged. "It's a good saucepan. My brother only buys the best."

CHAPTER 26

WITH THE HELP of the witches, Meaghan got the unconscious wizard into a chair. A half a roll of duct tape later, he wasn't going anywhere.

The witches cast some spells to reinforce the duct tape and block any spells he might try to cast. Natalie held her hands to his head to feel for serious injury but didn't detect anything. Meaghan declined Natalie's offer to fix his nose.

"Not yet. Let him suffer a bit," Meaghan said. At Natalie's raised eyebrow, Meaghan said, "Don't look at me like that. I'm not going to torture him or anything. We can do the good-cop bad-cop thing on him when he wakes up. I'll yell at him, scare him a little, and then one of you can offer him some comfort by putting his nose back together."

Natalie and Kady took off to check on Jamie after Meaghan shared her concerns about him. Two other witches left to find Russ and escort him home.

Several derogatory comments were made about the

Order's general magical abilities, but it was clear to Meaghan that the witches were not taking any chances with this guy. The incident with Emily and Jamie had shaken them.

"Borrowed magic," said Lynette, the witch with the silver bouffant, shaking her head. "I can't believe Emily was foolish enough to use someone else's magic."

"Is that really bad?" Meaghan asked.

"Well, it's dishonest," Lynette answered. "And kind of icky when you get right down to it. Like wearing shoes from thrift shops."

"What's wrong with that? I wear thrift shop shoes all the time," said Marnie, a younger witch about Kady's age. Tall and slender, she had a ring in her nose, black hair cut in a severe angled bob, and wore a Harley T-shirt and plaid bermuda shorts.

"It's like wearing jail underwear," Meaghan said.

"Jail underwear?" asked another even younger witch. With a start, Meaghan realized it was Emily's plump, ponytailed receptionist.

"Um, yeah," Meaghan answered. "I have a friend back in Phoenix who's a municipal court judge. She says the best way to scare female defendants straight is to tell them if they do time they'll have to wear jail underwear. Bras and panties. Laundered but worn by other prisoners."

The three witches in the kitchen pondered this a moment. They shuddered.

"Yeah," the ponytailed witch said. "It's kind of like that. If jail underwear made you crazy powerful."

"Does she do that as a habit? Use borrowed magic?" Meaghan asked.

The young witch shook her head. "Not that I've noticed.

I've never seen her that powerful before. If it's a habit, she's hiding it well. At work at least."

"And she was out all week after the thing on Monday?"

The witch nodded.

Meaghan said to her, "You know, I'm sorry, I don't know your name. We didn't really have a chance to chat when we met last week."

The girl beamed at her. "I'm Sarah. That was totally awesome how you stood up to her."

"Thank you. Your coworker, the blond girl, is she a witch too?"

Sarah shook her head. "Chloe? No, but she says she'd like to learn how to hex Emily."

Marnie and Lynette burst out laughing.

"Yeah, I'll bet," Meaghan said. "So what's Emily's deal? Why does she hate Jamie so much?"

At that moment, Russ appeared in the hole where the kitchen door had been, flanked by Anna and Emma, the two young witches assigned to protect him.

"Holy shit, Meg, what did you do?" he asked, eyes wide.

She snorted. "I didn't do it, dumbass." She pointed at the wizard taped to the chair. "Voldemort here did it."

Russ walked towards the unconscious wizard. His jaw dropped. "Then who did this to him?"

"I did." She held up the saucepan, which she had kept close just in case. "With this."

Russ goggled at her. "You took him down with a saucepan?" He thought about it a moment. "It is a solid pan."

"Perfect for gentle simmering and personal defense," Meaghan said.

"Wow," Russ said, circling the bound wizard. "Damn.

Remind me not to piss you off in the kitchen." He looked up at her. "Is Dad okay?"

"Slept right through the whole thing. He's still asleep. Natalie and Kady are over at Jamie's keeping watch." She glanced up at the clock. "We should probably check in. Would somebody call them and make sure everything's okay?"

"I'll do it." Marnie pulled a cell phone out of the back pocket of her shorts and walked into the living room.

"Jamie?" Russ asked. "What's he got to do with it?"

"Nothing, I hope," Meaghan said. "But Emily got her extra power last week from these guys and used it against Jamie. And they're working for somebody we don't know. It seemed prudent to keep an eye on him in case hometown politics were involved."

Russ ran his hands through his hair. "What a freaking mess. Bastard couldn't pick the lock?" He sighed and sat down across the table from the wizard. "Hometown politics?"

Meaghan shrugged. "Jamie's heir to John's throne. It's fair to assume the guy who tossed John out hasn't forgotten that. I don't know much about Fahraya, but I do know politics."

"And you were afraid you couldn't do this job," Russ said. "Feeling more confident?"

She smiled. "Yeah. I am. A bit. I think Mr. Wizard here wanted to scare me. Kind of surprised him when I got pissed off instead of quivering like a damsel in distress."

"Heh." Russ laughed. "Yeah, I bet. I've seen you get mad. It's not pretty."

"He tried to hex me too. He was even more surprised when that didn't work."

Russ frowned. "He did? The Order know all about Matthew and word's been out for a while that you'd probably be taking over for him." He appraised the young wizard. "And there are ways they could have tested whether magic worked on you without tipping their hand like this." He looked back at Meaghan. "They set this kid up."

Meaghan glanced at the unconscious wizard and felt the tiniest spark of compassion. He was just a kid. "Why would they do that?"

Nobody answered. They all stared at the wizard for a moment and then Marnie trotted back in.

"What'd I miss?" she asked. "What are we doing?"

"The Order set him up," Sarah answered. "We're wondering why."

Meaghan pulled her eyes away from the wizard. "Is everything okay with Jamie?"

Marnie nodded. "Natalie and Kady are putting up a bunch of protective spells to be safe but no sign of trouble."

"So, they only came after me and sent someone who didn't know he couldn't hex me. Set him up to fail," Meaghan said. "Although they probably didn't expect him to fail this badly. What are they up to? Trying to scare me?"

At that moment, as if on cue, the wizard groaned and lifted his head.

He looked around at the assembled witches and Meaghan. His eyes widened. He was visibly shaking.

"Hey, sunshine," Meaghan said brightly. "Time to wake up. Welcome to my home. Try anything, and I do mean *anything* and I'll trade the saucepan for something pointy. My brother buys good knives too." She pulled up a chair and sat down in front of him. "Kid, you're in the deep shit right now. You don't like witches? They don't like you, either. And five of them are staring at you right now. I'm the least of your worries."

He screwed his eyes shut and began to chant what sounded like Latin in a squeaky voice.

Meaghan gently flicked his broken nose with her index finger. He yelped.

"Knock it off, Merlin. That doesn't work on me. Remember? And the nice ladies here have hexed the crap out of the airspace around you." She stared at him, trying to read his face. "The Order set you up, sweetie. They sent you here to fail."

His eyes flew open, wide with fear, and he jerked against the tape holding him to the chair. Meaghan saw nothing on his face but raw terror. What happened to the smug bastard who blew down the kitchen door?

"How old are you anyway? Sixteen, seventeen?"

He continued chanting.

"You really weren't top of your class at Hogwarts, were you?" Meaghan sat back. "Keep it up and I'll give you to the witches. If I could kick your ass this hard without magic, think what they can do to you."

That seemed to take the fight out of him. He slumped back against the chair and began to cry.

"Look at me," Meaghan said. He didn't respond.

"C'mon," Meaghan continued. "I need to take a look at your pupils and make sure they're the same size. Make sure I didn't scramble your brains too hard. The less trouble you give us, the more likely we'll be to get you medical attention if you need it."

He finally looked up. His face was chalky white, his eyes

red and brimming. Confusion and terror fought for control of his tear-stained face.

Something's wrong with this, she thought. He seemed like a different person from the wizard who had attacked her. This was a terrified, half-starved kid. The tiny spark of compassion Meaghan had felt for him ignited into a feeble flame. Time for some good cop.

"Tell you what," Meaghan said. "Let's at least get that nose fixed up for you. That's easy enough. Ladies?"

Lynette stepped forward. "I got this."

Meaghan suspected Lynette was experiencing the same feeling. Something was off. The kid seemed to have no idea what was going on. No defiance, only confused fear.

Lynette placed a hand on the top of his head. He flinched at her touch, as if expecting to be struck. She gave his shoulder a gentle squeeze with the other hand. "This won't hurt," she said in a soft voice. She moved her hand from his shoulder and held his mangled nose delicately between her thumb and middle finger. She breathed a few soft words Meaghan couldn't make out. With a sigh, the boy slumped in the chair. After a moment he sat back up.

"Better?" Lynette asked.

He nodded at her, his eyes wide with wonder. "Thank you," he croaked.

Sarah handed her a damp paper towel. Lynette dabbed the blood off the boy's face and then gave Meaghan a meaningful glance. "Girls," Lynette said to the other witches, "I need to talk with Meaghan and Russ for a sec. Keep an eye on him."

She pulled Meaghan into the hallway and Russ followed.

In a low voice, so only they would hear, Lynette said, "He was possessed."

Russ whispered back, "You sure?"

Lynette nodded. "I can feel the residual energy. That boy doesn't have any power at all. Whoever came after you wore his skin and then abandoned him when the spell didn't work."

Russ shook his head. "The bastards sacrificed a pawn."

"That's exactly what they did," Lynette said. "I don't know how he got mixed up with the Order, but we can't send him back. Even if he wants to go. Which I don't think he does. I sensed a lot of fear and pain."

Meaghan nodded. "He's not going anywhere until we know what we're dealing with. Come on. Time for a new strategy."

CHAPTER 27

MEAGHAN STEPPED BACK into the kitchen followed by Russ and Lynette. The boy sat slumped in the chair, staring at the floor. Just a kid, Meaghan thought. Another lost boy. This time without Matthew to rescue him.

The boy's stomach growled.

"You hungry?" Meaghan asked him. "Of course you are. Starved is probably more like it. If you'll eat, we'll feed you."

He shook his head and continued to stare at the floor.

Meaghan shrugged. "Suit yourself." She looked around the room. "Would you ladies like something? Russ, would you whip something up for our guests?"

Russ stared at her for a long moment, then nodded. "I'd be happy to."

Without asking the witches what they wanted, Russ began frying bacon. Meaghan smiled. Russ had gotten the message. Threats weren't going to work. Time to see what basic kindness could do. Bacon was hard to resist even if you weren't a starving teenage boy.

"Russ, isn't there some pie left over from dinner? That strawberry pie Natalie made?"

"Yeah, Meg, there is. Damn, that was good stuff," Russ said.

"Sarah, would you grab the pie out of the fridge?" Meaghan asked. "And grab the bowl of whipped cream. And there should be a jar of fudge sauce right near it. Hot fudge on pie. Sounds weird, but it's so yummy. Natalie's kind of a genius."

"Got it." Sarah scurried to the fridge.

The young wizard's stomach growled louder.

Meaghan turned back to him and smiled. "We do like to eat well around here. My brother's an awesome cook. If you change your mind, let us know."

"There's also some leftover burgers in the fridge," Russ called out from the stove. "I cooked them rare so they'll still be good reheated. Grass-fed beef from a guy I know up the road. This bacon would be good on top of a burger. Or I could fry some eggs or make pancakes."

"Ooh, I know," said Lynette, catching what Russ and Meaghan were up to. "There's nothing like a bacon cheese-burger with a fried egg on top. It's a messy pile of joy."

The young wizard whimpered and licked his lips.

"Lynette, you're as bad as Natalie," Meaghan said, laugh-ing. "If I hadn't already had a huge dinner, I'd be right there with you. I'll have to stick with pie."

Russ added, "Fried onions would be good on that burger too. Can somebody slice up an onion while I get the burger fixings together? Anybody want me to fry up some hash browns while I'm at it?"

The wizard groaned as his stomach growled even louder. The kitchen was beginning to smell like a gourmet diner.

The witches helped Russ prepare a small mountain of food, while Meaghan swept up broken glass, chattering the whole time about her favorite dishes. What finally shoved the boy over the edge was the smell of Russ's home-baked hamburger rolls warming in the toaster oven. He began to sob, loudly, uncontrollably, his stomach roaring. Meaghan sat down in front of him and held half a cheeseburger to his mouth and he couldn't stop himself. He ate it in three ravenous bites. If she hadn't pulled back in time, he'd have bitten her fingers off.

Lynette took over, feeding him like a baby. A few forkfuls of potatoes followed by a bite of the pie. Meaghan poured him a small glass of milk, the full-fat raw stuff that Russ got from another guy he knew up the road, and held it up to the boy's lips. He gulped it down.

"Can I have more, please?" he gasped.

"Not yet, honey," Lynette said, gently wiping his face with a damp paper towel. "You're so starved you'll get sick if we give you any more right now."

Meaghan smiled. She could hear the maternal concern in Lynette's voice and see the boy respond to it. It was one thing to hate witches in the abstract. It was another thing altogether to hate a kind, motherly woman who called you "honey," fixed your broken nose, and fed you good food when you were starving.

"See?" Meaghan said. "We're not so bad."

He began to cry again. "Hunger is pure, gluttony is a sin," he gasped.

"Pfft," Meaghan sputtered. Gluttony? The kid ate half a burger and drank a small glass of milk. No wonder he was so pathetically thin. "Russ, did you hear that?"

"I did," he answered, his voice grim. "Kid, this isn't gluttony. This is high-quality food, lovingly raised and produced, and skillfully prepared. This is a sacrament. Every bite is a gift from the earth."

The wizard sobbed, snot bubbling from his nose. Great, Meaghan thought, they'd scared him again. But he was all softened up. Time to get some answers.

She held a paper towel up to his nose. "Blow," she said. He obeyed like a child.

"Feel better?" she asked when his sobs had subsided a bit.

He gave a tiny nod.

"There are some things you need to know," Meaghan said, "before I start asking you questions. First, I'm impervious to magic. It flat out doesn't work on me. And the Order knows that. Or suspects it. And they could have checked it out for sure without coming near me. Whoever sent you here to hex me wanted you to fall on your face. Do you understand?"

He stared at her, eyes wide. "Nobody told . . . I . . ." He broke down again. "I don't know why I'm here."

Meaghan nodded. "That's what I thought. I don't want to hurt you. I really don't. Unless you make me. If you behave, so will I. Deal?"

He nodded again, biting his bottom lip.

She gave him a moment, then helped him blow his nose again before asking, "What's your name?"

"Caleb," he said in a tiny voice.

"Caleb what?"

"Just Caleb."

"You don't have a last name?"

He shook his head. "I don't know."

"What are your parents' names?"

"I don't know."

Meaghan raised an eyebrow. "You don't know? Are they still alive?"

"I don't know," he said in a small, timid voice.

This kid is breaking my heart, she thought. "Caleb, how old are you?"

"I'm twenty, I think. About twenty." He looked at his feet again, his face turning pink.

No name and he doesn't know his birthdate, she thought. Did these Order freaks kidnap him as a child? Was his face on a milk carton somewhere?

Meaghan nodded. "You're a little older than I thought. Why did you join the Order?"

"I was raised in it," he said shyly.

Meaghan raised an eyebrow. "I thought you guys avoided women. How did that work?"

"My parents. My father gave me to them."

"What did your mother have to say about that?" Meaghan asked, feeling sick. This was even worse than kidnapping. There was no loving family out there searching and hoping. They'd handed their son over to the bastards.

"My mother obeyed him. She didn't say anything," he whispered.

"Not anything?"

He shook his head. "A wife must submit to her husband.

My father commanded her silence." His jaw clenched. "He never let her talk," he said, his voice louder, angrier.

There it was. Even as she felt her eyes prickle with tears, Meaghan knew she'd found a way in.

"And she put up with that?" Sarah asked, shocked.

Caleb blushed darker. "I guess. I don't know. I don't remember her very well."

"How old were you when your father gave you to the Order, Caleb?" Meaghan asked gently.

"I was about five, I think, I don't really remember."

Another abused kid torn from his mother and abandoned by his father. He'll fit right in around here, Meaghan thought. "Do you like being in the Order?"

He met Meaghan's eyes with a confused look. "What do you mean?"

"You're an adult now. You get to choose. Do you like being there?"

He looked baffled, utterly confounded, at the idea that he had a choice. "I was pledged. I'm pledged to the . . ." His voice dropped to a whisper. "The Power."

"The Power?" Meaghan asked, feeling a chill run down her spine. Was this the Big Bad pulling the strings? "Is that where the magic comes from?"

Caleb nodded.

Melanie had been right about that, Meaghan thought. The Order had a patron.

Meaghan continued her questioning. "It's my understanding that the Order has started using magic only recently. Is that true?"

"No. Well, sort of. The Order is much stronger with the Power." He yawned deeply, one of those huge yawns that come with extreme fatigue. His eyes were glassy, like he was about to fall asleep.

He must be feeling safer, Meaghan thought. Now what do I do with him? There was a lot more she wanted to learn from him. And she couldn't throw him back to those cold-hearted bastards who'd done this to him.

Crap, she thought. I've adopted a damn stray. Just what I need. "Caleb, it's getting late and we're tired. I can't let you leave, you know that, but let me confer with the ladies and see if we can make you more comfortable. Is there anything you'd like to ask me?"

He looked up shyly. "May I use your bathroom?"

Yup, Meaghan thought. He was here to stay.

CHAPTER 28

LYNETTE AND MEAGHAN cut Caleb loose from the chair. The resistance had drained out of him. Lynette, in a kind but firm voice, ordered him to behave and reminded him he was surrounded by powerful witches. With a meek nod, he followed her to the hall bathroom and she stood guard outside the door.

While Caleb was in the bathroom, Meaghan and the witches quickly agreed on a plan. Lynette and Marnie would spend the night. Sarah and the other two witches, Anna and Emma, the quiet ones who'd looked after Russ, would check in with Natalie, then recruit more witches to guard the Keeles.

"We can't let him go to sleep or he'll go into a coma," Anna said. "I bet he has a concussion."

Emma shook her head. "That's totally a myth. So long as his pupils are the same size and he's not barfing, he's fine to go to sleep."

Anna shrugged. "Well, that's what I've seen on TV."

"Is any of the stuff about witches on TV right?" Emma shot back.

"No," Anna said, staring down at the table.

"The lawyer stuff's all wrong too," Meaghan added, trying to make Anna feel better.

Anna and Emma, Meaghan learned, were fraternal twins and, despite the squabbling, inseparable. They borrowed Russ's car and drove home to pick up their own car and some of their younger brother's clothes for Caleb. When Meaghan asked why they couldn't zap themselves home, they told her that materializing out of thin air, like the witches had done on their initial arrival in the kitchen, took a lot of magic. They only traveled that way in dire emergencies.

Meaghan didn't ask about brooms. In her experience, something that stereotypical had to be wrong.

Meaghan put clean sheets on the guest bed, while Russ scrounged up a new toothbrush and found a T-shirt and gym shorts for Caleb to use as pajamas. By this point, Caleb swayed with weariness. Lynette helped him into the oversized clothes and tucked him into bed. She even kissed him on the forehead.

Within moments he was out cold. Lynette and Marnie put up protective spells. Russ made coffee and Marnie took the first watch.

It was now well past midnight. Meaghan was exhausted, the surge of adrenaline that cleared away the tequila long gone.

And still Matthew slept on.

Meaghan had a few things to wrap up before she could go to bed. She sat around the kitchen table with Russ and Lynette as they assessed their next steps.

"It's horrible," Lynette said. "That poor boy. He's covered

in bruises and scars. They did even worse than starve him." She shook her head. "He is not going back to them."

"No," Meaghan said. "Of course he isn't. And at this point, I'm not sure we could get him to go even if we wanted him to. Between you and the food, I think we made a big impression. I thought you were gonna read him a bedtime story after you tucked him in and kissed him goodnight."

With a snort of laughter, Russ got up and poured himself a mug of coffee. He could drink the stuff any time day or night and sleep like a baby, Meaghan remembered. If she drank coffee at this hour, even as tired as she was, she'd be awake all night.

"The problem," Meaghan continued, "is we still don't know why they sent him. And what they can make him do. Until we know for sure that he's not a threat—"

"That boy is not a threat," Lynette said, with a scowl.

"On his own, I agree with you, he's not a threat. He's a beaten-down, starved kid. But they controlled him like a puppet earlier this evening." She gestured at the broken kitchen door. "Remember? You didn't see him. I did. Whoever was pulling the strings was pretty damn threatening."

"He can be saved," Lynette said. "I know it."

"I agree. But the protective spells have to stay up for now, until we know what we're dealing with. And the good news is the best way to make sure he's not a threat is to keep him here with us."

More witches arrived. Meaghan was too tired to catch any names. But based on the admiring looks, the newcomers had heard either about her showdown with Emily or how she'd brought down a wizard with a saucepan. Or both.

Meaghan said goodnight and dragged herself up the

stairs to her room. She brushed her teeth, dropped onto her bed still in her clothes, and fell asleep almost immediately. And dreamed.

She stood on the sunny front porch. The dark forest crowded around the yard and she had a sense of things moving within the tree line. Meaghan saw a figure approach through the now-familiar distant shimmer and her heart leapt with joy. She thought it was her mother, coming to see her again.

But she was wrong. As the figure came into focus, Meaghan saw a man about her age who she didn't recognize. Short and stocky, with a round open face and sleepy looking eyes, he was bald except for a salt-and-pepper fringe on the sides and around the back.

He wore a tan leather jacket, straight out of the seventies, with a black polyester collared shirt and plaid pants. He had a gold chain around his neck.

With a pudgy hand, he waved hello. "You gotta be Meaghan. You look so much like your dad." He smiled. "Prettier, though," he added. "I bet you hear that a lot. Both parts." He held out his hand. "I'm Lou."

Lou, she thought, shaking his hand. The journal she'd read this morning. Matthew had mentioned him. "Hi," she said cautiously. "I've seen your name in my father's journal, but it didn't provide any details."

The man nodded. "Okay, so you're dreaming right now and when you wake up you'll—"

"My mom came to see me last week in a dream. I know how it works and I'm past the skeptical stage. What's up?"

Lou looked startled. "Well, aren't you the fast learner. Matthew said you were a sharp kid. " He finally let go of her hand and said, "Can we sit?"

"Sure," Meaghan said.

Lou plopped down in a wicker armchair. "Oh, yeah. That's the stuff. It's a long walk."

"From where?"

Lou smiled. "Aw, I can't tell you that. No peeking beyond the veil, right? I'm the man who did this job before your dad. I found him and broke the news to him. Then I got myself whacked a couple of days later, so I wasn't much help."

Meaghan nodded. "He mentioned that he wished you'd found him sooner. Did you visit him like this?"

Lou chuckled. "I tried. For a long time, Matthew assumed he was crazy and I was a delusion, so he ignored the dreams. And even once he got his act together, he was never all that good with dream contact. Not like this."

He stared at her, as if weighing his next words. "Your dad was good at this job, but not without some big growing pains. But you? I never seen anybody like you. Even I didn't slide into it this easy and I grew up knowing I had to do it."

He looked away from her and pointed at the movement within the tree line. "They're scared of you. You're the most non-magical being they've ever had to deal with. At the same time, you got no problem accepting the truth about the world. In less than a week, you own the job in a way your dad and I never managed."

Meaghan watched the tree line with Lou. She still couldn't see what was moving. "Who are they? The ones so scared of me? The Order? This power thing Caleb mentioned?"

Lou sighed. "They're part of it, but they aren't the only ones who want to keep humanity under their magical thumbs. You're a harbinger of things to come. And that scares them."

"A harbinger of what? Everybody becoming impervious?"

Lou nodded. "Yeah, but that's only part of it. There's also the fear. If you can't control people with magic, then you control them with the fear of it. With fear of the supernatural."

Meaghan frowned. "But most people don't fear magic or supernatural stuff anymore. They don't believe in it."

"Really? They don't? Think about it. There's still plenty of us who want to believe in things that go bump in the night. I mean . . ." He thought a moment. "Okay, look at the ghost hunters. Why do they bother? Well, partly because there's something to it. Enough people have had odd experiences to suggest something's going on."

Meaghan nodded, wondering where he was going with this. "You would know."

"Well, haunting's a different . . . department, I guess. I can't go really go into it." He plopped a booted foot on the coffee table. "You'd think being dead would take care of sore feet, but no." He sighed. "Where was I?"

"Ghost hunters," Meaghan said.

"Right. Ghost hunters. They mostly break down into two groups. You get the rational ones who are open to the idea of the supernatural, but they don't automatically assume every slammed door or cold spot is a ghost. They look for simpler reasons, *natural* reasons first. They rule out stuff. They try to gather evidence. They want to figure out what's going on and if it's only leaky windows or a warped door frame, they're okay with that. You know what I mean?"

Meaghan nodded.

Lou continued. "They may get scared from time to time, get the creeps from stuff they encounter, but they don't fear ghosts just because they're ghosts. They may not understand what they're seeing, but they don't crap their pants just because they see it. Like you, they don't scare so easy, but unlike you, they can still be affected by magic."

Meaghan smiled. "And the other kind lock themselves into a spooky building at midnight, turn the lights out, and scare the shit out of each other. They believe implicitly in the supernatural, but are still terrified when they think they've encountered it. They manage to be credulous and surprised at the same time."

Lou nodded. "And that makes them easy to manipulate and control. Even without magic. Add magic and they're sheep. But you . . ."

"I manage to be impervious *and* unimpressed."

Lou laughed. "Exactly. You get them coming and going."

"While I'm having my cake and eating it too." They both laughed.

"The best the magical bad guys can do," Lou continued, "is hex the world around you, but if you're shielded with a good protective spell they can't even do that. They can't hurt you with magic, and they can't scare you with it either."

Meaghan stared at the tree line. "But I'm only one person."

Lou shook his head. "No, you aren't. That's what I'm here to tell you. Think about it. Seven billion plus humans on the planet. Being one in a million's not as big a deal as it used to be. It means you got seven thousand people to keep you company."

"How do you know it's one in a million?"

He shook his head. "I don't know what the exact odds are. I'm only trying to make a point. Being impervious is a genetic trait. More people means more chances for the gene to spread. You're the tip of an evolutionary iceberg. Enough people like you and they're screwed."

Meaghan gave him a skeptical look.

Lou pulled his foot off the coffee table and leaned forward in the chair. "Look, magic makes a world stagnant. There's no reason to innovate when you can just mutter some fancy words and wave your hands around. But non-magical humans, which is most of us, can't do that so we keep coming up with new ways to do stuff. I love the movies, the books where the vampire, wizard, whatever, the supernatural bad guy, starts gloating about weak, puny humans. And yet there's seven billion of us living in the sun while they skulk around in the dark. We're doing something right."

"I guess," Meaghan said.

"The magical realms are in big decline, have been for a long time. Gods and monsters still walk among us, but the smart ones? They don't advertise. They keep a low profile to stay off the radar of people like you. Like us. And there's more of us every day. This isn't a one dies, one gets chosen deal. You aren't alone. This doesn't have to be a solo gig."

"So I may not be stuck in Eldrich for the rest of my life?"

Lou smiled. "Stuck? Is that what you call it? From where I'm sitting it looks like you finally got yourself a home."

"I miss Phoenix," she said. "It's sunny and warm. And new. There's no dark forests hemming you in. No witches, wizards or fairies, either."

"Well, none that advertise at least. And you were all alone."

Before Meaghan could think of a comeback, the dream dissolved and she woke up.

CHAPTER 29

GRAY LIGHT FILLED the room. Meaghan could hear rain pattering on the roof and against the windows. She sat up and her head began to pound. The adrenaline hadn't washed away the tequila. It had simply rescheduled it to a later time.

As hangovers went, it wasn't terrible, simply a headache and general malaise. Her stomach seemed okay. But the older she got, the less booze it took to make her feel bad the next day. It didn't matter if she spaced the drinks over several hours with a lot of food and paid careful attention to hydration.

She felt like crap. "Aging sucks," she mumbled.

It was a few minutes past nine. She threw on some clean-ish clothes from the top of the laundry pile, looked in the mirror, decided she didn't care how she looked, and went in search of coffee.

The kitchen was in full swing with Russ at the stove. He

took one look at Meaghan and poured her a large mug of coffee. "Here. Want breakfast?"

"Unh. Let me caffeinate first." Meaghan shuffled to the table and sat down.

Lynette and Caleb were already seated. Caleb, clad in a T-shirt and jeans, looked like a different person. He looked healthier, for one thing, with a little more color in his cheeks. His long shaggy brown hair was still damp from the shower. He was eating breakfast under Lynette's watchful eye.

"Small bites, Cal. We still need to ease you into it. Lots of small meals until you put on some weight." She smiled up at Meaghan. "Morning, sweetie. Sleep well?"

"Unh," Meaghan replied. "I'll tell you when I wake up."

"Meg's not a morning person," Russ said, joining them with a plate in his hand. "I made extra toast if you want it."

"Okay." Meaghan picked up a slice of the heavy brown toast off of Russ's plate, took a small bite, and chewed it carefully. "How's our house guest doing?"

"He's coming along," Lynette said. "He had a good night's sleep and a shower, and now some breakfast." She plucked a strand of hair off his forehead. "Cal, what would you like to say to Meaghan?"

He swallowed the food in his mouth, but did not put down his fork. "I'm sorry I broke your kitchen door, Meaghan."

"Apology accepted," Meaghan said. "I know you didn't mean to do it. So, you're Cal now?"

"Um, I guess." He stared down at his plate. He then looked at Lynette for approval and she smiled back. "It's like being a whole new person."

Marnie strolled in from the living room with two mugs. "Can your dad have another cup of coffee?"

"Sure," said Russ. "How's he doing?"

"He's as happy as can be. He thinks I'm someone named Liz."

Meaghan and Russ exchanged a look. Marnie missed it.

Refilling the mugs, Marnie said, "Hey, Cal, you want me to give you a haircut?"

"Um," he said, looking again at Lynette. She nodded.

"Don't worry," Marnie added. "I cut hair for a living. My day job."

"Okay," Caleb said softly.

"Leave me a card," Meaghan added. "I'll need a trim pretty soon." She may have been attacked by wizards, and she was being guarded by witches, and the whole world had turned on its head, but she wasn't passing up any leads on a good hair stylist.

Marnie nodded. "Will do." She carried the coffee back out to the living room.

Meaghan thought of what Lou had said in her dream about finally coming home. She was still skeptical about herself, but Caleb—correction, *Cal*—sure seemed to be home. But it was probably too much to hope for that they could neutralize the rest of the Order with good food and free haircuts.

The caffeine was beginning to do its stuff. Meaghan felt a bit better. She plucked another slice of toast off Russ's plate.

"So, what's on for today?" she asked.

Through a mouthful of food, Russ said, "We're waiting for you to tell us. You're the leader."

"Me? Tag, I'm it?"

"Every army needs a general," Russ said.

Meaghan snorted. "Who do I look like? George Washington? Buffy, the Vampire Slayer?"

Russ shrugged, and tucked another forkful of food into his mouth. Through it, he said, "More like George. Buffy's much younger than you are."

"Bite me," Meaghan replied. Russ smirked.

"He's right, you know," said Lynette. "The Order came after you."

"Yeah, but with a weapon they knew wouldn't work." Meaghan eyed Caleb. "They sacrificed a pawn. Sorry, Cal, but that's what you are to them. But, they really couldn't expect that would be enough to scare me away, could they?"

Face red, Caleb met her eye. "They think women are weak and easy to frighten."

Meaghan stared back. "Do you think women are weak and easy to frighten?"

Caleb shook his head vigorously. Eyes wide, he said, "Not anymore I don't."

Even Meaghan had to laugh. "Yeah, I bet you don't." She got up and poured another cup of coffee. Sitting back down, she said, "But, I still don't get it. Why scare me? I don't have any power. Any ideas, Cal?"

"The Power likes fear and pain," he said softly. "They used to . . . hurt us, the younger ones." He swallowed hard, his face now white. "As a way to . . . to *feed* it."

Meaghan felt a fresh wave of hatred for the Order. "And they thought they could scare me off while giving the Power a tasty meal. And all it cost them was you."

Caleb looked stricken.

Meaghan continued smoothly. "Which makes them morons because now that we have you, we're going to put the Power on a diet. We want you to feel safe and be happy."

He exhaled with relief. "You won't make me go back?"

Meaghan smiled to herself. Solemnly, she said, "We will not make you go back. You have a home here if you want it."

Lynette scowled.

"With us or with Lynette," Meaghan said. Lynette's face smoothed. It was clear to Meaghan that Lynette had already decided Caleb was going to live with her and that was that.

While Matthew dozed on the sofa, Marnie ran home to grab her styling tools for Caleb's haircut.

"Have we heard from Natalie yet this morning?" Meaghan asked, as Russ set a plate of scrambled eggs in front of her. "Or Jamie? I still think this has got something to do with Fahraya."

Russ shook his head. "Natalie said not to worry. She put up a bunch of protective spells around the house and she lives right around the corner from him."

"Oh, yeah," Meaghan said. "Right. Amulet maintenance."

Russ nodded. "It's a good thing they get along so well."

"So, who keeps John's amulet working?"

Lynette sighed. "Poor John. What a tragedy. We all pitch in as needed, but his amulet is less finicky. He doesn't need as much magic to be human."

"Because of . . . his wings?" Meaghan asked.

"You know about that?" Lynette asked.

"Found the pictures."

"Awful thing," Lynette said. "How his own brother could—"

Meaghan cut her off. "His brother? The guy who cut off John's wings, who tortured him and killed his wife and made his son watch was John's *brother?*"

Russ plopped down in a chair next to her. "Yup. That's him, the bastard."

"How did Dad get involved?"

Before he could answer, Marnie arrived and whisked Caleb out to the back porch for his hair cut.

With Caleb gone, Meaghan asked Lynette the question she'd wanted to ask since she first sat down. "Are we safe with him here? Any sign that they're controlling him or eavesdropping?"

Lynette shrugged. "I don't know. I'm not feeling that weird energy I felt last night when I fixed his nose. And I haven't detected anyone trying to break the spells we put up last night. So, I'm pretty sure they aren't doing anything to him with magic. But they had the poor boy most of his life."

"And there's no telling what awful things they did to his head during that time," Meaghan said.

"Exactly. All we can do is keep an eye on him." Lynette glared at Meaghan. "We aren't sending him back."

"Like you'd let me," Meaghan said with a smile. "I'm right with you on this. That kid is not going back to those assholes. We keep him close and let them come for him if they want him." She pushed the remains of her breakfast around on her plate. "It'd help to know what they're up to. I still think this is about Jamie. I'm calling Natalie."

As she stood up, the phone rang. Meaghan felt her stomach clench as she answered it. *Bad news*, a little voice whispered in her mind. She heard a sob and then Natalie's panicky voice. "They took him. Oh, God, they took him. I couldn't stop it. I tried—"

"Natalie, breathe. Who took who?"

Her voice shaking, Natalie said, "Jamie. The Order. They took Jamie. They're going to the gateway in the woods. To Fahraya."

CHAPTER 30

MARKED BY A stone circle deep in the forest, the gateway to Fahraya was about a twenty-minute drive from the Keeles' house, assuming a driver followed the posted speed limit.

Accompanied by Lynette, Caleb, and Russ, Meaghan pushed her car, an Audi sedan, to a smooth ninety on the straight sections of road but had to slow for the curves. The Audi cornered well and she knew how to drive fast, but if she lost control on the rain-slicked road and wrecked the car, they had no hope of getting Jamie back.

Russ called Natalie back on Meaghan's cell and routed it through the dashboard phone system. They lost the cell signal about five minutes into the trees, but Natalie had enough time to tell them the basics.

Three Order wizards, dressed in normal clothing instead of their usual gray robes, arrived at Jamie's house, with Emily

Proctor leading the way. While the wizards ducked out of sight, Emily, carrying a fruit basket, rang the doorbell.

Seeing her alone and holding a gift, Patrice assumed that Emily was coming to try to make peace. Wanting to confront Emily about what she'd done to Jamie, Patrice opened the door. Augmented with the Order's power, Emily shattered Natalie's protective spells. She tossed Patrice across the room with a wave of her hand while the wizards pounded up the stairs to find Jamie.

Natalie, sitting in her kitchen, felt her spells breaking and ran, barefoot and in her pajamas, through the alley joining her backyard to Jamie's and got there in time to see them drag Jamie down the stairs, also in pajamas, fighting them every step. Patrice, bleeding from a cut lip, her wrist broken, huddled in the hallway trying to shield the kids.

They choked Jamie until he stopped struggling, handcuffed him, and threw a pillowcase over his head. Natalie tried to hex them, but they shoved her out of the way and dragged Jamie out to an SUV idling in front of the house.

Emily tried to follow them but got blasted backwards by one of the wizards. Without her borrowed magic, Emily was helpless from Natalie's wrath. Natalie pinned Emily against the wall, threatened her, and within moments Emily told her where they were headed with Jamie. Natalie called Meaghan for help while Patrice tried to calm her hysterical children.

The Keeles lived several miles closer to the Fahrayan gateway than Jamie and Patrice did. Russ knew a few short cuts and thought they could head off the wizards. The twins had followed Meaghan in their car, while Marnie stayed behind to protect Matthew.

Anna's little hatchback couldn't keep up with the Audi

and the twins soon fell behind. Natalie was sending out word to all the local witches to get there as fast as they could, but materializing into the forest was tricky and required preparation. Meaghan and Lynette would need to stall the wizards until help arrived.

"Why the hell are these bastards driving? Why didn't they get there with magic?" Meaghan asked as she thundered down the road.

"The gateway," Lynnette said. "You can't materialize too close with all the background magic leaking out of Fahraya or you'll get sucked through. You can't get any closer than about a quarter of a mile. You have to walk the rest of way."

"So? It's only a short hike. It would still get them there faster."

"I know why," Caleb said. "The magic from the Power needs to be recharged and it takes time and a sacrifice. Driving gives them time to . . ." He shuddered. "To do things to him. To scare him and hurt him. They're giving that back to the Power."

"Everything I hear about these fuckers makes me hate them more," Meaghan said. "So, how does the Power feel about rage? Does it like to eat that?"

"It doesn't like it when you fight back," Caleb said. "That's why they only feed it with the younger and weaker ones."

"You fought back?" Russ asked.

"Tried to."

"Jamie's no coward," Russ said. "They attacked his family and I'm betting on rage instead of fear no matter what they do to him."

"Can that help us?" Meaghan asked.

"Depends," said Lynette. "It might slow them down a

bit, but once they get there, they can boost their power with the magic leaking through the gateway."

"Lots of power in Fahraya," Russ said.

"Then we have to get there first," Meaghan said.

The last mile was unpaved and muddy, not enough to mire the car, but she had to slow down to keep from bottoming out in a pothole. The Audi wasn't built for rough roads and if she ripped out the transmission or broke an axle, Jamie would be long gone before they got there.

"Is this the road they'd use?" Meaghan called to Russ.

"Probably not. There's a longer road that's paved almost the whole way. They think they've got a head start."

The rough road curved to the left into a small clearing. Meaghan slowed to a stop. A few boulders lay in a rough circle with two taller, vaguely rectangular stones forming a doorway of sorts. The tallest stone was no more than waist high.

There was no sign of another vehicle. "It's not exactly Stonehenge, is it," Meaghan said. "Is there another gateway they could use?"

Russ shook his head. "No. This is the only way into Fahraya around here. The other gateways are in Europe."

They climbed out of the car. Meaghan pulled Matthew's old double-barrel shotgun out of the trunk, loaded it, and handed the box of remaining shells to Russ. "Stick close in case I need to reload."

Russ took the box and stared wide-eyed at his sister. "You know how to use that?"

"I do."

"You any good?"

"Hell, no," Meaghan said. "That's why I like shotguns.

You don't have to be good. You just have to fire in the general direction of what you want to hit."

She walked towards the circle and, holding the gun to her shoulder, surveyed the area. No sign of anyone but them. "Lynette," she called. "What's your magic like up here?"

"Give me a second." Lynette stood next to the car, eyes shut, feet firmly planted, hands out with her palms facing down. She took several deep breaths, then opened her eyes. "I'm good. Had to ground first. Wooh, I forgot how strong the Fahrayan stuff is. They'll need to keep Jamie human as long as they can before they shove him through. If he changes out here, they'll never be able to control him."

"Won't they go with him?"

In a rush, like he wanted to get it over with, Russ said, "They can't. Humans can't enter Fahraya unless they're impervious. Too much background magic. Guess I should have told you that on the way over."

"So, it's me who has to go get him if we don't stop them here." Meaghan nodded. "Yeah, I figured it'd be something like that."

CHAPTER 31

MEAGHAN COCKED HER head at the faint sound of a motor. "They're coming. Lynette, we need some fireworks. And shield Russ and Caleb. If I get close, I'll pull Jamie's amulet off and we'll worry about getting it on him later."

Meaghan strode to the circle and stopped before it. She took a solid stance and lifted the gun to her shoulder. "Russ, stay clear until I call for more shells."

A silver SUV, its windows tinted dark, drove towards them from the opposite end of the clearing. Two men got out of the front seat. She couldn't see inside the SUV, but Meaghan assumed the third wizard was in the back seat with Jamie.

They weren't wearing the Order's usual gray robes. And they looked a lot bigger than Caleb, and healthier. No starvation for these guys. Saucepan not gonna get it done this time, Meaghan thought. She could feel the fear trying to bubble up, trying to eat away at her anger. She pushed it back down.

The two wizards started chanting and waving their hands. Her fear evaporated. How arrogant were these guys? How much evidence did they need that she was impervious?

"You shitheads are bone stupid. Enough with the magic already." She cocked the shotgun. "You're not taking him. Let him out of the car and be on your way."

The biggest one walked closer. He was about Meaghan's age, dark hair flecked with gray and close cropped to his head. He could have been handsome except for the malice on his face. He wore cruelty like other men wore cologne. "Keele's *daughter*," he sneered. "Go away, little girl. Before you break a nail."

Meaghan snorted. "Little girl? Break a nail? Where are you from—1955? Screw you, asshole. You go away. Before I blow your balls off."

"She'll do it, Cooper," Caleb shouted. "She's mean and strong and not scared of you." His voice was shaking with rage. Lynette and Russ were holding him by both arms to keep him from running to Meaghan's side.

Cooper ignored him. "My associate is holding a very sharp knife to the Fahrayan's throat," Cooper said. "Or, more accurately, to the powerless human's throat. Interfere further and my associate will sever his carotid artery. You didn't specify that we let him out of the car alive. Put the gun down."

"Fine," Meaghan said, lowering the gun, but not letting go of it. Was he bluffing? If Jamie's uncle wanted him dead, he would have hired the Order to assassinate him. Sending him back to Fahraya required more effort. Uncle wanted him alive. But she couldn't risk being wrong. One quick stroke of the knife and Jamie would bleed out in seconds.

The other wizard continued chanting and waving his

hands, then abruptly stopped. Cooper smiled, a horrible malicious grin that bore no human feeling. "And the barrier is complete. Your gun and the witch can't touch us now. All the way down, girl. Put it on the ground at my feet."

Slowly she crouched, reached forward, and set the gun on the ground. With a flick of his hand, Cooper sent it skittering out of her reach.

"You go with it. On your knees." Cooper's evil smile spread wider. "Where you belong." He was enjoying this.

Meaghan knelt, with a wince. Her knees were creaky, but the mud cushioned them a bit. She still retained one advantage. Cooper underestimated her. If she confirmed his beliefs about women, he'd drop his guard.

"Caleb," Cooper called. "You're safe now. Come with us."

"No," shouted Caleb, his face twisted with rage, tears streaming down his red face. "I'm never going back to you."

She needed to buy some time until the other witches arrived. "Please. Don't hurt us," she cried, putting a perceptible tremor into her voice. It wasn't hard. Her body hummed from the adrenaline coursing through her blood. The wizards had been facing forward when doing the protective spells. Maybe the barrier was only on one side and arriving witches could get through. It was a slim hope, but all she had. "Why are you doing this?"

And he fell for the bait. It was all she could do not to snort her derision. How did villains still not get this?

"Our client, the King of Fahraya, sent us to bring the false heir. He broke the treaty and must answer for it," Cooper said.

"The treaty?" Meaghan asked, kicking herself internally for waiting a week to start reading her father's journals. She would have pretended she hadn't known what he was talking about anyway, but it galled her to have to ask this pompous asshole because she honestly didn't know. While on her knees no less.

"Did Daddy's brain rot too fast for him to prepare you?" Cooper asked in what he probably thought was a gentle tone. "Poor thing. So outmatched."

Time to reel in the glib sonofabitch. "I don't know what I'm supposed to do," Meaghan wailed. "Please don't hurt me." She saw something moving in the trees. She buried her face in her hands and pretended to sob.

"There, there," Cooper said. "So weak. Not at all like your father."

Yeah, she thought. Matthew never had to learn how to manipulate sexist morons. She lifted her head, hoping Cooper didn't notice her complete lack of tears. Natalie and two witches she didn't know were creeping up on the SUV from behind. She caught Natalie's eye and saw her nod and circle her hand emphatically. Stretch it out, Natalie motioned.

Meaghan threw herself at Cooper's feet and wrapped her arms around his legs, shaking with fake sobs. By now, Russ had to know she was faking it. Caleb's continued silence was a good sign. She didn't need the distraction. She wanted Cooper and the other wizards focused solely on her.

Cooper's face twisted in disgust. "Don't touch me, bitch." He swung his fist and hit her in the side of the head.

Meaghan fell onto her side. His blow hurt, but at least she was off her aching knees. She looked up and saw Natalie and the two witches next to the SUV. More were creeping into the clearing. The wizards were soundly outnumbered.

A huge boom rocked the clearing as Natalie blasted the

back doors off the SUV. The wizards spun around. Meaghan took advantage of their distraction, and lunged for the shotgun as she scrambled to her feet.

Jamie rolled out of the SUV, shirtless, his hands cuffed behind his back. His chest and back were covered with bloody gouges. The pillow case was gone, replaced by a cloth gag. He landed on his feet, roaring inchoately with rage, the third wizard right behind him. Jamie spun and with a graceful kick to the chest knocked the wizard off balance.

The wizard recovered quickly and shot a spell at Jamie, who doubled over and fell to his knees. Cooper and his companion turned away from Meaghan and ran back to the SUV.

Meaghan, forgetting the wizards' barrier spell, fired the shotgun at their backs, praying she didn't hit Jamie. The buckshot hit the spell wall, never hitting Jamie or the wizards. The rebound almost knocked her off her feet, but no pellets hit her. Lynette must have put up her own barrier.

Cooper and the two wizards began chanting and waving their hands. Jamie tried to struggle to his feet, then fell to the ground as if pushed. An invisible blow struck him and he curled into a ball, gasping for breath.

Meaghan could see a glint of metal in Cooper's hand. Even though the magical barrier wouldn't affect her, if Cooper had a knife he could cut Jamie's throat before Meaghan got close enough to make a difference. Even if she could get close, these wizards were not half-starved boys. Any one of them could kill her with a single blow.

The witches and Meaghan advanced on opposite sides. Cooper swept his hands high and Jamie was pulled to his feet. As Meaghan drew close enough to see the bloody wounds on Jamie's torso, she realized in horror what they were. The wizards had carved symbols of some type into his flesh. He was still trying to fight but could no longer control his own body. Surrounded by the wizards, Jamie lurched towards the circle as he fought the movement of his feet.

The magical barrier now surrounded the wizards and Jamie. Meaghan could see flashes of light where the witches' spells struck it. The wizards had reached the stone circle. They raised their hands, chanting in unison, and blasted one of the boulders forming the ring into gravel. At that moment, Jamie turned his head and saw Meaghan. She couldn't save him and they both knew it.

"I'm coming for you," she shouted. "You stay strong. I'm bringing you home."

He nodded, but his face was heavy with defeat.

With a triumphant smile, Cooper grabbed Jamie's amulet from behind, as the other wizards chanted. Cooper pulled the thong tight around Jamie's throat and planted his booted foot on Jamie's backside, below his cuffed wrists, and shoved. There was a blinding flash of light, and Jamie was gone. Cooper, wearing a vicious grin, raised the amulet for Meaghan to see, and then with a flourish of hands, the wizards disappeared too.

CHAPTER 32

"GOT HIM!" MEAGHAN heard Lynette's triumphant shout and whirled around.

"Got what?"

"Jamie. I put a tracking charm on him." She rushed forward to Meaghan's side and put an arm around her. Meaghan hadn't felt herself falling, but now found herself on the ground with Lynette, Russ, and Caleb crowded around her.

"You're tracking Jamie?" Meaghan asked.

"Yes, hon," Lynette said. "Take a second and breathe."

More worried faces appeared, leaning over her. She saw Natalie, Kady, Sarah, and several other unfamiliar women. "Why am I on the ground?" she asked.

"Because you're freaking awesome," Kady said.

That jerked Meaghan out of her faint. "No, I'm not awesome. Not a bit. Goddammit. That shithead was right. I wasn't ready." She held out a hand. "Get me off my ass."

Several hands leaned in and hoisted Meaghan to her feet.

"I pick a fight with Emily and give her a perfect chance to attack Jamie. I waste a whole damn week not dealing. And then I bring a shotgun to a magic fight. Jamie's gone and it's my fault." Meaghan was so ashamed and angry at herself she could barely breathe. She kept seeing that defeated look in Jamie's eyes before they shoved him through the gateway.

Natalie shook her head. "It's not your fault. Or mine. It's Emily's fault. And it's time to beat some answers out of her."

Meaghan nodded. "She here?"

Natalie motioned with her head. "Back there. Chained to a tree."

"With magic?"

"Not entirely. My bike lock helped. And the twins are ready to blast her into cat food if she so much as twitches."

"Patrice and the kids?" Meaghan asked.

"Safe. They're surrounded by protective spells and some seriously pissed-off witches."

Meaghan nodded.

"And John's bee hives," Natalie added.

Meaghan raised an eyebrow. "They're with John? Is that a good idea? What if they come after him too?"

"From what I could get out of Emily, John's not considered a threat. Not without wings. And even if they come, the wizards wouldn't get through the swarm."

"The swarm?" Meaghan asked. "Can John control his bees?"

"He talks to them," Russ said. "Gives them good hive boxes. He doesn't control them. They just seem to like him a lot. They're very loyal. He thinks it's why the honey's so good."

Meaghan nodded. She'd reached a saturation point on

weirdness, she decided. It was all starting to roll off her. John had watch bees. Why not? He used to have wings, after all. His son still did.

His son. She forced herself out of the lethargy that kept trying to take her. "Lynette, tell me about this tracking charm. I couldn't figure out what you were doing back there."

Lynette gave a worried smile. "I know. I'm sorry. You wanted fireworks, but I knew they'd put up a wall first thing. The Order are good at big showy stuff and barriers, but not the smaller more personal magic. I started it the moment the truck pulled up. I could feel him in there and honed in. I can feel him now." Her eyes filled with tears.

"He's still alive?" Natalie asked breathlessly.

Lynette nodded and a tear slipped down her cheek. "But in pain. And scared. He's still fighting it, but the fear is taking him."

"The ritual," Russ said, nodding. "Oh, hell. That's got to be it. They'll do the same thing to him they did to John. Jamie was sentenced to it as a kid, but Dad got him out before they'd hurt him too bad."

"How long does it take?" Meaghan asked.

"Well, the good news, if you can call it good, is it's not a fast way to go. They broke John down over a couple of days. It's the Fahrayan version of capital punishment, meant to deter the worst crimes." Russ shook his head. "We gotta get him home."

"How much time does he have?"

Russ stared into space, watching something unfold in his mind. He turned, took a few steps away from everyone, and threw up his breakfast.

"Russ," Meaghan said. "Pull it together. How much time does Jamie have?"

"A couple of days at least. But . . . oh God, Meg. I saw what they did to John. And what it did to him. He was a Fahrayan warrior, a king. Jamie's a nice kid with an office job."

She dragged Russ away from the group by the arm, grim determination etched on her face. "Don't talk like that again," she hissed. "I need everyone to believe he's fighting hard and we can get him home. No giving up. Ever."

He stared back at her for a long moment, really stared, like he was seeing her for the first time. He nodded. "I know he'll fight hard. I just hope it's hard enough." Louder, so the rest could hear him, he said. "Got it, Meg. What's the plan?"

Meaghan walked back to where she had fainted and picked up the shotgun. "I go to Fahraya. With John. We get Jamie back. But first, I need to talk to Emily. And somebody contact Melanie. I need a Troon who has experience with Fahraya to translate. As much as I want to charge in there, we have work to do first." She headed for her car. "Everyone who needs a ride, come with me. Natalie, bring Emily to my house. We'll make that our base of operations. We'll be safer if we concentrate our fire power. Split the troops as you see fit. One group to help you with Emily. One group to move John, Patrice, and the kids to my house. Somebody grab that SUV and take everybody far enough away so they can zap themselves wherever they need to go."

Kady saluted.

Meaghan smiled, feeling a tiny spark of hope. "For that Miss Smarty Pants, you're in charge of clearing everybody's calendars and thinking up a reason why none of us go to work tomorrow."

Kady nodded. "On it, boss. Staff retreat. I'll call Buzz Hallam to cover anything I can't put off."

"Let's move." She put the shotgun in the trunk and climbed into the driver's seat. "Russ, on the way home, tell me everything you know about Fahraya, and this damn treaty I should already know about."

CHAPTER 33

B Y THE TIME they got home, Meaghan knew the basic outline. The treaty, such as it was, had been negotiated by Matthew to get John and Jamie out of Fahraya alive. V'hren, John's brother, agreed, in exchange for John's exile, to allow John and Jamie to live. If they ever attempted to return to Fahraya, V'hren would consider it an act of war and be entitled to execute them.

Even with these broad brushstrokes, Meaghan could sense the presence of something larger and darker pulling strings. V'hren's victory seemed too complete, his path to power too straight. John had been well liked by his people and strong, but V'hren had somehow managed to undermine and overthrow him in mere days.

There had to be more to the story.

As Meaghan suspected, she was the only one who could save Jamie. Under Fahrayan tradition, only the parties to an agreement or their kin could petition the king for its enforcement. John had no credibility without his wings. Jamie, as a presumed traitor, wouldn't be allowed to argue his own case. Matthew certainly couldn't do it. And Russ would get fried by all the magic. Unless John and Jamie had family she didn't know about, that left Meaghan.

Melanie and Sid were waiting for them on the back porch. "I'm coming with you to translate," Sid announced, as Meaghan approached him. His little blue face was screwed up with worry and something else.

Resolve, Meaghan thought. "Are you sure you want to do this?" she asked Sid, handing the shotgun to Russ as he passed her. Russ made a face, took the gun from her carefully like it might explode, and headed upstairs to lock it up in the attic gun cabinet.

Sid nodded. "You need a translator. I speak the best Fahrayan." He looked down at the floor. "Jamie's my friend," he said, fighting back tears.

"Thank you, Sid. We'll get him home. If you're sure you want to go, I could really use your help."

He beamed at Meaghan, his snarky demeanor of the day before utterly vanished. Melanie walked over, put her arm around him, and kissed him on the cheek, pride and worry fighting for control of her small face. She stepped back and carefully, with trembling hand, adjusted the collar of Sid's jacket.

She was Sid's mother, Meaghan realized. Parent. Whatever the Troon called the Troon who bore them. Or hatched them. She had no idea how they reproduced. Another race I know nothing about, she thought, angry at herself again.

"Melanie, I need the Fahrayan treaty and any notes Matthew wrote on it," Meaghan said. She told herself she couldn't get those lost days back. Self-loathing was an indulgence she couldn't afford at the moment. "You know his files better than I do."

"I'll go find everything I can. Sid can help me." Melanie grabbed Sid's hand and they entered the house.

Meaghan followed them into the kitchen. Marnie was sitting at the table.

"Where's Matthew?" Meaghan asked her.

"In his room. Asleep. He's been asleep since you left."

Meaghan nodded. "Good. Would you go upstairs with Melanie and Sid and help them hunt down some files?"

"Okay, boss." Marnie trotted out of the kitchen.

Boss. Now Marnie was calling her that. At least with Kady it was functionally true. It was like the first time a store clerk called her "ma'am." Meaghan had looked over her shoulder to see who the clerk was talking to. *Ma'am* was a real grown-up. Not Meaghan.

Natalie arrived, shoving Emily through the door in front of her. "What do I do with this?" she asked. "I know what I'd like to do."

Emily stared at the floor, shaking with fear. She wouldn't meet Meaghan's gaze.

Good, Meaghan thought. She should be scared. "Basement," Meaghan said. "I'll be down in a bit. With questions." She waited a beat for effect. "Questions, Emily, you would be wise to answer with a minimum of bullshit. If Jamie dies, I'll let the other witches dispense justice any way they see fit."

Natalie scowled. "Emily, you don't want to know what I'll do to you. He's family." She shoved Emily hard toward the basement door. "Move."

Meaghan took a couple of deep breaths. She had to stay

ahead of the fear trying to overtake her. She could only do that if she kept moving. Okay, she thought, what do I do next . . .

A gentle tap on her shoulder made her whirl around. Caleb stood behind her. "Can I help?" he asked.

Oh, God. What to do with Caleb? He wasn't working for the Order anymore, Meaghan felt confident about that. If Russ and Lynette hadn't held him back, he would have charged and attacked the wizards in the clearing. But, they still didn't know if the Order could control him or use him somehow.

No point in tiptoeing around it. "I don't know if we can trust you yet, if it's safe to let you help."

His face fell. Meaghan took his hand and squeezed it. "I know you wouldn't betray us on purpose. But I don't know if they can listen through you or still control you somehow. Do you understand? We want to trust you, but we aren't sure about what they can make you do."

He nodded slowly. "It's not me you don't trust, it's them. What they can do through me." He met her eyes. "And considering it was only last night I broke into your house, I wouldn't trust me either."

Meaghan smiled at him. "I know you'd never help them on purpose. If that was you pretending to hate them back in the woods, then you're one hell of an actor. Sit tight for now. We'll figure out something you can do to help."

"Okay. I'll wait for Lynette. She went to get Jamie's family." He sat at the table and stared up at her for a long moment. "You can do this. I know you can. It's okay to be scared, but stay angry too."

She stared back at Caleb. "The wizards cut symbols of

some type into his chest and back. Any idea what they were? Have you seen them do that before?"

Caleb frowned. "I've seen them cut people up but not like that. I don't know what those were."

"Meaghan," Natalie shouted from down in the basement. "You want to talk to her now?"

"Yeah," she shouted back. "I'll be down in a second." She squeezed Caleb's shoulder as she passed.

Down in the basement it looked like a mashup between an estate sale and a scene from a mob movie. A bare light bulb hung from the ceiling. Witches milled around looking through the piles of stuff. Sarah, the young witch who worked in the council office was working her way through a box of books.

Emily was tied to an old wooden chair with whatever the witches had found, which included a plaid bathrobe belt, a few bungee cords, and a string of Christmas tree lights. In the jumbled mess, someone had found an aluminum clip-on task light and Natalie was shining it into Emily's face.

"Natalie, stop doing that," Meaghan said.

"I'm gonna break her," Natalie said.

"No, you're going to blind her along with me." Meaghan found an old desk chair, rolled it in front of Emily, and sat down. "You're making my head hurt with that thing. And it already hurts from all the damn tequila I drank last night and getting punched by that wizard. What's next? Beating her with rubber hoses?"

Sarah looked up from her books. "I found a box full of old garden hoses under the picnic table. Should I pull them out?"

Meaghan rubbed her temples. "No. Nobody's getting out

any hoses. How about we start with talking?" She stretched her neck to the left and felt a satisfying pop. "Oh, that's better. So, Emily, what the hell? Why did you do this to Jamie?"

Emily narrowed her eyes and began muttering, trying to cast a spell. Natalie groaned and smacked the back of Emily's head. "Give it up, already. We cast dampening spells and Meaghan's impervious. Remember?" Natalie rolled her eyes. "She's like this at work too. She gets a little frigging power and makes everybody miserable. She never knows when to stop."

"When I get out of here, you'll all pay," Emily snarled. "And Sarah? You're fired."

"No, she's not," Meaghan said. "You know how hard it is to fire non-appointed staff. The civil service review board will just overturn it. What are your grounds? 'Sarah helped thwart my evil plan'?" She leaned back in the chair. "And saying how you'll come after us later doesn't exactly provide me with strong incentive to make sure you live through this."

Emily swallowed hard but didn't say anything. Natalie stared at Meaghan, her mouth open.

"How do you like those ugly politics?" Meaghan asked. "Do I have your attention now? Why did you help them take Jamie?"

"He's one of *them*," Emily said. "Those filthy insect men." She shuddered. "They're all the same. He can pretend he's human, but he's not."

"You hate him because he's Fahrayan? Or because he's not human?" Meaghan asked, genuinely confused. She'd expected some kind of personal grudge, not bigotry.

"He's a monster," Emily said. "Nobody sees it but me."

Natalie stepped forward and slapped her.

Meaghan raised her hand. "Natalie, not now."

"Why not? You heard her," Natalie said, her voice shaking with anger. "The bitch."

Meaghan stared Natalie down. "Plenty of time for that later. Right now I need information. If she won't talk, I'll let you have her."

Emily smirked at Natalie.

Meaghan reached forward and slapped Emily herself. "Don't for a minute think I'm protecting you," Meaghan said, with icy calm. "I'll throw you to whatever wolves I can find if it suits my purpose. Right now, the only monster I see is you. What's your problem with Jamie? Specifically?"

"He hurt me. He took my family away," Emily said. Meaghan's cold threats seemed to frighten her more than Natalie's theatrics. She squirmed in her chair, her eyes now glistening with tears.

"Jamie? How did he hurt you?"

"He's one of them. They're wrong. Everything about them. They look like fairies, but they're killers. They made my family hate me." Emily began breathing heavily, her voice rising in tone and volume. "I told everybody I didn't do it. I didn't hurt him. But they blamed me and they thought I was crazy."

An emotional dam seemed to break inside Emily. "They gave me back," she cried. "I finally had a family and they gave me back." She dissolved into shaking sobs. "Because of them. What they did. And he'll start it again unless I stop him."

Meaghan gave Natalie a questioning look as Emily wept. Natalie, eyes wide, shook her head and shrugged.

"Emily," Meaghan said, her voice gentle now. "Who got hurt? Can you tell me?"

With a sob, Emily said, "My little brother. They had him right after they adopted me. I was eight and he was three."

"They being your mom and dad?"

Emily nodded.

The mood in the room had shifted. The anger was gone, replaced by horror and pity. This was a side of Emily no one had ever suspected.

"Emily," Meaghan said. "Take a minute and breathe. Somebody grab some tissues and make a cup of tea."

Sarah clattered up the stairs, her face pale and strained. This was not the satisfying comeuppance everyone anticipated.

The basement was silent except for the sound of Emily's bubbling sobs.

We don't have time for this, Meaghan thought. Jamie was getting farther away by the moment. She kept seeing that defeated look on his face.

"Emily," Meaghan continued, not waiting for the tissues and tea, "you made a deal with those wizards, didn't you. More power for giving them access to Jamie. Is that right?"

Emily looked up. Even as she wept, she tried to sneer at Meaghan. "Bug Boy has to go answer for his crimes now," she sniffled. "For what he did to me."

"Which is what? Who hurt your brother?"

"*They* did. The *Fahrayans*," she spat. "In the forest. The car broke down. We were on the side of the road. Toby saw them flying, like fairies, and he ran into the trees. I went after him and when I found him they were swarming all over him and they were slashing at him with their little knives and spears. I threw rocks at them and screamed and they flew away. Then Daddy came and Toby was all bloody and I was still holding a rock." She paused to catch her breath, wild eyed and staring at some internal movie playing in her head. "And they blamed me. I told them what I saw and they took me to the hospital and I never saw them again. Any of them. Ever again."

Oh, God, Meaghan thought. Another traumatized child? What is it with this town?

"Emily," Meaghan said. "Think. Jamie wasn't even born when that happened. The Fahrayans hurt him too. They killed his mother right in front of him. He had nothing to do with it. Beyond coming from the same place."

Emily shook her head. "That's not true. The wizards told me the real story. How it was Jamie's grandfather who ordered the attack on my brother and how they're plotting to go back and start it all again. His father, the drunk, he can't go back because they took his wings, so Jamie would take over unless we could stop him. Unless we could prove he broke the treaty and send him back to face justice for what they all did." She stared up at Meaghan, her face tear stained but defiant. "But he was too careful. So they asked me to take his amulet and force him to change so they finally had the grounds to go after him."

Meaghan heard a heavy tread at the top of the stairs and looked up. John walked slowly down the stairs, staring at Emily with narrowed eyes.

"Is this her? The one who helped them take my son?"

"Yes," Meaghan said. "She was telling us why."

"I hear some of it. They lied to you, witch. They take my son to kill him so he won't take power from my brother. My father punished them, the ones who hurt you. He staked their wings to the ground and cut their throats in front of us all."

John walked slowly towards Emily.

She drew back and hissed at him. "They took my family away."

John nodded. "They took my family too. They killed my wife, they hurt my son, they hurt me. And now you hurt my son and his family. What do you think I should do to you?" He stared down at her and Emily glared back.

Meaghan shivered. Even in his degraded state, John was imposing.

Emily was the first to look away. Meaghan saw a small grim smile flit across John's mouth and then it was gone.

"I think I leave you to Patrice," John said. "You took her man and scared her babies after she let you in her home. If this were Fahraya, she would cut your throat and hang your head from her door. I think Patrice will do something worse to you if Jamie dies." The grim smile returned. "That girl is more tough even than my wife. And she loves my boy. You should fear her more than the witches."

John turned away from Emily and addressed Meaghan. "I know why they took Jamie. We don't need her. We will go to Fahraya. Tonight. Before they hurt him too much." He looked down at his feet, his face red. "Like they hurt me."

Meaghan felt her gut flutter. No, no, she told herself. This is no time to be crushing on the former king. "Okay." She called out to the witches. "I assume there will need to be magic done to make it happen. Get on it."

Sarah crept down the stairs with the tea and the tissues. "What did I miss?"

"Cruella's got a backstory and Meaghan and John are going to Fahraya," Natalie said. "Now we need to figure out exactly how my mom shrank Meaghan's dad to Fahrayan size back in the day and find John some tiny clothes."

Emily sobbed quietly, forgotten, while Meaghan, John, and most of the witches scrambled up the stairs. Meaghan stopped halfway up and turned back to Sarah. "Clean her up a little, will you? But don't untie her. I think Jamie's wife wants a word."

Emily cried louder.

"Okay," said Sarah. "What's she going to do? Fire me?"

CHAPTER 34

O NE OF THE witches was assigned the task of making something for John to wear after he took off his amulet. Meaghan didn't need tiny clothes because they were shrinking the space around her.

She didn't understand this at all. They couldn't shrink Meaghan, because magic didn't affect her, but somehow they could hex the space around her and create a bubble, as Natalie described it, of this world's reality to surround her.

This being witchcraft, a funky crystal amulet was required to maintain the bubble.

"So, what happens if I take the amulet off over there?" she asked Natalie. "I get big? I'm a giant? Then I could swat the little bastards out of the sky. Right?"

Natalie shook her head. "Wrong. You'll be a giant crater. Or at least that's what you'll create." She held the crystal between her palms and mumbled something, then turned her attention back to Meaghan. "You'll actually be all the tiny human bits surrounding the giant crater."

"I'll explode?" Meaghan's voice grew louder. "I'll blow up?"

"Oh, yeah," Natalie said. "Big time."

"I thought magic didn't affect me. How can it make me explode?"

Natalie sighed in an annoyed way. "Okay, fine, technically, I suppose, it doesn't make *you* explode. Only the space around you. It's that explosion that makes you explode."

"Why? Why does anything have to explode?" Meaghan asked in a strangled voice.

"Big thing suddenly occupying tiny space, weird physics, wonky magic?" Natalie shook her head. "Hell, I don't know how it works. Just trust me on this. Little Meaghan becoming big Meaghan means cat-food Meaghan."

Meaghan shook her head. "This day gets better and better. Make sure you hang that thing on something sturdy."

"Don't worry. I'll put some big magic on it. It'll only come off if you take it off."

"Let's hope it doesn't come to that."

"Yes," Natalie agreed. "Let's hope."

Trying not to think of the nuclear option that would soon be hanging from her neck, Meaghan went to find Melanie. She had homework to do.

Melanie and Sid were still in her room sifting through boxes. Melanie looked up. "There isn't much." She pointed at the table, on which sat a manila folder, a small scroll of some sort, and a narrow cardboard gift box about the right size for a watch or bracelet. "The treaty and some Fahrayan weapons John gave to your father soon after they met."

Meaghan picked up the box and lifted the lid. Inside she saw a tiny stone knife and spear.

"Be careful," Melanie said. "Those are very sharp." She held up a small blue finger wrapped in a Band-Aid. "Even after all this time."

Meaghan put the box down and poked at the scroll with her index finger. "What is this? Parchment?"

"Dried snakeskin," Sid piped up from the floor, where he was looking through a file box. "It's written in blood."

Meaghan pulled her finger away from the scroll like she'd been burned.

Sid laughed. "You can always count on Fahrayans to bring the *grrrr*." He pantomimed a slashing claw. "No medium bond recycled for those guys."

"Blood on snakeskin? How big are the damn snakes?"

"Oh, you know, regular sized," Sid said casually. He waited a beat for effect. "For this world."

Meaghan did a quick mental calculation. "Holy hell. So, let me get this straight. I'm walking into a power struggle between warring brothers in a brutal Stone Age world full of giant freaking snakes and flying badass warriors with razor-sharp weapons who write their treaties in blood, wearing a necklace that will turn me into a nuclear bomb if I take it off?" In the company of an alcoholic man I'm crushing on hard and shouldn't be, she added to herself.

"Um, yeah," Sid said nodding. "That kind of sums it up."

"And you still want to come along?" Meaghan asked.

Sid swallowed hard, his bravado faltering a bit. "Well, the way you describe it, maybe not so much." He took a deep breath and the resolve returned to his small blue face. "But I'm going anyway. You need me. Jamie needs me."

"You aren't wrong about that." She stared at the scroll, puzzled. "Is that our size or their size?"

"They split the difference," Melanie answered. "They made a large ceremonial version they gave to Matthew that's big enough to handle in our world. Quite like a billboard actually. Took several of them working together to roll it up and fly it through the gateway. There's a typed translation in the folder. The blood came from the signatories, including Matthew. Although as I recall, much of it was John's. From where they took his wings."

Meaghan bent over and peered at the scroll but couldn't bring herself to touch it. "That's . . . beyond horrible. We don't need to take it with us, do we?"

Melanie shook her head. "I cut a tiny strip for John to carry with him. For totemic effect, I suppose. To remind V'hren what he agreed to."

"No journals?" Meaghan asked.

"Not that I could find in these boxes. I know Matthew made notes about what happened over there, but I don't know what he did with them. We can check over in his office but it will take some time. He wasn't great at filing."

"Time we don't have." Meaghan sighed. Of course there aren't any notes, she thought. That would make things too easy.

"John and I can both give you some background on Fahraya if that will help."

"It will." Meaghan fought back the panic that was trying to take her. Too much, she thought. It's too much too soon. Damn it, Dad. I need your notes. I can't do this alone. "Let me look at the treaty first."

"There's not much to it. Technically you and John will

be breaking the treaty simply by entering the gateway, but considering the circumstances, I think it's safe to say that V'hren broke it first." Melanie grimaced. "Assuming V'hren still honors the treaty."

Sid appeared engrossed by something he'd found in one of the boxes. Taking advantage of his distraction, Meaghan leaned closer to Melanie and whispered, "I'll do my best to take care of Sid and bring him home safe."

Melanie took Meaghan's hand and squeezed it. "I know you will," she whispered back. "If I keep Sid from going, he'll never forgive me. If he gets hurt, I don't know if I'll be able to forgive myself." Melanie's small orange eyes filled with tears and she turned away.

That makes two of us, Meaghan thought. She picked up the manila folder, but before she could open it, she heard shouting. She didn't know the words, but she recognized the inflection. John was swearing at the top of his lungs in what had to be Fahrayan.

Still holding the folder, Meaghan ran into the hallway, her heart pounding. Lynette stood in front of the bathroom door, holding a towel and laughing. She saw Meaghan's stricken look and smiled at her. "It's fine. Just a little magical cleanse." To the bathroom door she said, "Better now?"

John stumbled out of the bathroom, wet and naked except for a towel wrapped around his waist. He saw Meaghan, turned bright red, and shoved past Lynette into the guest bedroom across the hall.

"Lynette," Meaghan said, voice shaking. "What the hell? I thought he was being killed in there."

Lynette shook her head. "Relax. We only pulled the alcohol out of him. Freshened him up a bit so he can function over there."

"You . . . he's . . . *cured?*" Meaghan's gut fluttered. If he wasn't a drunk anymore, they could— she cut off that line of thought before it got any further.

Lynette brought her right back to the ground. "No, he's not cured. Not in the least. We merely did a very rapid detox to get rid of his current physical need for alcohol. The emotional need hasn't gone away. But this way at least you won't have to tote a bottle of gin with you to keep him from seeing hairy monsters. Other than the hairy monsters that are already there."

"You mean *other* than the giant snakes?" Meaghan asked, her voice pitched much higher than she intended. Snakes— normal sized snakes, at least—didn't really bother her, but she could do without giant ones. And spiders. She didn't like spiders. The only things worse than spiders were scorpions.

John appeared in the guest room doorway, wearing jeans but no shirt, and rubbing his hair with a towel.

Meaghan tried not to notice his bare chest. For an aging alcoholic, he was remarkably fit. She flashed on the memory of Jamie naked. Something deep in her brain wondered if the size of certain body parts was a family trait.

She felt her ears and cheeks grow hot and knew she was blushing. His face, she thought, keep your eyes on his face.

Lynette shifted her gaze back and forth between the two of them like she was watching a tennis match. She wore a small knowing smile.

Meaghan shoved her attention back to the matter at hand. She held up the folder. "I need to read this. Alone. Once I do, John, I need to talk to you."

John nodded.

Meaghan desperately wanted to shift attention from whatever was going on between her and John. "Lynette, I . . . maybe . . . do you still feel Jamie?"

Lynette nodded. "I do. Loud and clear. He's scared but defiant. Some pain but not too bad yet."

"Can you make that connection go back the other way? Can you send him a message?"

Lynette tilted her head to one side and frowned, staring at the ceiling. "That's an interesting question. Let me think about that. Do your reading and I'll go talk to Natalie."

"I'll go downstairs and see the babies and Patrice for now, okay?" John gave Meaghan his shy smile. "While you read?"

Meaghan softened. That smile got her every time. "Okay. I'll find you when I need you." She smiled back. "They're nice kids."

John nodded and turned back into the guest room to grab the T-shirt lying on the bed.

Lynette grinned again, in that knowing way. "He's quite a man," she said in a low voice so John couldn't hear.

"Don't look at me like that," Meaghan said, blushing again, as she turned and fled back to her bedroom.

CHAPTER 35

MELANIE AND SID went downstairs and Meaghan was finally alone. She shut the bedroom door and leaned against it with her eyes shut. This was the first moment she'd had all morning to catch her breath and think about the task ahead.

"What am I supposed to do?" she asked the empty room. "How am I supposed to fix this?" Meaghan had never felt so outmatched in her entire life. She felt the tears well up. Then her body decided that tears took too long and she had to run for the toilet to keep from vomiting on the floor.

After what felt like a very long time, Meaghan's gut was empty. She flushed the toilet, then leaned back against the bathtub, the porcelain cool on the back of her neck. She felt so shaky she didn't trust her legs to support her.

Meaghan had no idea how she was going to rescue Jamie. No idea what she was going to say or do. The risk was huge, the likelihood of success minimal. *I don't have a chance in* hell, she thought. If I fail, he's going to die and me along with him.

But there was nothing to be done about that. She was the only one who could save him. If she left him there to die, in agony, far from home and surrounded by enemies, she'd be as good as dead anyway. She could see no way forward from such a cowardly act, other than crawling into a liquor bottle and drinking herself to death. Like John had been trying to do for the last eighteen years.

In that moment, Meaghan grasped the brutal simplicity of the task before her. Get Jamie home or die trying. Perversely comforted by her limited options, she got up from the bathroom floor and brushed her teeth.

Meaghan picked up the folder from the bed where she'd dropped it in her dash to the bathroom. She sat at the table, where Melanie had left the treaty scroll. She shoved the dreadful scroll aside with a grimace. Snakeskin and blood. She shook her head in disgust. But even if she wasn't repulsed by it, the scroll was in Fahrayan and she couldn't read it anyway.

She opened the folder. It contained two typed single-sided sheets of white paper, probably written on a manual typewriter judging by the bumps she could feel on the back of each page.

It was more a list of bullet points than a formal legal document. The Fahrayans, as far as she knew, didn't have a legal system, at least not a very sophisticated one based on John's grisly comments about Patrice hanging Emily's severed head from her door. So, if it wasn't legally binding in the sense Meaghan understood, was there something magical about the use of the snakeskin or the blood? Or were there so many giant snakes and bleeding bodies lying around that it was easier than rustling up paper and ink?

Ugh. More questions for John. Read, she thought. Quit thinking and read.

There wasn't much to the treaty. V'hren was declared the rightful ruler of Fahraya. John was ordered into exile and agreed to never return or attempt to avenge his losses. Jamie wasn't even mentioned by name, only as "heir or issue" of John. There was no specific ban she could find on John or Jamie changing into their Fahrayan form so long as they didn't do it in Fahraya.

Okay, she thought. There was something to work with. Emily made it sound like the Order was relying on Jamie's forced change as the grounds for dragging him back. But merely changing into his Fahrayan form wasn't enough to violate the treaty unless done for the purpose of returning from exile.

Jamie only entered Fahraya because V'hren sent hired wizards to kidnap him and physically shove him through the gateway. There was no intent by Jamie to return. Jamie was only in Fahraya because V'hren had brought him there.

It couldn't be that easy. Could it?

Probably not in Fahraya where justice was dispensed with a sharp knife. V'hren had gone to a lot of trouble to bring Jamie back for public execution. Meaghan doubted that he would simply give up because she pointed out that he had violated his own treaty to do it.

She kept reading. V'hren's responsibilities were simple. Leave John and Jamie alone and continue to punish any attempts by his people to enter the human world.

So, that must have still been going on, she thought, even

though John's father killed the raiders who attacked Emily's adoptive brother. Had that been the source of friction between John and V'hren? That V'hren supported raiding and John didn't? That was probably part of it, but being brothers, John and V'hren were likely acting out a whole bunch of crap going back to childhood.

This treaty wasn't going to help her. And there was no time to hunt through Matthew's office to find his missing journal. She needed the details from someone who was there.

She wished she could talk to her father. But she knew she couldn't unless he was having one of his rare lucid moments and even then he got dates and people confused.

So, Matthew was out. That left John and . . . who else would have been around? Vivian was dead. Lynette had mentioned cleaning up John when he first got here, so she might know something, but she couldn't have been in Fahraya.

But there would have been a translator. Melanie, Meaghan thought. Maybe Melanie was there. If Meaghan was right, Melanie was the only person actually present during the treaty negotiations who had not been undergoing torture and who was not now dead, demented, or kidnapped. Maybe she could give Meaghan some solid details instead of merely background information.

Feeling a flicker of hope, Meaghan shoved the treaty back into the folder and headed for the kitchen. It was crowded with people. Waiting for her, she realized. For her orders. The panic began to bubble again. The house was too full of people watching her every move. She needed a little distance.

"Melanie, let's talk," she said. "In Matthew's office. Russ, you got the key?"

Standing at the stove, Russ dug in his pocket and held

out his key ring. "The padlock key. It's pretty stuffy in there. Open the windows and air it out a little."

She nodded as she took the keys.

"Take the pitcher of lemonade in the fridge with you so you can start replacing all those fluids you just lost."

Meaghan sighed. "You heard?"

"We all heard," Russ said. "Sounded like you were barfing up a lung. Ready to eat yet?"

Her stomach growled, right on cue.

"I'll bring something over in a minute," Russ said before she could argue.

"Where's Lynette?" she asked.

"Out on the porch with John, Patrice, and the children," Melanie said.

"And Natalie? Please tell me she's not in the basement tormenting Emily."

Russ said, "I could, but I'd be lying."

"Natalie," Meagan shouted. "Get up here. I need to talk to you." She turned back to Russ. "Where's Caleb?"

"Sarah and Marnie took him to the movies to get him out of the way."

Meaghan raised an eyebrow. "He was okay with that?"

"It was his idea," Melanie said. "He thought it would be safer for all concerned to remove himself from the situation. Until we know more about what the Order may have done to him."

Natalie clattered up the steps. "Yeah, boss."

"Who else is down there?" Meaghan asked.

"Gretchen."

Meaghan stared at her, drawing a blank. Too many names to keep track of.

"You know," Natalie said. "The nice little grandma lady who walked you through the new job paperwork?"

Meaghan nodded. "Right. I know who you mean."

"Well, she and Emily go way back. I think she hates her more than I do," Natalie said with a smile. "Gretchen's way meaner than she looks."

Meaghan sighed. "Well, that's just great. Patrice been to see Emily yet?"

Natalie shook her head. "No. She's been busy introducing the kids to Grandpa. When I told her what he said about her cutting off Emily's head, she smiled and said 'I like how he thinks.'"

"Oh, this keeps getting better and better," Meaghan said. But she didn't have time to worry about what Patrice might do to Emily and she realized she didn't care. This crap is changing me, she thought. Into someone who scares me a little. Out loud, she said to Natalie, "I need to talk to you too. In the garage. Let's go."

CHAPTER 36

MEAGHAN CLIMBED THE rickety stairs at the back of the garage to her father's office, followed by Melanie and Natalie. The padlock was old and rusty, but the key turned easily. Meaghan removed the padlock and pushed open the door.

The odor of dust and mildew permeated the air. Gray, rainy daylight filtered into the room through two large windows in the far wall. With a bit of effort, Meaghan pushed up the lower sash of each grimy window.

"Leave the door open," she called over her shoulder. With the windows opened and fresh air flowing, she took a moment to survey the small room.

Every inch of wall space was covered with photos, artifacts, and yellowing newspaper articles. A large bookcase covered most of one wall. It overflowed with dusty books, some of them legal tomes she recognized, but most were old and tattered. A small bust of George Washington sat on the top of the bookcase.

On the other side of the room, stacks of files covered a battered oak desk, and the dented steel filing cabinet next to it. An old leather swivel chair sat behind the desk with two straight-backed wooden side chairs placed in front of it. A slouchy tattered gray armchair sat beneath the windows.

"Have a seat," Meaghan said, gesturing to the wooden chairs. "We don't have time to dig through this crap and find Matthew's missing journal, so I need to talk somebody who was there." She looked at Melanie. "Did I guess right? You were there?"

Melanie nodded.

"Good. I need to know exactly what happened. Unless V'hren is way more reasonable than he appears to be, arguing the treaty won't be enough."

"No," Melanie said, sitting down. "It won't."

"But do we know if it's still the same guy in charge?" Natalie asked. Like Meaghan, she was roaming around the room, taking it all in. "What if there's somebody new trying to tie up all the loose threads?"

Meaghan marveled at her own obtuseness for a moment. It never occurred to her that V'hren might be dead. "Natalie's right. It's a violent place. How do we know he's not dead? It's been eighteen years. We could be dealing with somebody else."

Melanie shook her head. "We aren't. There isn't much information coming out of Fahraya, but we do know V'hren is still in power. And that he's growing increasingly erratic."

"How do we know that?" Meaghan asked, running her index finger along the dusty spines of the books on the shelf in front of her. More than a few were in Latin. She thought getting out of the house would help, but this was worse. Here she was surrounded by visible evidence of how much she didn't know.

"We have an inside man," Melanie said. "V'hren's son. Jhoro leads the resistance, if you can call it that. There's only a handful of them left. He's been a fugitive, under a death sentence, since John was exiled."

"Wait," Meaghan said, turning to face Melanie. "I found a photo in one of the boxes in my room. John with two boys in Fahraya, Jamie and a nephew. Is that him?"

"That's him," Melanie confirmed.

"What was he, fifteen, sixteen, when John left?"

"Fifteen, I believe," Melanie. "Which by Fahrayan standards is manhood. Extended childhood is a luxury Fahrayans can't afford."

"Why didn't he escape with John and Jamie?" Meaghan asked. "Why did they leave him behind?"

Melanie shook her head. "They didn't leave Jhoro behind. He refused to go. Not everyone supported V'hren, and they weren't ready to hand Fahraya over to him without a fight. They needed a leader and Jhoro was the logical choice."

"But he was only a kid," Natalie said. "Fifteen and he's the guy in charge?"

Melanie shook her head again. "Human fifteen and Fahrayan fifteen are not the same. At fifteen, Jhoro was taller and stronger than John and already a skilled hunter. And V'hren's heir. With John and Jamie gone, the resistance looked to Jhoro as their de facto king."

"Can we count on Jhoro's help when we get over there?" Meaghan asked.

"Maybe," Melanie said. "If you can find him. And if he wants to help."

"Why wouldn't he help?"

Melanie stared at the floor and didn't answer.

"Melanie, why wouldn't he help?" Meaghan asked again.

Natalie said, "Well, it's obvious isn't it? With Jamie out of the way, V'hren's the only guy between Jhoro and the big chair. And if V'hren's a complete bastard in how he kills Jamie that makes Jhoro look like a better alternative." Natalie looked at Meaghan. "Right?"

"Yeah, sadly, that sounds about right to me," Meaghan said. "Melanie?"

"Jhoro is a better man than that," Melanie said. "Much more like John than V'hren. To the point that V'hren never quite believed that Jhoro was his. Jhoro may want to rule, but he'd never step on Jamie's broken body to get there. Unlike his father."

"So then why not help us?" Meaghan asked.

"Because John is as good as dead to them from the shame of losing his wings," Melanie answered, looking at the floor. "And because you're Matthew's daughter. Many, including Jhoro and his companions, blame Matthew for what happened to John."

"Matthew? How is it Matthew's fault? He *saved* John," Meaghan answered, indignant.

"And according to some, John only needed saving because Matthew's presence gave V'hren an excuse to move against him."

Meaghan felt the panic rise again. Was Matthew really to blame for what happened to John? Was that even possible? If Matthew, with more than twenty years of dealing with this shit, had screwed up that badly, what hope did Meaghan have of saving Jamie?

Seeing the look on Meaghan's face, Natalie steered her across the room and gently pushed her into the arm chair.

The warm weight of Natalie's hands on her shoulders steadied Meaghan, and her panic subsided a bit. It was still there but muted enough so she could function.

Breathe, Meaghan told herself. Keep breathing. "I need the whole story, Melanie. Not bits and pieces. What the hell am I walking into? All of it. Now."

Before Melanie could answer, they heard footsteps on the stairs and Russ appeared with a tray of sandwiches. "Lunchtime," he said, in a cheery voice, then he saw Meaghan's face. He scowled. "What the hell have you been telling her?"

"Nothing yet," Meaghan said. "They were just getting started." She glared at Melanie. "Right?"

CHAPTER 37

T HE CURRENT ROUND of trouble started not long before John's exile. But the roots of the story lay in the first contact between Fahraya and the human world. Fahraya wasn't a separate world or dimension, like most of the other worlds accessed through the Eldrich gateways. It was a bubble of space time, a tiny dimension clinging to the human world. It had no separate existence.

Its inhabitants had once been human until a magical accident split them off from the wider world. Magic, much like radiation, could force genetic mutation, causing strange results. The people developed wings and became smaller, although many other species in Fahraya did not. Like the giant snakes, which were only giant relative to the now tiny human residents.

"So how long have they been on their own?" Meaghan asked.

"We don't know for sure," Melanie said. "The magic accelerates genetic change, so the split could have been relatively recent, but they're a Stone Age culture which suggests they've been alone for some time. You've looked at the treaty scroll?"

Meaghan wrinkled her nose and shook her head.

Melanie smiled. "It's pictographic. Fahrayan is not a written language. Their history and folklore are passed on orally, through sagas and stories, chanted or sung. All the written treaty does is reference, through crude pictograms, the much more detailed song that contains the agreed-upon provisions."

"So, no writing," Meaghan said.

"No writing, no metalworking, no agriculture, no manufacturing," Melanie answered. "The usual lack of progress found in magical cultures, although the Fahrayans are a somewhat different case. Their world is so harsh, so poor, that without magic they couldn't survive. Unlike worlds and species that never grow because they use magic as a crutch."

"It's a total dump," Natalie said.

Melanie nodded. "It's not fairyland."

"So, why can't they magic up a better world?" Meaghan asked.

"Because they aren't practitioners, like witches and wizards, who use magic as a tool. They're a magical species," Melanie explained. "Without magic they can't exist, at least not in their current form. But they have very limited ability to manipulate it."

"So, who's doing the magic?" Meaghan asked, confused.

"Nobody is," chimed in Natalie. "The magic is just there, like background radiation. The Fahrayans are used to it, they evolved with it, and their bodies can't function properly without it. They can't fly without magic. But the rest of us—humans at least—can't go there without getting fried."

"Unless we're impervious," Meaghan said.

"Exactly," Natalie said.

Meaghan scowled. "If they need magic to fly, then how the hell do they get around over here? Emily says a bunch of them attacked her brother. And I saw Jamie with my own eyes. And other people have seen them or there'd be no stories about fairies with wings, right?" As she said Jamie's name, Meaghan felt the panic bubble up. She pushed it back down.

Melanie jumped in. "The Fahrayans lose their ability to fly if they get too far from a gateway. Their wings are ridiculous if you understand typical avian anatomy. They shouldn't be able to fly at all with them, but somehow they do. Much like dragons."

"Dragons? They have *dragons* over there?" Meaghan shuddered. "I'm still trying to get used to the giant snakes."

"Relax," Melanie said. "No dragons in Fahraya. Entirely different world. But the same principle. The wings are too small and attached in the wrong way to lift a beast of that size off the ground. Which is why dragons are now creatures of myth in this world. Not enough magic left to let them fly."

"But the Fahrayans are so small they don't need as much magic," Meaghan said, trying to disregard Melanie's comment about dragons. One monster at a time, she thought. If I die in Fahraya, at least I won't have to worry about any dragons. "And the sightings and attacks have all occurred near gateways." She craned her head to look at Natalie. "And city hall's sort of a gateway, right?"

Natalie shrugged. "More a magnifier, but the same general idea."

Without the gateway magic or some other source of magic, the Fahrayans were incapable of flight and lost their disproportionate strength. The farther they got from a gateway, the weaker they got.

"So, without magic, they're defenseless," Meaghan said. "How do the amulets work? And don't tell me 'by magic' again."

Natalie smiled. "They're pretty cool. My mom came up with them."

The amulets worked by dampening the magical mutations and activating residual human DNA. When Jamie told Meaghan that the amulet made him human, he was half right. He was already human, mostly. The amulet merely suppressed the genetic changes that made him Fahrayan. Vivian had believed that Jamie could be made human permanently, but the spell would require a blast of magical power far in excess of anything in the human world, even near the gateways. So, they made do with the amulets, which were an astonishing bit of magic in their own right.

Russ, this time managing not to make a sound on his way up the creaky wooden stairs, appeared with another tray of food, a pot of coffee, and a reproachful look at Melanie and Natalie. "Are you still freaking her out?"

Yes, Meaghan thought. "No. I feel better," she told Russ. *Liar*, she thought. "How are things in the house? Is the wicked witch of the basement behaving herself?"

Russ shrugged. "I assume everyone's still alive down there, but I'm kinda trying to stay out of it."

Meaghan nodded. "Has Patrice been down to talk to her?"

Russ shook his head. "Not yet. I think she's letting her stew awhile. Patrice is one tough lady. I'd be a wreck if I were in her shoes." He set the tray down on the desk, bustled around for a minute pouring coffee and handing out cookies, then grabbed the nearly untouched sandwich tray and left.

"So," Meaghan said. "Back to business. The Fahrayan gateways are relatively new, right?"

"Relatively," Melanie said. "They opened up in the mid-nineteenth century."

"Is that normal?" Meaghan asked. "Gateways popping up like that?"

"No," Melanie answered. "Not in the least. We're still not sure why it happened."

"Not *totally* sure," Natalie muttered.

Meaghan looked at Melanie for a reaction, but Melanie's face was unreadable. Even when they claim they're telling me everything, Meaghan thought, they're still holding shit back. But, for now, she'd have to be okay with that.

When the first gateways opened in England, Melanie explained, the tiny winged warriors found themselves in the middle of Romanticism and the Victorian Age. Since magical gateways tended to exist in clumps, they appeared in the spots already reputed to be fairy strongholds.

"Fairy folklore has existed for centuries," Melanie added. "But fairies didn't have wings until the Fahrayans arrived." Somehow, the brutal Stone Age Fahrayans were converted in human imagination into the graceful, charming, childlike inhabitants of a paradisiacal fairyland.

And, the Fahrayans didn't do much better gaining an accurate first impression of humans. The Victorian fairy hunters were not the most sensible of people. Their idealized view of the Fahrayans led to an idealized view of their behavior, allowing the Fahrayans to steal them blind whenever they crossed paths. The idea began to root in the Fahrayan psyche that the giant humans were easy pickings.

Those who flew far enough from the gateways to lose their magical boost generally didn't come back. The few who managed to return told stories of fearsome giant predators like foxes and badgers and house cats. Owls and hawks in particular were feared. The Fahrayans had evolved their magical wings because it was the best protection from the fearsome creatures of their world, none of whom could fly. But in the human world, death could come screeching from above, from creatures with far more impressive flight capabilities.

"Those who wanted to raid into the human world dismissed the tales as raving or lies, and pointed out how easy it had been to steal food and small objects from the humans they'd encountered," Melanie said.

"But they were all bubble-headed Victorian fairy hunters," Natalie added. "Not exactly a complete picture of humanity, you know?"

The Fahrayans with more realistic views of humanity urged caution. It was safe to assume, they argued, that if Fahrayans could travel back and forth through the gateways, then so could the giant birds of prey. Or the giant people themselves. Best to stay clear of them altogether.

Melanie sighed. "The one thing, I believe, that all Fahrayans shared, however, was an utter lack of comprehension of how vast and complex the human world really is."

The cautious faction won the day and taboos about entering the gateways were established. But the stories and the desire for the treasures seen in the human world remained. It became an illicit rite of passage for adolescent Fahrayans to sneak into the human world. Respect for the taboos faded, although the occasional encounter with an owl was enough to instill a healthy respect for the inherent danger of the other world. Which made it even more attractive.

"That all changed with John's father," Melanie said. "Zayhna."

Zayhna and his bravest friends, barely out of childhood, their heads full of tales of glory and treasure, of brave Fahrayans outwitting the hapless giants, snuck through a gateway and found themselves right in the middle of a bloody World War II battlefield.

Natalie shook her head. "Jamie never told me any of this. Not even in high school when he took that stupid European history class I had to help him with."

"That's because he didn't know the story," Melanie said. "At least not the details. Zayhna was the only survivor and he was so traumatized he could barely speak about what he'd seen."

Melanie believed, based on her research, that an artillery blast probably hit near the gateway as the Fahrayans crossed through, killing several and scattering the rest. The remaining Fahrayans didn't last long. The few soldiers who saw them assumed them to be hallucinations brought on by battle stress and told no one. It was rumored in the magical worlds, but never confirmed, that a few had been captured alive by the Germans and taken to a secret lab in Berlin.

When he could finally speak of what he'd seen, Zayhna was adamant that humans were not the silly, hapless giants found in Fahrayan stories. The humans he observed were warriors, like the Fahrayans, but with weapons of inconceivable power and savagery. If the giants were angered, they could easily destroy Fahraya.

"Zayhna believed all contact with the human had to end," Melanie said. "When he took power from his father, he reestablished the taboos and this time backed them up with substantial penalties. The worst of which . . ." She trailed off as she lowered her face into her small blue hands.

Meaghan heard her sob softly. Natalie jumped up and put

her arms around Melanie. After a moment, Melanie pulled herself together and blew her nose loudly. "We have to get Jamie home. Quickly."

Melanie, unable to meet Meaghan's eye, quickly rattled off Zayhna's penalties. Any foray into the other world would result in a savage public beating. Attempting to attack or plunder from the humans would result in public execution. Finally, any contact that might invite an incursion or invasion by the humans would bring down the most fearsome punishment of all. The perpetrator would be publicly tortured to death in an ancient Fahrayan ritual reserved for only the most heinous of crimes.

After a few days of scourgings and beatings, while the priests performed rituals to block the soul's passage to the afterlife, the victim's wings were cut off, the tongue ripped out, and if male he was castrated, if female her womb was cut from her. Finally, the victim was carried high in the air above the rocky terrain and dropped, with the corpse left for the snakes and other beasts.

"Is that what they did to John?" Meaghan asked, feeling sick.

"Well, not all of it. Fortunately," Melanie said. "But, yes, that's the punishment V'hren imposed on John. And now on Jamie."

Natalie wore a look of horror. "Jamie . . . he . . . they *can't*." She began to cry and it was Melanie's turn to comfort her.

Meaghan buried her head in her hands. "Let me guess," she said. "John got himself in trouble by somehow getting mixed up with Matthew."

Melanie sighed. "There's more to it, but basically yes."

"And that's why Jhoro won't help us. Won't help *me*."

"Maybe. I don't know that for sure. He may view every

enemy of his father as a friend by now," Melanie said. "But you need to hear the rest of the story."

Meaghan nodded but didn't look up.

The ritual hadn't been performed in centuries and Zayhna invoked it now only as a way of instilling fear in his populace. Zayhna had entered the gateway a bold young man, full of energy and bravado. In a few hours, his youthful exuberance disappeared. Terrified by what he had seen, he became grimly determined to protect his people, even willing to sacrifice their goodwill and respect in order to do it. The risk was too high to allow anyone else to enter the human world.

"Wait a minute," Meaghan interrupted. "So then who was stupid enough to attack Emily's brother? John said his father had them executed, so obviously the ban was still in place."

"Zayhna didn't want his people to know how vulnerable they were, so he blocked them from the gateways but didn't really explain why," Melanie said. "Most Fahrayans accepted it, but there are always a few who think they're clever enough to break the rules and not get caught. Zayhna never imposed the ritual on anyone, but he did have several would-be raiders executed over the years."

"So, no plot?" Natalie asked. "Emily and her brother were just random victims?"

Melanie nodded. "Wrong place, wrong day."

CHAPTER 38

I T WAS INTO this world that V'hren and John were born. Meaghan was surprised to learn that V'hren was the older brother. Succession was not dependent on birth order in Fahraya, but nonetheless, Zayhna's selection of John as his heir infuriated V'hren.

"But Zhara was the greatest source of conflict between them," Melanie said.

"Zhara?" Meaghan asked.

"John's wife and Jamie's mother."

"Ah," Meaghan said. "Of course. So your standard brother-versus-brother crap. But what's that got to do with Matthew?"

"I'm getting there," Melanie said.

"Get there faster," Meaghan said with a glare.

According to Melanie, V'hren believed John had stolen everything that rightfully belonged to his older brother. His father had chosen John as his heir and Zhara had chosen John as her mate. Even V'hren's son liked John better. "Jhoro's mother died in childbirth," Melanie said, "and V'hren blamed John. If John hadn't—in V'hren's mind at least—stolen Zhara, V'hren would not have had to settle for an inferior woman. He ignored Jhoro. He even suggested that Jhoro was not his, that his wife had been unfaithful."

Natalie scowled, her tears now subsided. "Gee. I can't imagine why Jhoro liked Uncle John better. With V'hren, it's always somebody else's fault, right?"

Melanie nodded. "V'hren's tendency to bitterness and his sense of entitlement were the primary reasons Zayhna had not chosen him and the same reasons why Zhara rejected him."

"And somehow that was all John's fault," Meaghan said. "So if he was such a jerk how was he able to turn everybody against John overnight?" *And when the hell are you going to get to the point?* "Big picture version, okay?"

"Upon being passed over, V'hren immediately began a whisper campaign against John. Trying to convince whoever he could that John was reckless and would be a bad king." Melanie fidgeted in her chair, trying to avoid Meaghan's gaze. "But ultimately the most useful fiction that V'hren planted was that John would conspire with the giants and destroy Fahraya."

"And somehow Matthew stumbled into the middle of that and gave V'hren the opening he needed," Meaghan said.

John had followed his father's edicts regarding the human world but wondered whether such rigid isolationism was the solution. Fahraya was so poor and had so few resources that if the old stories of the riches to be found in this other world, stories now taboo, held even a grain of truth, then, if navigated with care, it could be a source of a far better life for his people.

Following Zayhna's death, John, the new king decided to make a quiet foray into the human world to learn more. The punishments would stay in place, and these visits kept secret, until he knew more. The risk was huge. It didn't matter that he was the king. If he was found out, he could be brutally executed. But the reward—he could give his people a better life. Plus, he'd be hailed as a hero and live on in the sagas.

"So," Meaghan said. "Not entirely a selfless act."

"Not entirely," Melanie said.

"And V'hren wasn't completely off base suggesting John was reckless," Meaghan added.

Melanie sighed. "No. He wasn't."

Armed to the teeth, John, under the guise of a long hunting trip, slipped through a gateway into the human world and found himself in Eldrich. Face to face with Matthew and Vivian, who were on their way back from a visit to Troon, accompanied by Melanie. "There's not much more to tell," Melanie said, with a sad smile. "You already know how the story ends."

Melanie translated between Matthew and John the best she could. Despite the language barrier and size difference, John and Matthew became fast friends. Vivian made her first amulet and a few weeks after his initial visit, John, in human form, was escorted around Eldrich.

Matthew showed him maps and photos, and impressed upon him the size and complexity of the human world. They tested how far from a gateway a Fahrayan could go before losing his strength and ability to fly. Matthew, wearing his own amulet, made a stealthy visit to Fahraya and met John's family. During one final visit to Eldrich, John decided it was time to change the edicts to allow carefully planned visits to Eldrich and access to the wider world under Matthew's guidance and protection.

"And somehow that went sideways," Meaghan said.

Melanie nodded. "Yes, it did. V'hren had a spy who saw

John enter the gateway. And somehow V'hren got wind of what John and Matthew were up to. When John returned, ready to announce his decision to open the gateways, V'hren was waiting for him."

"But why didn't John explain—"

Melanie cut off Natalie's question. "He tried. But V'hren had done such a good job sowing the fear of an invasion—a fear that seemed to be supported by John's furtive actions—that no one would listen. V'hren declared John a traitor and took control as king. His first act was to order John's execution. And because John's family had met Matthew during his secret visit, V'hren condemned them, as well."

"They tortured Jamie's mother too?" Meaghan asked, feeling sick. "Jamie had to watch that?"

Melanie sighed. "The few remaining shreds of V'hren's sanity saved her from that at least. He had loved her once and still had enough feeling that he couldn't bring himself to do that to her. Claiming it as an act of benevolence and mercy, he simply had her wings bound and had her dropped into a ravine near the gateway. She died instantly. As horrible as her death was, at least it was over quickly."

"But he started the ritual on Jamie, didn't he," Meaghan said. "I saw the photos."

"Jamie watched his mother die and his father tortured, and endured a few hours himself before Matthew and I arrived and stopped it."

"And I'm betting John blames himself for what happened," Meaghan said. "It's not the physical abuse that broke him but the guilt. It's why he let Matthew raise Jamie."

Melanie simply nodded. The three women sat silent for a moment.

"What happened to Jhoro?" Meaghan asked.

"Jhoro escaped into the hills with a few of his friends before his father could seize him too," Melanie said. "As you know from the photos, Jhoro met Matthew during his initial visit so he was complicit in the crime and subject to the same penalty."

"But," Natalie said, "Jhoro's his son. V'hren couldn't do that to his own son."

"Oh, yes, he could," Melanie said, her face grim. "And he would have, and still will if given the opportunity. Jhoro has been a fugitive over half his life trying to evade V'hren's wrath."

"He wants to torture his own son to death?" Natalie said, fury in her eyes. "What an *asshole*."

Melanie smiled. "Indeed." She lowered her head and rubbed her eyes with both hands. "He was always that. But—"

Meaghan cut her off. "There's something else at work here."

Melanie raised her head and stared at Meaghan for a long moment. "Yes. I believe there is."

"Manipulating people to create fear and resentment," Meaghan said. "Inflicting pain. Where have we seen that before? That's who the Order is really working for. I'm thinking V'hren has the same boss." She slumped in the armchair and stared at the ceiling. "So, we're dealing not only with a megalomaniacal sociopath, but also an evil force that's using him like a sock puppet?"

"Yes, I'm afraid we are," Melanie said.

"Well, at least it puts the giant snakes back in perspective," Meaghan said. "Time to talk to John."

CHAPTER 39

M EAGHAN FOUND JOHN sitting on the front porch, Liddy playing at his feet and Ben asleep against his chest. After all the years without knowing his grandchildren, it was like John couldn't get enough of them.

Liddy was chattering a mile a minute about Disney princesses while drawing on a yellow legal pad with a mismatched assortment of pens. John gazed at her, a look of wonder on his face, as he patted and stroked Ben's small back.

Watching from inside the screen door, Meaghan felt her eyes sting with tears and stepped back before John could see her. Seeing his loneliness eased for a moment made her realize how bad it must have been for him all those years, alone with only his bees for company. To believe that the horrors inflicted on him and his family were his fault, no matter how good his intentions. No wonder he drank.

She thought of Matthew's lonely years, of the estrangement between them, and how foolish it all seemed now. If

John and Meaghan somehow managed to save Jamie and they all got home alive, it would be John who best understood what his son had endured. He'd have to put his guilt and shame aside, and step up and be a father again. She wondered if he was up to it. And if Jamie would be able to accept his father's help after all these years.

Of course, it's all moot, she thought, if we don't get back alive. Which we probably won't. With a sigh, she wiped her tears away with the back of her hand and blew her nose on the crumpled tissue she found in her pocket. Keep moving, she told herself. No crying.

Meaghan pushed open the screen door and stepped out on the porch.

Liddy looked up from her drawing. "This is my Grandpa John. Are you going to get my daddy back?"

Meaghan nodded. "Soon, kiddo. And your grandpa's going with me. But first I need to talk to him. Where's your mom?"

"She's sad. She misses my daddy. She went inside with the ladies," Liddy said.

"Patrice is talking to *her*, downstairs," John said. Ben wriggled and began to whimper. John murmured and rocked him until Ben settled back into sleep.

With Ben quiet again, John returned his attention to Meaghan. He wore the same look of wary shame that Meaghan had seen Jamie wear after his secret was first revealed. "Now you know my story I think. You still want to go to Fahraya with me?"

"Well," Meaghan said with a weak smile. "I don't really want to go at all, but since I have to, you're coming with me."

She felt her face flush and the tingly rush of blood

through her body she always felt when he was near. A hell of a time to be weak in the knees, she scolded herself.

John spoke to Liddy. "Little honeybee, go find one of the ladies for me, to take your brother, while I talk to Meaghan, okay?"

Liddy nodded, jumped to her feet, and headed for the door. She stopped on the way to accept a one-armed hug from John. "Don't leave to get Daddy until I get back," she said.

He smiled at Liddy, the same wide free smile Meaghan had occasionally seen from Jamie. Years of care dropped from his face. "I promise. Now go buzz buzz and find Lynette or maybe Russ, okay?"

Liddy smiled back and ran into the house. They heard her shout "Russ!" at the top of her lungs. John shook his head, still smiling. He shifted the baby to his other shoulder and then looked up at Meaghan, who was leaning against the porch rail.

"We are going when it gets dark in Fahraya, yes?" John asked her.

Meaghan nodded. "Around midnight our time."

"It's dangerous after dark, but worse if they see us right away." He stared at her intently for a moment. "Don't worry. They chant for many hours. Hurt him a bit, try to scare him, but we got time. Lynette is telling him we are coming."

"So, the connection does go both ways. Good." Meaghan sat down on the porch steps instead of one of the chairs. Those were too close to John. She was giddy enough with several feet of space between them.

"That's a good idea you give to Lynette. It's not like words she sends, more like feelings, but it's enough. The hardest part of the first day is fearing what is to come. We give him hope to fight with." The baby stirred again. "Shh, little man. Your father is coming home, I promise."

"I wish I had your confidence," Meaghan said, the tears again trying to surface. She wouldn't be able to push them down much longer.

"You are like your father. You'll know what to do when it's time."

"What about you? Are you okay to do this? I know what . . ." she faltered. "I know what they did to you and what they were going to do. Are you sure you can go back there?"

He stared into the distance, silent, rubbing Ben's back. Finally, he spoke. "I think I should have gone back a long time ago. To finish with my brother. But instead I drink and feel sad for myself, and now my son, he pays for it." He shook his head. "You promise me, when you come home you make it right with your father. He was a better father to my son than I was, but he always wanted to be father to you."

The tears now arrived despite Meaghan's efforts to hold them back. She felt her face screw up. Her chin wobbled and, mortified, she heard herself whimper.

John moved to sit next to her on the porch step. He held the baby in one arm and Meaghan in the other, trying to comfort her. "Don't listen to stupid me. I make you cry. Shh."

She leaned her head on his shoulder and sobbed.

Lynette appeared in the doorway, followed by Liddy.

"Take the baby, okay?" John asked. "Take them back inside with you."

Meaghan heard Liddy ask, "Why's she crying?"

"She's had a busy day, honey, and she's tired," Lynette

answered. "You cry sometimes when you get tired, don't you?"

"Does she need a nap?"

"Yes, I suspect she does. Now let her sit with your grandpa a bit, okay?" Lynette plucked Ben from John's chest and herded Liddy back into the house.

Now John put both arms around Meaghan and stroked her hair while she cried. After a moment he scooped her up into his lap so he could hold her closer.

"You'll be okay, shh, it's okay," he murmured.

Her tears tapered off and Meaghan became acutely aware of his body pressed against her. But she didn't pull away. With his arms around her, holding her close, Meaghan felt safe for the first time since Natalie's frantic call that morning. She knew it was an illusion, but she was grateful for the momentary comfort.

"Better now?" John asked.

She hiccupped and sniffed. "I need to blow my nose."

"In my pocket." He gestured at the pocket on his T-shirt with his chin, keeping his arms wrapped around her.

She carefully plucked the tissues out of his pocket, feeling his heartbeat under the soft, worn cloth. In that moment, she knew if she didn't pull away, she would kiss him. And that would be a disaster. She had to stay focused.

Red-faced, Meaghan scrambled out of his lap and to her feet. She blew her nose loudly. "Thank you. I'm sorry to be such a baby."

He gazed up at her, a knowing smile on his face. "You are so like my Zhara." After a moment he added, "My wife. Jamie's mother. She never liked to cry either. So strong, my Zhara."

"I don't feel very strong at the moment," Meaghan said, still sniffling as the words tumbled out in a rush. "I feel like I'm about to go stumbling into something I don't understand and unless you've cooked up a doozy of a plan that you haven't told me about yet, I don't know what to do. You say I'll know what to do, but I . . . I don't."

John didn't reply. She could see his lips moving like he was sounding out words and she realized he was trying to translate what she'd said.

"I'm sorry. I know I talk too fast," she said.

"Nuh," he said, smiling at her. "I hear too slow. I don't know what 'doozy' is, but I get what you say. I'm thinking of a plan, but it's not ready to tell yet. And Matthew had no plan back then and he got me and Jamie out alive. You'll do the same I think."

John stood up. He was standing on a lower stair so their eyes were level. He reached out and stroked her bare arm with his calloused fingers. Meaghan felt an electric rush where he touched her.

She took a step back. "I . . . it's . . . this can't happen," she stammered.

"Why not?" He stepped up on the porch, close enough to touch her again. "I made myself alone for so long and today I know how stupid it was." He stepped even closer. "It's a long time alone for both of us."

Damn you, Russ, she thought, why did you tell him that? Only Russ knew the details of her nonexistent love life. Meaghan took another step back. One more and she'd be backed up against the door frame. "If we . . . if I let you . . . then what happens if we do make it home? Do you stop drinking? *Can* you stop drinking?"

Now John took a step back. His face grew red and he stared at the floor. The shame was back.

Meaghan hated herself for a moment as she watched his reaction. But she'd been down this road before, with her father and with Greg, her long-ago boyfriend with the heavy fist. One detox didn't change a thing. She wouldn't subject herself to the betrayal, violence, and broken promises ever again. Her body might be ready to trust him, but her mind knew better.

"I'm sorry," he said, his voice stiff. "I am stupid to think . . . I have to talk to Patrice." He fled down the front steps and around the side of the house.

"God, I sure handled that well," Meaghan muttered.

"Handled what?" Russ appeared on the other side of the screen door.

Meaghan yelped and whirled around. "Goddammit, Russ. Don't sneak up on me like that."

"I didn't sneak up on anybody. I was making as much noise as I could. Didn't want to walk in on a private moment," Russ said. "Did you kiss him? There's a pool going."

"Did I *what?*" Meaghan felt her cheeks flame. "Wait, did you say there's a *pool?* You assholes are betting if I'll kiss him?" She glared at him through the screen. "There's nothing going on. Nothing."

"Sure. Right. Nothing's going on. And it's not a bet on if you'll kiss him but when." Russ pushed the screen door open. "Move. Let me out. Did it ever occur to you that something going on may be exactly what you need? It's sure something he needs. John's had more social interaction today than he's had in the last eighteen years."

"He's a drunk. I don't need that crap in my life and it's not my job to fix him." She refused to meet Russ's eye.

"You don't think people can change?" Russ asked. He plopped down on the settee. "Oh, that's good. I've been on my feet all day."

"I do think people can change, but only when they're ready. I'm an idiot if I think I can convince him to change on my timetable." She sidled over to the settee and sat down next to him. "You know that. Good intentions won't fix him. It's not a freaking fairy tale. One kiss won't break the evil spell."

Russ refused to take the bait. "I'm not saying he doesn't come with a hefty pile of baggage. But at our age, who doesn't? I've got three ex-wives and you've got such raging commitment issues you haven't been on a date in ten years."

"I don't have commitment issues," Meaghan said.

Russ snorted. "Right."

"I can't believe you started a pool, for God's sake."

"I didn't start it," Russ said, with a smirk. "Lynette did. After she saw you ogling John in the hall after his detox."

"I wasn't ogling him," Meaghan said, blushing yet again. "And why the hell is my love life so damn fascinating all of a sudden? It's not like we don't have bigger things to worry about."

"That's exactly why," Russ answered. "We *do* have bigger things to worry about. But we've done all we can from here and there's nothing to do now but wait until midnight. Giggling over you and John gives us all something to do besides weep with fear."

"Well, at least you can check that off the list. I've taken care of the weeping. But then I'm betting you nosy little jerks already know that. Some fearless leader I'm turning out to be."

Russ reached over and took her hand. "Don't sell yourself short. You're impressing the hell out of us all. If it was me knowing I had to go to Fahraya, I'd be hiding under the bed whimpering. Jamie would be screwed."

She gave him a wan smile. "You would not. I'm doing what anyone would do in this situation. If Jamie was counting on you, you'd step up. Everyone here would do the same. I'm nothing special."

Russ shook his head, serious now. "No. You don't get it. There are plenty of people who'd chalk it up as hopeless, leave him there to die, and get on with their lives."

"But what kind of life would I have if I let him die? If I didn't do everything I could to bring him home? If I didn't die trying?"

"You'd have John's life. He lived and his wife died. He couldn't save her, and as far as he's concerned, he let that happen to her. He didn't die trying to save her and he's been punishing himself ever since. If that were you, would you want the first person who made you think forgiveness might be possible—that there might be a way forward with your life—shut you down cold without a chance to prove yourself?"

"No. That would be awful," Meaghan said with a sigh. She squeezed her brother's hand. "How did you get so wise? For once I'd like you not to know me better than I know myself."

CHAPTER 40

T HEY WENT BACK in the house. Russ started rounding up dinner for the troops and Meaghan went to find John.

John and Meaghan's not-so-romantic interlude on the porch had kept her from asking the questions she had for him. Meaghan still needed the information, but first she needed to apologize. Not for her doubts about his ability to stay sober, she still had those, but for her abruptness in how she conveyed them.

If someone was driven to drink by a terrible grief, by a devastating upheaval in his life, could healing that emotional wound, could finding the forgiveness he so desperately needed, be enough to give him the strength to stop drinking? Was there a difference, she wondered, between someone who drank too much because even one drink was too many, and someone who drank too much because the pain was simply too great to bear without it?

Could she really equate John, the deposed king who'd had his family, throne, and pride all stripped from him, who'd endured days of torture, with Greg, the heavy-fisted lunkhead who drank too much because it was the most interesting thing he knew how to do?

And then there was Matthew. He drank because he thought he was losing his mind. He drank because he'd lost his family. Because his wife couldn't accept what she saw happening to him.

Meaghan had always treated alcoholism like a one-size-fits-all malady. If Greg couldn't, or wouldn't, stick with sobriety, then that meant no one could. But her father had. He'd been sober for over thirty years. And who knew what had happened to Greg? Could he be sober somewhere, living his life?

The violence Greg had inflicted on her was unacceptable in any context and she knew she'd been right to leave him. And she knew that if John had shown the slightest inclination toward violence over the years, Russ wouldn't be so glib about a potential romance. Russ was still living in Arizona when Greg assaulted her. It was Russ who took her to the hospital, Russ who wanted her to file a police report, Russ who begged her not to go back to him. And when Meaghan finally left, it was Russ who helped her pack.

If there was no physical risk to her, and John hurt only himself quelling his pain and guilt—if it was only about the drinking—maybe slamming the door and never looking back was shortsighted. Maybe she owed it not only to John but to herself to give him a chance to prove her wrong.

She found him sitting on the back porch, staring at the ground. He didn't look up when she approached. She sat down next to him.

"Meaghan, I—"

At the same moment, she said "John, I—"

"You go," he said.

Meaghan took a deep breath. Sitting this close to him, she

could feel the warmth of his body and found it hard to maintain any kind of emotional detachment. Her physical attraction to him confused her. Usually the mere hint of a drinking problem was enough to turn off any incipient feelings. Like flicking off a light switch.

"I'm sorry," she said. "I could have handled that better. But your drinking . . . it does concern me. I have history. Bad history and as much as I . . ." *Want to tear your clothes off and have sex with you right here*, she thought, her face reddening. Instead she said "as much as I like you, I can't be around you if you're still drinking."

"I know," he said. "Your father and Russ tried to help me long ago and I know Matthew drank too much once too. But I am always too . . . too drunk," he said, with a wry chuckle. "Too drunk to listen. I am not your best choice. I know this. You need someone you can trust. He's not me."

The brief flash of humor was gone, replaced by a look of such sorrow that Meaghan, without consciously realizing it, took one of his calloused hands into her own. "He might be you," she said softly. "But we don't know that yet. Either of us. And the only way to know is for you to get the help you need and stay sober for a while. You need to be able to trust yourself. And I don't think you've trusted yourself for a very long time."

His eyes filled with tears and one fell before he could blink it back. He wiped it away with the hand Meaghan wasn't holding. "Huh, now it's my time to cry, I guess."

"I've been doing enough crying for everybody, but I'm happy to share," Meaghan said. "But don't expect to sit on my lap while you do it."

John laughed and the tension ratcheted down a bit. "So, what do we do?" he asked.

"We go get your son back and if we don't die doing it, then you need to get sober."

"I'll do it for you," he said, squeezing her hand.

She shook her head. "No. You can't do it for me. You have to do it for yourself. It has to be something you want, not something you think I want. Do you understand what I'm saying?"

"Yeah. I do. It is something I want. I have wanted it for long time now, but I was too proud, too sick to ask for help. Those witches make my head more clear than it's been for a long time. I missed all those years with my son and his wife and the babies. I don't want to miss any more."

Meaghan teared up. "Oh, crap, now I'm blubbering again." She sniffled, her nose starting to run. "I need my hand back so I can blow my nose."

John smiled and released his grip. He groped in his shirt pocket. "You take all my tissue."

"Don't worry. With my nose I've always got one buried in a pocket somewhere." She found a crumpled tissue and blew her nose. "I still have a lot of questions I need to ask you. That's why I came to find you in the first place. Before I got all weepy."

"And before I got all . . . what's the word . . . lovey?"

It was Meaghan's turn to laugh. "Now presenting Weepy and Lovey in the touring company production of *Surviving Fahraya*."

"Touring company?" John asked, puzzled.

"Dumb joke, not very funny. Tell me about the giant snakes."

CHAPTER FORTY-ONE

GIANT SNAKES, GIANT spiders, giant things that sounded suspiciously like scorpions . . . Fahraya had a lot of giant creepy crawlies. What it didn't have was arable land, abundant water, or natural resources in any significant amounts.

Natalie was being complimentary when she'd called it a dump.

The seasons never changed. It was always about seventy degrees during the day, about fifty at night. The weak sun rose and dropped in the same place at the same time every day. There were no oceans, no lakes, no rivers, no mountains—only low rocky hills riddled with caves and bisected by the occasional shallow ravine.

Vegetation was limited to low shrubs, sparse plants, and fungi growing among the rocks. The people survived by hunting and gathering. They made all their clothing, weapons, and tools out of stone, bone, sinew, and hide. Some of their water came from rainfall that collected in natural tanks in the rocks, but most of it sprang from magical springs that moved at whim, so the Fahrayans couldn't even build permanent settlements. They were nomads, living in caves and following the shifting water.

"It's just a tiny little place," John said. "Not like this where there is always more to see. Fahraya just . . . ends." The farther one flew from the populated area, the darker and colder it grew. The world slowly dissolved. There was a point where the magic stopped working and Fahrayans lost their ability to fly. The ground there was flat, with no distinguishing characteristics, only endless gray sand. No one traveled farther on foot because there was no point. Even the land appeared to fade into a gray void.

"It's like that old episode of *The Twilight Zone* about the omnipotent kid who makes the entire world outside of his town disappear," Meaghan said.

John looked at her blankly. "The twilight zone?"

"Old TV show. Sorry. Ignore me when I say stuff like that," Meaghan said. "I can see why the human world would be scary but enticing at the same time." She glanced around the backyard. The grass needed to be cut, at least what grass was visible between the weeds and dandelions. A few tired fold-up lawn chairs sat on the cracked concrete pad that stretched out from the porch. "Well, maybe not this particular little piece of the human world."

John smiled, then got serious again. "My father, he saw terrible things and he didn't know it was only a little part of this world. He was so scared for us that he didn't look for more or let us look. Others saw only things to steal." He shook his head. "My brother saw only a way to scare everybody to follow him and get revenge on me."

"And what did you see?" Meaghan asked.

"I saw a better life for them. But I was wrong."

"No, you weren't. I think your father and your brother were wrong. Your brother's still wrong."

"He has to fight big snakes and fight Jhoro and I sit here with a full belly and a pretty girl next to me." He grinned at her. "You are right. This is better."

Meaghan blushed. *He thinks I'm pretty*, part of her mind gushed. The rest of her mind rolled its eyes. With no clear mental consensus on how to respond, Meaghan ignored John's comment.

"So," she asked, "what do you think your brother is up to? Why grab Jamie now? Why hasn't he come after him sooner? And how did he get mixed up with those . . ." She was about to say "assholes" and edited herself. "Those stupid wizards in the first place?"

John shook his head. "I don't know. In our stories, wizards are trouble. They bring evil. They are not friends to Fahraya. To work with them . . . is very bad." He sighed. "He was jealous even when we were boys, but we were still brothers. We hated each other, but we loved each other too. You know?"

She nodded.

"But he changed when my father picked me. His mind got bad, I think. He was more than jealous. He began doing evil things, crazy things. Maybe now he's losing the fight with Jhoro and he wants to look strong. Jamie is easier to take and kill than Jhoro. Maybe even V'hren won't kill his own son."

"I don't know," Meaghan said. "I mean I get why V'hren

wants Jamie, but I'm still not seeing the need to manufacture a reason to grab him. And it's not even a good reason. The treaty doesn't prohibit either of you from changing between human and Fahrayan while you're here. There's got to be more to it."

John nodded. "I see what you mean. Maybe he gets these wizards and Emily to make Jamie change to scare you into going away?"

"Yeah, maybe, but there are other ways they could have done that. And it doesn't make sense strategically. I'd be even more useless right now without the heads-up. At least now, everybody doesn't have to waste time convincing me this stuff is real." Sitting this close to John, she could feel the warmth of his body. He smelled of laundry detergent and something clean and pungent like a freshly cut pine tree. They were as close as they could get without actually touching. "Maybe I'm over-thinking it. But I still feel like there's a big piece here we aren't seeing."

John shifted position slightly so their thighs barely touched. It was such a subtle movement she wasn't sure he was even aware of it. Meaghan felt a quiver between her legs. Down girl, she thought. No time for that. She eased a fraction of an inch away from him, breaking contact. He didn't follow her or even seem to notice.

"You know," he said. "Maybe these wizards give V'hren power like they do for Emily. And they lie to him. Tell him he can do things he can't. Like they tell Emily she can make spells on you."

"Power to do what? Fahrayans don't practice magic, do they? Are they even capable of it?"

"Power to do nothing good, I think. Our stories tell how

wizards had a great war and how they destroyed the rest of Fahraya—the gray place now—by stealing all the magic there. Fahrayans learn as babies that making spells is very evil and it can bring back the wizards to take the rest of the magic and then we'll die."

"So," Meaghan said, "how's that work with you and the witches then? You seem to get along fine with them."

John shrugged. "Some witches in our stories but mostly wizards. And this world is so different. Humans don't need magic to live like the Fahrayan do. The witches here heal and bring babies and only sometimes are bad. I know now that witches and wizards can be good or evil. But in our stories . . . wizards are always bad. All of them." He sighed heavily. "To work with wizards . . . If the people knew this . . . My brother, the boy I knew, he died a long time ago and left a crazy man in his place."

"The Order definitely take after the wizards in your stories," Meaghan said. "So, working with the Order is a big risk for V'hren, but worth it to him to get Jamie back to Fahraya. And the wizards tell Emily they need her help to manufacture a treaty violation to bring Jamie back, but what they come up with doesn't violate the treaty."

Meaghan's mind was churning. She could feel the outlines of something but could not quite see it. "There's something Caleb keeps talking about, something he calls the Power."

John looked at her blankly. "Caleb?"

"The wizard who broke in last night."

"You trust him?"

"Yeah, I do. He says he doesn't know how he ended up in my house and I believe him. The guy who broke in was scary. Caleb isn't. Lynette said she could read different energies in the room like another wizard had been there. She thinks he got there in Caleb's body, then abandoned him after confirming that I was impervious."

"This is the guy you knock down with the cook pot?"

"Yeah, that's the guy," Meaghan answered. "Russ says he's glad I finally found a use for cookware other than cooking. It's a less dangerous way for me to use it, he says."

John laughed, a full throaty sound that sent a tingle down her spine.

"Yeah. Ha ha," she said. "As I was saying, Caleb talks about something he calls the Power. How it feeds off pain and fear. Melanie thinks whatever this thing is, it's where the Order has gotten their magical abilities. Russ says they were a joke only ten, fifteen years ago, but now they're major players."

John nodded. "And you think V'hren is getting something from it too. He's feeding it my boy, maybe, for power." His eyes narrowed. "Last time, I walked away from my son. Not this time."

"It's getting close to dusk," Meaghan said. "Only a few more hours. We need to eat before we go and sleep if we can."

He smiled at her, but it was grim and strained. He stood up. "I'll go see what they give me to make clothes. And shoes. This time I will need shoes in Fahraya. I never wore them before. You don't walk when you can fly."

CHAPTER 42

I T WAS JUST before midnight and time to go through the gateway.

John went first. He asked them to give him a few minutes to check things out before following. No one argued with him. He was keeping his composure to a degree Meaghan doubted she could manage if she were in his place. But those first steps into Fahraya would be overwhelming and if he needed a moment to pull himself back together, Meaghan would see that he had it.

John stripped off his amulet and shrank to his Fahrayan size. Melanie gave him the tiny knife and spear she'd found and he dressed in the doll-sized trousers, tunic, and cloak that the witches had made for him. They'd even made shoes, gluing padded leather oblongs, roughly the shape of a foot, in the center of two scraps of chamois.

John wrapped his feet and lower legs in the chamois, then bound it in place with heavy black thread, cord sized in his small hands, to make crude boots. He wrapped the small strip Melanie cut from the treaty scroll around his waist like a belt.

Dressed and armed, John walked through the gateway.

Lynette placed a tracking charm on John similar to the one she had on Jamie. She stood with her eyes shut, as if listening and after a few seconds, motioned to Meaghan and Sid that it was safe to follow. Lynette had driven up in her son-in-law's truck camper and was planning on monitoring the gateway until they returned.

Meaghan wore her usual jeans and T-shirt, and a gray fleece jacket wrapped around her waist. On her feet she wore the sturdy hiking boots in which she'd walked over half of Arizona. She carried a pack containing water, matches, a first aid kit, a rain poncho, and some food, mostly high-energy nutrition bars and Russ's homemade jerky. She also carried the typed translation of the treaty scroll.

Sid wore his usual mélange of trendy children's attire, all boys' clothes this time with the exception of a pink Hello Kitty T-shirt. He also wore a fedora, a la Indiana Jones.

"Nice T-shirt," Meaghan said, with a smile. "That should strike fear in their hearts."

"Yeah, ha ha, Miss Thing. What's that around your waist? A dead sheep? Fahrayans are terrified of house cats, in case you didn't know."

"Sid, nobody's scared of Hello Kitty. Not even mice."

Troon were like camels and Sid, despite his love of coffee, could go for several days without eating or drinking, so he carried nothing with him. He had his own amulet that would allow him and his clothing to enter Fahraya at an appropriate size.

Meaghan didn't ask Sid if his amulet had the same explosive qualities as hers.

Natalie assured Meaghan that she wouldn't feel a thing going through the gateway. It would be like stepping through a doorway. The magic of the gateway combined with the amulet would activate the spell and shrink the space around her. It wouldn't affect her at all.

"Unless I take it off," she reminded Natalie.

"Right. Unless you take it off," Natalie confirmed. "And you're the only one who can do that. It's like the ruby slippers. Someone else tries and they'll get zapped."

"And if I take it off, I explode."

"The space around you explodes."

Meaghan glared at her.

Natalie looked away and said, "Not that it makes a big difference for you, I guess."

Meaghan sighed. She was really starting to hate magic.

Russ stood next to her, his brow furrowed and deep lines etching his face. "Just don't take the goddamn thing off, all right?"

He exhaled raggedly, his eyes shiny. Meaghan could see him struggling not to cry, trying to be brave. After a moment, he said, "Okay, Dorothy, off to Oz you go. But remember, there's no place like home."

Meaghan smiled back and took his hand. "I'll leave a trail of breadcrumbs, Hansel."

He tried to smile, failed, and instead threw his arms around Meaghan and hugged her so tightly she could barely breathe. "Be careful, Meg. Please. I just got you back. Don't leave me again."

She heard the tears in his voice. "Don't cry," she said in

his ear, "or I'll start again. We'll be back before you know it. Does Dad know we're going?"

Matthew had slept through most of the day, only awakening to eat lunch and wander around the house for a little while, confused by all the activity.

"Don't know. He's really been out of it today. I'll try to explain it when I get home."

Meaghan stepped back from Russ and pushed a strand of hair off his forehead. His eyes were red with tears and the circles under them stood out like bruises. "You look hammered. Go rest. You've been on your feet all day. Don't worry. I'll be back. With Jamie. You can't get rid of me that easily."

"Damn," Russ said, with a forced smile. "And here I thought I was getting my quiet house back."

Sid held out his small blue hand. "Ready, darling? Let's go dazzle the savages."

She took his hand. "Our amulets won't meld or something if we go through at the same time and blow us up, will they?"

Sid looked perplexed. "Nat," he called. "Any boom boom if go through together?"

"No. Quit worrying." Natalie waved them on. "Just don't take it off. That's almost the only thing that will make it explode."

"*Almost?*" Meaghan shouted. "What do you mean almost?"

With a laugh, Sid dragged her through the gateway into Fahraya.

CHAPTER 43

MEAGHAN HADN'T BEEN sure what to expect. Flashing lights, the sensation of moving at high speed, something dramatic.

But, no, Natalie had been right. It was like walking into another room. It was kind of anticlimactic. It didn't feel like another world. The sudden change in scenery might have been disconcerting, but it was so dark on the other side she couldn't see a thing.

Meaghan stepped on Sid's foot.

"Ow, watch it," he said.

"Can you see anything?" she asked.

"Of course I can. Oh, wait. Right. Humans have totally crappy night vision. I forgot. Grab the back of my jacket."

She reached down for his collar.

Sid chuckled. "My jacket, sweetie. Not my ass."

Meaghan let go like she'd been stung. "Are you standing on something?"

Near her, to her left, she heard John's voice. "No. Troon are bigger here. Sid is taller than me now."

"And I suppose you can see everything too with the super night vision?"

"Yeah, like this I can. I forgot how good I can see at night." John took a deep breath. There was the slightest tremor in his exhale. "Too good, I think for what there is to see."

She heard Sid's voice. "Hey, big guy, you okay?"

"Okay," John said. "So far. But I never walked here much, mostly flew, so I need to think about how we should go."

"C'mon, Dorothy," Sid said, grabbing her hand. "Follow me. I'll follow him. Can you see anything yet?"

"Not really, but it's not quite as dark. There's no moon. Where's the light coming from?"

"The rocks are phosphorescent in spots. It's not bright light, but it's enough. Even for human eyes once your night vision fully kicks in. Honestly, you humans, you're so high maintenance I don't know how you've done so well. You can't even see in the dark and the light at the same time."

They moved slowly, Meaghan stumbling over the rocks. There was the faintest hint of a trail, but in the dark she was having a hard time following it even with Sid's assistance.

"How far do we need to go?" Meaghan asked. Before Sid or John could answer, she stumbled over another rock and nearly fell. "God, I already hate this stupid place and I can't even see it."

"Doesn't get much better," Sid mumbled. "At least this way you can't see the wildlife."

"There's wildlife?" Meaghan asked, her voice rising a few notes. "Those scorpion things?"

"No," Sid said. "I'm just messing with you. If something

does show up, I'm sure John can kill it with his spear, right, big guy?"

"It's been a long time since I hunt." John's voice sounded distant even though he was standing only a few feet away. "Long time since I fly."

"Uh oh," Sid whispered. "We're already starting to lose him."

Meaghan picked her way carefully to where John stood. She slipped her hand into his. She could feel a faint tremor. "You okay? I can't imagine how hard this must be for you, but we need you to stay strong. Jamie needs you."

John sighed and squeezed her hand. "Zhara died over there." He pointed at a dark gash to their left. "Where the ground falls. They dropped her. She made no sound. No scream. Only falling."

Meaghan let go of his hand and slipped her arms around him. She had no idea what to say so she just held him close.

"They were waiting when I came through the gateway. They had Zhara and Jamie. She died first and didn't have to see what they did to me." His body stiffened and he pulled away. "It's quick to fly but slow to walk. We must keep going."

Without a sound he clambered up the rocks and within a moment disappeared in the gloom.

"Can you see him?" Meaghan asked Sid.

"Yeah. No problem. He's out ahead of us a bit, but I've got even better night vision than he does. This is going to get harder on him the closer we get, you know."

"Well, of course it is," Meaghan said. "He lost his wife, his whole way of life. The memories must be overwhelming."

"No. It's not the memories," Sid said. "It's the shame."

"But it wasn't his fault," Meaghan said.

"Try telling him that."

"But he was trying to help his people. There's no shame in that."

Sid sighed. "That's not the problem. It's his wings. He let them take his wings."

"He didn't let them do it," said Meaghan, indignant. "They did it to him. After torturing him for days. I saw the pictures."

Sid shook his head. "Doesn't matter. In his mind the fact that he's still alive means he didn't fight hard enough."

"But that's crazy. He had to stay alive for Jamie."

"No. You're looking at this like a human, not a Fahrayan. John doesn't think he saved Jamie. He thinks he shamed him. Which is why he let your father raise him. In John's mind, he wasn't a man anymore. He had no right to be a father."

"But what the hell was he supposed to do? They hurt him. On purpose. How does that shame anybody but V'hren?" Meaghan asked, furious. "John is better off human if this is how Fahrayans treat each other."

"Right," Sid said. "Because the same crap never happens in your world. John's like the hundred-pound girl who gets slut-shamed for not being able to fight off her two-hundred-pound rapist. It wasn't only his wings they took. They took his honor. They took his dignity. They took from him what made him a man. And he's been punishing himself ever since even though there wasn't any way he could have stopped them." Sid paused a moment to catch his breath and scan the horizon for John.

"They took everything from him but his life," Meaghan said, fighting back tears.

"Exactly," Sid said. "I think that's why V'hren was willing to let John go. If John had died, he'd be a martyr. Instead he's a joke. The wingless king. Just the sight of him walking into their camp will be enough to bring down the derision of all."

"Then he's not walking in. We are," Meaghan said. "You and me. John's our guide, but he shouldn't have to face V'hren. Once we get there, he can hang back and wait for us."

"Yeah, good luck getting him to do that. Facing V'hren is why he came." Sid scanned the horizon. "Dammit, where the hell is he? We're getting closer to the camp. I can see the glow of the cook fires from here." He pointed to the horizon. "See?"

"No," she said. "I can't see a damn thing. What the hell is he doing? He's just handing himself to them." She felt sick with fear. Even with all her doubts and the short time she'd known John, the thought of losing him was too painful to contemplate.

"Yes," Sid, said, serious now. "That's exactly what he's doing. He's offering himself in exchange for Jamie."

"But he can't," she said. "They'll kill him."

"And Jamie too if you can't convince V'hren to let him go. John chose this plan. It's what he always intended to do."

Her rising panic segued into fury. "Always intended? *Always intended?* He sure didn't act like it when he was getting all cozy with me on the back porch. He talked like we had a future, that sonofabitch. He's not dying here. I'm getting him home so I can kill him myself." Part of her was aware that she was spilling all this stuff to gossipy Sid, but she was too enraged to care.

"Ten years. Ten freaking years of celibacy," she ranted, "then his majesty slinks into my life with his sad blue eyes and his shy little smile, gets me all hot and bothered, and now he's going to hand himself over to these shitheads? No way in hell will I let that happen."

"Atta girl," Sid said. "I knew you wouldn't let John go without a fight. Even if it's him you're fighting. I always thought it was a stupid plan. So what's the new plan?"

"Get them both back. Kick everybody's ass. Do we have any element of surprise at this point?"

"Not if you keep hollering. My ears have almost stopped bleeding, thanks for asking."

Meaghan took a deep breath. "Sorry. I'm . . . it's . . . I'm upset."

Sid put an arm around her shoulder. In her head, he was still much shorter. She imagined him standing on a rock and her stomach felt better.

"Of course you're upset," Sid said. "I'm sorry. I thought you knew."

"Does everybody else know about John being a noble idiot?" She looked down to talk to Sid, then remembered she had to look up.

"No. Only me and Melanie. And now you. I sort of assumed John had talked to you."

"So Russ doesn't know," Meaghan said.

"No. He would have stopped John too. He has the same heart you have. Humans always want to believe there's another way."

"That's because a lot of times there is. I wish I could see something." She scanned the horizon, but all she saw were more rocks giving off their dim light in the blackness. "How far away are we?"

Sid screamed as something attacked her from behind. She felt a piercing pain in her arm and then everything went black.

CHAPTER 44

MEAGHAN HEARD SOUNDS, voices she thought, but unlike any she'd heard before. Like an aria written for fingernails on a blackboard. There was a music of sorts to it but at a frequency that felt like a chainsaw inside her skull.

The grating sounds jerked her out of her stupor. Now that she was fully conscious, the voices, while still not pleasant, were more bearable. Like a swarm of bees arguing with a tree full of cicadas. Her head would be aching from it, she thought, if her arm didn't hurt so much.

"Meaghan!" Sid cried. At least it sounded like him. It was still so dark she could barely see him.

"What the hell happened?" she asked. She tried to sit up, but the pain in her arm exploded and she fell back.

"You got bit by a . . . a thing," Sid said.

"A thing? Like a snake?"

"No. More like those scorpion thingies you hate so much." Sid took her hand. "You scared the shit out of me."

"Where are we?" She felt odd, feverish. Fatigue washed over her in waves.

"In a cave. They dragged you in here after John killed that thing."

She felt a sudden panic. John. She was supposed to be saving Jamie and John, not lying here like an invalid. She tried to sit up again. "John? Is he here?"

Sid pushed her down. "Lie still. Give it a chance to work."

"Give what a chance?" Meaghan's voice was weak and raspy. A spasm shook her. "What's happening to me? Where's John?"

"They gave you an antidote to the venom. But you need to lie still and let it do its thing."

"Who's they?" Her words slurred. The world spun and the blackness took her again.

When she awoke, gray daylight filled the cave and the pain in her arm had lessened. It still hurt but at a distance, like her arm was on the other side of the room. She felt lighter, like she could float. Float to the sky, she thought, like a big balloon. Like the Goodyear blimp. She giggled at the mental picture.

Meaghan sat up. Her arm felt much better. Someone, Sid probably, had dug the first aid kit out of her pack and bandaged the wound. Her head—it was like the opposite of a headache. She felt awesome. Her head felt huge and full of light and very far from the ground.

"Shit, I think I'm high," Meaghan said to no one and then started howling with laughter. Then she decided to simply howl. Which made her laugh even more.

"Ahem." A deep voice interrupted her.

Meaghan looked in the direction of the voice. Matthew,

but younger, his hair dark and eyes shining with the fierce light she remembered, sat on a rock a few feet away.

"Uh oh," Meaghan said. "Am I dead?"

"No, kiddo. I am." Matthew smiled at her. "About damn time."

"You're dead? I'm sorry." Meaghan knew she should be feeling grief, but he was right there talking to her, looking better than he had in years.

"Don't be. I was sick of being a turnip and you needed my help. So I died. Right after you walked through the gateway. I'd have been wearing diapers in a couple of weeks anyway. Like being a baby in reverse. Damn undignified way to go."

"So, you're really dead? I'm not just imagining this?"

Matthew shrugged. "Well, you are imagining it, I suppose. But that doesn't make it any less real or me any less dead."

Meaghan stared at him for a moment, then nodded. For now she'd take him at his word. She was too loopy to do anything else. She'd grieve when she got home, she knew. If she got home. "Okay. Am I asleep?"

Matthew shook his head.

"Am I high?" she asked.

"Like a van full of hippies on their way to a Dead show." He grinned. "It's the antidote. As much venom as you got, if you weren't impervious, you'd be dead. You only got the biological whammy, not the magical one too. But they needed to give you a lot more antidote than usual to counter it and the antidote includes some hallucinogenic mushrooms."

"Shouldn't I be seeing freaky stuff? I'm not seeing anything freaky but you. And even you look normal, except for being dead . . . and a lot younger." She giggled. "Shit, you're younger than me right now."

"I'm monopolizing your perception at the moment. It's the first time I'm communicating like this, and I'm not very good at it—taking up too much brain space. Otherwise you'd be seeing more freaky stuff."

"Seeing you this young is pretty freaky, Dad."

"For both of us, honey. Believe me. But hallucinations aren't the only things this stuff causes. This being a weird magical place, these particular mushrooms also have strong psychic properties."

"But I'm impervious."

"Psychic isn't magic. It's organic. Something in the brain. Everybody has the equipment, but most can't use it. This stuff activates it. But it's not magic."

Meaghan nodded. ESP was not a hard sell after everything else she'd encountered in the last week. "So are you going to have to jet out of here in a minute like Mom and Lou did?"

"Nope. Not now. I was hanging around hoping you'd take a nap so I could talk to you and then you conveniently got dosed with Fahrayan peyote. I can be here until you come back down." Matthew paused, serious now. "If you want me here, that is."

"Hell, yeah, I want you here," Meaghan said. "I don't have a clue how to deal with this mess. I'm sorry I was such a bitch for all those years."

Matthew waved his hand. "You weren't any bitchier than I deserved. No need to apologize. I'm sorry I was such a crappy father."

Meaghan smiled. "No need to apologize for you, either. I get it now. I'm too high to be mad."

"And I'm too dead to be mad. I've been this way for only a few hours and already I see how pointless all the resentment is."

She smiled back. "It really is. I love you, Daddy, and I'm glad you're here." She realized she was crying. "There I go again. But it's all good. I should have gotten bit by a giant scorpion and dosed with funny mushrooms years ago." An earlier part of the conversation finally caught up with her. "So, who exactly gave me this antidote?"

Matthew pointed at the entrance of the cave. "There he is now. The fugitive son himself. Meet Jhoro."

Tall, lean, and blond, Jhoro was as handsome as Jamie, despite the dirt and those crazy dreadlocks. He appeared to be clean shaven, which even in her impaired state she found odd. He certainly had plenty of hair on his head. His wings were drawn in close so she couldn't see much of them. He wore animal skin leggings and a loin cloth and that was it. Nothing covered him from the hips up but grime.

Meaghan struggled to her feet, gave him a goofy smile, and waved. "Hey gorgeous, thanks for the 'shrooms." And she started giggling again. She knew she should be more freaked out than she was, but everything was so funny. And sunny. And her brain was all runny. "I'm turning into Doctor Seuss," she said.

Jhoro looked over his shoulder and barked something with the singing buzzsaw voice she'd heard earlier. Sid appeared behind him, then dashed to Meaghan and threw his arms around her.

"Oh, honey, I was so worried, you've been out of it for

hours, and they weren't sure how the antidote would work on you." He paused to take a breath and then examined her face. "You're stoned off your ass."

"Oh, yeah. Like . . ." She looked over her shoulder to where Matthew was sitting. "Dad, how did you phrase it? Van full of hippies off to see the Dead?"

Matthew nodded.

Sid gripped her arms. "Meaghan, sweetie, who are you talking to?"

"My dad."

"Your dad's not here. He's back in Eldrich."

Meaghan shook her head to indicate no, then kept shaking it because it was fun. "Ooh, that makes me dizzy," she said and stopped. "No, he's here. He died a little while ago and now he's here as a . . . ghost? Spirit?" She looked back at Matthew. "What are you? Technically?"

"Hallucination, I suppose. Technically. Not that it really matters. No one can see me right now but you."

Meaghan looked back at Sid. "He says he's technically an hallucination."

"No kidding," Sid said, eyes wide. "What's in that antidote anyway?"

"Lots and lots of magic mushrooms," Meaghan said, smiling. "Well, not magic like *magic,* because that wouldn't work on me, but lots of fun druggy stuff. You going to introduce me to your smokin' hot friend over there?"

"Oh, right." Sid buzzed something at Jhoro and bowed. Jhoro bowed back and replied to Sid. Then Sid turned to Meaghan. "Meaghan, meet Jhoro, son of V'hren."

Meaghan giggled some more. Jhoro was disconcertingly handsome, even with the grime and animal skins. She waved again. "Hey. Pleased to meet you." The clean face in the midst of the Stone Age bothered her. She leaned closer to Sid and whispered. "How does he shave?"

"No body hair," Sid hissed back.

Meaghan's eyes widened. "None? Wow." She giggled, leaned closer, and whispered, "*Anywhere?*"

Sid shook his head. "We are so screwed."

Jhoro buzzed something at Sid, who nodded back. Jhoro stuck his head out of the cave, called to someone, and turned back. He spoke to Sid again.

Sid turned to Meaghan. "Meggy, you're a little too high to do what we need to do, so he's going to give you something to mellow you out a bit."

"Not if it means I can't talk to Dad. I need him on this. You tell him."

Sid shook his head. "Fine." More buzzsawing ensued and then Sid turned back to her. "He says that the drink won't keep you from speaking to your spirit guide. You'll still—as close I can translate this—see whole—but with less distraction."

Meaghan looked at her father. "What do you think?"

Matthew nodded. "Take it. I know the stuff he's talking about. I took a little trip of my own with John back in the day. You'll still feel good but a little more grounded."

Meaghan turned back to Sid. "Okey dokey, artichokey," she replied and burst out laughing again.

Sid shook his head in disgust.

"Don't get sniffy with me, Caffeine Boy," Meaghan responded. "I've seen you after too much coffee. The only thing different is the hallucinations. Unless coffee makes you hallucinate?"

"Coffee does not make me hallucinate," Sid said.

"Think of all the great stoned-out Meaghan stories you'll be able to tell."

"If we get home," he said.

"Nope," Meaghan replied. "When we get home. Trust me. I'm going to have a plan."

"You don't have it yet?"

"Nope. But I know I will." She grinned up at him. "Sid, honey, I can't get used to you tall. The plan is on its way. Can't you feel it? We're golden. We can't lose."

"That's the mushrooms talking."

"And they're talking sense. I say we listen."

Sid threw up his hands and walked away. Matthew laughed out loud.

Jhoro entered with a small cup, made from an animal horn or some type of bone. He held it out to her. She took it and sniffed. It smelled awful, like a dead fish wrapped in a dirty gym sock.

"Just throw it back," Matthew said. "It tastes like shit."

"Smells like it too." She held her nose and drank it down fast. And started to cough. "Damn, Dad. Calling this shit is an insult to shit."

Meaghan felt it work almost immediately. Like music from an audio speaker set too loud, the sensations in her head had been distorted. The awful drink dialed back her high enough so the distortion cleared. She still felt great but less giddy.

"Well?" Sid asked.

"Better. Still on a trip but at a more leisurely pace." She turned her head back and forth. There was a nimbus effect around objects that was new, but otherwise she felt relatively normal.

"Anything else I should expect?" she called to Matthew.

"Oh, yeah. The heavy psychic stuff should be hitting you any time now."

"There's more?" she asked. Before Sid or Matthew could answer, the psychic wave broke over her head, and the mysteries of existence were revealed. Speechless, Meaghan collapsed and the world grew black again.

CHAPTER 45

MEAGHAN WOKE UP knowing she'd received some profound truth, that she was the beneficiary of a greater wisdom than she'd ever known. If only she could remember what it was.

There was a moment of oneness, of completion, of . . . something. Like a dream she couldn't quite remember, it remained out of her grasp. She could feel the basic shape of it, how it made her feel, but the details dissolved like cotton candy.

"And now it's gone." Meaghan sat back up. "Shit."

"What's gone?" Sid asked. He crouched next to her, fear coming off him in waves. She could feel his fear, actually feel it. Like heat rising from a Phoenix sidewalk in July.

"Divine wisdom. Ultimate answer. Ultimate question. That kind of stuff. What was it Jhoro said—see whole? I did. All at once. And now it's gone." Had Matthew gone with it?

Her heart in her throat, she looked around the cave. Matthew stood near the doorway, leaning on a large boulder.

"Oh, thank God," she said. "Dad's still here." Turning back to Sid, Meaghan asked, "How long was I out this time?"

"Only a few minutes," Sid said, eyes wide.

"What happened? Something bit me, right?"

"One of those giant scorpion thingies came out of nowhere, stung you in the arm, and was going in for the kill." Sid shuddered. "Then John comes tearing up the trail, jumps on top of the thing, and skewers it with his spear."

"He killed it?"

"Oh, yeah. He was crazy frantic by the time he got to you. Then Jhoro and his guys appear from out of nowhere and bring you here. They'd been following us since we arrived."

"And they decided to help us?"

Sid shrugged. "I think they decided to help John. They were all pretty damn impressed at how fast he ran back up here and how quickly he killed that thing. They rely so much on their wings they don't have a real good sense of what they can do with their feet. John won back some respect, I think."

"Is he still here? Or does he still think handing himself over is a good plan?

Sid couldn't meet her eyes. "He left as soon as Jhoro told him you'd be okay."

Meaghan took Sid's hand. "Don't worry. I won't start ranting again. At least now we have some allies and I've still got Dad. Help me up. It's time we got moving. Where's Jhoro?"

"Outside."

"Is he coming with?" Before Sid could answer, Meaghan said. "Of course he is. I can feel it." She shut her eyes and concentrated, feeling for Jamie and John. She could sense individual lives pulsing all around her. She wasn't reading their minds, exactly, but she knew all she needed to know about them.

Jhoro felt like a roaring fire. He was easy to find. No fear there, only resolve and righteous anger. And love for John. Seeing his uncle again had freed something in his heart. But the rest of them—the fear was so pervasive it was hard to pick out individuals. The people of Fahraya were terrified and had been for a long time. Even Jhoro's companions struggled with it although the fear was tempered by their utter trust in Jhoro. They would follow him wherever he led regardless of their fear.

"Seeing whole," she murmured. So this is what Jhoro had meant.

Meaghan pulled Sid into a one-armed hug and, on tiptoes, planted a kiss on his blue cheek. She felt full of light. Her head no longer felt huge, because huge implied a boundary, something that could be compared to something else. Huge was a concept that simply didn't apply because there were no boundaries, no separation. Her mind contained and was embraced by the whole of creation.

Closing her eyes and breathing slowly, she concentrated. She soon found Jamie and John. Jamie, exhausted and racked with pain, struggled to hold back the despair that threatened to engulf him. He hadn't given up yet but couldn't hold out much longer. He was waiting for Meaghan to save him. She was his last hope.

For John had already given himself up, Meaghan knew, and had failed in his plan to offer himself for Jamie. Now they both were at the mercy of V'hren. She could feel John's shame pummel him like angry fists. He felt no fear for himself, only for Jamie, but his self-loathing cut through Meaghan like a knife. Whatever they were doing to him, it wasn't causing him physical pain, beyond bumps and bruises. He'd been roughed up a bit but wasn't being tortured like Jamie, not physically at least. His torment lay deep inside his mind.

Meaghan tried to let them know, deep in their bones, the way she knew them at this moment, that she was on her way and they'd soon be home. Then with a calm that would have astonished her only a day before, she put her fear and concern aside. She would crumble if she focused on their misery for too long. They needed her to be strong. She had to keep moving.

"Time to go, Dad," Meaghan said. "You too, Sid. I need you to translate."

Matthew nodded and walked out into the daylight.

"Are you still talking to your invisible father?" Sid asked.

"Yeah. Let's do this." She walked out of the cave and into the weak sunlight. The nimbus effect around each object was gone, replaced by a clarity of vision that made even barren, lifeless Fahraya look beautiful.

"Do what?" Sid asked, following close behind her.

"Save Jamie and John. Thwart V'hren. Help Jhoro. Liberate Fahraya."

"Are you high?"

Surveying the landscape, Meaghan said, "You know I am. Wow. With a head full of drugs, I'm liking this place a lot more. It's kind of beautiful, in its way."

"That's definitely the mushrooms talking. Think up that plan yet?"

Meaghan shook her head. "Not yet. But something will

come to me as we go along." She gave Sid a wide, dazzling smile. "Trust me."

"So says the stoned lady. What's Dad think about it?"

She turned to look at Matthew. He shrugged.

"He's noncommittal at the moment. Seriously, don't worry. I'm a lawyer. I'm always making up shit at a moment's notice." She heard Matthew snort with laughter as she looked around the deserted landscape. "Where is everybody?"

"Hiding, scouting, hunting—the usual stuff they do," Sid said. "There's only a few of them so they don't do a lot of hanging around. When you can fly you get gone in a hurry."

Meaghan frowned. "I thought they were coming with us. Sure felt like it."

Sid gave a hollow laugh. "They aren't suicidal. They're outnumbered and don't want to end up like John and Jamie. And despite taking care of you for the last few hours, they still don't trust you."

"Why not?" Meaghan asked. She was surprised that she didn't feel her usual indignation, only curiosity.

"You're a giant from the other world. They've spent their whole lives hearing what a threat humans are. Their whole society fell apart because of John buddying up with your dad."

"Hmm. Yeah. I can see why they'd think that." A thought began to churn in her head.

"I'm sure they're watching," Sid said. "If you do pull this amazing plan out of your ass, maybe then they'll side up with us. But I wouldn't count on them."

Meaghan ignored him. "Dad? What was that you used to say?"

"I used to say a lot of stuff, honey," Matthew said. "You need to be more specific."

"It was something like if you can't make people respect you, then at least make sure they fear you."

"Yeah, okay," Matthew said, his voice cautious. "Where are you going with this, Meg?"

Sid threw his hands in the air. "Here we go with invisible Dad again."

Meaghan ignored Sid some more. "I'm an evil giant wearing a nuclear necklace. An evil giant *lawyer* wearing a nuclear necklace. Scary things should be scared of me."

Matthew shook his head. "Don't joke about the amulet. I assume Natalie told you what will happen if you take it off? That's the kind of bluff you don't make unless you're ready to back it up."

"Well, it's not Plan A."

"So, what is Plan A?" Sid asked. "Please tell me you have an idea other than you exploding and taking us all with you."

"Plan A is the plan I haven't come up with yet."

Sid buried his face in his hands. "Oh, God. We're all gonna die."

"Don't be such a drama queen," Meaghan said. "We'll be fine." She pointed ahead of them. "That way. I can feel them."

CHAPTER 46

S ID HAD THE presence of mind to bring along Meaghan's backpack and refused to go until she drank a bottle of water and ate some of the food Russ had packed for her.

The food and water grounded her further. The loopy effects of the hallucinogens were finally gone, but she could still see Matthew and feel Jhoro. He wasn't far.

And she could feel stirrings of something else. Something wrong. She wanted to ask Matthew, but she could barely find the words to express it to herself. Meaghan finally dismissed it as anxiety. Even if her mind didn't have the sense to be afraid, her body knew what lay ahead.

The Fahrayan encampment may have been close by air, but for Meaghan and Sid it was a slow, arduous hike over the rocky terrain. There was no trail, only a haphazard path formed by empty spaces between the rocks. After half an hour of frustration, they stopped trying to walk around the rocky outcrops and scrambled over them instead.

"How long has John been with them you think?" she asked Sid. "It couldn't have been much faster going for him."

"You were out for hours after he left. If he waited until dawn to enter the camp, they've had him a couple of hours at least. Long enough to beat the shit out of him." Sid looked grim. "They only did half the job last time."

"That's not the feeling I'm getting. He's not in physical pain, at not least not yet. It's all mental. His plan to offer himself for Jamie didn't work and now he's torturing himself worse than they ever could. "

"For the only non-magical person around, you're sure getting creepy with the long-range sensor thing." Sid tripped and would have fallen if Meaghan hadn't grabbed his arm. "Can we stop a minute?"

"Sure. Want some water?

Sid shook his head. "I don't need it. Save it for yourself. You'll dehydrate long before I do. Got any other insights on John?"

Meaghan smiled at him. "I thought this psychic stuff was creepy."

"It is but in a useful way."

"What girl doesn't love to hear that," Meaghan said. "I'm creepy but useful."

Sid found a large flat boulder and sat. "Turns out these boots weren't make for walkin'," he groaned. "Look at it this way. Better creepy and useful than creepy and superfluous."

"I guess." She rubbed her arm.

"You hurting?" Sid asked.

"A bit. Not terrible."

"Hang in there," Sid said. "We gotta be getting close. Is Matthew still along for the ride?"

"Yeah. He says he likes Fahraya a lot better now that he's dead."

"Well, that's a comfort, I suppose. Maybe we'll like it better dead too."

Meaghan shook her head. "Sid, they have no fight with you. We may die, but you won't. So quit worrying."

"Yeah, no worries. Because there won't be any ass kicking waiting for me at home if I let you guys die." Sid stood up. "I'm in this to the end, same as you."

They trudged on in silence until they could detect the aroma of smoke and hear the murmur of voices. They crouched low and crept closer.

They almost fell over Jhoro. He grabbed them each by the arm and pulled them flat to the ground, next to him. In the cave, he hadn't been close enough for Meaghan to notice the stink. But here, lying next to him, she nearly choked from the physical assault on her sense of smell. Sweat, blood, and smoke all rolled together into a body odor that could peel paint off walls. Her eyes began to water.

"There you are," Meaghan said, breathing through her mouth. "I knew you were around here somewhere. You're going to help us." It wasn't a question. She could feel the resolve radiating from him. "Thank you."

Jhoro looked at her blankly. Sid translated. Jhoro flashed her a dazzling smile, whispered something to Sid, and crawled away. Considering the grime and stench, she was surprised by how perfect and white his teeth were.

"He said to stay here and he'll be right back."

Meaghan shook her head. "We need to get down there now."

"Don't worry. We'll be there soon enough."

Jhoro slunk back, this time accompanied by a dark-haired Fahrayan. Another looker, Meaghan couldn't help but notice.

Sid, Jhoro, and the other Fahrayan, who was called Finn, whispered back and forth for a while. Meaghan sensed a deep emotional bond between Jhoro and Finn. They'd been out here fighting together for years, Meaghan thought, so it made sense. There was something else between them, but before she could grasp it, Jamie's pain exploded in her mind, drowning out everything else. Meaghan curled into a ball, gasping, as electric agony burned along her spine. She could feel his screams as well as hear them.

They were slashing at his wings, hacking them from his body.

We're on our way, she told him as soon as she could think through the pain. Soon. I won't leave you here. I'm taking you home. She felt him teeter on the brink of defeat, then something stirred in him. She felt him dig deeper inside himself for strength. "Dad," she whispered.

"Right here," Matthew said, suddenly at her side.

"Can Jamie hear me? Can he sense me like I sense him?"

Matthew shook his head. "Probably not. If he does, it won't be anywhere near as strong and he won't know where it's coming from."

She had just gotten her breath back when John's shame knifed through her. Seeing his son suffer his fate was unhinging him, and driving him deeper into the abyss opening in his mind. She could feel his sanity slipping away. She was losing them both. She had to get down there.

She started to rise to her feet. Sid grabbed her and hissed something at Jhoro, who moved over to her. Meaghan simply stared at him. We don't need words for this, she thought. I'm going and you can either get out my way or kill me. You won't stop me any other way.

Jhoro scrutinized her with his deep blue eyes, so similar to John's and Jamie's.

After a long moment, he nodded and gestured for them both to go. He and Sid whispered back and forth for a minute, and then Jhoro crawled away.

Sid grabbed her arm. "We stay low until we're on the other side of this outcrop so they have time to get under cover. Then we walk down into the camp. They'll do what they can to help, but they won't sacrifice themselves."

Meaghan nodded. "Somebody needs to keep fighting. I get it. His obligation is to his men."

They crawled to the other side of the outcrop. All they had to do was stand up and they'd be plainly visible to the Fahrayans below.

"Ready?" Meaghan whispered.

"No," Sid hissed back.

"Too bad." Meaghan stood and waved at the crowd of Fahrayans. "Here we go."

CHAPTER 47

O N HER WAY down the rocky slope, Meaghan had time to ponder her aversion to scorpions and wonder whether she was giving them a fair shake. The one that bit her did her a huge favor. Even with a head full of drugs, Meaghan felt anxiety bloom in her gut. Without the high, she would have been batshit crazy with fear.

There were hundreds of Fahrayans, men and women, all of them beautiful and terrifying, clustered below them. The women were only marginally less intimidating than the men. Tall, strong, and armed to the teeth, they looked like angry Olympic sprinters. Not a fairy prince or princess in the bunch.

Except for the wings.

Meaghan now understood how someone could confuse a Fahrayan with a fairy.

It was the wings.

Up until now, Meaghan had only seen Fahrayan wings in relatively bad office lighting, old photos, and in a poorly lit cave. Nothing prepared her for how they looked fully extended in sunlight— delicate, iridescent, and utterly impossible. Even angels were portrayed with more solid, practical wings.

Someone already predisposed to see fairies would be so dazzled by those wings, particularly when sprouting from a tiny man or woman, that the Fahrayans' more unsavory characteristics—like the dirt and the smell and the razor-sharp stone weapons—could be easily overlooked.

You're the giant here, Meaghan reminded herself. Even if they're all taller than you right now. Don't let them rattle you.

She could feel Sid's terror rolling off him in waves. She took his hand. "I thought you were the Fahrayan expert."

"I learned Fahrayan from Melanie. And Jamie," he squeaked in a high strangled voice. "This is different."

"You aren't going to freeze up on me, are you?" Meaghan asked, already knowing his answer.

Sid puffed up a little, his vanity overcoming his fear. "I'm not going to freeze up. I've been in scarier places than this."

"Good, because I haven't. I'm counting on you and Dad to keep me on track. You're as big as these guys right now, remember?"

"Yes, but inside I'm still small. I'm like a Great Dane who thinks he's a Chihuahua."

"Yeah, but they don't know that."

"Somehow I think they do," Sid squeaked, his fear reasserting itself.

"Here's a secret," Meaghan said, squeezing his shaking hand. "They're even more scared than we are."

Terror swirled around her, monolithic and palpable. Within it, Meaghan could feel Jamie throbbing like an exposed nerve. He was close and aware that somebody was coming down the hill.

A Fahrayan woman stepped in front of Meaghan and buzzed something at her, scowling. The crowd closed in behind her.

"Keep moving," Matthew said to her. "Stare her down. Don't let her turn you back. You have to be the alpha dog here."

Sid swallowed hard and stopped, but Meaghan kept going, pulling him behind her, until she stood in front of the Fahrayan woman.

Meaghan stared up at her. The woman was several inches taller, younger, and appreciably more fit. Meaghan's only advantage was attitude. She knew backing down would be fatal. "Move," Meaghan said. "You won't turn me back. Don't even try."

The woman stood her ground and buzzed something back.

"She's says they don't want you here," Sid breathed.

"Too bad." Meaghan took a step closer, still staring. Eye contact was critical.

The Fahrayan woman fingered her stone knife, appraising Meaghan, who stared back.

Neither woman moved for a long moment.

Meaghan could feel the Fahrayan woman's terror under her surface arrogance. The woman was using all her control to master her fear but was close to cracking. Meaghan's intimidation evaporated. So much fear. Time for another approach.

"Let her save face," Matthew whispered.

Meaghan's glare softened. "My fight isn't with you. Please. Let me help them."

Taken aback, the woman stared a moment longer, then with a slight bow, stepped aside. Taking her cue, the crowd parted and provided Meaghan and Sid their first clear look at Jamie.

CHAPTER 48

MEAGHAN GASPED. EVEN though her new senses told her he was still alive, her eyes refused to believe it. There was so much blood. No one could be that battered and still live.

Naked, he slumped between two higher outcrops, his arms stretched over his head, tied by each wrist to what looked like bones hammered into crevices in the looming rocks. Ugly red gashes cut across his body, joining the crusted symbols the wizards had carved into his chest the day before. His wings, now cut from his back, hung like blood soaked curtains from the outcrops where they were tethered. Blood ran down his legs and puddled at his feet. His head was bowed and she couldn't see his face.

A man about John's age stepped forward, twined his hand in Jamie's hair, and jerked up his head. He leaned close to Jamie and spoke.

Jamie opened his eyes, vivid blue in his bloody, bruised face.

He saw Meaghan and smiled as best he could with cut and swollen lips. She felt hope and relief flare up in him again.

Then John's shame and guilt crushed her so hard she felt her knees buckle and she would have fallen if Sid hadn't supported her.

John was kneeling nearby, hands bound behind his back, head down, a stone spear tip pressed against the nape of his neck. She knew he registered her presence but was too ashamed to look at her. She could feel the madness biting into him, could sense the deep, dark pit into which his mind had been cast. In his present state, John was no help at all.

"Time for that plan," Sid hissed.

"Yes, Meg, it's time," Matthew said to her. "Trust yourself."

"Is that V'hren?" Meaghan asked, inclining her head in the direction of the man who still gripped Jamie's hair.

"I don't know," Sid said.

"Yes," said Matthew.

"It's him," Meaghan confirmed for Sid.

She closed her eyes, feeling out toward V'hren.

The oddness she'd sensed on the hike from the cave, the unsettling energy she'd dismissed as anxiety, now hit her but a thousand times stronger than what she'd felt before. Something twisted and vile, living but not alive, something wrong in every way a thing could be wrong assailed her now, and it was all she could do not to fall to the ground, curled in a ball, weeping in terror.

She took a deep breath and tried to steady herself. "V'hren's dead. Or as good as. I don't know what that thing is, but it's not human or Fahrayan. Even if V'hren's still alive in there, something else is in charge."

Matthew grimaced. "Whatever it is it's strong and it doesn't want me here." He began wavering like she'd seen her mother and Lou do in her dreams. "I'm sorry. I'll try to get back. You can do this."

And then he was gone.

Meaghan was alone. It was all on her now.

She tried to quell her panic, but it was raging like a wildfire. If it weren't for Jamie's wordless plea, deep in her mind, she would have turned and fled. Instead, her body shaking, Meaghan took a step forward. She was having a hard time controlling her legs and her breath was shallow and ragged. The horrible presence began to wrap tendrils around her mind. She felt doubt and fear and self-loathing churn inside her. She fought it, pushing it away, but it continued to search for a way in.

The V'hren thing grinned at her, the cruel twist of his lips a mockery of a smile. He stared into Meaghan's eyes, his blue eyes washed out and flat like a corpse. Once he was sure he had her attention, he pulled Jamie's head back even farther with the hand still twined in his hair. He drove the heel of his other hand into Jamie's face.

Jamie cried out in pain, blood bubbling from his broken nose.

Meaghan felt a fierce wave of maternal protectiveness rush through her, scouring away her panic like a desert flash flood scoured a canyon, replacing it with a righteous anger. The probing presence in her mind recoiled and fled.

"Enough," Meaghan shouted. Her heart raced. She was still shaking but from adrenaline now, not fear. Her instinct to protect Jamie was so pure, her anger so fiery, it left no room inside her for fear, no room in her mind for the thing that stood before her.

V'hren's cruel leer melted from his face. For a moment he looked shocked and unsure, then his vicious smile returned. But Meaghan could see it was forced, that she had unnerved him when she pushed him from her mind.

Fear, she thought. It's my fear he wants. She remembered what Caleb had said about the thing he called the Power feeding on fear. Whatever it was, it had consumed V'hren so effectively that it now wore him like a coat. But Caleb had also said it didn't like its food to fight back, that it didn't like the fierce rage now coursing through her.

When angry, Meaghan had the tendency to let her mouth get out ahead of her brain. Over the years, she had damaged relationships beyond repair with vicious words and had learned through bitter experience when to bite her tongue. She had to stay cool. Fahrayans respected strength. She couldn't let them see her lose control. To Sid, she said, "Start translating."

She stood tall, chin lifted. With the most imperious air she could muster, she began to speak. "I am Meaghan Keele and I come from the other world. Eighteen years ago, you entered into a treaty negotiated and signed by my father, Matthew Keele, a treaty you are now violating. Release these men," she said, gesturing at John and Jamie, "allow us safe passage back to the gateway, and in return, I will allow your world to survive."

Sid was translating as fast as he could. But V'hren's sudden cold laughter told Meaghan that V'hren knew what she'd said without the translation. Everyone else was looking at Sid. V'hren and Jamie were looking at Meaghan.

John's head was still bowed, but Meaghan noticed that the guard had pulled back the spear a bit. Damn it, John, she shouted at him in her mind, snap out of it. I need you.

V'hren confirmed her suspicions by answering her in English. A buzzing, sizzling, harmonic- laden English, but lacking his brother's thick accent and stilted syntax. "Go ahead and destroy this world. I'm almost done with it. Soon, I'll see your world burn too and you with it. Power-less. Lonely. Afraid. I know what you feel for them, would-be husband and would-be son, and I'll destroy them both— slowly—while you watch." He looked at Jamie in disgust. "I'm almost done with this one. Even weaker than his father."

"I knew you weren't V'hren," Meaghan said. She'd been right all along. Something else was pulling the strings. "I think I know what you are and I'm not afraid of you. Hurt them anymore and I will find a way to end you. Count on it."

V'hren smirked at her and then surveyed the crowd with-out speaking.

Meaghan glanced over at John. His head now up, he stared at V'hren through narrowed eyes. Meaghan felt a thread of defiance weave itself into John's shame. It wasn't much, but it gave her an opening.

The guard standing behind John stared at V'hren in con-fusion at the strange sounds coming out of V'hren's mouth. Taking advantage of V'hren's inattention and the guard's befuddlement, Meaghan ran to John. She lifted his face in her hands. This close she could feel how the thing inside V'hren had wrapped itself all around John's mind.

Magic, Meaghan thought. The bastard was using magic,

like John suspected. And it wasn't only John he was hexing. Now that Meaghan knew what to feel for, she sensed V'hren's tendrils twisting through the minds of the assembled Fahrayans. V'hren's magic mind control activated the fear and the fear fed the magic, creating a vicious feedback loop.

His magic didn't work on Meaghan, but V'hren had kept trying enter her mind until her furious intent to protect Jamie forced him to retreat. Maybe magic wasn't required to pull V'hren from John's mind. Maybe strong emotion could do it.

She didn't need the extra psychic boost to tell her what John needed most—forgiveness and a way forward. He needed to once again want something for himself.

Maybe some evil spells could be broken with a kiss.

Time for someone in Eldrich to win the pool, she thought.

Meaghan tilted up his face and bent over him. She brushed her lips against his cheek, then whispered in his ear, "He can't have you. You're mine." She gave him a gentle kiss. She pulled back and looked at him. No reaction.

Fairy tales used to be a lot darker, she knew. The chaste kiss was the sanitized stand-in for more primal behavior. In the oldest tales, the prince woke Sleeping Beauty with a body part other than his lips. In a few versions, the prince, like a drink-spiking date rapist, didn't bother to wake her at all.

Meaghan was no princess, John wasn't particularly charming, and both had lost their innocence a long time ago. Screw the Disney version. She pushed down on his shoulders. His knees bent until his backside rested on his heels. She straddled him and pressed her breasts against his chest. Wrapping her arms and legs around him, she kissed him again. This time she opened her mouth, used her tongue, and took her time. In a moment, he began to kiss her back. She felt V'hren flinch and withdraw. John's shame and guilt evaporated, replaced by desire.

John was back in the game.

CHAPTER 49

MEAGHAN HEARD V'HREN shouting but she kept kissing John until the guard pulled her off him. John wore a big goofy grin. She could feel joy and lust rolling off him in alternating waves.

The spell—V'hren's spell at least—was broken.

Meaghan smiled back at John. She felt great, her initial euphoric confidence returned. With an imperious glare, she shook off the Fahrayan guard and strutted over to Sid, who was staring at her with his mouth open. "I told you I'd have a plan," she said. "Translate everybody both ways. I want V'hren's people to hear everything."

The assembled Fahrayans looked back and forth between her and V'hren, as confused as John's guard had been. Meaghan reached her new senses out to the mob, moving beyond the noise in her head made by Jamie, John, and Sid. Fear predominated, but under it she could feel the faint stirring of other emotions. Disbelief, anger, disgust, worry, compassion, hope—all sparked throughout the crowd of Fahrayans. Not much, but enough that with some fanning she might be able to coax a flame.

V'hren spoke to the mob in Fahrayan, as Sid translated for Meaghan. "My people, you see how the false king and false prince flaunt their complicity with the giants. They violate our laws, they violate the treaty I made with them. It was out of love that I spared my brother and his son those many years ago. His son now invades our world, plots against me, lays the groundwork for an invasion by the giants. My brother follows him, the emissary of the giants at his side. You witnessed their brazen display. You heard her threaten to destroy our world."

When Sid reached the final sentence of his translation he looked over at Meaghan and grimaced.

"Damn it," she muttered to Sid. "He got me on that one." She could hear the murmur of the crowd, felt some of them wanting to believe V'hren. But in many others, she felt a subtle vibration of doubt.

Their bullshit meters are starting to register, she thought. V'hren screwed up by speaking English. Let's see if he's dumb enough to make the same mistake twice.

Meaghan turned so that she could address V'hren and the crowd at the same time. "There appears to be a mistranslation." She looked over at Sid and mouthed "Sorry." He nodded.

"What I intended to say," she continued, "is that if you release them now and allow us safe passage home, I will not destroy *you*." She glared at V'hren. "I was threatening you, V'hren, not them." She swept her arm toward the crowd. "We have no complaint with your people. Only with you."

Meaghan had spent a few years as a criminal prosecutor, long enough to know how to sell her case. She moved closer to the crowd. Time to work them like a jury. "Your king's version of the truth is a lie. A flat-out lie and he knows it."

She pointed an accusing finger at V'hren. "Your king sent dark wizards to seize the prince, to kidnap him from his home." This drew a collective gasp from the crowd when Sid translated it. "They hurt the prince's wife. They threatened his children. They likewise attacked me in my home, but I drove them back in a bloody battle."

Meaghan paused a beat to let Sid catch up and the words sink in. The last bit wasn't exactly a lie, she thought. Yes, it was only one wizard and he was a half-starved kid that any self-respecting Fahrayan could have snapped in half, but there was blood from his nose after she hit him with the saucepan. So, close enough.

"The prince has no plan to invade," she continued. "No plan to return to Fahraya at all. He has a human family—a wife, a daughter, an infant son. He is a respected and important man in our world. The king bases his allegations solely on the prince's temporary transformation to his Fahrayan form. A transformation forced on him by a witch working for the dark wizards." Another gasp rose from the crowd. "Directed by the wizards, this witch tore from the prince's throat the amulet he wears in our world to take our form and size."

The crowd murmured. She could feel their outrage beginning to rise. They had been afraid for so long that it was a feeble anger but enough to visibly weaken V'hren, at least to Meaghan's informed eyes. He staggered slightly as he moved away from Jamie to address the crowd.

"She lies," he shouted in Fahrayan. "She and my brother, the traitor, traveled willingly through the gateway in violation of a treaty that protects you from the giants."

Meaghan continued, her voice calm and steady. "A treaty already broken by this man." She pointed the accusing finger again. "A treaty broken by this man in his attempts to manufacture grounds on which to bring the prince here." She paced back and forth. "The dark wizards hired by this man . . ." She pointed again. "They entered the prince's house through deceit and tore him from his bed where he lay with his wife. They beat him. They bound his hands. They tortured him with their dark magic, carved their evil symbols into his flesh, and tried to cut his throat when he resisted. He fought them bravely and fiercely but was finally overcome by their magic. The prince only entered Fahraya because he was forcibly pushed through the gateway."

She paused again for Sid to catch up. V'hren was seething but said nothing. Meaghan had him. Plain and simple. The crowd was nodding as she spoke. She was winning them over.

"I freely admit that John and I entered the gateway. We had no choice. What father would leave his son to such a fate? What father would not do everything he could to protect his son and save his life?"

The father standing in front of you, she knew many of the Fahrayans were thinking. *The one who would torture his own son to death if he could only get his hands on him.* She stared back, at her ease, as V'hren glowered at her. *You opened the door, moron*, she thought, *and you let me walk right through it.*

The guard standing behind John had lowered his spear

again, his attention fixed on Sid as he translated Meaghan's words. John rose to his feet. The guard lifted the spear, barked a few words, and stepped forward. John whirled and glared at him. The guard lowered the spear, stepped back, and stared at the ground. A second guard held up both hands, palms toward John, and said something to him. John nodded and the second guard approached him and cut his hands free.

Now free from V'hren's influence and free from his guards, John strode over to Meaghan. Even dressed in clothes sewn out of rags and remnants from somebody's quilting bag, John looked richer and grander than the skin-clad Fahrayans. Except for the lack of wings, he looked every bit the king he'd once been.

"You are not my brother," he said to V'hren in English. His extra vocal cords added the strange harmonics Meaghan had heard in V'hren's voice but without the buzz. Whatever V'hren now was, he wasn't accustomed to speaking English, despite his proficiency. V'hren knew English better than John but wasn't as good at speaking it with a Fahrayan voice. "Who are you?"

"Your worst nightmare, you pathetic drunk."

John barked a grim laugh. "You do not come close to my worst nightmare. My worst nightmare is seeing my Zhara fall silent from the sky and hearing her hit the ground. For a long time I thought there was nothing worse. Until today. Until I see what you do to my son."

"You wingless freak," V'hren hissed.

"Wings you cut from my back." He turned his head and smiled at Meaghan. "Wings I don't need anymore. Not as a human man." He returned his attention to V'hren, pinning him with his cool, regal stare. "I wonder now, was that

V'hren who did that or you? When did you slither into his mind? Were you in him even then?"

And V'hren fell for it. John dangled the bait and V'hren leaped. Meaghan was impressed.

"I didn't own him yet, but I was close. Watching. Whispering in his ear. But what he did to you was all him, his choice, out of his free will. His bitterness, his fear, his darkness, his cruelty. All those things he gave to me in one bloody banquet, a meal that let me claim him as my own. But I was the one who let you and your whelp live because it suited me. All that shame and guilt and self-destruction. I was aging you like fine wine. Then you met *her*." He glared at Meaghan, then twisted his lips into that mockery of a smile. "If it's any consolation, your brother has suffered more than you over the years. He still lives deep inside me, feeding me, a parasite I will not let die because his misery amuses me."

Meaghan registered Sid translating all this into Fahrayan in the background. So, finally, did V'hren. He turned to Sid and screamed, "Stop." When Sid didn't stop, V'hren waved his hands, screeching something that didn't sound like English or Fahrayan. He made a slashing motion, like the one Meaghan had seen Emily make, and Sid dropped to the ground.

CHAPTER 50

MEAGHAN SCREAMED. MORE loud gasps and cries from the crowd. She heard Jamie shouting.

She ran to Sid and dropped to the ground next to him, shaking his body. "Can you hear me?"

No response. She had no idea where to feel for a pulse so she placed her hand on his chest, in the middle of his Hello Kitty T-shirt. She felt his lungs rise and fall and rise again.

Meaghan sagged with relief. At least Sid was still alive. "He's breathing," she shouted loud enough for John and Jamie to hear.

John nodded, then glared at V'hren. "You are even more stupid than my brother. You hexed him. Like a wizard. Now they all know you're not one of us."

The mood of the crowd was audibly shifting. Meaghan could hear the angry buzzing, like a swarm, their fear giving way to anger. V'hren tried to attack John but stumbled and fell to one knee.

John turned to the crowd and spoke to them in Fahrayan.

Meaghan took advantage of V'hren's distress to move closer to Jamie. He was conscious, his breath loud and ragged. But he was so exhausted his legs could no longer hold him up. His hands were stark bluish white, the blood cut off by the unsupported weight of his body hanging from his wrists.

Meaghan rifled through the pack for Matthew's old clasp knife. Russ had added it to the pack "just in case." She found it, dropped the pack, and ran to Jamie. He was too tall for her to stand at ground level and reach the leather thongs binding him.

She gripped the folded knife between her teeth and with adrenaline-fueled strength, she scrambled up one of the outcrops. She slipped and felt a sharp stab in her knee and the skin scrape off her right palm. She ignored the pain. If she didn't get those thongs cut, Jamie could lose the use of his hands.

Finally, high enough to reach him, she opened the knife and cut the thong binding his right hand, leaving all his weight on his left wrist. Meaghan slid down the outcrop, her hands slick with blood, and her legs shaking. She knew she wouldn't have the strength to climb the other one.

Wrapping her arms around him, she tried to hold him up enough to take the strain off his still-bound left hand. "I can't make that climb again. I'm sorry."

"You kissed my father," he rasped. "What the hell was that?"

Struggling to support his weight, she said, "I had to get that thing out of his head. You can yell at me when we get home. Right now, we got bigger problems."

He stared at her a moment, then said, "Give me the knife."

Meaghan used her shirt to wipe off the blood from her torn palm and pressed the knife into Jamie's freed hand. Leaning on Meaghan, panting with the effort, his fingers numb and clumsy, Jamie sawed at the thong until it snapped. He and Meaghan fell to the ground in a heap.

She held him close for a long moment. "I've got you," she whispered in his ear. "I won't let him hurt you anymore." She felt his body shudder against her. "I've got you."

Pulling away from him, she cradled his battered face in her hands. "Can you translate for your father? I need to know what he's saying."

Jamie nodded. "I'll try. My Fahrayan's pretty rusty. He was repeating what Sid translated before . . ." He swallowed hard. "What V'hren just said. And he's telling them that something evil has infected V'hren. Something that's been in charge of him for a long time."

"How are they taking it? Do they believe what John's saying?"

"They saw V'hren hex Sid." Jamie's eyes filled with tears. "Is he okay? It's my fault he's here and—"

Meaghan cut him off. "He's okay for now. He's here because he's your friend and wanted to help." She pulled Jamie closer. "None of this is your fault. None of it. I know you're tired and hurt and want to go home, but we—me, your dad, and Sid—need you to keep it together for a little while longer. Can you do that?"

Jamie nodded.

V'hren regained his feet and began speaking to the crowd.

Jamie tried to translate as V'hren spoke. "Um . . . the giant she brings evil magic and tries to make you see things that aren't there. I'm your king. Would you believe the . . . wingless one over me?" Jamie stopped, exhausted with the effort. "They hit me hard a few times on my ear and I think they messed it up. There's a lot of ringing and it's hard to hear. I need to get closer."

Meaghan nodded. "Can you stand?"

"If you help me." With a grimace and a few pained grunts, Jamie got to his feet. Supported by Meaghan, he hobbled closer, then sank to the ground.

She grabbed her backpack and pulled out her remaining water bottle, uncapped it, and handed it to him.

With shaking hands, he held the bottle to his mouth and drained it. "Better," he said.

Meaghan surveyed the crowd. Most were transfixed by V'hren and John, but a few were staring at Jamie. She realized she couldn't feel their emotions anymore. The drugs had worn off. She was alone in her head for the first time in hours. She had to know what V'hren was saying.

She sat down on the ground behind Jamie, supporting him with her body, arms around him like she'd hold a small child on her lap. She could feel the blood from the stumps of his wings soaking through her shirt and bra, but if he couldn't lean back on her, he'd collapse. "I need you to keep translating."

He slumped against her, wincing as her shirt rubbed the raw wounds on his back, and nodded. "Um . . . liar, false king, he tries to steal back what he lost by consorting with the giants . . . oh shit, he noticed you cut me down. He's calling the guards."

Meaghan felt Jamie tense and curl into her. The shaking became shuddering and she didn't need a head full of mystic mushrooms to feel his terror. She wrapped her arms around him and held him tight, feeling that fierce maternal protectiveness sweep through her again. If the guards came, she'd fight for him to her last gasp.

But the guards didn't move. They wore the same narrow-eyed scowl she'd seen on John's face when V'hren has first spoken to her in English.

"Look," she said to Jamie. "They aren't obeying him."

Jamie didn't respond. He was unravelling in front of her eyes. The pain and terror of the previous day and night, combined with the physical toll on his body from injury and blood loss, were overwhelming him. That he was still functional at all was testament to his extraordinary strength, but he was at the far reaches of that strength. She hated having to ask him to give more, but without Sid, and without her drug-induced extra sense, Jamie was her only link to the battle of wills going on between John and V'hren.

"Honey, I know you're exhausted and in pain and it's not fair of me to ask, but I need you to keep going. I know it's hard, but I need to know what they're saying."

With a moan, Jamie lifted his head and nodded. "My father is telling them why he went to Eldrich in the first place. Better life, food, water. He's telling them that I didn't want to come back here. He's telling them about . . . he met Patrice and my kids?" Jamie looked up at her, shocked.

"After you got grabbed. They hid out at his house while I tried to stop the wizards at the gateway. They're at my house now. The kids love him and he really helped Patrice keep it together after they took you. He stepped up. I'll tell you more later, but now I need to know what he's saying."

"He says he doesn't want to be their king either, knows he can't because he's not a Fahrayan man anymore. But there's another . . . Jhoro? My cousin? He's still alive?"

Meaghan nodded. "Yeah. He helped save my life after a scorpion attacked me. He's close, watching and waiting for his moment."

"This would be a good moment," Jamie murmured.

V'hren glared at Meaghan and Jamie.

Meaghan glared right back. You don't scare me, she repeated like a mantra. You don't scare me.

But he scared Jamie, who buried his face in Meaghan's shoulder and began to sob. V'hren's face screwed up into that rictus of a smile as Jamie's terror flowed into him. He'd found a new food source.

Meaghan felt hatred for V'hren flare in her chest. This was a different anger than she'd felt earlier. Before it had been pure, fueled by her desire to protect Jamie. This was darker and revolved around her sudden desire for revenge, to hurt V'hren like he'd hurt Jamie, who now clung to her like a terrified child.

V'hren stood taller, a gleam in his eye.

He enjoyed the taste of hatred too.

Jamie, she thought. She had to focus on protecting Jamie. The anger that surprised and weakened V'hren had come from a place of protection and love, not hate and fear. The thing inhabiting V'hren had mentioned how much it enjoyed the original V'hren's bitterness and cruelty, and John's shame. And now her hate.

If negative emotions fueled him . . . In a sudden flash of understanding, she let all the pent-up maternal desire, all the longing she'd stuffed so deep inside her since she'd lost her chance to be a mother, rush over the young man weeping in her arms. A fierce love for Jamie swept through her and she rocked him like a baby.

"Shh. I won't let him hurt you anymore." Now she was weeping too, overcome by the feeling rushing through her. She looked up at V'hren and saw the shock on his face.

Meaghan thought about the suffering the thing controlling V'hren continued to inflict on what remained of the actual man. V'hren, who felt abandoned and passed over, who had only wanted what he thought belonged to him, who had enforced against John's family what John conceded was valid law. V'hren, who even now writhed in torment deep within this creature who wore his skin. V'hren, who, even in the depth of his bitterness and despair, with a monster whispering in his ear, had spared the woman he once loved not from death but at least from the more hideous aspects of the fate to which her husband's actions had consigned her.

Meaghan knew firsthand how loss could twist a person. In her case, she'd closed herself off from human contact and spent ten long lonely years refusing even to feel her pain, growing colder and harder with each day. She could have chosen to channel her longing into another course, she could have given that love to a child who needed it, she could have given it to friends, to family. Instead she grasped her hurt close like a bitter treasure to be protected at all costs, the highest cost being her loss of a functioning heart.

She felt a flicker of compassion for V'hren. What he'd done had been monstrous, but he had paid for it, continued to pay in unimaginable torment as a prisoner inside his own body. He had done terrible things, not because it amused him, like the creature now controlling him, but out of fear and pain and loss, manipulated by a monster. And he'd been denied any chance at all to atone for what he'd done. Maybe if this thing hadn't been whispering in V'hren's ear, darkening his thoughts, maybe none of this would have happened.

Meaghan looked V'hren in the eye and let the compassion grow into a warm flame.

V'hren shrieked with rage.

"Don't hate him," she shouted to John. "It makes him stronger."

"I don't hate him," John answered. "I pity him, at least what is left of him. He was not always bad. Not as a boy. And this *thing*, that wears him." He gestured dismissively at V'hren. "Hating it is like hating a disease. It can't help what it is."

V'hren whirled on John, desperate now. "I can give them back to you," he said in English. "I can give you back your wings and make you a man again. All you have to do is ask. I have the magic to do it."

John wavered. "My wings?" His eyes narrowed. "What is . . . how do you say . . . the catch?"

"Give me your son. His life for your wings. Let me finish the ritual. They won't even have to know you agreed to it. You can be king again."

Meaghan felt Jamie stiffen in her arms.

John said nothing, staring at V'hren, his expression unreadable.

Jamie moaned in fear.

Meaghan held him close. "Don't you dare even think it," she said. "He'd never do that to you. He loves you. You're worth a lot more to him than wings." She hated herself for it, but she felt a tiny trickle of doubt as John's silence continued. He wouldn't, she thought, feeling sick. He couldn't, could he?

Finally, John shook his head, a sad smile on his face. "That's not worth even an answer. How can you ask me such a thing?

What father would do this to his son? I would not give him to you even to save my own life. If I let you have him, I will have no life even if I still live." He snorted. "Wings. You're a fool. Like my brother. There is more to being a man than wings. Better a wingless freak than the twisted thing you would make me. A thing like you."

John now gazed on Meaghan and Jamie, huddled together. "I think, brother, I understand you now. I came here to offer my life for my boy to go free. And you laughed at me, made the people laugh at me, and you crawled inside my mind, burying me in my shame. And I let you do this to me, because I thought it was what I deserved. But now I know why you wouldn't kill me in his place. You can't let me give myself to die for him because it's a good death. It has honor. It gives you no way into me, no way to take me like you did my brother. But, if you can get me to trade my son, let you hurt him more and kill him, for my wings? This act is so evil it would let you enter me and have a way into the human world. I think this is your plan. To use Fahraya to get to the human world."

John smiled at Meaghan, the broad free smile that made the years and pain drop away from his face. "She doesn't need me to have wings. Why feel shame for losing something I don't need any more? I don't need wings to be a man, Fahrayan or human, no matter what anyone thinks."

And I don't need a womb to be a mother, Meaghan thought. Just a functioning heart. "See?" she murmured in Jamie's ear. "I told you. He loves you. It's time to get you home."

CHAPTER 51

MEAGHAN HEARD A voice speaking Fahrayan. Fal-tering at first but growing stronger. She craned her head around to see Sid, sitting up as he spoke. She felt a dizzying rush of relief.

Sid dragged himself to his feet and, still speaking, walked toward John. He gave V'hren a contemptuous look, and once at John's side, grabbed his hand and raised it victoriously.

"What's he saying?"

Jamie, who seemed energized by Sid's recovery, pulled himself up and sat without support. "He's telling them about the deal and about my father turning it down flat and why."

The murmur of the crowd grew louder. After eighteen years of living in fear of V'hren, of having their thoughts clouded by magic, the Fahrayans were waking up, many nodding as Sid spoke, and staring at John with growing admiration.

And then V'hren made his move. Much like it had when Meaghan witnessed Emily attack Jamie, time seemed to slow.

She saw V'hren pull a stone knife from his belt and run at John, knife raised, as Meaghan screamed a warning. Sid and John, turning toward her, saw V'hren nearly on top of them. Sid, who in his present form was bigger than John, shoved John aside as V'hren swept his hand down to strike. Instead of hitting John, V'hren plunged his knife into the middle of Sid's chest. Sid fell to the ground.

Jamie and Meaghan both screamed. Even in Jamie's weakened state, Meaghan had to use all her strength to keep him from throwing himself at V'hren. John rose to his feet, and in one flowing movement, plucked the knife from Sid's chest, grabbed V'hren, and cut his throat.

And for a moment, silence. It had all happened so fast that it took a moment for the crowd to register what John had done. Then, a collective gasp rose, and they erupted— cheering, crying, screaming.

John ignored the pandemonium and tossed the knife away, dropping to his knees at Sid's side. Meaghan pulled Jamie to his feet and half-supported, half-dragged him to where Sid lay.

Sid's eyes were open as he smiled up at John. The pink T-shirt was soaked with the blue blood that oozed from the hole in his chest. "Is Jamie okay?" he wheezed. He began to choke and John put his arms around him and pulled him up into a semi-reclining pose. Sid coughed spasmodically, then spit up more blue blood. He was drowning inside.

Jamie grabbed his hand. "Hey, buddy. I'm here. You hang on until we get home and Natalie can fix you up."

Sid shook his head. "I'm done, sweetie. Circling the drain. But your shithead uncle's going with me, so it's all good." More coughing shook him. "Where's Meg?"

Meaghan took his other hand. "Right here. Don't you talk like that. You're going to be fine." Even as she said it, she knew it wasn't true. Sid was dying in John's arms. Even if John and Jamie could still fly, they wouldn't be able to get him to the gateway in time to save him. As it was, without help, it would be a grueling trek simply getting Jamie over the rocky pathless terrain to the gateway, let alone Sid.

With all eyes focused on Sid, V'hren was forgotten. Then Meaghan registered the screaming from the crowd. Sid's eyes widened and he gave a thready hoot. Meaghan followed his gaze and saw V'hren, standing, covered in the blood that ran from his gaping throat. John had nearly decapitated him. But there he stood, his mouth twisted into a horrible parody of a smile.

As Meaghan screamed, one of V'hren's bloody lifeless hands shot towards Jamie and twined itself into his hair. V'hren pulled Jamie onto his knees and dragged him away from Sid. V'hren's other hand clasped the stone knife John had discarded. A hideous grin stretched across his dead face, he lifted the knife to strike.

Then a figure swooped down, like a giant bird of prey attacking, and pulled the knife from V'hren's hand, knocking him to the ground.

Jhoro had finally chosen his moment.

Matthew had described a Fahrayan warrior in flight as a "helluva thing." Try glorious, Meaghan thought. Terrifying, awe-inspiring. And sexy as hell. No wonder they equated losing their wings with losing their manhood. Nobody who was proportionally sized would ever mistake Jhoro for a child-like fairy.

V'hren stood up again, like a zombie in a bad horror

movie. Jamie scrambled away on hands and knees as fast as he could, a look of horror on his battered face. V'hren took several fast steps and reached for the back of Jamie's neck. His dead fingers grabbed but couldn't get a grip.

Jhoro swooped out the sky, wrapped a muscular arm around V'hren's neck, and pulled him into the air. A few wing strokes took them to the rocks surrounding the natural bowl where the assembled Fahrayans watched, transfixed. Jhoro made a lazy circle, climbing the air currents to about fifty feet above the ground, and then he dropped V'hren's struggling corpse.

For a corpse it had to be. Meaghan had seen up close how deep and savage the cut across V'hren's throat had been. John had struck a killing blow that V'hren could not have survived. Whatever inhabited him now manipulated his body through dark magic or sheer force of will.

Meaghan held her breath, waiting to see if V'hren would rise yet again.

He didn't disappoint. After a quick moment on the ground, V'hren launched himself into the air, his wings broken and askew but still effective. He shot towards Jhoro, who watched in horror as his father's corpse flew toward him. Jhoro hovered until the last moment, then he dove straight downwards at speed. V'hren howled in rage and dove after him.

A moment before he reached the ground, Jhoro did a tight forward roll so his feet now faced downward. He braked slightly with his wings. Using his legs like springs, he pushed off the ground at an angle and shot back into the sky.

V'hren's broken wings and broken body lacked the dexterity to copy the maneuver. He crashed headfirst hard into the ground and lay still, face down, his body broken and contorted. Jhoro landed beside him and probed the corpse with his spear. When V'hren didn't respond, Jhoro rolled him over.

The impact had crushed the top of V'hren's skull, caving in his bloody forehead. One eye was gone and the skin below it was peeled back to expose the cheekbone. Something that looked like gray cottage cheese and raspberry jelly smeared his neck and chest.

Jhoro stared for a moment, nodded, and then launched himself back in the air.

Brains, Meaghan thought. Those are his brains smeared all over him. He's not getting up from that. She turned her head, willing herself not to vomit. After several deep breaths, the nausea passed.

She felt Sid squeeze her hand. She turned her attention back to him.

"Showoff. Stealing my death scene," he gasped. "Take care of Melanie. She didn't want me to go in the first place. Neither did you. So don't feel guilty. Tell her too. Tell everybody how awesome brave I was. Get Jamie over here and give us a minute alone, okay?"

John caught her gaze. He still kneeled at Sid's head, supporting him, his arms around him. Silent, John gestured with his head to indicate Jamie's position, a worried look on his somber face.

Jamie crouched a few yards away, a rock held tightly in his hand, glaring at his uncle's corpse. "Stay dead, fucker, or I'll bash the rest of your skull in. Stay dead. You stay dead," he muttered.

He looked crazed and feral, like something had snapped

inside him. It hadn't even been two full days, Meaghan realized, since the cookout at her house, and the happy young husband and father was now a broken man. It would take more than medical treatment and rest to save him. She feared he might be so broken he couldn't be saved.

"Jamie," she said in a low voice, moving slowly toward him. "Honey. Sid wants to talk to you." She put a gentle hand on his shoulder. He grunted and lifted the rock to strike before recognizing her. The rock fell from his hand and he burst into huge racking sobs. "C'mon, honey," she said, holding out her hand. "Let's go see Sid."

Meaghan helped him hobble to Sid's side. She and John stepped away as Sid requested. A hush fell over the crowd as Jhoro landed next to her, followed by Finn, and several other young Fahrayan men. And a few women, Meaghan noticed. There were about a dozen of them, towering around her. She saw Finn slip his hand into Jhoro's and squeeze it for a moment before he let go. They exchanged a quick glance. The contact was meant to be surreptitious, and neither Finn nor Jhoro realized that Meaghan had witnessed it.

Startled, she realized what it was she'd felt between them earlier. They were far more than friends and comrades. They were lovers. And they didn't want anyone to know.

Your secret is safe with me, she thought. If you found love in this horrible place, as fugitives, good for you.

Meaghan felt the knot in her chest loosen. V'hren was defeated. Jhoro and his men would help them get back to the gateway with Jamie and Sid. The knot returned. Sid's *body*, she corrected herself. She dreaded facing Melanie. But at least now they could return Sid's body and give Melanie the small comfort of being able to follow whatever rituals the Troon observed at death.

Sid was gone, but Jamie was alive. Broken but alive. And John, somehow, was better. Not well, maybe, but better than he'd been since his exile. He'd made peace with his ordeal in time to help his son find a way forward. They only needed to hitch a lift back to the gateway and they would be home.

Where she could have a mug of Russ's coffee. And a bath. And sleep. She noticed in that moment her own fatigue and pain. Her arm ached where the scorpion had bit her. Her knee and right palm, injured climbing the outcrop to free Jamie, throbbed in counterpoint. Her clothes were wet with Jamie's blood. Every muscle hurt and she had a boom thumper of a headache.

"I'm too old for this action hero shit," she mumbled. Jhoro looked down at her with his gorgeous smile. She smiled back.

They were going to be okay.

And then V'hren sat up.

CHAPTER 52

J AMIE, BY SID'S side, let out a blood-curdling wail. With a roar, John threw himself at V'hren. An instant later, Jhoro followed.

But V'hren, now on his feet, had one last trick to show them. He conjured a magical barrier. Before John could grab V'hren, a bright light flashed and John was thrown through the air. Meaghan screamed and ran to him, her heart pounding.

John was stunned but otherwise unhurt. She helped him up. He wrapped her in a crushing hug for a moment. "Stay with Jamie," he said before letting her go and running toward V'hren. She ran to Jamie, who was huddled over Sid, and she threw herself on top of both of them.

John shouted something at V'hren in Fahrayan. V'hren grinned back, his mouth stretched in a horrible rictus across his bloody face.

V'hren's head lay on his shoulder at an impossible angle and

Meaghan realized his neck was broken. Yet he still stood. He slashed one hand through the air.

Meaghan didn't want to believe her eyes. It looked like V'hren had ripped a tear in the space in front of him. Meaghan saw a wavering, black vertical line several feet long. V'hren made a pulling motion and the line widened into a gaping hole. With a last ravenous look, he stepped through the gap and was gone.

The ground shook beneath their feet. With a roar, the gap widened. She felt a sudden wind rush past her. Dust and small stones were carried up in the flow and pulled into the gap. Within moments, the wind increased to a gale and, in a rush of panic, Meaghan realized what V'hren had done. Melanie had described Fahraya as a bubble of space time, but Meaghan saw now that it was more like a balloon, and V'hren had torn a hole in it. Fahraya was collapsing.

Meaghan, gripping Jamie and Sid, shouted to John. "We have to go! *Now!*"

John stared at the gap, the blood drained from his face. She knew he saw the same thing she did and understood what it meant. If V'hren couldn't have Fahraya, no one could.

John shouted something to Jhoro, Finn, and the rest of Jhoro's followers. Finn, already airborne, scooped up Meaghan. Jhoro grabbed Jamie, and launched into the air, followed by another Fahrayan who had Sid's body. She heard more shouting and over Finn's shoulder saw the assembled Fahrayans arise en masse and fly in different directions toward the various gateways.

"John? Where's John?" she shouted at Finn. He pointed behind them. One of Jhoro's men carried John through the air.

They were headed for the Eldrich gateway, flying hard against the headwind caused by the atmosphere rushing into the gap. It was like flying into a hurricane.

It had taken Sid and Meaghan hours to get from the gateway to the settlement. At the rate Fahraya was ripping itself apart, they had mere minutes to make the return trip.

Meaghan could feel Finn struggle against the roaring wind, his heart pounding as he sprinted for the gateway. She clung to him. Fahrayans were all around them, those without passengers moving much faster. Meaghan felt a hand reach for her arm. She resisted, then looked over at Jhoro and saw that he now shared Jamie with another Fahrayan, each tightly gripping one of Jamie's arms.

"Oh shit oh shit *oh shit*," she cried as she squeezed her eyes shut and let the hand take her arm. Scared beyond rational thought, Meaghan now dangled between two Fahrayans as they flew.

By the time they got to the gateway, it was all the Fahrayans could do to hold course in face of the howling, roaring wind. Large rocks flew through the air and she heard screams and knew that someone had been hit.

John grabbed her and shouted in her ear. "Go. You go now."

"No," she shouted back. "I'm not leaving you here."

"You're the only one big enough to take Sid through. You go now. I'll be there soon. Once my people are through."

A leaf the size of a comforter blew through the gateway and nearly hit them. The gap was starting to pull debris from the other side. She nodded.

But before she could go, he pulled her close and kissed her hard, as if trying to compress his passion into a moment. He pulled away.

"Don't you die," she shouted. "I want to do that again."

"That's what I hope," he shouted back. He helped drape Sid's body across her shoulders in a fireman carry and shoved her toward the stone pillars that marked the gateway. Struggling against the wind and Sid's weight, she staggered through. She stumbled as she felt Sid grow suddenly lighter and smaller.

She and Sid fell into the clearing. Lynette and Natalie were waiting, swaying in the growing wind, mouths hanging open in shock.

"What the hell's going on?" Natalie shouted over the roar of the trees as she ran to Meaghan.

"End of the world," Meaghan shouted back. "Fahraya's collapsing. Once everybody's through, we have to close the gateways."

"Everybody?" Lynette shouted. "What do you mean?"

"Everybody. The whole damn population's coming through the gateways. Then we need to shut them. All of them. Soon. How do we do that?'

Natalie shook her head. "There's no way to do it." Then her face fell. "Except, maybe . . . but you can't."

"Can't what? If we don't stop this, it's taking this world with it." Out of the corner of her eye, Meaghan saw a steady stream of Fahrayans, now tiny, zoom past.

Natalie stared in shock at the tiny Fahrayans flowing through the gateway.

"Natalie, goddammit, how do we shut the gateways?"

Natalie turned back to her, a dazed look on her face and tears in her eyes. "There's only one way I can think of. You do it. You shut them. You go back in and right before the end, you take off your amulet."

CHAPTER 53

S O, MEAGHAN THOUGHT. It *is* up to me to the save the goddamn world. I knew it.

She stared at Natalie for a long moment, saw the tears streaming down her face, and then nodded. "Okay."

What else could Meaghan say? She was dead anyway. They all were if she couldn't get those gateways shut.

I'm about to die and I'm too tired to care, Meaghan thought. She couldn't even summon up tears to match Natalie's. I should be scared, she thought. But maybe her emotional flatness was for the best. It had to be done. She had to do it. All the tears in the world wouldn't change it.

Meaghan had always assumed that when death was imminent, she'd be afraid. But now that she no longer had to rely on hope, now that she actually knew there was an existence after death, she discovered the fear was gone.

Her only regret was John, what her death might do to him. Jamie needed him, his people needed him, and Meaghan hoped that losing her wouldn't throw him back into his self-destructive spiral.

And then there was Russ. He'd lose his father and sister within two days. She knew he'd have plenty of support, but it would still be heartbreaking. She wished she had more time to prepare, more time to say her goodbyes. But there was no time.

At least she wouldn't have to face Melanie.

Meaghan sent Natalie off to fetch amulets for John and Jamie, and to contact the local witches to start making more. She also ordered Natalie to send out word to the covens near the European gateways to warn them about the Fahrayan diaspora coming their way.

Meaghan grabbed Lynette's arm before she could follow Natalie. Pulling her close, she said, "Sid didn't make it. Get him somewhere out of the way for now. I don't want Melanie to find out this way, in the middle of all this panic."

Lynette nodded, pulled her into a tight hug, and then stepped back. "Jamie?"

"Alive but in very bad shape. They took his wings." She heard Lynette gasp. "Are Patrice and the kids here?"

"No. At your house."

"Good. They shouldn't see him until you can clean him up a little. Dealing with all this will be hard enough on him without . . ." She felt her throat tighten with tears. "Lynette, he's so broken. He needs a little room to remember who he is. He won't want Patrice to see him like this."

Lynette nodded. "Meaghan, I have bad news."

"I know. My dad died."

Lynette jerked back like Meaghan had punched her. "How did you know that?"

"He came to see me. Long story—a giant bug bit me, the

antidote includes a lot of funny mushrooms, and Dad was able to talk to me while I was high. Tell Russ he's okay. He's glad to be himself again."

Lynette nodded, tears rolling down her face. "Russ is here. Tell him yourself."

"He's here? Oh, shit. He's going to fight me on the amulet. And he can't. I have to do this."

Too late. Russ was running for her at top speed. Before she could say anything, he'd wrapped her in a huge bear hug. He was weeping. "Meg. You did it. Meg."

Meaghan pushed him away enough so she could see his face. "I know about Dad. He came to see me after he died and was with me for a lot of it. He's young again, and happy. Will you do me a favor and help Lynette with some stuff? I have to go back through and check on John."

She saw Lynette make a face like she was about to protest. As Meaghan pulled Russ back in for another hug, she gave Lynette her fiercest glare and shook her head. Then she pulled away and ran for the gateway without a backward glance.

Waiting for a slight lull in the stream of Fahrayans pouring through the gateway, Meaghan ducked as low as she could and crawled through. When she stood it took her a moment to register what she saw.

Over half the sky was empty and black. Not the black of space, because no stars were visible. It was simply empty. A void. The dim sun still hung in what was left of the sky, but it looked stretched. The whole scene looked stretched, like a surrealist painting.

John stood a few feet away, working hard to maintain his balance in the roaring wind. The stream of Fahrayans was becoming a trickle with Jhoro and Finn pushing, dragging, and carrying people through the gateway.

There wasn't much time left.

Trying not to be blown off her feet, Meaghan stumbled over to John. She wrapped her arms around him and put her mouth next to his ear so he could hear her. "You need to go," she shouted. "They need you on the other side."

"Not till these are through." He gestured at the handful of Fahrayans working their way through the gateway. "You go back and wait for me."

"No." Meaghan swallowed hard. Now that it was time, the fear and loss rose up in her throat. In that moment, she realized how much she didn't want to die. She couldn't tell John the truth because he'd want to stay and she wasn't strong enough to force him to go. She wasn't sure she could let him go at all. "I have to be the last. I can close all the gateways by taking off my amulet as I go through."

"No! You'll die," John shouted, gripping her closer.

Time to lie. "No, I won't. Not if I time it right. The explosion will push me through as it closes." Meaghan forced back the tears rising in her eyes. "I'll be fine. But I have to be the last one through. So, you have to go. Now."

She heard a muffled shout behind them. The only Fahrayans left were Jhoro and Finn. Jhoro, Finn wrapped in his arms and buffeted hard by the wind, flew through the gateway.

"They're through. Go!" She shoved him toward the stone pillars.

His eyes not leaving her face, John walked slowly backward and then he was gone.

Meaghan was alone.

CHAPTER 54

WITH ONE ARM wrapped around a stone pillar, Meaghan gripped the amulet tightly in her hand and waited for the end, Fahraya dissolving before her eyes.

The ground shook and groaned. The black empty sky now stretched down to consume the land itself. What remained of the sun looked like a star painted by Van Gogh. Streamers of light whirled around it and rushed toward the vast emptiness. Debris from her world flowed like a stream through the gateway. Leaves the size of bed sheets and twigs the size of logs blew past.

If she didn't close the gateways, soon trees and people and cars and buildings and then the whole planet would be sucked into the void consuming Fahraya. She wondered if, unchecked, the destruction would then spread to other dimensions through their gateways. If so, she wasn't saving only the human world but possibly multiple universes.

At least I'm dying for a good reason, she thought. Now

that she didn't have to put on a brave face, the tears fell. She didn't want to die alone. She wanted her father to come back and guide her through death and into wherever it was he now existed.

At that moment, her wish granted, she saw Matthew approach her across the disintegrating ground. Like her mother and Lou, her father appeared to be walking across a desert from a far distance. Wherever it was he walked, it was sunny and still. There was a shimmer like heat rising from asphalt and now he stood before her, still not affected by the roaring gale that blew around him.

"Are you here to take me to the other side?" she shouted.

"No, Meg. I'm here to shove you back through when you pull off the amulet. Vivian flipped when she heard Natalie tell you to blow the gateways with you still inside."

"You mean I'm not going to die?"

"Not today, kiddo. It's not your time. There's too much for you to do back home." He pointed at the gateway. "But we have to time it exactly right."

"Won't you get blown up if you stay?" Meaghan shouted.

"Nope. I'm dead, remember? I can't get any deader." Matthew stepped closer to her. "This takes some big juju for me to get corporeal enough to do this. We only get one shot at it."

"Mom was corporeal when I saw her in my dream."

"No, she wasn't. You only dreamed that. You're awake this time and not tripping. The only reason I can be here at all is because reality is falling apart."

Matthew shut his eyes, concentrated, then reached out and put his hands on her shoulders. "I can steady you while we do this. Let go of the pillar."

Meaghan did as he told her. The wind still blew around her, but she was steady on her feet. "I'm good. Now what?"

"When it's time, you snap that cord around your neck and I give you a big push backwards."

"What was that thing controlling V'hren? Is it coming back?"

"I don't know. It's gone for now, but I don't think for good."

Meaghan nodded. "How much longer?"

"Any second."

"When will I see you again?"

"I'm pulling in some big favors to be here, so probably not for a while. I'll send Mom along later to check in. You ready?"

"Yeah."

"Okay, wait . . . wait . . . *now!*"

Meaghan yanked the amulet and felt the thong snap. Matthew gave her a mighty push as he pulled the amulet from her hand. Then pressure and darkness, followed by the sensation of movement, of flying backwards very fast, until she felt herself hit the ground.

A flash of light. Hands touching her. Arms around her.

Somebody kissing her.

Her eyes flew open and there was John, crying and laughing at the same time. She threw her arms around his neck and pulled him on top of her.

She didn't come up for air for a long moment.

Then she registered the voices all around her. Wailing and shouting. It sounded like a bus station. But weren't they in the woods?

John helped her up. Still dazed, Meaghan looked around.

The clearing was full of filthy, naked people. Not Fahrayan but human. "How'd Natalie get those amulets together so fast?" she asked.

"No amulets," John said. "We're human."

"You're what?" She gazed at his throat. He wasn't wearing an amulet. "What happened?"

"You flew backwards out of the gateway, big boom, bright light, and here we are. Don't know why."

She heard Russ scream her name. He shoved John aside and grabbed her into another monstrous bear hug. He was sobbing so hard he couldn't speak.

Natalie followed hard on his heels. Then Lynette. They both threw themselves on top of Russ and joined the hug.

Then Meaghan heard a keening wail cut through the rumbling of the crowd. A howl of pain and grief.

Melanie, she thought. She knows about Sid. Meaghan pulled herself out of the hug and looked around for Melanie. But the cries were coming from someone else.

She saw Jhoro cradling Finn's limp body in his arms, tears streaming down his face, wailing in a tear-choked voice. Blood covered Finn's chest, pouring from a gaping wound near his heart. His eyes were still open, staring blankly at the sky.

"Oh, no," Meaghan murmured. "Not Finn. Poor Jhoro." She didn't add her insight into how deep Jhoro's grief must go. She vowed to keep his secret.

Which, it turned out, wasn't really all that secret.

"He's singing Finn's death song, as his mate," John said, in a quiet voice, standing at her side. "The song I never had a chance to sing for Zhara."

Meaghan tore her eyes off Jhoro and Finn. "You know about them?"

John shrugged. "I talked to his people. Everyone knew."

"Everyone knew? Then why were they hiding it?"

John shook his head. "I know what you think. We don't see it like humans. It's okay. It means some of us get to have a second baby. I don't know why they hid it."

Meaghan felt a small hand slip into hers. She looked to see who it was. Melanie smiled up at her.

Guilt rising in her throat, Meaghan said, "Melanie, I'm so sorry. He was so brave. You need to know how brave he was."

"Was? He still is brave, my little Sid. He's in Lynette's camper. He wants to see you when you get a moment."

"Wait. He's . . . Sid's not dead? He's still alive?" Meaghan started to cry. "I thought he was dead when he got hexed and then he got back up and then he took a knife to the chest and he said goodbye and how is he still alive?"

"He's one tough Troon, that's how. We heal very quickly. It takes a lot more than a knife to the chest to kill a Troon."

"But," Meaghan said, "he was dying. He said he was circling the drain and that V'hren was stealing his death scene."

Melanie smiled and shook her head. "That Sid. He does have a flair for the dramatic. Note that he called it a *scene*."

Relief washed over Meaghan. "He was *faking?* I'm so glad he's alive, but when I get my hands on him I'm going to kick his rotten little butt."

Melanie laughed. "He said he thought the pathos would play well for the crowd."

"Jamie," Meaghan remembered. "Sid wanted to talk to Jamie."

"Pep talk. He wanted to let Jamie in on the secret because

he didn't think Jamie could take much more." Melanie's smile vanished. "I'm not sure it helped."

"Can I see him?" Meaghan asked. "Where is he?"

"In the camper with Sid." Melanie sighed. "Give him a little time. Natalie is cleaning his wounds. The visible ones at least." She peered around Meaghan to where John stood. "John, he's going to need you. You can't fade away again."

John took Meaghan's other hand. "Not this time. I'll be with him even if doesn't want me."

Meaghan turned back to John. "Do we know if everyone got out before the—" She stopped, unable to finish her question.

John sighed. "Not yet. The other gateways are far away. And my people are alone with no one to speak for them. The witches are trying to get news."

"Wally and a few other Troon with some skill speaking Fahrayan are on their way," Melanie said. "But without both sets of vocal cords—"

"It will be hard for them to speak," John said. "And they have no wings." He looked around the clearing at the bemused Fahrayans. "I remember how hard it was for me to be human when I first got here. How hard it is to no longer fly."

Meaghan stared at him a moment. "And what about you? Are you okay?"

John shook his head. "I don't know." He turned his head and stared into her eyes. "I wonder if I'm their king again. If nobody has wings, then I don't need them. But right now? Now I really want to be alone in my little house with a big bottle of gin. I don't know yet if I'm a man you can trust."

Meaghan nodded, a lump in her throat. Because she

knew now how much she wanted him to be that man. The thought of him sliding back into being the town drunk was more than she could bear. And he needed to be more than merely a man she could trust. He needed to be the man his son and his people could trust. It was a lot of weight to balance on his fragile new sobriety.

"One day at a time, right? That's what they say," she finally said. "Let's get through today."

CHAPTER 55

THEY GOT THROUGH that day and then several more until a couple of weeks had passed.

Meaghan slept for the better part of two days and then began reading her father's journals in earnest. She wasn't getting caught unaware again. She had a job to do. No more screwing around.

She kept her distance from John. He had work to do and didn't need the distraction. And she didn't need the temptation. He had to stay sober for a while.

Russ advised her not to even consider a romance with John until he could bring her at least a ninety day sobriety chip from AA. "And make sure he has a sponsor," Russ warned. "He can't skimp on that. Dad had three false starts before he finally admitted he couldn't do it on his own and got himself a sponsor. And remind him that if he hurts you, I'm kicking his ass. Hard."

Meaghan merely smiled. John could mop the floor with

Russ. Everyone—including Russ—knew it, but she appreciated Russ saying it anyway.

Jamie, with some string pulling by Meaghan, was placed on short term disability leave and wouldn't be back to work for a while. The raw emotional bond forged between them in Fahraya seemed to have evaporated. He wouldn't look Meaghan in the eye or talk about what had happened to him. He was furtive and ashamed, not only with Meaghan but with Patrice as well.

Patrice's boss, the doctor who ran the local clinic, was the son of a witch and clued in. After treating Jamie's physical injuries, he told Patrice to take a few weeks off and get Jamie out of town for a while. Buzz Hallam, whose law firm was handling Jamie's workload, had a remote cabin on the New York side of the state line. Patrice left the kids with Natalie and took her wounded husband away from Eldrich. Jamie was human now, so there was no amulet to worry about.

Emily returned to work the same day Meaghan did. When Meaghan got home from the forest, she found Emily still locked in the basement. No longer bound to a chair, Emily was sleeping on an old camp cot she'd found. Meaghan, still wearing clothes stained with Jamie's blood, woke her and told her to leave. Emily snarled a response about making everybody pay. Meaghan said nothing, responding only with a cold, heavy-lidded stare. Emily, silenced by the look in Meaghan's eyes, fled up the basement stairs and out of the house. So far she'd kept her distance, but Meaghan suspected it wouldn't last.

Jhoro, nursing his grief for Finn, moved in with Meaghan and Russ. It seemed she'd gotten more than one surrogate son during her time in Fahraya. He told John that he wanted to make sure Meaghan was safe from whatever had taken over his father. Meaghan suspected that he was feeling lost without Finn and unsure what his role was now that John appeared to be king again. Being her protector gave him something to do.

She and Russ were glad for the company. Jhoro helped fill the void left by Matthew's death. Russ had been a caregiver for a long time and didn't quite know what to do with himself with Matthew gone. Jhoro had a sweet goofy charm under his rough exterior and, unlike Jamie at the moment, was happy for a little parenting. A lot of parenting, actually, considering she and Russ had to teach him how to use the toilet, bathe, and eat with a fork, among other things.

At Jhoro's insistence, Finn was buried in the stone circle that marked the closed gateway. Jhoro cleared the brush and, with Russ and Caleb's help, replaced the unimpressive standing stones with larger boulders. It now looked like a proper mystical site even if the magic had been drained from it.

The now-human Fahrayans were gathered in Eldrich and the surrounding area. Most of those who survived had come through the Eldrich gateway. There had been only about a thousand of them to begin with and by the current headcount, about half of them had perished when Fahraya was destroyed. Or at least they weren't accounted for yet, despite the best efforts of the European witches and the Troon to find them.

Unlike the Eldrich gateway, the European gateways were not so remote. The one in England sat right on the edge of an exclusive new housing development. The local coven managed to gather up the confused Fahrayans before they attracted too much attention and, by detouring through Troon, got them safely to Eldrich.

The gateway in Germany, in the Black Forest, wasn't quite as close to major population centers, but was still surrounded by tourists. Melanie observed signs of wind damage near the gateway but no Fahrayans. The French and Romanian gateways showed similar wind damage and also no Fahrayans. The popular theory was that those gateways had been destroyed before the fleeing Fahrayans could get to them.

Meaghan hated government conspiracy theories because of her familiarity with how government actually worked. But she had to wonder. It had long been rumored that a few Fahrayans from John's father's doomed raid had been captured by German troops. If the story was true, then somebody who wasn't part of the magical world might know of their existence. What if the missing Fahrayans had arrived but been grabbed before the witches got to them?

But there was so much work to be done dealing with the Fahrayans who could be accounted for that there was no time to worry about what might have happened to the others. Meaghan had seen firsthand what V'hren's hole in reality had done to Fahraya. Considering how little time they had to evacuate, the most likely explanation was that the lost Fahrayans were dead.

Trying to feed and shelter nearly five hundred bewildered new humans with no modern living skills was a logistical feat that took up all of John's time, as well as the time of Lynette and every witch who didn't hide when she called for help. For now, it was barely manageable between home placements and the refugee camp that had sprung up around John's house. Without magic, it would have been impossible.

A more permanent solution would have to be found before winter.

The Order and whatever V'hren now was—Meaghan felt sure that what Caleb called the Power had been the thing possessing V'hren—were still out there, which concerned Meaghan quite a bit. Everyone was so busy dealing with the Fahrayans that she hadn't pushed the issue, but Meaghan knew she needed to learn more about the war her mother and Natalie had mentioned. John had also mentioned a great war waged by wizards told of in Fahrayan folklore. And whatever had possessed V'hren could do magic and was working with wizards. So far, nothing had turned up in Matthew's files, but she could feel the connections even if she didn't yet know the details. She suspected that the Order and the Power weren't finished with them yet.

So far, the Order had made no obvious effort to contact or control Caleb. Lynette kept a watchful eye on him, as did the other witches, but detected no signs of Order interference. Caleb moved in with Lynette and worked by her side, gaining weight and growing visibly happier every day. The Fahrayan children, in particular, adored him. He was almost as much a stranger in the modern world as they were, and he understood, better than anyone else in Eldrich, what it was like to have your whole world disappear in a moment.

And so the days passed and after two weeks, a fragile new normal asserted itself. Then John called early on Saturday morning. He had, he said, something he wanted to talk to her about.

Meaghan showered, dressed, and waited for John to arrive, trying to control her nerves. They hadn't spoken since their return from Fahraya, when they'd agreed, in light of

John's renewed responsibilities to his people, that Meaghan and John's burgeoning romance would have to wait.

Much to Meaghan's relief.

Despite John's sober interlude, Meaghan was too familiar with alcoholism to believe that his sobriety could last without serious effort on his part, effort made much more difficult by the Fahrayan exodus. No matter how much she wanted him, they couldn't be together until they both knew he could stay sober.

She only hoped she was strong enough to resist him. She felt a funny little thrill in her gut when she remembered how it felt to kiss him. It had been so long since any man had even interested her, let alone touched her, that Meaghan knew if he pushed, even a little, she might not be able to say no.

John drove up a few minutes after ten. She heard the rattle of his old truck as she waited in the kitchen.

The house was empty. Russ had left shortly after dawn to take Jhoro fishing. Meaghan realized she hadn't been home alone since the day she'd first met John. It felt like it had been ages ago, but it was not quite a month.

She heard a gentle knock. Taking a deep breath in a futile effort to calm her nerves, she opened the kitchen door. John stepped through the doorway, smiling shyly.

And within moments she was in his arms, kissing him, with an urgency and need that shocked her. It had been so long, so many lonely years, and her resolve to wait evaporated like steam.

It was John who pulled away finally, taking several steps back from her. "Meaghan," he gasped. "We . . . I . . . wow. That's some kiss."

Meaghan, flustered, took her own big step backwards. "I'm sorry."

"Don't be," John said with a grin. "No one's been that happy to see me in a long time. But if I don't stop us, I think we'll do something we'll feel bad for after. It's too soon for us. I go to AA every day and my friends there they tell me it's too soon."

"You're going to AA?" Meaghan asked.

"Every day."

Meaghan's legs were shaking so hard she had to sit down. "Russ said to go at least ninety days and you need a sponsor before we . . ." She felt her face grow hot.

"I have a sponsor," he said. "A good one. Clued in so I can tell him everything."

"You have a clued-in sponsor?"

John smiled. "Yeah. I do. He's been sober a long time now. He was a big deal to his people once and then not any-more—like me—so he understands."

They sat in awkward silence at the kitchen table until Meaghan couldn't take it anymore. "You want some coffee?"

John sighed with relief. "God, yes."

Coffee served, Meaghan sat back down. Before she lost her nerve, she had to tackle the issue they were both avoid-ing. "About us, I . . . we . . . is ninety days enough?"

"That's what I'm here to talk with you about," he said, avoiding her gaze. "I keep remembering that kiss in Fahraya, to break the magic, and wondering . . ." He finally looked up. "I want to be with you, but I'm scared to death."

Meaghan let out her own sigh of relief. "Oh, God, so am I. Just terrified."

John laughed and she joined him. "I have to confess

something to you," he said. "I never . . . do the . . . you know . . ." His face turned red. "I've never been with a human woman. And never as a human man." He sighed. "It's been a really long time."

"For me, too," Meaghan said. "So, now what?"

John took her hand, his fingers warm and calloused. "My sponsor tells me he tells new members to wait awhile to be with someone new, but he knows nobody listens to that and I should let what happens happen. But . . ." He stroked her hand gently and stared at the tabletop.

"But what?" she asked, already knowing the answer.

"They say one day at a time, but I'm not even to one day yet. Sometimes it's one hour, one moment at a time. I'm so nervous it was all I could do not to drink before I come here today. I never thought I'd be the . . . the *king* again, you know? That they'd all look at me for the answers. I have to learn again how to do it." He finally met her eyes. "At the same time I have to learn again how to be sober. And how to be a father."

"And learning how to be with a woman again is too much right now." Meaghan nodded, disappointed but also relieved. "The other things have to come first." Only two months earlier she'd been so shut down she couldn't even admit how lonely she was. Since her emotional breakthrough in Fahraya, she was trying to mommy anyone who'd let her and was prone to bursting into tears at odd moments. "I get it," she said. "I'm not ready either. I have a lot of things I need to learn myself. I can wait. It's not like I'm going anywhere."

"I don't want to mess this up," John said. "It's too important for too many people, including you, that I don't fail."

The wall phone rang. John let go of her hand and she got up to answer it.

It was Natalie. "Boss, we've got a problem."

"Of course we do," Meaghan said. "Now what?"

"It's not a big problem," Natalie said. "More a nuisance really. Want to meet a new species?"

"What kind?" Meaghan asked, wondering if she really wanted to know.

"Wee folk."

"Actual fairies this time?" Meaghan looked at John and rolled her eyes. He laughed.

"Um, not exactly," Natalie. "Well, technically, yeah, but these aren't like Tinkerbell either."

"Okay," Meaghan said. "So what twisted representation of a beloved mythological figure are we dealing with this time?"

"Leprechauns," Natalie said.

Meaghan was silent for a long moment. "Are you shittin' me?"

"No, really."

"Whimsical little men in green suits guarding their pots of gold?"

"Um," Natalie said. "No, not really. More like grubby, foul-mouthed little loan sharks. There should be a file in the garage somewhere. Read up on them and I'll be over later today."

"Okay." What else could she say? This is my new normal, she thought.

"Oh," Natalie added, "if you see John, tell him they're roaming around the camp trying to introduce the Fahrayans to the world of bare-knuckle finance."

Meaghan sighed. "Will do."

She hung up the phone and turned to John. "You've got leprechauns out at your place trying to make loans to your people."

John's look grew dark. "Not for long, I don't. Not when I get my hands on the little bastards."

"You've met them?"

"Yes," he growled. "I have encountered them before. They infest. Like rats." He stood up and gave her a sad smile. "I have to go. King stuff to do."

"Yeah, I have some gatekeeping duties to get up to speed on myself."

They stared at each other for a long moment.

Meaghan pulled him close for a quick kiss, smiled at him, and then shoved him gently toward the door. "It's not like either of us has the time right now anyway. We'll get there. Go kick some leprechaun ass. I have reading to do."

ACKNOWLEDGEMENTS

FIRST AND FOREMOST, thank you to my father, Ray Kirwan. This book would not exist without his support and encouragement. Next, a big thanks to my beta readers Rick Wysocki (frederickwysocki.com), Brenda Moyer, Andrea Garland, and Jen Treadway. Also thanks to my editor, Susan Lindsey of Savvy Communication LLC (savvy-comm.com), and to James T. Egan of Bookfly Design (bookflydesign.com.) Finally, thank you, Lindsay Buroker (lindsayburoker.com), for your advice and assistance.

A NOTE TO READERS

IMPERVIOUS IS THE first of seven books in the City of Eldrich series. More information about the series is available at laurakirwan.com.